D0546599

Dear Reader,

You've asked for it, and you've finally got e-story about being inadvertently infected with the vampire virus, was first released, I've gotten e-mails from fans begging me to put my Shadow Falls novellas in print. You want to be able to hold that book in your hands, you tell me. You want to see it on bookshelves. And so it is!

Almost Midnight is a compilation of all four of my previously published e-novellas. You can follow Della through *Saved at Sunrise* where she's rescued by the hot shape-shifter who vied for her attention. In *Unbreakable* your heart will break for all that Chase Tallman endured before he became the mysterious and alluring new vampire whose presence stirred up trouble at the camp and caused all kinds of havoc for Della. Ahh, and let's not forget the lovable Miranda, who until now felt lacking in her supernatural potential. In *Spellbinder,* you learn that deep down this witch is a force to be reckoned with. And if her ex, Perry, doesn't come around soon, there's a new sexy warlock who'd be happy to take his place.

But there was someone else in my fictional world of Shadow Falls who kept tapping on my mind and insisting she wanted her own story. She wasn't even a likely candidate. Frankly, most of the time, she wasn't even likable. She was Kylie's nemesis—someone everyone wanted to root against. Yet even archenemies have stories. Some of them, like Fredericka Lakota, even deserve to be redeemed. In *Fierce,* you'll not only get inside this werewolf's head, but into her heart. You'll see her struggle to overcome her past, and you'll see her win the future—and the hot guy—she truly deserves.

Enjoy your stroll through the enchanted world of Shadow Falls—a world where friendship, romance, and laughter make everything a little more magical. And prepare yourself for one last book in 2016, where Miranda's new powers will be challenged, her heart finally won, and there will at last be a graduation that brings this amazing journey to a close.

Thank you for being a fan.

Happy Reading!
C. C.

Praise for the Shadow Falls Series

"Hunter sucks you in . . . an amazing roller-coaster ride."   —*RT Book Reviews*

"The Shadow Falls series belongs to my favorite YA series. It has everything I wish for in a YA paranormal series. A thrilling tale that moves with a great pace, where layers of secrets are revealed in a way that we are never bored. It continues a gripping story about self-discoveries, finding a place in the world, friendship, and love. So if you didn't start this series yet, I can only encourage you to do so."   —*Bewitched Bookworms*

"Ms. Hunter handles this series with such deftness, crafting a wonderful tale that speaks to the adolescent in me. I highly recommend this series filled with darkness and light, hope and danger, friendship and romance."
      —*Night Owl Reviews* (Top Pick)

"Jam-packed with action and romance from the very beginning, Hunter's lifelike characters and paranormal creatures populate a plot that will keep you guessing till the very end. A perfect mesh of mystery, thriller, and romance. Vampires, weres, and fae, oh my!"   —*RT Book Reviews* on *Taken at Dusk*

"An emotional thrill ride full of suspense, action, laughter, multiple love stories, and an intriguing variety of paranormal species. I could not put this book down and can't wait to start the next book as soon as I finish this review."
      —*Guilty Pleasures Book Reviews* on *Awake at Dawn*

"There are so many books in the young adult paranormal genre these days that it's hard to choose a good one. I was so very glad to discover *Born at Midnight*. If you like P. C. and Kristin Cast or Alyson Nöel, I am sure you will enjoy *Born at Midnight*!"   —*Night Owl Reviews*

"The evolving, not-always-easy relationships among Kylie and her cabin mates Della and Miranda are rendered as engagingly as Kylie's angst over dangerous Lucas and appealing Derek. Just enough plot threads are tied up to make a satisfying stand-alone tale while whetting appetites for sequels to come."
      —*Publishers Weekly*

"With intricate plotting and characters so vivid you'd swear they are real, *Born at Midnight* is an addictive treat. Funny, poignant, romantic, and downright scary in places, it hits all the right notes. Highly recommended."
      —*Houston Lifestyles & Homes* magazine

"I laughed and cried so much while reading this . . . I LOVED this book. I read it every chance I could get because I didn't want to put it down. The characters were well developed and I felt like I knew them from the beginning. The story line and mystery that went along with it kept me glued to my couch not wanting to do anything else but find out what the heck was going on."
                                        —*Urban Fantasy Investigations*

"This has everything a YA reader would want. . . . I read it over a week ago and I am still thinking about it. I can't get it out of my head. I can't wait to read more. This series is going to be a hit!"   —*Awesomesauce Bookclub* on *Born at Midnight*

"The newest in the super-popular teen paranormal genre, this book is one of the best. Kylie is funny and vulnerable, struggling to deal with her real-world life and her life in a fantastical world she's not sure she wants to be a part of. Peppered throughout with humor and teen angst, *Born at Midnight* is a laugh-out-loud page-turner. This one is going on the keeper shelf next to my Armstrong and Meyer collections!"   —*Fresh Fiction*

"Seriously loved this book! This is definitely a series you will want to watch out for. C. C. Hunter has created a world of hot paranormals that I didn't want to leave."   —*Looksie Lovitz: Books and Wits*

"*Born at Midnight* has a bit of everything . . . a strong unique voice from a feisty female lead, a myriad of supporting supernatural characters, a fiery romance with two intriguing guys—mixed all together with a bit of mystery—making *Born at Midnight* a surefire hit!"   —*A Life Bound by Books*

"Very exciting, taking twists and turns I never expected. The main character grows very well throughout the story, overcoming obstacles and realizing things she never thought possible. And the author masterfully ended it just right."
                                        —*Flamingnet Book Reviews*

"I absolutely LOVED it. Wow, it blew me away."
                                —Nina Bangs, author of *Eternal Prey*

"Fun and compulsively readable, with a winning heroine and an intriguing cast of secondary characters."   —Jenna Black, author of *Glimmerglass*

ALSO BY C. C. HUNTER

Born at Midnight

Awake at Dawn

Taken at Dusk

Whispers at Moonrise

Chosen at Nightfall

Reborn

Eternal

Almost Midnight

* * ✦ * *

C. C. HUNTER

ST. MARTIN'S GRIFFIN ✠ NEW YORK

ALMOST MIDNIGHT. Copyright © 2016 by Christie Craig. All rights reserved. Printed in the United States of America. For information, address St. Martin's Press, 175 Fifth Avenue, New York, N.Y. 10010.

www.stmartins.com

The Library of Congress Cataloging-in-Publication Data is available upon request.

ISBN 978-1-250-08100-1 (trade paperback)
ISBN 978-1-4668-9285-9 (e-book)

Our books may be purchased for use in promotional, educational, or business use. Please contact your local bookseller or the Macmillan Corporate and Premium Sales Department at 1-800-221-7945, extension 5442, or by e-mail at MacmillanSpecialMarkets@macmillan.com.

Turned at Dark was originally published in 2011 by St. Martin's Griffin.
Saved at Sunrise was originally published in 2013 by St. Martin's Griffin.
Unbreakable was originally published in 2014 by St. Martin's Griffin.
Spellbinder was originally published in 2015 by St. Martin's Griffin.

First Edition: February 2016

10 9 8 7 6 5 4 3

Turned at Dark

Sixteen-year-old Della Tsang had never seen a ghost until she saw her dead cousin zip across the street and duck into the alley. If it hadn't been for the streetlight spitting out its spray of wattage overhead, she might have missed him.

And if it hadn't been for a scar that ran along his chin, she might have thought it was just someone who looked like Chan. Then again, it was after midnight. But she *had* spotted the scar. A scar she'd sort of given him when they'd been six, jumping on the trampoline and he'd collided with her head.

Hardheaded Della had been her family nickname after that. Sometimes Della wondered if she'd really been obstinate then, or if the name had just been another thing for her to live up to. Being of Asian descent, there were high expectations, sometimes too high. But because she and her sister were half-white, her father insisted they work twice as hard to prove that their parents' love hadn't tainted the family tree.

A pair of headlights moving down the road pulled Della's attention from the alley where Chan had disappeared. Not that she completely believed it was Chan. Did she?

The car drew nearer, and thinking it was Lee to pick her up, Della stepped off her best friend Lisa's front porch, leaving the sound of the party still going on behind her.

At least twice a month, Della and Lee tried to sneak away so they could be together for an entire night. She knew her parents would freak if they knew she and Lee were sleeping together. It wouldn't even matter that they were practically engaged. But at least Lee had gotten a stamp of approval from her father. Luckily, she agreed with him, too. Not that she agreed with her father on everything. However, Lee was everything Della wanted in a boyfriend—hot, popular, smart, and, thankfully for her father's sake, Asian. It didn't even bother her that Lee wasn't totally into the party scene.

She gave the alley one last look. It couldn't have been Chan. She'd attended his funeral less than a year ago—had seen his casket being lowered into the ground. She remembered she hadn't cried. Her father had insisted she not. She wondered if her father would be disappointed if he knew that very night, while alone in bed, she had cried her eyes out.

When the car drove closer, Della realized she'd been wrong. It wasn't Lee. She watched as the car moved down the street, past the alley. She stood there, staring, suddenly feeling alone in the dark, when her phone beeped with an incoming text.

Pulling it out, she read the message. *Parents still up. Will b late.*

Frowning, she repocketed her phone and her gaze shifted back to the alley. What would it hurt to just . . . go check? To prove that ghosts didn't exist.

Moving slowly in the shadows, she neared the alley. The cold of the January night seeped through her leather jacket and the soft tap-tapping of her footsteps seemed loud. Maybe too loud. No sooner had she cut the corner than she heard yelling. She stopped short. Her breath caught at the sight of the fight—or out-and-out war—taking place. The sound of fist hitting flesh filled the cold darkness and she saw bodies being tossed up in the air like rag dolls.

Della might not have been familiar with this darker side of life, but she immediately knew what she'd stumbled on. A gang war. Her heart jumped into her throat. She had to get out of here and fast.

She stepped back, but the heel of her shoe twisted and she lost her footing. Her leg shot up in the air and she went down with a loud thud.

Slamming butt first, her hands went back to catch herself. She felt a sharp pain in her palm, no doubt from a piece of glass from a broken beer bottle a few inches away. Wincing, she muttered, "Shi . . ." The one-word curse hadn't yet left her lips when the dead silence suddenly drew her attention upward. The fighting had stopped and at least six guys, young, about her age, starting moving toward her. Moving oddly, as if . . . Their posture reminded her of a pack of animals coming to check out their prey.

Della's focus shifted from the group's strange body movements to their eyes. Her heart jolted when she saw their eyes glowing burnt orange. Then low growling noises filled the shadows. "What the—"

Before she could finish her sentence, they were upon her. "Human. Yum," one of them said.

Tension filled her chest. "I'm leaving." She jumped to her feet.

Suddenly, she heard footsteps behind her, and knew they had her surrounded. The growling escalated and for a second she could swear the sounds weren't human. She turned, hoping to find a path to run, but instantly something grabbed her around her middle and a cold wind blasted against her face. She felt dizzy, disoriented, as if she were suddenly traveling at high speeds like she was on a roller coaster. She tried to scream, but no sound came out. Darkness surrounded her and it took a second to realize she had her eyes closed. She tried to open them, but the rush of air coming at her stung so badly she slammed them shut. What the hell was happening? Now it felt as if . . . as if she were flying.

Or falling. No, not falling—someone, or something had her.

Her lungs screamed for air, but what she thought was an arm wrapped around her stomach and cut off her ability to breathe. She tried to yank herself free, but her efforts were futile. Whoever had her was built of steel, and his flesh felt cold, hard. Something wet seemed to ooze from her hand and she realized it was her blood from where she'd cut herself.

Right then, the cut started to burn. Burn badly, as if someone had just doused it with rubbing alcohol. The searing pain seemed to follow her arm upward, all the way to her chest, and for a second, her heart didn't beat. She gasped, hoping to breathe, but nothing seemed to get through to her lungs. Refusing to let the fear stop her, she forced the words out, "Let me go, you asshole!"

A jolt shot through her body as her feet hit the ground. The arm released her. Her knees buckled, but she caught herself at the last second and shot her eyes open. Blinking, she tried to focus, but everything appeared blurry.

"Breathe," someone said and she recognized the deep, masculine voice. Recognized Chan.

Ghosts did exist?

No, they couldn't.

A couple more seconds later, her vision cleared and holy mother of pearls, she was right. Chan stood directly in front of her. Nausea hit. Her palm still burned. She grabbed her middle, bent over, and puked all over the front of her dead cousin.

"Oh, shit!" He lurched back.

She stood upright again and stared, thinking that any minute now she'd wake up. Or maybe it wasn't a dream. Had someone slipped something into her drink tonight? She pressed her palms into her eyes and didn't care that she was probably smearing blood from the cut on her hand all over her face.

When she dropped her hands, Chan stared, only now his black eyes glowed a bright green color.

He jumped back from her. "You're bleeding!"

"You're dead." She pressed her bloody hand on her middle, hoping to squelch the nausea and wipe away the sting.

He pinched his black brows together and stared harder. "Friggin' hell! You're turning."

"No, I'm not! I'm standing still. In one spot," she snapped. "Then again, I do feel dizzy." She closed her eyes and then popped them back open again.

"You needed help so I . . . I didn't know you'd cut yourself or—"

"I did not need your help, I would have . . . I would have figured something out."

He shook his head. "Still hardheaded, huh?"

She hugged herself. "What just happened? No, what *is* happening?"

She looked around and saw they were no longer anywhere near Lisa's house or that dark alley where she'd gone looking for . . . "You're dead, Chan. How can you be here?"

He shook his head and stared at her forehead. "If I'd known you were bleeding, I wouldn't have . . . I should have known you were a carrier. But if I hadn't got you out of there, the dogs would have eaten you alive."

She stopped listening and tried to make sense of the crap that had just happened. She remembered seeing the gang fight, then she fell, and then she'd been surrounded, and . . . "Oh damn, am I dead?"

"No. But you're going to think you're dying in just a bit. You touched me with an open wound. Your virus is turning live now. That's why you're feeling like you do." He stopped talking and put his nose in the air. "Damn, the hounds are looking for us. I've got to get you out of here." He reached for her and she jumped back.

"Stay away. You've got puke all over you."

"It's your puke."

"I don't care. I don't want it on me. I think—" Whatever she thought went out the mental window. Once again, the wind whipped her hair around her shoulders. The long strands flipped around so hard, it stung when they slapped against her face.

Della's head hurt something fierce. Was this her official first hangover? How many beers had she had; only one, right? She never drank more than . . . She opened her eyes, and found herself staring at her bedroom ceiling. She knew it was her bedroom, because she could smell the vanilla-scented candles and the Lemon Pledge she faithfully polished her furniture with every Friday. And her pillow still smelled like Lee, from when he'd dropped her off at home from school on Monday and no one was home. She loved how he smelled.

But how had she gotten home from the . . .

Fragments of memories started forming—Chan, the gang fight, flying.

Flying?

She jackknifed up. Her head nearly exploded. "Crap," she muttered and told herself it had been a dream.

"Hey, cuz."

His voice came at the same time the nausea did. She turned and for the second time puked all over her dead cousin.

"Ahh, gross," Chan said, but then he snickered. "I guess I deserve this. Not that I meant for this to happen. I really didn't." But then he laughed again.

Della wasn't laughing. "What's happening?" Tears, partly from the frustration, partly from the pain, filled Della's sinuses. She forced them away. She wiped her mouth with the sleeve of her shirt and saw her leather jacket tossed over the foot of her bed.

Chan put a hand on her shoulder and gave her a nudge. "Lie back down and I'll explain."

"There was a gang war," she muttered, trying to remember.

"Yeah, vampires and werewolves. I went to watch. It's cool to watch us take out a few dogs."

Her phone, sitting on her nightstand, beeped with an incoming text. She tried to reach for it, but moving hurt. Another surge of tears filled her throat.

"It's your lover boy," Chan said. "This is like the tenth text he's sent. I think you missed your hookup date." Chan shook his head. "So my little cousin is getting it on with a guy, huh? I feel like I should go beat him up or something."

She dropped back on the bed.

"Do you want me to text him and tell him you're okay?"

"I'm not okay!" Talking made her head pound worse. Realizing she was talking to a ghost make it pound twice as hard. Pain shot in the back of her eyes and she closed them, wishing for relief.

"What's wrong with me?" she muttered to herself and not to Chan, because logic told her that Chan wasn't really there. Someone must have put something in her drink at that party. Yeah. That had to be it.

She heard a chair being pulled up beside her bed. "You're not going to believe this, and that's to be expected. It will take a while to soak in. You see . . . I'm not dead. I . . . well, our family carries this virus.

It's dormant and you can go your entire life and not even know it, but if and when we come in close contact with a live carrier, especially when there's blood involved, the virus can turn active."

"I got a virus?" She swallowed another bout of nausea.

"Yup."

"Bird flu?" she asked.

"Not quite."

"West Nile?"

"No. Vampirism."

She opened one eye—that's all she could do—and peered at him. She would have laughed if she didn't feel as if she were dying. "I'm a vampire?"

"Not yet, it takes four days. And it's not going to be easy. But I'll help you through it."

"I don't need your help." She was her father's daughter, always figuring out how to help herself. Della closed her one eye. Another pain shot through the back of her head, and she realized the way she had to help herself right now was to get help. But not from a ghost. Using every bit of energy she had, she got to her feet. The world started spinning.

"Where are you going?" Chan caught her right before she fell on her face.

She started to ignore Chan, because he wasn't real, but what the hell. "Gotta get Mom." Whatever someone put in her drink was pretty powerful stuff because she was sitting here talking to a ghost about vampires.

"I can't let you do that." Chan pushed her back on the bed—not that it took much effort. She had about as much energy as a snail on Xanax, skinny-dipping in a cup of chamomile tea.

"Mom?" Della screamed.

Della wasn't sure if she'd been in the hospital three hours or ten. She wasn't feeling any better, but at least she'd stopped hallucinating. Chan had disappeared. He hadn't appeared since her mom found her in the fetal position, throwing up again.

The nurses came in and out of her room, trying to force her to drink something. She didn't want to drink anything.

"What the hell did she take?" Della heard her father mutter.

"We don't know she took anything," her mom answered.

"Why would she do this to us? Doesn't she know how this will look?" her dad asked.

Della considered trying to tell them one more time that the only thing she'd done was drink one beer. Earlier she'd almost confessed her theory that someone might have put something in her drink, but stopped when she realized that would've gotten Lisa in trouble. Best to keep her mouth shut, and take whatever punishment came.

"I don't give a damn how it looks! I just want her to be okay," her mom said.

It was the same argument, different version. Mom hated Dad's pride. Della didn't like it either, but she understood it. She hated making mistakes, too. And on top of that, she'd seen the one-room apartment over a Chinese restaurant that her dad and his sister had been raised in. Her father and his family deserved to be proud of what they'd accomplished. And it hadn't happened by making mistakes.

Della heard the hospital door open again. "Why don't you take a coffee break, I'm going to be here for a while," a female voice said. Della thought she'd heard the voice earlier. Probably a nurse.

The sound of her parents leaving filled the room. Della felt an overwhelming gratefulness toward the nurse for sparing her from having to listen to the argument, but she didn't have what it took to express it.

"You're welcome," the nurse said, almost as if she'd read Della's mind.

Della opened her eyes. The nurse stood over her.

Blinking, Della tried to focus, but then something weird happened. She could see . . . something on the woman's forehead. Weird crap. Like lines and stuff, like some kind of computer-jumbled pattern. She blinked hard and slowly opened her eyes again. It helped. The odd stuff was gone.

Della went to push up and realized something else that was gone. The cut on her hand. How had it healed so fast?

The nurse smiled. "Has anyone talked to you yet?"

Della forced herself to reach for the large cup on the hospital table. "About drinking my water. Yeah."

"No, about what's happening to you." The nurse took the cup from Della's hand. "Don't drink anything. It'll make you sicker."

"Sicker? Have they figured out what's wrong?"

The door swished open and a doctor walked in. He moved to the side of her bed and stared down at her. "Does she know?" he asked the nurse.

"Know what?" Della blurted out.

"I don't think so." The nurse ignored Della's question.

"Know what?" she asked again.

"Her parents aren't live carriers?" the doctor asked.

"No," the nurse answered.

"Would you stop talking about me like I'm not here?"

The doctor met her gaze. "Sorry. I know this is hard." The intensity of his stare disturbed her. For some reason, everything about him disturbed her. Which was odd. She didn't normally instantly dislike people. It generally took at least fifteen minutes and a good reason.

She started to close her eyes, and bam, the weird crap appeared on the doc's forehead.

The doctor growled, a real growl. Della recalled the gang members doing—

"Someone knows." The doctor nodded back to the door.

The hospital door swung open so hard, it slammed against the wall and sounded as if it took a chunk out of the plastered wall. Della glanced up, but the doctor blocked her view.

"What the hell are you doing to her?" Chan stopped on the other side of the bed.

"Shit," Della said. "It's happening again." And when she glanced at the nurse that crazy thing was on her forehead again. It was as if Della could see inside the nurse's head, like in some cheesy B-rated movie.

She could see the front of her . . . brain. Yup, it looked like a brain, only it wasn't just wrinkled. It had strange-looking zigzaggy lines, a cross between bad modern art and ancient hieroglyphics.

"What's happening?" the nurse asked.

"I'm . . . seeing ghosts." Della had to force herself to stop staring at the woman's brain. She looked at Chan and now he had something on his forehead, too. Only his brain looked different.

"We're trying to help her," the doctor answered Chan.

Della's breath caught. "Can you see him, too?"

Chan snarled at the doctor, exposing his teeth, and she recalled the insane talk about vampires earlier. "She doesn't need your kind of help, werewolf!"

"Did you do this to her?" the doctor asked. "Are you the one who infected her?"

"Yes," Chan seethed. "But I didn't know she was bleeding, and if you must know, I didn't have a choice. It was snatch her up and get her out of the alley or let you dogs kill her!"

The doctor frowned. "Have you at least explained it to her?"

"I tried," Chan said. "She's not buying it."

"Buying what?" Della asked, blinking furiously, trying to get the crap off everyone's forehead. "He's dead," she snapped.

"We have to get her out of the hospital before Phase Two hits," the nurse said.

Phase what? Nothing was making sense now.

The doctor looked at Della. "Look, your cousin isn't dead. He's . . . a vampire and thanks to his carelessness, like it or not, you're about to become one, too."

Della's head started to pound again.

"I have to go," Chan said. "Her parents are coming up in the elevator."

"Wait," the doctor said to Chan, "If I get her released, will you see her through this?"

"I don't need anyone's help!" Della insisted.

"Of course I will," Chan said. "She's my cousin."

The nurse looked back at Della. "When the turn is complete, I want you to call this woman." She handed Della a card. When Della didn't take it, the nurse placed it in her hand.

"Call who?" Chan asked as he backed toward the door.

"Holiday Brandon. She's the director of the Shadow Falls Camp. She can help."

"Oh, hell no! Della's not going to that stupid camp to get brainwashed by the government."

The nurse's shoulders tightened. "They don't brainwash anyone. They'll help her decide what's best for her."

"I know what's best for her. She's going to come live with me."

Live with Chan? Della struggled to keep up with the crazy conversation. Then she heard the elevator bell ding as if it were right outside her door.

"And fake her death, like you did? That's why she thinks you're a ghost, right?" The nurse shook her head. "Is that really what you want for her? To have to walk away from her entire life, her family?"

Chan didn't answer. Della only saw a blur appear where he'd stood. The door swung back open and caused another chunk of plaster to rain down on the floor. The doctor and nurse looked back at Della with pity, sympathy. Della scowled at them.

"The nurse's right," the doctor said. "Call Shadow Falls. Trust your cousin to help get you through the next few days, but after that, don't believe everything he tells you. You look like a smart girl. Make up your own mind. With proper planning, we can live normal lives."

"We?" Della asked.

"Supernaturals," he said and pointed to his chest. "Werewolf." He motioned to the nurse. "Fae. And you're vampire. There are others, but you'll learn about them in time."

Della slumped back onto the pillow. "So it's official?" she muttered.

"What's official?" the nurse asked.

"I've lost my mind."

"You need to eat and drink something," Della's mother said and handed her a cup with steam billowing above the rim.

Della had been out of the hospital for a day. Her head pounded like a mofo, her body hurt like the worse case of flu she'd ever had. And mentally she was slipping. Her assessment no longer hinged on the fact that she saw Chan. It hinged on the fact that she was this close to believing him. She was turning into a vampire. And, according to Chan, the first two days were a stroll down Easy Street in flip-flops compared to what the next two would be.

She pulled the cup of hot tea to her lips, pretended to drink, hoping to appease her mom. The nurse, and then Chan, had told her that eating or drinking anything would make things worse. Oh, Della hadn't taken them at their word. Nope. She had to go prove it.

She'd never heard of anyone puking up a vital organ, but odds were she was missing a lung right now. Thank God she had two.

"Lee called again," her mom said, straightening Della's covers.

"Is he coming over?" Della managed to ask, torn between wanting to see him, and not wanting him to see her like this. Upchucking a lung didn't leave one looking their best.

"I told him he could, but he said his mom was worried you might be infectious."

"She never liked me." Della closed her eyes.

"Why would you say that?" Her mom stood up.

Because I'm half-white. "I don't know," Della lied and opened her eyes. "Because I'm too ballsy."

Her mom squeezed Della's hand. "You are too ballsy. Too independent. Too stubborn. A lot like your dad. But I love him, too." She brushed Della's bangs from her brow.

When her mom left, Chan stepped out of the closet. He edged up against the bed. "You're about to hit Phase Three."

"How do you know?" she asked and oh, damn but every nerve ending in her body seemed to scream. If this was Phase Three, she didn't like it one damn bit!

"Your heart rate is increasing," he said.

Della pushed her head back into the pillow and muttered some ugly words.

"Listen to me, Della. This is very important. When your parents come in here, you have to act normal. Whatever happens, we can't let them take you back to the hospital."

"Why not?" she asked and moaned.

"There's too much blood there. You might lose it. Even the smell of blood might send you over the edge. The first feeds have to be controlled feeds."

Another pain wracked her body and she bit her lip to keep from screaming. "Can I die from this?" She bunched up a fistful of blanket and squeezed. She hated being scared. Hated it because it was a sign of weakness.

His black eyes met hers. "Yeah."

Another sharp pain exploded in her head. "Am I going to die?" Her thoughts shot to Lee. She wanted him to be here to hold her. If she died, she wanted to see him one last time. Then her thoughts shot to her little sister, Marla. Della had sworn to be there for her, to make sure no one ever bullied Marla, like they had her. For some crazy reason, Della knew her sister wasn't as strong as she was.

"No, you're not going to die," Chan said, but Della saw the doubt in his eyes. "You're too hardheaded. Hardheaded Della can't die. You hear me? You can't die, Della. You're going to be strong."

Two days later, Della slowly drifted awake. She'd slept fitfully for most of the past forty-eight hours. She recalled sitting up and pretending to eat when her parents came in, so she wouldn't get stuck going back to the hospital. And she remembered talking to Chan a few times. But she'd been so feverish and out of it that her memory was still hazy. She opened her eyes and quickly slapped her hand over them to block the sun spilling through her window. "Stop that," she seethed.

"Who are you talking to?" Chan asked.

"The sun!" she growled and nearly cut her tongue on her teeth.

"It pisses me off, too. We're night people now. But it's about to go down." Chan must have lowered the blinds, because the burning brightness faded. He continued talking. "As soon as your parents go to bed, we're going out. I need to educate you."

"Educate me in what?"

"Your new life."

She moved her hand from her eyes and looked around. The first thing she saw was the flowers. Red roses. Lee? Yes, she recalled her mother bringing them in and reading her the card. Lee said he loved her.

She smiled and realized she didn't hurt. Not her head. Not her gut. In fact, she felt . . . good. Strong. She felt more alive than ever.

"I'm well!" She stretched out her arms and did a little bed dance.

"Yeah, you made it. Scared me for a while there, but—"

"Where's my cell?" She wanted to call Lee.

"In the drawer, so I wouldn't have to listen to all the beeping. Your lover boy is worried about you."

Right then, all their talk about vampirism ran through her head. Did she really believe? And if she didn't, how could she explain Chan? She pushed it out of her mind, and decided to enjoy not feeling like day-old dog poop for a few seconds before traveling down that road. A road she somehow knew was going to cause her a lot of pain.

Sitting on the side of the bed, she remembered Chan propping her up on pillows and telling her to fake being okay every time he heard her parents walking up the stairs. She couldn't remember how well she'd done, but probably not too badly because they never bundled her up to take her to the hospital.

She stood, stretched, and looked down at the chair positioned by the bed. And bam, she was slammed with the memory of Marla, her little sister stepping inside the room. She'd held Della's hand and cried. Cried silently because even her sister knew how her dad hated weakness. Marla's words played like sad music in Della's head. *Please don't die, Della. You're supposed to help me, help me learn to be strong like you.*

A big ache filled Della's chest. She was so glad she hadn't died and let Marla down.

Looking at the window, she had a vague memory of . . . standing on the roof.

"Did we go somewhere?"

"Yeah, you were getting cabin fever—needed to sort of test your wings. You did good, too."

Suddenly, she recalled moving at amazing speeds and feeling the wind in her face. What was real?

Her stomach growled. "I'm starved," she muttered.

Chan pointed to a big plastic cup with a straw. "You didn't finish your breakfast."

She reached for the drink and sipped. A thousand different flavors exploded in her mouth. Berries, dark chocolate, tangy melon. Flavors she didn't even recognize, but somehow knew she couldn't live without now that she had sampled them.

"What *is* this?" She licked her lips and immediately started drinking again.

His right brow arched. "It's what you'll be living on from now on. Blood."

She almost gagged, then stopped herself. She'd bitten her tongue before. "Blood doesn't taste like this." She yanked the top off and stared at . . . at what looked like blood.

"How can . . ."

"Nothing will taste like it did before. Don't you remember gagging on the chicken soup your mom brought you?"

She looked at her cousin and vaguely remembered trying to eat the soup. "Tell me you're lying."

"Sorry. Everything is different now. No use in me trying to sugarcoat things. Just accept it."

She stared down at the thick red substance in her cup. "This can't be real."

"It's as real as it gets."

"Oh, God!" She put the cup on her nightstand and stared at it. "What kind of blood?"

"AB negative. O is better, but I couldn't find any."

"That's . . . that's human blood?" Her stomach churned.

He nodded. "Animal isn't nearly as good. But you'll learn about that in time. I have a lot to teach you."

She cupped a hand over her mouth and stared at the cup. But even as the thought of drinking blood sickened her, even as a part of her vowed not to become this monster, her mouth watered for another taste, another swallow.

She hadn't ever known real hunger or thirst, but this . . . the feeling that said if she didn't finish what was in that cup right now she might die, had to be the closest thing she'd ever experienced.

Chan went to grab the cup. Before she knew what she was doing she lunged, knocked him across the room, and grabbed the cup.

He laughed. "I figured as much."

She finished the drink, and looked up at Chan. "I need more."

"I know. Right after you turn, you're ravenous. I think I put down fifteen pints my few first days. But you're going to have to wait until after your parents go to bed."

"I want it now," she hissed, not even recognizing her own voice.

"They didn't card me?" Della said, following Chan into the club several hours later. The place was dark, lit up by only a few candles, but amazingly she didn't have much trouble seeing. Or hearing. Noise, crowd noise, the chattering of different conversations, and people shifting in their chairs, came at her from every direction, but somehow she could shut out the parts of it that she didn't want to listen to. However, the ambience didn't stem from the noise or the lighting. Energy vibrated in the place. Della felt it, felt it feeding her, like some forbidden drug.

"The only card you need for this place is right here." He touched her forehead.

Immediately, Della remembered the weird things she'd been seeing on everyone's forehead. She grabbed his arm. "What is that? The forehead thing?"

He grinned. "It's your ID. All supernaturals have the ability to read brain patterns, and eventually you'll learn to tell who is what. And if you concentrate just a little bit you can get behind their shields and know if they're friend or foe."

He pointed across the room. "Look at the guy in the green shirt. Tighten your eyes, and stare at his forehead and tell me what you see."

At first all Della saw was his forehead and then . . . "I see . . . swirly lines."

"Now look at my pattern. Do you see the similarities?" Chan asked.

"Yes. But they're not identical," she said.

"Not identical, but he's vampire. Brain patterns are like tracks in the snow—sooner or later, you'll be able to know what kind of animal made that print."

She nodded and glanced around the room.

"Look at that big guy's pattern, the guy in the black coat," he said.

She did. The pattern was completely different. Horizontal lines and . . .

"Now look deeper. Keep staring. Open your mind."

She concentrated and what she saw was black and dark and gave off the impression of danger. She took a step back.

He laughed. "It's okay. He's not going to hurt you. Not here, anyway. But meet him in a dark alley, and who knows."

"I wasn't scared," she insisted, but she knew it was a lie and she heard her own heartbeat speed up as if punctuating the fib.

"You should be. He's werewolf and not someone you want to associate with."

Della remembered. "The doctor. He was a werewolf and he didn't seem . . . bad."

"They are all bad." He looked around. "There's a fae, the pretty brunette in the pink dress. Well, she's half fae, half human."

Della tightened her brows and recalled the pattern of the nurse in the hospital. "I think I sort of understand. But if these people don't get along, how come they come to the same bar? And why would they work together?"

"Because some supers think we should live as one big happy family. Like humans who want to live alongside lions. And I admit I've had my fair share of fun toying with a few breeds." He wiggled his brows. "Especially humans. It's fun to play with our food."

Della took a step back. "You're human. How can you . . ."

"I told you earlier, I'm not going to sugarcoat it. I'm not human anymore. Neither are you. You need to start looking at humans as prey because that's all they are for us."

Della put a hand over her mouth. "The blood earlier, you didn't . . . hurt anyone."

"Got it from a blood bank." He glanced away, almost too quickly, as if he were lying. "Oh, see the little guy in the black shirt? Check his pattern out, but . . . if he looks this way, glance away, quick."

Emotions swirled around Della's chest. She stared at Chan.

"Look at him, Della. This is important. You need to know this shit."

"Why?"

"Because he's a shape-shifter. You need to be able to recognize them so you can stay clear of them. They are one pissed-off breed. All that changing forms messes with their psyche. Most of them would just as soon kill you as speak to you in passing."

Her emotions were again swarming in her chest.

"Don't worry," Chan said. "Where you're going to live, you won't—"

Della recalled vague snippets of conversation about leaving her family. She couldn't do that. "Chan, I . . ."

"I'm taking you back to Utah with me. It's a vampire community. I'm actually thinking about joining a gang, and if you want to, we both can—"

She shook her head. "Even if I wanted to go with you, my parents would never let me go."

"Which is another reason we're here. There's a guy here, a mortician, he's going to help us fake your death. How do you wanna go, car crash? Maybe you fall and hit your head when you get out of the tub. He's really good."

Della stood there staring at him, the dark candlelit atmosphere making it seem surreal. Instantly, she remembered how Chan's parents had been devastated at his funeral, how his little sister and hers had cried. How Della had wanted to cry, but her daddy kept looking at her and reminding her she had to be strong.

"No," she said to Chan. "I won't do this."

"You don't have a choice."

"No!"

And just like that, Chan disgusted her. She had to get away from him. Away from everything he was telling her. She shoved him hard. Harder than she intended to. She saw him fly across the room. She didn't wait to see him land, or even to see if he was okay. She took off, darting between tables until she saw a door and ran for it. That room was even darker—only two or three candles were placed on a bar. She darted away from the light, hoping to hide, hoping to lose herself in the crowd.

Suddenly a guy grabbed her by her forearms. "Slow down, sweet-cakes. You okay?"

Sweetcakes? She looked at him, but with the tears in her eyes her vision wasn't quite focused. Suddenly his forehead opened up and she saw his pattern. She didn't know what he was, but when she looked deeper, she got a sleazy feeling.

He leaned closer. His breath smelled like onions. "I ordered this for me, but I think you need it more." He placed a warm shot glass in her hand.

She was about to drop it away when the smell hit her. The exotic flavors. She brought the glass to her lips and swallowed it in one gulp. It was better than any alcohol she'd ever tasted. Even better than the blood she'd drunk earlier.

"What was that?" She licked her lips to collect the last taste.

"O negative. Freshly drained." The guy smiled. "My name's Marshal. How about we go back to my place? I got some of this stuff at home, too."

The seediness of his presence suddenly overwhelmed her. "Ever heard of statutory rape, you pervert?" Della seethed, realizing the guy was older than her dad.

"Need some help?" asked a girl who suddenly stood beside them. Dressed goth, her eyes brightened a gold color. Della tightened her brows to read the girl's brain pattern, and decided she was most likely a werewolf. The girl grabbed the man.

The man shoved the girl down and grabbed Della. Della lost it and tossed him across the room the way she had Chan, then she took off for another door, but not before looking back and seeing the girl who'd helped her give her the thumbs-up. Della couldn't help but wonder if Chan was wrong about werewolves.

"Don't believe everything he tells you. You look like a smart girl. Make up your own mind." The doctor's words played in her head, but she didn't have time to think. She heard the dirty old man spouting out orders to someone to find her and bring her back so he could teach her a lesson.

She'd learned enough lessons for one day, Della thought. She ran faster, knocking over tables and chairs, and occasionally the chairs weren't empty. "Sorry. Sorry," she said as she went, moving through the dark, crowded spaces. She smelled beer, and heard the clinking sound of ice swirling in drinks. The club was like an old house, a lot of cubbyholes and tiny rooms filled with card tables for people to group together. The interior felt as if someone had just kept building on, creating an almost mazelike atmosphere. She moved aimlessly, through one door, then another, or maybe it wasn't so aimlessly.

She followed something. She just didn't know what it was until . . . until she did know. The smell.

Blood.

She entered another room, and three men lay stretched out on beds, needles in their arms and blood being drained from their bodies.

Her first thought was that they were being forced to give up their life-sustaining substance; her second thought was . . . yum. Her stomach grumbled and she licked her lips. Then her last thought sickened her. She took a step back, afraid of the urges vibrating through her body, but then the smell entered her senses and her mouth watered.

"If you're wanting to buy it, you'll have to go to the bar," said one of the men. "We work for Tony and we'll get our ass burned if we start selling by the pints in here. But if you want to take one of our cards, we can talk later."

Della watched as one man got up, pulled a needle out of his own arm, and sealed off the bag with some kind of plastic clamp. But the ripe smell of all those exotic flavors filled the room. She watched as he put the blood on a metal tray.

"Hungry, aren't you?" he asked and he smiled at her. She tightened her eyes and saw he had a pattern similar to the nurse. Was he fae?

She inhaled, the smell again filling her nose. Realizing they offered to sell her the blood later, she concluded that they obviously weren't being forced to give up blood. Somehow that made her desire for it less hideous.

Her heart raced. Her stomach grumbled and she dove over the man, her only goal, her only desire to get her hands on that bag of blood.

She got it. The other men stood up from their beds. The needles were yanked from their arms, blood spilling on the floor as they stood. She hissed at them, thinking they would attack, but they all backed up, as if she frightened them. She knew she frightened herself. The deep, angry sounds parting her lips were unlike any sound she'd ever made.

Moving backward, she found the doorknob and made it outside the door, but a loud ear-pinching noise filled her head. Alarms. She held the plastic bag of blood close to her chest and ducked between crowded tables. Heads turned and followed her every move. She realized that perhaps the others were like her and could probably smell the blood. But she still didn't care. She needed this. Had to have it.

Suddenly, she felt someone grab her arm and yank her across the room. She fought, but her attacker's strength matched her own. The alarms kept ringing, she heard people running away from her and some toward her. Whoever had her continued to pull her across the room. She glanced up and didn't see a door, no way to escape. Would she die here because she'd stolen blood? She tried to pull away, but couldn't. And then they crashed through a window, shards of glass fell around her, and in seconds they were flying.

"That was so stupid," Chan said. "You so could have gotten us killed."

She closed her eyes tight, preventing her weakness from showing, but on the inside, where it counted the most, the tears fell. What was happening to her? What kind of monster had she become?

In a matter of minutes, she and Chan stood outside her house. Normally he landed on the roof and they crawled in her bedroom window. Not this time. She clutched the blood to her chest as if it were a precious stone.

"If you want it, you'd better drink now," he said, his frustration evident from his posture to his tone. "Your parents are up and pissed."

The bag of blood in her hand was still warm. Somehow its scent leaked out of the plastic and filled her nose. Della looked back at her house. "How do you know they're up?"

"Focus. Your sensitive hearing should already be working."

She looked up at her bedroom window. "I can't hear . . ." And suddenly she could. Her mom cried and her dad muttered about how he planned to find a good drug rehab. She stared back at Chan. "I'm not using drugs?"

"Yeah, but you're doing things you've never done, so they just assume. My parents did the same thing." He sighed. "But it doesn't matter what they think."

"It does to me," Della snapped back.

He shook his head. "Can't you see how impossible living here will be? It's not like you can keep your blood supply in the fridge. You're not going to fit into their lifestyle now."

She shook her head. "I can't . . . I can't walk away from . . . Lee. I can't leave my sister. She needs me." And whether she wanted to admit it or not, she loved her parents, too.

"Hardheaded Della," he muttered. "I should have known you'd have to find it out for yourself. So go . . . walk in there with your blood and see if you can explain it." He threw up his hands as if exasperated. "I'm leaving. Going back to Utah. How are you going to get blood tomorrow or the next day? You can't live with humans anymore. You can't."

"They're my family," she said.

"Not anymore. I'm your family. Other vampires are your family. You'll see. You don't belong here."

She looked down at the bag of blood. Her hands shook. Her chest hurt with emotion.

"Ah, screw it," Chan said and the fury in his eyes faded. "Give me the blood. I'll bring it to you later. Go deal with your parents. But I'm telling you, I can't hang around here to supply you with blood forever. Sooner or later, you're going to have to leave them. You'll see. I don't care how hardheaded you are. Sooner or later, you're going to have to accept my help."

Della refused to cry. No matter how harsh, how bitter her father's words were. She sat there on the sofa, her chin held high, taking the insults. Each one hurt a little bit more. But damn it to hell and back. She wouldn't cry. Her father continued, telling her how *she was a disappointment to him and his family legacy. How she'd brought shame down on her family name. How he would never be able to stand proud in public again.*

"Go to your room and think about what you have done!" he finally demanded.

She left. She couldn't get away from him, or her mom, fast enough. Her mom had stood stone-faced and let him say those horrible things. All of it a lie. She wasn't taking drugs, or selling her body to different men to feed her obsession. She'd given her body to one, Lee, whom she loved, who loved her. When she got to her room and slammed the door, she tried to swallow the shame, the anger, the fury that filled her throat.

Then the sweet smell of roses filled her nose. Her gaze shot to the arrangement. Suddenly, all she could think about was Lee. She needed him to hold her, to tell her it would all be okay. Rushing to the window, she flung it open and stared down at the grass two stories below. She stood on the edge for several seconds, unsure how she did this, but desperation made her jump.

Landing on her feet without feeling any of the impact of the jump, she took a deep breath and started to run. At first, it was slow, then faster and faster still. Soon she wasn't even sure her feet touched the ground. As the wind whipped her hair around her face, Della formed a new plan.

She didn't have to go live with Chan in Utah; she and Lee could get their own place. They had talked about it already. They would work part time and go to school. They could do this.

In less than five minutes, she stood in front of Lee's house. She saw his window, but it was dark. Of course it was dark, it was two in the morning, but she didn't care. She leapt up, grabbing hold of his ledge, and then she forced the window up. Thankfully, it wasn't locked.

When she climbed inside, Lee sat up. He blinked, stared at her with his dark brown eyes, and then he ran a hand through his hair. "Della?"

She moved closer. "I . . . I had to see you. I missed you."

"Are you okay?"

"Yeah, I'm fine."

"Your mom said the doctors didn't know what was wrong with you."

"They didn't, but I'm well now and I've been thinking . . . I want to be with you. I want to get our own apartment like we talked about."

He stared at her, his hair mussed. He wasn't wearing a shirt, and he looked good. Sexy. She moved to the edge of the bed.

"How did you . . . get inside?" He looked back at the window.

"It was unlocked."

"But it's the second-story window." He scratched his head.

She sat down beside him. "I love you, Lee. I want to be with you, always." She reached out to touch him. His skin was so hot, and felt so good. She just wanted to lie down beside him, have him hold her.

He flinched and pulled away. "You're cold. *Really* cold."

His words brought back something Chan had said when she'd been half out of it. Something about her body temperature changing, about how she couldn't let her parents take her temperature anymore.

"What's wrong with you?" he said, scooting away. "You must still be sick."

"No," Della said. "I'm fine, I'm just . . . I mean . . ." What did she mean? Was she going to tell Lee the truth? "I'm not contagious," she said.

"What did you have?" He eased away, when all she wanted to do was to get closer. She wanted him to hold her, to kiss her and make her forget everything that happened these last few days. He raked a hand through his black hair. "You should probably go. If you get caught here, you know how it will look."

"It will look as if we're sleeping together. Which we are. And I don't care if people know anymore."

She put her hand on his shoulder.

"But I do care," he said. "Don't touch me." He pushed her hand away. "I . . . I'm sorry, but I don't like how you feel right now. Something feels . . . off about you. It's hard to explain, but you just seem really weird right now. I think you should go home and talk to your parents, get the help you need."

It hit her then. Hit her like an eighteen-wheeler without brakes. Lee would never like how she felt. If he was afraid of some kind of flu, how would he feel about her being a vampire? About her drinking blood?

Tears filled her throat, but like the daughter her father had raised her to be, she didn't let a single tear fill her eyes. "I see." She stood up.

"See what?" he asked.

She moved to the window and swore she wouldn't look back, but she couldn't help it. She turned and met his eyes. For some reason, she suddenly saw something in Lee that she hadn't seen before. She saw her father. And yet . . . "I love you. I will always love you." And with that she jumped out of his upstairs window. She heard him call her name, and pull back the covers.

But she was gone before his feet touched the floor.

When she got back to her room, she sat on the edge of her bed. Her stomach growled, her mouth watered, and she knew she needed . . . blood. Where was Chan? Had he taken her O negative pint for himself? Had he abandoned her? She jumped up and went to the mirror and stared at herself. Her eyes were no longer dark brown, but golden. Bright hot yellow as if something inside her burned. And yet she was cold. Too cold for Lee? She noticed her two canines were . . . sharp.

Her pulse raced and she heard Chan's words bounce around her head. *You can't live with humans anymore. You don't belong here.*

Her chest ached and this time she did cry. Tears crawled down her cheeks. Accepting what she had to do, she grabbed her suitcase and tossed in a few things. When Chan got here, she would be ready. Then, realizing she couldn't leave without . . . without at least seeing her family one more time, she tiptoed out of her room and headed down the stairs. Her parents' door was closed, but she eased it open just a bit. Just enough to see them one last time. Her mother was asleep on her father's chest. Her mother might not like her father's pride, but she still loved him. She loved him because down deep she knew that her father had forsaken his pride to marry a white woman. In truth, he loved her mom more than his pride.

Her throat tightened as she silently closed the door. Then she moved back up the stairs, but instead of moving toward her room, she went to Marla's room. The door wasn't closed. She stepped inside and moved to the edge of the bed. Her sister rolled over and opened her eyes.

"You feeling better?" she asked.

"Yeah." Della tried to keep her voice from shaking.

Marla smiled that sleepy smile of hers that made her look younger than fourteen. "I told Mom you wouldn't die, because you wouldn't leave me. You'd never leave me." She dropped down on her pillow and drifted back to sleep.

Tears filled Della's eyes and the pain of knowing she'd never see her sister again made her heart break. She got up and walked out of the room. She closed the door and saw her packed bag. She'd left the window open, hoping Chan would see it and come back. A breeze entered. It felt . . . colder. Unnaturally cold. Chills tiptoed up her spine.

Something fluttering across the wood floor caught Della's eye. She looked down at the card. She picked it up and saw the name *Holiday Brandon* scribbled across the card. Below the name was a telephone number and the words SHADOW FALLS CAMP.

Vaguely, she remembered the doctor and nurse telling her she could call someone, someone who could help her decide the right thing to do. But she couldn't call a stranger and ask for help. Or could she?

Her thoughts went to her sister and Della reached for her phone and dialed.

"Shadow Falls Camp," a woman answered. Della couldn't speak. "Is someone there?" asked the sleepy voice. "Who is this?"

Another stream of tears silently slipped down Della's cheek. "My name is Della Tsang and I need help."

Saved at Sunrise

◆

Chapter One

"Do not put yourselves in any jeopardy. Your job is to infiltrate the gang by showing interest in joining, find out if they're using murder as a rite of initiation, and then get out. Alive."

"That's my plan, too." Della Tsang answered with sass, looking up at Burnett James, one of the Shadow Falls Academy owners who also just so happened to work for the FRU—Fallen Research Unit—which was basically the FBI of the supernatural world.

"We don't want you to bring anyone in. We don't want you to take care of the bad guys." Burnett continued staring right at her.

Afternoon sun poured into the window of the Shadow Falls office behind him. The crystals sitting on shelves caught the light and cast rainbow-colored mirages on the wall. They danced and shifted as if magical. And maybe they were. Crap like that happened all the time here.

"Actually," Burnett said, drawing Della's attention back to him, "we don't think this is the group, but if it is, with your testimony, we'll have enough proof to get a search warrant and we're pretty damn positive we should find all the evidence we need to convict."

Burnett, six feet plus, with dark hair and eyes, was a hard-ass who worried way too much, but being a vampire like herself, Della respected him and his hard-assness.

She just wished the respect was mutual. Seriously, didn't he trust her? Didn't he know she could friggin' take care of herself? Did he really have to go over this *again*?

"I understand, sir." Steve, the brown-haired, brown-eyed, great-bodied guy sitting next to her spoke up when she didn't. For the first time, Della noticed his voice held a hint of a Southern accent that wasn't just Texan.

Della glanced over. Steve gave Burnett his complete attention. What an ass-kisser.

Steve was evidence that Burnett didn't trust her. Why else would Burnett insist Steve go with her? She didn't need the shape-shifter. He was just going to slow her down.

"Wait," Burnett said, pacing across the office again. "Let me re-phrase that. I don't want you to just get out alive. I want you to get out just the way you went in. Not wounded, not bruised, and for God's sake, don't leave any dead bodies behind. You got that?"

"Now you're taking all the fun out of it," Della smarted off.

Burnett growled. "I'm not joking and if you can't take this seriously then get your vampire butt out of here, because I'm not playing around."

Della slumped back in her chair, knowing when to shut her mouth. She really wanted to do this assignment for the FRU. Wanted to win Burnett's respect. Everyone needed someone to impress. And since impressing her parents wasn't an option anymore, she'd settle for Burnett.

Not that impressing anyone was the only reason she wanted to go. Even before she'd been turned into a vampire, she'd considered a career in criminal justice—something that allowed her to kick butt. Of course, her parents had frowned on that. They had her earmarked to be a doctor. They had her earmarked to be a lot of things.

But not a vampire.

Not that they knew what she was. The way Della figured it, if they went bat-shit crazy just because she'd stopping eating rice—which after being turned tasted like curdled toe jam—how the hell were they going to accept that she was a blood-drinking vampire? The answer was obvious. They wouldn't, couldn't accept it.

Lucky for her, she'd been accepted into Shadow Falls—a boarding school for supernaturals—and didn't have to worry what her parents thought about her choice of careers, or whether she ate her rice or not. And yet . . . now Della couldn't help but question if they ever thought or worried about her at all. Did they sit down to eat dinner and notice her chair was empty? Did her mom ever forget and set an extra plate at the table?

She doubted it.

Yes, they came to the parents' day visitations, but they were always the first to leave, and eager to do it. Especially her father, the man Della had spent her entire life trying to impress.

A daddy's girl, her mom used to call her.

Not anymore.

No doubt her sister had taken over that role.

Turning vampire hadn't been Della's choice. It was one of those things life slapped on your ass and you just had to accept it. Which meant she'd had to accept that her family would never be able to accept her. Not that it really bothered her. Not anymore.

She was so over it.

"Am I making myself clear?" Burnett asked, yanking her back to reality.

"One hundred percent," Della said, working hard to keep her attitude from spilling over.

"Yes, sir." Steve nodded.

Yup, an ass-kisser.

"Okay, you got your orders?" Burnett said. "You know where to go and what your cover is? They expect you to meet them at four in the morning. Don't be late, don't be too early. Don't let them lure you back to their compound. The policy, if they follow their own policy, is that three of the members will meet with you to talk. You get the information about joining, you get out."

"Got it." Della held up the brown envelope. *And you've gone over this ten times.*

"Then go get your things." Burnett eyed Della. "And please, don't make me regret sending you on this."

"You won't," Della said.

Della and Steve stood to leave.

"Steve," Burnett said. "Give me a few minutes."

Della looked from Steve to Burnett. What the hell did he need to talk with Steve about that couldn't be said in front of her?

Burnett shifted his gaze to Della and then cut his eyes to the door.

Frowning, Della shot up from the chair and left. She stopped about fifty feet from the porch, holding her breath and not moving a muscle. Hoping Burnett wasn't still listening, she tuned her own vampire hearing and waited to discover what the hell was up. The afternoon sun spilled over the trees, casting shadows on the ground as she stood frozen in one spot.

"I'm trusting you to keep Della safe," Burnett said.

Della inwardly growled at Burnett's chauvinistic approach and fought the need to rush back in there and give him some lip. *I'm the one who's gonna have to protect* his *butt!*

"I do not believe this is the gang we're looking for." Burnett's voice carried well. *"Or I wouldn't be sending you two. This is just a clearance check. But that doesn't mean this group isn't dangerous."*

"Don't worry," Steve's deep voice answered. *"I'll keep her in my sight at all times."*

Like hell you will. She already had a plan of doing a little side trip, and she didn't need Steve tagging along.

At six that evening they arrived at the cabin the FRU had rented them right outside the vampire compound. To call the place a dump would have been like calling one of those roach-coach vans fine dining.

Of course, she and Steve were supposed to look like a couple of supernatural teen runaways. She supposed it would have looked suspicious if they'd rented anything with even part of a star attached to its reputation. But damn, this was supposed to have been a fun trip.

She wasn't a prima donna, but sleeping on a mattress that was more dust mites than filling, with sheets that looked as if they hadn't been changed in a year or so wasn't her idea of fun. The bed's covers were half on and half off the mattress, and the pillow sported an indented greasy spot in the center as if someone with not-so-clean hair had slept there.

Or maybe died there.

As disgusting as that thought was, one even worse hit. Someone had probably done the humpty dance on that bed.

Yuck.

She could probably get a disease sleeping on it.

Walking back into the tiny living area, she found Steve staring at the sofa with about as much distaste as she had while gaping at the bed.

"Come to think about it, I'll take the sofa," she said. "And I don't want to hear any shit. There ain't no one going to get past me."

They had flown here. Not on a jet. Him as a peregrine falcon—which meant he was fast—and her as a, well, a vampire—which meant she was faster. Vamps and shape-shifters were the only two species who could really fly. Well, an occasional witch, but Miranda, her Wiccan roommate, swore they really didn't travel around on brooms.

However, Steve and Della's mode of transportation also meant they really hadn't spoken since they'd left Shadow Falls, with the exception of when they'd first walked into the cabin and he'd insisted she take the bed. And why? Because if someone came through the door he would stop them.

That downright pissed her off. She almost called him on being a complete chauvinistic pig, but then realized that if she wanted to sneak out later, she wouldn't want him traipsing into the living room before morning and finding her gone.

Since he came across as the type with manners, and morals and stuff, who wouldn't come into a girl's bedroom—at least not without an invitation—she'd kept her mouth shut.

Face it, she'd take the odds of him finding her gone to the odds of those mattress germs finding her body, hands down.

Steve cut his soft brown eyes to her and a knowing smile spread his lips. He ran a hand through his brown hair, which he wore a tad longer than most guys. The strands fell right back into place, looking instantly styled. She doubted he went to some professional salon to get that look, but it almost appeared like he did.

His smile widened and he tucked one hand into his jeans pocket. The stance made the muscles in that arm bulge. "So what you're saying is that the bed is worse than the sofa?"

"I didn't say that." She tried not to laugh, but something close to it slipped out of her mouth. She tried not to stare at his crooked smile and what it did to his lips and eyes. Or how his muscled arms looked like a safe place to fall. She'd give anything, even half a bra size to make him . . . ugly. And unlike her two roommates at Shadow Falls, she didn't have much bra size to offer.

She continued to stare at him. She could have dealt with an ugly guy much better than one who looked like he'd just walked off of some men's soap advertisement. And hell, she thought, breathing in his aroma, you'd think after spending the last two hours as a bird, he wouldn't smell like he used some spicy-smelling men's soap, but he did.

He smelled . . . awesome, and that ticked her off, too.

If she were a witch like her bigger-boobed roommate, Miranda, she'd change him into a repulsive fowl/foul-smelling guy. And she'd also make him less . . . nice. She didn't like nice.

The only nice person Della had grown fond of was Kylie. And she was so nice, even Della couldn't hate her. Well, right now, Della did hate her. Hated her for leaving. And if she didn't get her butt back to Shadow Falls soon, Della was going to drag her friend back kicking and screaming. Sure, Kylie had gone to meet her newly discovered grandfather and learn more about her species, but plain and simple, she belonged at Shadow Falls. Someone had to keep Della and Miranda from killing each other. And no one was better at that than Kylie.

"We could both sleep on the sofa," Steve said, and damn if he didn't sound serious.

"Not even in your dreams, bird boy!" she snapped.

"Ouch," he said and chuckled. "I only meant your head at one end and mine at the other. Only our feet would be touching."

"So you've got a foot fetish, do you?" she asked before she could stop herself.

Humor brightened his eyes. With him positioned right in front of the bare window, and the last rays of the setting sun beaming in, she got a good look at those eyes. Were those flecks of amber and green in his brown pools?

His gaze lowered to her Nike-covered size sixes. "I don't know, I haven't seen your naked feet."

Hearing him say the word *naked* with what sounded like a deep Southern accent, deeper than Texas, made her stomach flutter like she was twelve again and had never been kissed. Good Lord, what was wrong with her? Since when did she find a Southern accent seductive?

She stuck one foot behind the other. "And you won't see them naked," she snapped, not liking that they'd been here less than five minutes and they were already . . . flirting. At least it felt like flirting.

And Della Tsang didn't flirt.

Not anymore.

His gaze rose from her feet. "We'll see about that," he said.

They stood there staring at each other for a second. Then he spoke up. "You want to go grab a bite to eat?"

She frowned. "I brought a couple pints of AB positive with me in my bag." Which she needed to put in the fridge. While most vamps preferred their blood warm, Della liked it better cold. When your core temperature was 92 degrees, you appreciated things colder than yourself.

"Yeah, but I need food. Something hot and greasy. Nutrients for whatever the hell is gonna go down tomorrow morning."

Steve had been set up to play as her shape-shifter boyfriend, a guy she'd met after running away from home. They didn't allow anyone but vampires into the gang, but if she got accepted, and he could prove his worth to them, he would be brought in as an "extra." Basically someone they sent out to do their dirty work. Which was part of the reason it pissed her off that Burnett insisted he come. Extras were considered expendable.

"Don't worry, I'll protect you," she said.

"That just warms my heart." He put a hand over his wide chest. "Come on, go with me to grab a burger."

He made it sound like a date or something. Frowning, she was about to call him on it when she remembered seeing a Walmart not far from there and close to some fast-food joints. She could pick up a set of sheets, a blanket, and some extra-strength Lysol spray and maybe be able to sleep on the bed. That meant she could skip out on the foot-loving, Southern-speaking Steve. She wouldn't be gone long. She only needed a peek. A peek at the life she'd been cheated out of.

"Fine." She lit out of the room.

He lit out with her, and within seconds had transformed into a hauling-ass peregrine falcon. She wasn't certain, but she thought she'd heard this was one of the fastest birds that existed. It wasn't a half-bad-looking animal, either. Its feathers were a blend of browns, tans, and black. Its eyes were striking, round, with large black pupils that seemed to take everything in. And when it stretched out its wings, it almost looked like it had leopard spots.

Della didn't know a whole lot about shape-shifters, but she'd heard once that one sign of their power was they could shift quickly. He'd shifted into a bird pretty damn quickly. Not that she was impressed or anything.

Sort of like flirting, Della Tsang didn't get impressed. Not about guys.

Not anymore.

Not since she'd turned vampire, turned cold, and had her heart shattered into tiny little bitty pieces by the guy who was supposed to love her forever.

Della landed with a thud on the pavement in the back of Walmart. Steve, still a bird, landed elegantly beside her. His wings stretched out wide.

Immediately, he started turning back into human form, and as always when a shifter turned, sparkly bubbles began floating around.

One of his transformation bubbles lingering in the evening air popped on her arm and sent a tiny electric current up her elbow, zinging like she'd walked on carpet and then touched something metal.

"What are we doing here?" Steve asked, looking confused.

"Bedding and disinfectant." She brushed off her elbow, then looked up. The sky was darkening, and the stars hadn't yet come out to play. Lifting her nose in the air, her vampire sense of smell caught the hint of werewolf under the strong scent of motor oil.

"Something wrong?" Steve asked.

"A few werewolves, but not too close."

He frowned. "Damn, let's grab what you need, snag me a burger, and get the hell back."

She smirked. "You scared of a couple of werewolves?"

"Scared, no. But we don't need any trouble right now." He started walking.

She moved with him. "Sometimes trouble is fun."

"Yeah, but let's save our energy for any trouble that finds us tomorrow."

"Anyone ever accuse you of being boring?" she snipped.

"No, but I'll admit, I'm more of a lover than a fighter."

She kept an eye on the dark shadows, making sure something didn't lurk there. "Please, that's so lame."

"Lame, but true." Humor sounded in his voice.

"I'll stick with lame," she muttered.

She imagined him smiling again, but afraid she'd be pulled into his smile, she didn't chance looking at him. Hearing the laughter in his voice gave her stomach flutters. Or was she just hungry and needing some blood?

Entering the store, they made fast work of buying two flat sheets, a couple of pillowcases, two blankets, and some disinfectant. And Steve tossed in a bag of chips. At the fast-food place next door he got his burger to go, but he wolfed it down as they left the joint to find a desolate spot for him to transform so they could head back.

He'd finished the burger when they started down a dark alley behind the strip center. She noticed he stuffed the sandwich wrapper in his pocket. The guy didn't even litter, never mind the alley was covered in trash. They only got about ten feet down when they heard a scream.

A life-or-death-sounding scream.

Chapter Two

Della stopped, her gaze zipping around to locate the screamer. Steve jerked her into the dark shadows. A woman suddenly appeared at the other side of the alley running like the devil was chasing her. And he might've been, because someone slapped the pavement right on her heels.

A male someone.

"What are they?" Steve whispered, standing so close she could feel his words against her cheek.

They were too far away to note the pattern in their foreheads which marked a person's species—something all supernaturals could see—but Steve obviously trusted her sense of smell. She inhaled and tried to find the scents in the air besides the spicy male soap that filled her nose. "Humans."

"Good." He took off down the alley.

The girl screamed again as the attacker tackled her. Della, plastic bag in tow, beat Steve to the scuffle. The man on top of the female shifted back and forth, using the woman as a punching bag. Della snagged the creep off the obvious victim and tossed him a good five feet in the air. Not enough to kill him, but hopefully enough to hurt when he came down.

Blood oozed from the woman's nose and mouth. "You okay?" Della asked and crouched beside her. When the scent of blood filled her nose, Della had to work at not letting her eyes start to glow from hunger.

"Yeah." The woman sobbed out the word. "He's my husband, but he's drunk." She wiped blood from her lip. "He gets mean when he drinks."

But he wasn't the only one drinking. Della could smell booze on the woman's breath.

"This wasn't your problem," a deep voice seethed from behind Della. If she hadn't been so intent on the woman, she'd have heard him coming.

Della glanced up. Looming over them stood the drunk husband, who she obviously hadn't thrown nearly hard enough. Of course, that could be fixed.

He reached for Della, fury in his eyes and alcohol on his breath. "But you made it your problem now, bitch!"

Before she could shoot up, Steve caught the man by the arm and swung him around.

Fists started flying. Della heard what sounded like a few punches hitting bone. She could swear the jerk got a punch in on Steve. Bolting to her feet with plans to end the fight, Steve ended it first. He threw a hard right. The woman's dear old husband took that right directly to the face and fell over cold.

It would have been nice to savor the moment of success, but a pair of flashing blue police lights appeared at the end of the alley. Steve turned to Della. "We need to get the hell out of here."

Della grabbed her bag and they took off at a sprint. In the distance she heard the cops yelling for everyone to stop. They didn't. They couldn't.

Burnett hadn't been specific about them not getting arrested, but she had a feeling he'd frown upon it.

"Police! I said stop," the policeman yelled again. Footsteps echoed behind them, making their way down the alley.

They cut the corner into a side alley, and Della didn't know if they had time to get the hell out without the officers seeing their escape.

The refrigerator at the cabin didn't have an ice machine. She supposed she should be glad it had one ice tray with five pieces of ice in it. She emptied the five tiny cubes into a new pillowcase and handed it to Steve. His eye was almost swollen shut. "Hold it against your eye," she said.

They'd gotten away from the police, but barely. She stared at Steve's injury.

"Why didn't you change into something and maul his ass?" she bit out.

"You don't transform in front of humans," Steve said. "That's the number one shape-shifting rule."

"I'd think the number one rule would be to protect yourself."

"You'd think wrong," Steve said.

She shook her head. "They were both drunk, who would've believed them?"

He cut his eyes up to her. "What about when the cops showed up?"

She frowned, seeing his point, but still not liking it. "Put the ice on your eye." After a second she said, "So you're supposed to let them use you as a punching bag?"

Steve dropped the ice from his face. "He got one punch in, and who was the one on the ground when we left?"

Della groaned. "You should have let me handle him."

Steve ignored her and reached up to touch his eye. "Hey . . . this will look good for tomorrow. I'm a badass shape-shifter, not afraid to fight."

Della rolled her eyes at him the way Miranda rolled hers at everyone. "But you just broke one of Burnett's rules. You're gonna come back bruised."

Steve grinned. "I'll tell him you did it."

Della plopped down on the old pine chest that served as a coffee table. "He'd know that wasn't true, even if he couldn't hear your heart lie. If you pissed me off, I wouldn't have stopped at a black eye. You'd be black-and-blue all over."

"Now that's just an outright lie. I don't think you'd hurt me." His Southern accent came out again.

"And you'd be wrong." She paused. "Where are you from?"

"Where do you think I'm from?" He smiled as if her question pleased him.

And she knew why. She'd shown some personal interest in him. She shouldn't have done that because he might think she actually liked him or something.

"I think you're from somewhere where they talk funny," she smarted off, and shot up to get her blood from the refrigerator. She found a cup, rinsed it out—twice—poured her dinner into it, and sat down at the kitchen table.

He dropped into the second chair at the table. "I'm from Alabama. My parents dragged me to Dallas two years ago."

"You don't like Texas?" she asked and frowned when she realized she'd done it again, shown a personal interest. Then again, maybe she should give herself a break—they were on a mission together, and she was pretending to be his girlfriend. If someone asked something, she should be able to answer it.

"Since I went to camp this last summer, I do. Before that . . . not really. The school in Dallas was some fancy prep school—not even for supernaturals. That school fit my parents' way of thinking and life, but I don't do fancy schools very well."

She couldn't see him in one, either. Not that he didn't seem smart, he did. But he was just easier going than someone who wanted to put on airs.

A few more questions popped into her mind, but she hesitated to ask. She turned her cup in her hands.

The silence must have felt awkward to him as well, because he continued. "My dad's a lawyer and CEO for an oil company, Mom's a doctor. And I'm an only child who's not supposed to care what I want but just grow up, become what they want me to be, and make them look good in the human world."

"They're shifters, too, right?" she asked.

"Yeah, but you'd hardly know it. I don't think my mom has shifted in a couple of years. Dad does it just to relieve stress, but they like living in the human world."

"And you don't?" Della asked, thinking about how often she wished she could go back to the human world and be one of them. Sure, she appreciated the powers, loved knowing she could kick ass. But she wished that gaining these powers hadn't meant losing so much of her life. Or rather the people who were in her life.

"I don't want to run off and join a damn compound or anything, but I'm proud of what I am. I can abide by the rules, not exposing myself in front of humans. I don't have a problem with rules, but I don't want to hide from this part of myself."

"I don't blame you." She didn't think she could hide, either. Not now.

"I'm not really complaining about them," he said. "I mean, as long as we don't have to see each other very often we forget that we're all disappointed in each other."

She knew all about the feeling of disappointing your parents. Exhaling, she looked at the pillowcase, which was bunched up at the end and held the five pieces of ice. He'd brought it with him to the table, but wasn't using it. "You should use that. That's all the ice we have."

He put it against his eye and stared at her with the other. "What's your story?"

"No story here," she lied.

He leaned his chair back on two legs. With half his face hidden behind the hanging pillowcase, he looked accusingly at her with his uninjured eye. "Liar."

She swallowed and stood, picking up her cup.

It didn't stop him from talking though. "You think I don't see you on parents' day? You look completely miserable when you see them come in." He dropped the ice from his eye. "The only time you look more miserable is when you watch them leave."

She frowned, not liking that her feelings about her parents had been so visible. "You're not fae, you can't read my emotions. So stop trying." She took two steps and then looked back. "I'm calling it a night."

He dropped his chair down. "It's still early." Their gazes met. "I'm sorry I said what I did. I just thought . . . I told you about my parents and . . . We don't have to talk about that. Choose a subject and we'll talk about whatever."

Ignoring the soft pleading in his voice, she went to the Walmart bag she'd dropped on the sofa. She pulled out one sheet, one blanket, and snagged the other pillowcase. "We have to be up at three thirty. Don't bother me."

She sprayed the bed three times with disinfectant, made it, and then used the old bedding to make it look like she was under the blanket. If he peeked in, he'd hopefully assume she was out cold—pun intended.

It was, Della thought, the thing she hated most about being a vamp. Drinking blood she could handle, but when someone accidentally brushed up against her and flinched at her body temperature, she felt . . . like a monster.

She knew why, too. It had been the thing that kept Lee from touching her after she'd been turned. *You just don't feel right,* he told her. *You're cold. I think you're still sick.*

A crazy thought came. Would Steve not like how she felt? She pushed the thought away, because seriously, it didn't belong in her mind. Tilting her head to the side, she listened for the shape-shifter. When she'd been making her bed, she'd heard him doing the same to the sofa. He must be sleeping now, because she could only hear the very subtle sound of someone breathing.

The conversation they'd had earlier about his parents floated through her head and whispered across her heart with a tug of emotion. He almost sounded resigned to the bad relationship with his parents. Or was he just pretending—like she so often did?

Realizing she'd let Steve consume her thoughts, she blew out a deep whoosh of air. Then moving to the window, she quietly raised it. She stood there just a second, listening to the night's song, before she climbed out. She perched on the ledge a long second before she took off.

The dark September air felt cool, cooler than her skin. Her hair whipped around her head and scattered across her face, occasionally obscuring her vision. A sound, a slight wisp of air came from her left. Was something following her? She raised her head to catch any scents.

She didn't sense any other creature, but with so much wind coming at her, she wasn't sure if her sense of smell was accurate.

Without slowing down, she glanced back. Nothing but the night chased her.

She considered how close she was to the vampire compound and the rogue gang. Fear danced on her skin, but she pushed it aside. If it was them, she already had a cover for being there. Surely they would ask questions before they attacked. She hoped.

In a few minutes, she spotted the lake that ran by her parents' house and started descending. Her heart shifted from fear to something even more uncomfortable. Grief.

She came down a block from her house at the neighborhood park. Her black jeans and black tank top helped her blend into the darkness.

Moving in the shadows so no one would spot her, she saw lights on in her parents' dining room. Either her family was eating late, or they were playing board games. Her mom loved board games.

Easing between the bushes and the house, the neighbor's dog, the crotch-smelling canine Champ, barked from the neighbor's backyard. Then Della heard laughter.

Her father's laugh.

Her heart gripped and her throat tightened. She hadn't even seen him smile since she'd left for Shadow Falls. Easing in ever so carefully, she looked into the window.

The scene looked like something from a movie on the Family Channel, a family spending time together. A family she really didn't belong to anymore.

Tears prickled her eyes when she saw them. Her mom, her sister, and her dad playing Scrabble. They looked so happy, so . . . complete. Didn't they miss her, even a little bit?

A twig snapped behind her, and her heart rose to her throat. Della swung around. Champ, a mix of Lab and German shepherd, stared at her, or was he staring in the window? His tail slowly started thumping.

"How did you get out?" she whispered to the dog as she felt a tear slip down her cheek. He lowered his head, whimpered, and rubbed his snout against her knee. "What? No crotch smelling tonight? I'm hurt."

The canine looked up at her as if he actually missed her. How could that be, a neighbor's dog missed her when her own family didn't?

Moving out from behind the bushes, Della gave the dog another scratching behind his ears. She brushed a lingering tear from her eye and took off.

In less than five minutes, she landed at Lee's house. When the garage door opened, she flashed to the side of the house. As the car pulled out, she saw Lee in the driver's seat.

Where was he going? On a date? Her heart knew it. Her heart also said that she should just go back to the cabin. She didn't need to see it.

But she did.

Kylie had told Della a thousand times that she needed to move past Lee. Maybe this was the answer. Maybe if she saw Lee with someone else, she could let go. She could stop hoping that he'd come to his senses and would run back to her, begging for a second chance.

She followed him to a house on the other side of the subdivision. She waited for a few minutes in the shadows, still hoping maybe she'd been wrong. Maybe this was just one of his friends.

When he walked out with a girl, an Asian girl, at his side, the knot in Della's chest came back. This was the fiancée. The one he'd told Della his parents had pushed him into marrying. Seeing this should have been enough. Seeing how she clung to his arm. She should have left right then, but no. When they got in the car, she followed them to the restaurant.

The Red Dragon. It was a restaurant owned by some friends of Lee's parents. His mother had tried to get Della and Lee to go there several times. But Lee always said he didn't want to eat Chinese food. He had enough of that at home.

Why did he want Chinese food now?

She landed in front of the restaurant while Lee parked the car. She hid behind the tall dragon statue waiting to see them walk past. A hungry-looking kitten came slinking around the building. "Don't have anything. But there's a Dumpster in the back, I can smell it from here," she whispered and then she heard footsteps.

They were holding hands and the girl, Lee's fiancée, wore a big smile, her eyes bright with laughter. As they walked in the door, Della caught a whiff of Lee's cologne.

Anger surged in her chest. She'd bought that cologne for him last Christmas. Didn't he remember? Did he even care? How could he wear it for this new girl when Della had given it to him?

She waited a good ten minutes, telling herself to leave. Telling herself it was over. But when she tried to fly away, instead she swung around and headed inside.

She told the hostess she was looking for someone and walked past her into the spicy, sesame-scented air. She walked past a large fish tank with colorful fish swimming in circles as if looking for a way out. She continued past a couple and noticed the sound of plastic crinkling as they opened their fortune cookies. Perhaps she should snag one to see her own future.

Because God only knew what she planned to do when she found Lee. Part of her wanted to rip his heart out for using the cologne she'd given him to impress another girl. The other part wanted to drop to her knees and beg him to at least tell her he missed her.

All this time she'd believed Lee was engaged because his parents forced him into it. Now she didn't know what to believe. This didn't look forced. He actually looked . . . happy.

Leave. Leave. Leave. The voice of reason screamed in her head. But then she saw them at the back table. Candlelit table. Romantic table. She heard them talking. Not in English, but in Mandarin.

Della spoke Mandarin. Her father had made sure of it. But Lee had never spoken to her in that language. Right then Della knew for certain, she wasn't tossed aside because she'd turned into a vampire. She'd been tossed aside because she was half white.

She heard the girl talking about names. Names they would give their first child. Lee leaned in and kissed her. A romantic kiss that kicked Della right in the gut. From the happiness she heard in Lee's voice, and the way he kissed the girl, Della suspected this choice had been as much his own preference as his parents'.

A waiter must have dropped a tray of food because a loud clatter sounded right behind Della. She knew she should turn and flash away at the sound of the crash, but it was too late. She watched in horror as Lee pulled his hand away from his fiancée's and looked up. She saw his eyes widen at the sight of her. Was it a good widen or an "oh shit" widen? She didn't know.

Leave! Don't stand here and look pathetic. But her feet felt concreted to the restaurant floor and pathetic was all she could feel. Her gaze locked on his as he stood up and started moving toward her. Right toward her. And she knew she looked even worse than pathetic.

She looked pitiful.

Sad.

She looked alone and heartbroken.

Embarrassment and shame washed over her. But she didn't have time to let it engulf her. Someone grabbed her around the waist and pulled her close. Shocked, she looked up at . . . at Steve. He smiled down at her.

"I missed you already," he said and then he kissed her. Not a simple sweet first kiss, but one that involved tongue and . . . lots of desire.

Chapter Three

Della felt the embarrassment seep out of her as something else seeped into her. And it wasn't just Steve's tongue. It was . . . passion. It was the feeling of being alive. It was hope that her sad little life wasn't over. Since being a vampire, since she'd lost Lee, she'd thought she couldn't feel this anymore. Or maybe she just thought she wouldn't feel it anymore.

Someone cleared their throat. Realizing the familiar disapproving sound came from Lee, she put a hand on Steve's chest and reluctantly pulled back.

She met Steve's eyes briefly. She knew he'd kissed her to save her ass, but she also knew he'd enjoyed it as much as she had. The evidence was there in his warm brown eyes. Even with one of those eyes bruised, she saw the just-been-kissed heat in his gaze.

She turned to Lee. Only to realize she still didn't have a clue what to say to him. "Uh, hey. I . . ."

"What are you doing here?" Lee asked. "Besides making out in the middle of a restaurant?"

Hadn't he just been kissing his date?

As crazy as it was, Della saw something in Lee she hadn't seen before. Her dad. Or at least his disapproving attitude. Had Lee always been that way and she just now noticed? Or had he changed?

"What's wrong? Can't you talk?" he asked.

His words ran amok around her head and she couldn't decide how they made her feel or how to respond. And if she did decide she wasn't sure her tongue could take speaking orders, it was still in shock at having just had company—Steve's tongue.

"We were having dinner," Steve answered for her. "Actually, we're celebrating our three-month anniversary." His gaze went to Della.

"Three months?" Lee asked as if annoyed she'd started dating so soon. But hell, the guy was engaged. Where did he get off thinking . . . She opened her mouth to say something again but Steve jumped in first.

"I'm sorry," Steve said. "I didn't introduce myself. You must be an old friend of Della's. I'm Steve . . . ?"

Lee ignored Steve and looked at Della. "I thought you were at that school."

That school? Could he not even remember what school she'd been attending? "I am." She finally got two words out. "We . . . just slipped out."

"So you met him at school?" Lee asked and damn if he didn't sound upset. Anger started to spark inside her again. He had no right to be upset. None!

Steve spoke up again. "Love at first sight." He glanced at her and ran his warm hand around the curve of her waist and pulled her a little closer. His gaze shot back to Lee. "Still don't know how I got so damn lucky." If so much honesty didn't resonate from his voice, it might have sounded false. For a second she wished she had listened to his heartbeat—another little vampire talent. Had Steve been interested in her at first sight?

Lee's fiancée rose from her chair behind them and stopped at his side. Della couldn't help but notice how pretty she was—pretty in a very traditional Asian way. Her hair was longer, sleeker, and blacker than Della's. Her facial features were doll-like. Beautiful and perfect—a tiny nose, a bow-like mouth, and slanted black eyes that sparkled with intelligence. No doubt, Lee's parents had chosen well.

Or had Lee chosen her? Had he planned to break up with Della all along? He'd seemed pretty happy sitting next to her until Della showed up.

Not that he looked too happy now. He frowned when the girl slipped her arm through his, but he did the right thing and introduced them. "Mei, this is Della, and her . . . friend." The word *friend* came out sounding like a four-letter word. "Her friend who obviously likes to fight, if his black eye is any indication."

Della tensed, ready to tell him that Steve got that black eye standing up for her. Something she suddenly realized that Lee had never done. Not even with his parents.

"Actually," Steve spoke up again, "we were just wrestling around in bed and Della got me in the eye with her elbow."

Lee's shoulders tightened and all Della could think was, *Go Steve.*

Mei looked up at Lee and seemed to see his reaction. A tightness pulled at the girl's brow as she glanced back at Della. Della recognized that tightness as plain ol' jealousy. She'd felt it tug at her own brow every time she thought of Lee with someone else. Oddly, now Della felt . . . What did she feel? Angry. Hurt. Sad. But she didn't feel jealous. That meant something, Della knew that, but now wasn't the time to contemplate it.

"We should . . ." Her words got hung up when she met Lee's eyes again. The sad feeling swelled in her chest and she realized a better name for that emotion. Grief. She had loved Lee. Loved him with everything she had. And she'd given him her all—her heart, her body, her mind. Now she'd lost him. And now she grieved for what used to be.

"Go. We should go," Steve finished for her. "I already took care of the bill." Steve let go of her waist and held out his hand to Lee. "It was a pleasure to meet you."

Lee didn't take it. Which was super-awkward and not like Lee. He normally wasn't rude. Or was he? Had she missed that about him, too? Della nodded at the couple and when Steve's arm found its way back around her she let him guide her away.

They left the restaurant and it took a few seconds of the cold fall air hitting her face to realize she was still holding onto Steve. Holding onto him as if the ship of her life had been capsized. As if he was the only thing floating in the stormy waters to cling to.

The sense of weakness, feelings she could easily drown in, washed over her and sparked another flicker of anger. A big one this time.

She pulled away. Confusion bounced around her gut. The grief clung to her heart as tightly as she'd clung to Steve just a few minutes ago, but then the anger she'd experienced earlier returned. She opened herself up to that emotion. Anger she could handle, anger she could run with. So she let it roll around her, washing away the other emotions that made her feel weak and vulnerable.

She looked at Steve, who appeared happy, just the opposite of how she felt. "You followed me," she accused him.

The slight smile in his eyes dimmed. "I was obeying orders," he said. "We were told to stay together at all times."

"Damn it! I don't give a shit about orders. I don't like to be followed." A heaviness filled her chest and she recognized it as guilt. Guilt for . . .

"Then don't run away again," he said matter-of-factly and started walking to the back of the restaurant.

Damn it. Guilt for acting like an idiot with the person who'd just saved her.

She caught up with him. "I'm not finished talking!" she seethed.

He came to a quick halt and swung around. "But I'm finished listening. You can get mad all you want. I was trying to help." He took off again.

"I said I wasn't finished!" She flashed forward and shot in front of him, putting a hand out to stop him. When her hand met his warm chest, it reminded her just how cold she was and she pulled it away. She glanced up at him, he looked about ready to give her hell, but she spoke first.

"Thank you!" she growled.

His mouth opened as if to say something, but nothing came out. No doubt he was shocked at her declaration. And damn it, but she knew how he felt. She hadn't meant to say that—not that he didn't deserve to hear it, he did, but . . .

"Wow." He finally spoke. "I don't think I've ever heard anyone express gratitude in such a pissed off, angry tone."

"That's because I am angry. I'm furious. You followed me. Then you . . . you kissed me, with tongue, in front of everyone."

His brown eyes lit up with a smile again. He leaned in a little closer. His warm breath stirred against her forehead. "And it was really good, wasn't it?"

She glared at him and took a step back.

"Okay, if it's not for the kiss, what are you thanking me for?" he asked, sounding puzzled and yet interested.

Once again she shared his feeling, the puzzled one, that is. "I don't know," she seethed. But then instantly the answer dawned on her. He'd saved her from looking pathetic, from looking like a heartbroken ex-girlfriend.

"You are a real piece of work, Della Tsang." He reached out as if to brush a strand of hair from her cheek.

She didn't know if that was a compliment or an insult, but she slapped his hand just in case.

He laughed. "It really wasn't bad for a first kiss, you know. Usually they're kind of awkward. But that . . . that wasn't awkward. It was hot."

She thought about the kiss, the warmth of his mouth, the feel of his tongue. How he had tasted. "I'm glad you liked it, because it was your last," she snapped.

She turned to fly off. Her feet weren't all the way off the ground when she heard his reply.

"We'll have to see about that."

She gritted her teeth, continued toward the cabin, and fought the fear that if she wasn't really careful, he might be right.

And that would be wrong.

Wouldn't it?

Three thirty couldn't have come any slower. The new sheet, pillow-case, blanket, and Lysol helped, but she kept waking up every few minutes. With the cabin out in the woods, the only noises were a few animals. It should have been a fine place to get a good night's sleep.

However, being a vampire and basically nocturnal, she never slept well at night.

Earlier she'd blamed most of the tossing and turning on the thought of bedbugs. Funny how the idea of bedbugs kept shifting to Steve's kiss. Then Steve's kiss led her to think about her mixed-up, crazy feelings about Lee.

Was she over him? If so, why did it still hurt? But if she still loved him, why wasn't she jealous of Mei? Then Della's thoughts went to her mom and dad and sister playing board games without her. For some reason thinking about Lee and her parents helped block out the thoughts of the kiss.

Still in bed and staring at the stained ceiling, Della heard water running, which meant Steve was taking a shower. Before she'd gone to bed she'd given the shower a good spray of Lysol, and took a quick stand beneath the spewing water herself.

When she'd left the shower, Steve had been sitting on the sofa, staring at the bathroom door. Staring as if he hoped she'd be wearing something sexy.

Poor guy had been disappointed. Or she had thought he'd been for about two seconds, until his gaze had lowered and then traveled up again as a slow sexy grin appeared in his eyes.

"You were right," he'd said. "And you were wrong."

She liked the part about being right, but . . . ? "Wrong about what?"

That seductive smile shifted to his lips as his gaze lowered again, and stopped on her bare feet. "Right that I have a foot fetish. Wrong about me never seeing your naked feet."

She used those naked feet to run off to the bedroom. The second after she slammed the door, he'd called out that they needed to talk about the mission. She called back that they could do it in the morning. Then she'd dropped into bed.

Even five hours later, remembering the way he'd looked at her—at her feet for God's sake—made her feel all fluttery inside. Now, as the sound of water from the shower filled her head, so did images. Her mind went to him standing under a steamy spray of water. And she had the oddest desire to see his naked feet. And other things.

She groaned and pressed her palms into her eyes. Why couldn't he be ugly?

Taking a deep breath of resolve, she told herself to get over it. Besides, today was a new day. Slipping out of bed, she brushed her hair, and adjusted her bra. Feeling a tiny bit more in control, she went into the living room to wait her turn in the bathroom. She needed to brush her teeth, and they had to go over the plans for their mission. Then they needed to go do what they had to do. Catch themselves some bad vampires.

She didn't have time to think about how hot Steve was, or how his kiss had melted her insides like butter on a steaming ear of corn. It was time to think about kicking rogue vampire butt, not Steve's cute butt.

Drumming her fingers on the top of her knees, she saw the file they had to go over with their instructions sitting on the sofa. She really didn't need to review it. She'd read it a dozen times and memorized it. Because vamps could read a lie in a person's heartbeat, they'd come up with a form of the truth that hopefully wouldn't read as a lie. She, Della Tsang, had been turned vampire and was sent to a special boarding school. She wasn't big on the school's rules, so she and her friend Steve the shape-shifter had run off. But due to the known difficulties of obtaining blood for her, they had decided to join a gang.

The bathroom door squeaked open, and Steve walked out. He was . . . he was half naked, and bam, she was back to thinking about his cute butt. And . . . her gaze lowered. He had socks on.

For some odd reason, she recalled that someone had told her that Steve was already eighteen. He looked eighteen, probably a year older than Della. Muscles rippled over his chest and arms. She knew he worked out, but most of what he had appeared natural.

Her breath caught in her throat for a second. She'd seen him swimming and without a shirt, but something about seeing all that bare skin and him being freshly showered brought back the flutters. Brought back the memory of his kiss and of how his warm hands had felt in the curve of her waist.

He met her gaze and smiled as if somehow reading her mind. Moving to the chair, he slipped on a dark green T-shirt. *Thank goodness.*

"You ready to go over everything?" he asked.

"Need to brush my teeth." *Need to find my self-control and I'm pretty sure it's in the toilet.* She popped up and ran to the bathroom. When she came back three minutes later, she'd taken her frustration out on her teeth. There wasn't a speck of plaque on her pearly whites. And while she didn't find her self-control in the potty, she'd given herself a good talking-to about not acting like some hormone-crazed teen.

Sure she was a teen, and probably hormone crazed, but she didn't need to act like it.

Steve had the open file in his lap when she moved to the living room. She sat down on the opposite side of the sofa and he started going over the info.

She didn't tell him she already knew it because he might need to hear it. Five minutes later, he closed the file. "Okay, the thing to remember is if they insist I leave, I'll shift and hang around. I won't leave you."

Della cut her eyes to him. "Heartwarming, but if they insist you leave, I'll be fine. I can take care of myself. Besides, they know you're a shifter, Steve. Don't do anything that will ruin this."

"I won't do anything to ruin it. But I'm not leaving you." His tone came out determined, protective. "I'll be careful. They won't realize it's me."

"Yes they will. What about them knowing you're a shifter don't you get?"

He stared at her a long second before speaking. "So they're smarter than you, huh?"

She tightened her eyes at him. "What's that mean?"

"You didn't know I was there last night. You saw me twice."

She studied him, feeling puzzled. "I don't . . ."

"I was your neighbor's dog and then I was the kitten. If a shifter is careful what they become, we blend into the environment and are never suspected. Why do you think we're one of the most powerful of the supernaturals?"

First, they really weren't one of the most powerful supernaturals, vampires were, not that this was a competition. Then all of a sudden her chest tightened and her face heated remembering her short inter-action with the neighbor's dog. Hadn't she said something about him *not* smelling her crotch?

"Don't do that to me anymore." She stood up, went to the door, and glanced back over her shoulder. "It's time to go."

Della and Steve landed in the designated spot of the state park five min-utes later. A clearing, secluded from any road or human life, and sur-rounded by trees. A place where anything could happen and there'd be no witnesses. Della scanned the area, seeing only tall pines mixed with a few oaks and tons of thorny underbrush.

She didn't like it.

From just looking, one would think the area was abandoned. Only a few stars lit up the night sky. But one good nose of air told her the truth. They were here.

Hidden.

Waiting.

But for what?

To attack?

And while her nose couldn't count, she sensed there were more than three of them.

Did the gang somehow know Della and Steve were assisting the FRU? Or was this just the way the gang welcomed all potential new members?

A sense of danger brushed over her skin. As exciting as it was, fear crowded her chest. She remembered the pictures of those who had died at the hands of suspected vampire gangs. A mother and a child. An elderly woman. If this was the gang advocating murder for initiation, who had taken innocent lives, they needed to be stopped and the risk was worth it. Sure, Burnett didn't believe this was the gang, but he had to have doubts or he wouldn't have sent them on this mission.

"They're here," Steve whispered.

"I know," Della said.

A stirring of underbrush sounded to their right and then one to the left. And then behind them. Della spotted another vamp coming out from the trees right at them.

Friggin' great.

They were surrounded.

Chapter Four

"What a warm welcome," Della said, refusing to acknowledge her fear.

"She's sassy," said someone behind her.

"We can beat that out of her," said the vamp walking toward her as he eyed her up and down.

"I wouldn't try," Della said.

"I second that," Steve added, his voice deep and filled with warning.

The rogue tightened his gaze to check their patterns. "So you brought your pet with you, huh?"

Della heard Steve inhale and she reached over and touched his arm. Surely, he knew to let her deal with this.

"He's not my pet," she growled, offended for him more than she realized.

"Ah, I see," the lead rogue said, a filthy twinkle in his eyes. "So you're giving it up to this joker?"

"We've swapped bodily fluids if that's what you're asking," she countered, confident, and suddenly grateful they'd exchanged spit last night during that hot kiss.

The vamp grinned. "I like your spunk. Maybe you and I can swap some bodily fluid sometime."

Steve tensed beside her. "I wouldn't count on it," he said.

"And I'll second that," Della said.

The vamp frowned as if disappointed he couldn't intimidate them.

"You do realize first you will have to prove yourself worthy. If you are accepted, then your shifter here will have to prove himself, and even then he will only be considered an extra. Extras . . . don't last very long."

The rogue's insinuation struck a punch to Della's nerves, but she focused on what was important. The whole "prove yourself worthy" comment.

Was it going to be this easy? Was he just going to tell her right now what she had to do and they could leave? A tiny part of her hoped it wouldn't be so simple. She already disliked this guy and wouldn't mind teaching him a lesson.

"Exactly how do we prove ourselves?"

"Do you know how to fight?"

Hell, yes. "I can hold my own," Della said.

His gaze shifted to Steve. "Looks like shifter-boy likes to fight," he said, obviously referring to Steve's black eye.

"I can hold my own, too," Steve said.

"How strong of a shifter are you?" The rogue studied him as if assessing him.

"Strong enough," Steve answered.

The rogue laughed. "Then why did you stay human to fight? You're obviously not as strong as you'd like to believe."

"Don't let a little bruise fool you," Steve said, tilting back on his heels.

Della heard the confidence in Steve's voice, and while she'd assessed his ability to transform quickly, she honestly didn't know his strength. Yet somehow she sensed that like her, he was holding his cards close to his chest. Not cowering down to them, but not letting them know exactly what they were up against if they picked a fight.

The rogue laughed as if he didn't believe Steve. "Well, follow us. We have a little game going and we'll see how well you two do."

"What kind of game?" Della asked and cut her eyes around, taking in all the rogues circling them.

"A little hand-to-hand combat. If you do okay, we'll see about your pet. You game?"

"Now?" Della asked, remembering in detail how Burnett told them not to be lured anywhere. Already the vamps had proven they weren't good to their word because they'd stated only three of the gang members would meet them for a nonconfrontational interview.

"Now," the rogue said, pulling a knife from a side holster and wiping the blade on his dirty jeans. The guys to her left and right pulled out their knives as well.

Della heard a low growl, and although she didn't know shapeshifters growled, she knew it came from Steve.

She also knew that refusing the rogue's invitation wasn't an option. It was go, or have some hand-to-blade combat right now.

"Let's go, then," Della said, hoping whatever came next would provide a better escape.

Steve glanced at her and in his gaze she read his mind. *I don't like this.*

Well, neither did she, but she didn't see any other choice. She'd done a quick head count and there were twelve of them. She could probably take on five or six, but she couldn't take on twelve. Not with knives.

They were led to an old abandoned warehouse. Steve transformed into a black crow and moved slower. The rogues muttered curses that they had to slow down.

Della couldn't help but wonder if his choice of form hadn't been on purpose. Did shifting into a faster bird require more energy? And was he preserving it? Or was his ability to shift into certain kinds of animals a sign of power, and he was downplaying his abilities to the rogues? It occurred to Della that if she was going to work for the FRU, she needed to educate herself on all species.

It would have been helpful to know exactly what Steve was up to.

When they landed, she also noted Steve took several minutes to change. A hell of a lot slower than before. That's when she knew for sure he was downplaying his power to the rogues.

One of the vamps stepped close and said something about wringing the crow's neck. Della moved between him and Steve.

With Steve now in human form, they walked inside a dark building. Della could smell old blood and vampire sweat. While she couldn't see for shit, she could also smell the bloodthirsty crowd. No longer just twelve rogues to deal with, but more than fifty. Her chest clutched with fear and the realization that maybe she should have taken her chances back at the park.

The lights suddenly flashed on and the crowd hiding in the shadows appeared. In the middle of the room was a boxing ring. Steve looked at her, concern tightening his gaze.

The crowd cheered and Della looked back up. A girl was pushed into the ring. She looked scared, but also determined. Della tightened her brows and saw she was half werewolf, half vampire. Were being her dominant species. She was obviously an extra. And from her stance, Della also assessed she was a willing victim.

"And here I thought I was just going to get to kill a human or two," Della said, praying her voice didn't shake.

"Oh, we do that, too. But we change it up to keep it interesting."

Bingo, Della thought. They could leave now. Unfortunately, she didn't see that happening.

The girl turned and looked at Della with something akin to hatred. Della knew this was the girl she was supposed to fight.

The smell of dried blood in the air warned Della just how far this fight was supposed to go.

She looked at the leader of the rogues who had met them. "It's hard to fight someone I have nothing against."

"When she takes her first punch, you'll have something against her. She's not nearly as weak as she looks. Sort of like you, I'll bet." He pulled out his knife again. "Go fight her, Miss Sass, and let's see how good you really are."

Della swallowed a knot of fear, but she forced herself to ask. "Where does this end?"

"What do you mean?" he asked, but his smirk told her he knew exactly what she meant.

"I knock her out, it's over, right?" She was hoping.

His eyes brightened with plain ol' evilness. "What fun would that be?" He brought the knife up and stared at the blade. "It ends when one of you stops breathing and becomes a willing blood donor, that's when it's over. So the question is, will we be drinking your blood at sunrise or hers?"

"Hmm," Della said, and worked at keeping the horror from showing on her face. She glanced at Steve. He cut his eyes up to the ceiling. She didn't know what the hell the message was, but she hoped it meant he had a plan. Because, God help her, she couldn't think of one right now. And she was either about to kill someone, or be killed.

Chapter Five

Della got into the ring thinking there would be a bell, thinking she'd come up with a way out of this crap, but nope—on both counts. Before she had a chance to catch her breath, the girl attacked.

Della still didn't have a clue what to do. But when she took a fist to the cheek and it hurt like hell, she decided letting this girl beat the crap out of her wasn't a good plan, either.

Della ducked the girl's second punch. The crowd booed.

The were came at her again and Della grabbed the girl by the arm and unceremoniously tossed her across the ring. She landed hard, but was back on her feet in seconds. As the girl danced around throwing punches like some boxing queen, Della briefly found Steve in the crowd. He glared right at her and then cut his eyes upward again.

The second of lost focus cost Della dearly, for the girl struck again, this time kicking Della right in the ribs. Air whooshed out of her lungs as pain caused her to stumble back. That's when her gaze caught the slight opening in the ceiling, where an air vent had once been.

Okay, now she knew Steve's plan, but didn't he realize that these other vamps could fly, too?

Another foot came at Della's face. She grabbed the leg by the ankle and slung the girl outside the ring. Yelps and cries for blood echoed from the crowd. The girl landed in a group of vamps, but she must have been made of rubber, because she bounced back up and charged again.

She leapt into the ring. Her eyes glowed the notable orange color of a pissed-off were. She kicked up her foot; Della went to block it. A bad mistake, because she didn't see what the B with an itch had in her hands until it was too late.

The knife came right at Della's heart. Her only defense was to block it with her arm. The blade sliced into her forearm and it felt like a burn, hot yet cold at the same time. The smell of blood filled her nose.

Her own blood.

She heard the hungry cries from the audience.

The girl took a step back, but only to charge again. The knife was aimed right at Della's chest. A roar, not from the crowd, but from some exotic feline animal, rang in Della's ears.

Fury, hot red rage, filled Della's heart at the same time the knife sank into her chest, right below her collarbone. Amazingly, she felt more anger than pain. Grabbing the girl by the shoulders, she slung her. It looked like slow motion. Felt like slow motion, as the knife sliced its way out of Della's chest. Breath held in pain, she watched as the girl flew away, the knife, still in her hands, dripping blood from the tip of the blade.

Then Della saw the supersized lion, aka Steve, charging toward the ring, mauling anyone who dared get in his way. Go Steve! She pointed up and then with everything she had, she leapt straight into the air, barely fitting through the tight little exit. And right behind her, hauling ass, was a peregrine falcon.

She continued upward knowing the vamps, at least the ones who could fit through the tight opening, would be behind them. She ignored the burning sensation in her shoulder. Suddenly aware she didn't hear the flap of a bird's wings, she glanced back. Steve had returned to the roof, transformed into a dragon, and was in the process of breathing fire into the hole in the old building. Damn, but the guy made a nice-looking dragon.

Obviously, the building had some sort of insulation that wasn't fire resistant, because smoke started billowing out of the roof almost immediately.

In seconds, sparkles started popping off around the dragon and

Steve was back to being a peregrine. They flew off hard and fast. She kept looking back, praying the rogues weren't there. Thankfully, only the darkness chased them.

Suddenly, Steve started down.

"No," she screamed at him. "We need to keep going. They'll come after us!"

He didn't listen, but continued down and landed in a dark alley much like the one they'd been in last night. Six-foot-high wooden fences lined the pathway, as if too keep riffraff out. The overflowing garbage cans that smelled like spoiled fruit seemed to hold up the fences, some of which looked rotted. By the time she landed, Steve was already human.

"Shit," he said, grabbing her arm. The sweet smell of her own blood chased away the smell of garbage and filled Della's senses.

"You know," she said, flinching at the pain both in her arm and her upper chest, "you did good."

"You are not going to die!" he seethed.

"Who said anything about dying?" She found it hard to focus on him and she blinked a couple of times.

"You just complimented me," he said in a low growl. "That tells me how seriously hurt you are."

She grinned and she couldn't hold the gesture in place. "I'm not that bad, am I?"

"No, you're not that bad. Just stubborn . . ." he met her gaze, "and perfect," he said, but his voice sounded distant. "I need to get you to a hospital."

"No," she said, feeling her knees weaken. "I need blood and I'll heal. She didn't hit any major organs, or I'd be dead. Just get me blood, Steve. That's all I need. Vampires heal really quickly."

He frowned and pulled his phone out. "Don't you dare call Burnett!" she seethed, but her knees folded and she dropped to the ground. "Please," she begged, feeling tears fill her eyes. "I want to impress him. I can't let him down." She batted at her tears and saw Steve looking down at her with compassion.

Relief fluttered inside her when she saw him put his phone back into his pocket. "Thank you," she said. "Thank you," she repeated, but she'd no more gotten that last word out when she smelled the dirty scent that hinted at rotten meat. They had company. Not the rogue vamps.

Weres.

Oh, shit! She really didn't want to die today.

She stood up, her whole body trembled. She prayed she looked a lot more menacing than she felt. There were three of them, big mean-looking dudes. Hair so dirty she couldn't distinguish the color, and clothes that looked just as unclean.

They'd obviously smelled her blood and came looking for a bite to eat.

"Leave," Steve growled at them. "Or I'll kill you." Sparkles started popping off around him. A loud roar filled the dark alley. The lion had returned, only this time it was even larger, the size of a small van.

Two of the weres backed up, but one, obviously the most stupid, started running at Steve, his canines extended, his eyes glowing orange. Steve swatted one paw and knocked the were across the alley. He hit the fence with a loud thud. The two smarter weres ran like hell was on fire and chasing them.

It took Della a second to realize she hadn't done anything. She hadn't even growled at the intruders to help Steve stand against them. But how could she when it took everything she had to stand?

With the echo of the fading footsteps running down the alley, she watched the lion charge at her. But what she didn't understand was why everything was spinning. *Round and round the world goes, where it lands nobody knows.* Her mind created the singsong words in her head to go with the light-headed feeling washing over her. Just when she was about to get used to the light-headedness, black spots started popping off like firecrackers in her vision.

The last thing Della remembered was falling against the big beast and thinking that even as a lion, Steve smelled like some spicy male soap.

Della felt someone lift her head up.

Then she heard a male voice with a Southern accent as sexy as the voice was deep. "You either wake up and drink this or I'm going to have to call Burnett. You hear me? Wake up, sweetheart."

Sweetheart? Della lifted her eyelids and looked up at the dark-haired, soft brown–eyed guy sitting next to her on the huge bed. He had one hand behind her head and the other holding a cup up to her mouth. It took her a second to realize who he was. It took another one for her to remember everything.

The mission.

The vampires.

The weres.

Steve's kiss.

Oh, yeah, she remembered Steve's kiss.

"Thank heavens," he muttered when he saw her looking at him. "Can you drink?" He pressed the cup to her lips. "Just a couple of sips."

The sweet smell of blood filled her nose and she opened her mouth and sipped. It tasted so good, she took another sip.

Steve lowered her head on the pillow that was so soft it practically swallowed her head. She glanced up at his smile.

"I think you need to drink more, but we'll give you a few minutes," he said.

The silky feel of the sheets against her bare back and the soft pillow surrounding her head told her two things. One, they weren't back at the cabin, and two, she was practically naked.

She moved her gaze around and took in what appeared to be a fancy hotel room. Then she reached down to the sheet that covered her chest and lifted it up an inch to check for clothes.

Yup, naked. Well, practically naked. She still had on her red silk panties. And a bandage over her wound.

She dropped the sheet down against her chest and frowned up at him.

"Where are my clothes?"

"I threw them in the bathtub and rinsed them just in case any weres or other vamps were around. Didn't want them to smell you."

How could she argue with that? She couldn't. Well, she could, not every argument had to be based in logic, but face it, she was too tired to argue a logical point much less an illogical one.

"Ready for some more blood?" He held the cup out.

She wanted to say no, but she knew the blood was the only thing that would help her. Leaning up on her elbow, or trying to, she slipped back into the pillow. She looked up into his soft, concerned eyes and felt . . . she felt naked, weak, and vulnerable. This was so not her best day.

He reached down and helped her sit up. She felt the sheet slip down and she barely managed to catch it before it exposed her breasts. He held the cup to her lips and she sipped.

When he pulled the cup away, he smiled at her again—all sweet like. He wasn't even looking at her like she was naked under the sheet like most boys would. He was smiling at her like . . . like she was someone he cared about.

Definitely not her best day.

She didn't want him to start caring. Because then she might start caring about him. That was dangerous.

Closing her eyes, she leaned back and in few minutes she felt sleep claim her.

Chapter Six

Della felt a tickle against her temple and went to wipe it away. Then the tickle hit the back of her hand.

Her eyes popped open with a start. The tickle was someone's breath, easy in and easy out, wisps of air.

And that someone was Steve.

Steve, asleep in bed with her. Steve, on his side, sharing her pillow.

Steve, not even the least bit ugly, with dark long lashes resting against his upper cheek. His equally dark brown hair lay scattered across his brow.

Asleep, he looked younger, except for his five o'clock shadow. She tried to remember if she'd felt any of that stubble when he'd kissed her last night at the restaurant. She hadn't. But she wanted to run her fingers across his chin now.

Her gaze shifted downward to her chest, to her not-so-big boobs. The sheet had slipped down around her waist.

Frowning, she snatched the sheet up and wondered if Steve had been privy to the view before he'd fallen asleep. Of course he had, she realized, he'd been the one to remove her bra and play doctor when he dressed her wound. A depressing thought hit. Had he been disappointed that she wasn't bigger?

She stared at the two slight mounds now pushing against the sheet—finding a bit of hope that they were a little bigger than they used to be. In the last few months, she'd actually started to fill out a B cup. Not that she aspired to get to a C cup like Miranda and Kylie. But a full B or B+would be nice.

She glanced to her left side and lowered the sheet just a bit to see her bandage. It didn't look like a half-assed job. Shifting her shoulder, she realized it must have healed, because there wasn't even the slightest amount of pain. Then she looked at her arm where another bandage was.

She vaguely remembered Steve waking her up and making her drink blood two or three times. She also recalled him telling her yesterday that his mom was a doctor. Was he considering becoming a doctor himself? He should. The boy had what it took.

Reaching up, she loosened the bandage below her shoulder blade to see the wound. The cut still showed, but it was close to being healed.

"It looks good," a deep, sleepy voice said beside her.

She cut her eyes to the guy sharing the mattress with her and glared. "Get out of my bed."

He grinned. "Technically, it's my bed. I rented the room."

She frowned. "It's too early to be logical!"

He chuckled. "Actually, it's not early, either."

She sat up a little, holding the sheet to her chest, and vaguely recalled not being able to sit up earlier. "What time is it?"

He rolled over and looked at the clock on the bedside table. "Six."

"That's early," she said.

"In the afternoon." He ran a hand through his sleep-mussed hair and looked adorable doing it.

"Wait. It's six in the afternoon? Shit!" She sat up straighter. "I slept all freaking day? Burnett's probably livid. I was supposed to check in."

"I did."

She frowned. "You told him I was hurt!"

"No, well I did, but I downplayed it—a lot. I had to tell him you had to fight because the whole burning warehouse and sightings of giant lions made the news."

She recalled him turning into a lion both at the warehouse with the rogues and to fight off the weres. "You were spotted?"

"A drunk in the alley, so it's not too bad."

"Sorry," she said, remembering he was a stickler about following the rules and not shifting in a public place. And yet he'd shifted because . . . because she couldn't protect them.

"It's okay." His gaze went soft again, like he cared or something. "We got out alive. And we completed our mission. Now the FRU can go in and make some arrests in the gang."

She nodded. "I'm surprised Burnett hasn't been calling every fifteen minutes."

"I think he would have but he's got another problem on his hands."

"What?" Della asked.

"Supposedly Helen was attacked."

"Helen? Our Helen?" Helen was a bashful half-fae who Della couldn't believe anyone would hurt. "Is she okay? Who did that?"

"Burnett's been at the hospital with her. He said she was okay. I asked who did it, and he said they didn't know. But you know Burnett, he'll get them and when he does they'll get hell."

"Yeah, and I'd like to help him dish out that hell. Thank God she's okay." Della's stomach grumbled, embarrassingly loud, too.

Steve chuckled. "I think you're hungry." He bounced out of bed. "I'll get it for you."

Sitting up, she leaned against the bed's headboard and held the sheet to her chest. She watched him go to the small fridge and pull out a plastic bag with blood. But it wasn't the same blood she'd brought with her on this trip. That blood she'd left at the cabin.

Questions started floating around her head. "That's not my blood. Where did you—"

"My mom worked at this town's ER for a couple of weeks when we first moved from Alabama. There's a blood bank right down the street, that's why I chose this hotel."

His words bounced around her head. "You stole blood from a blood bank?" She shook her head. "You're never supposed to do that!"

"I didn't. Well, not technically." He moved to stand by the bed and handed her a cup.

She took the cup and stared down at it. The wonderful aroma filled her nose. "Is this O negative?" she asked, recalling how good it had tasted when she'd been semicomatose.

"Only the best for you." He sent her a crooked smile.

"I guess you can't take it back, can you? And if you try I might have to kill you." She took a big sip.

He grinned. "Drink up, and besides, I didn't exactly steal it."

She glanced at him from the cup's lip. He continued to stand there just looking at her. "What do you mean?"

"I went in to donate a pint and just left with it."

She licked the last drop of blood from her lips. "You're O negative?" No wonder he always smelled so good to her.

He nodded. With his grin now spreading to his eyes, he said, "You're welcome."

"I didn't say thank you."

"Yeah, but your appreciation was in your eyes."

She frowned, hoping to mask her appreciation. Then sitting up a little more, she drained the cup and set it on the bedside table. "Where are my clothes?"

"In the bathroom. They should be almost dry. I washed them out really good. But before you get dressed I need to put some more ointment on your cuts. One last time."

"I think I'm fine."

"Oh, you're fine," he said and smiled, "but your cut still needs one more dose of ointment." He moved back to the dresser and picked up a tube of something along with some other supplies.

He sat down on the edge of the mattress, put his supplies on the nightstand, and carefully removed the bandage from her arm. He squirted some medicine on a cotton swab and dabbed it on the cut. She studied the cut on her arm, and like the one on her chest, it appeared almost healed.

Then he reached up and nudged the sheet down. Not low enough to see anything, but low enough to hint at the breast below and to get to her bandaged wound. Gently, he pulled back the dressing and patted the medicine on the cut.

When she glanced up at him through her lashes he was staring at her. "You're beautiful, by the way."

She felt her face heat up. Okay, now he stared at her like a normal boy, thinking about how naked she was beneath the sheet. Yet, instead of being repulsed, she was . . . She was relieved to know he didn't find her unattractive. And he'd obviously seen almost all of her, too.

"If you tell anyone you saw me naked, I'll kick your ass."

He dropped the cotton swab on the nightstand and then reached over and tilted her chin up with his index finger. "I wouldn't tell anyone." His voice came out a little deep, and he sounded completely sincere.

He ran his finger over her lips.

"You aren't going to kiss me," she said.

"We'll see about that," he said and then he did it. He kissed her.

How it went from a simple kiss to him stretched out beside her, the sheet down at her feet and his shirt off, was a mystery. A delicious one.

His mouth moved from her lips to her neck and then lower. She moaned, lost in how good it felt. But when his hand softly, seductively slid down below her waist, she grabbed it, and swallowed a big dose of reality.

"I'm sorry," she muttered and sat up. "I can't . . . We can't."

She heard him inhale and she knew he was filled with want and desire just as she was. But supposedly it was even worse on a guy. It had always been hard on Lee before . . . before she let things go all the way.

The thought of Lee had her breath catching again.

Tears filled her eyes and all she could think was how she'd gone down this road already. She'd given herself to Lee and look where that'd led her.

"Go take a cold shower." She gave him her back and pulled the sheet over herself.

He took several deep breaths of air, and after a few long seconds he said, "I didn't mean . . . I was just going to kiss you. Shit," he said, his voice filled with self-loathing. "I never meant to take advantage of the fact that—"

"You didn't." She closed her eyes. "Didn't take advantage. I went there with you. But . . . we shouldn't have . . . gone there."

"To soon?" he asked.

"Too everything," she answered. *Too good. Too real. Too much like it meant something really special. Too much to have to deal with losing later on.* "If you're not going to shower, I am. We need to get back to Shadow Falls."

She hated the anger in her tone and hoped he understood it wasn't because of him. It was because of her. She simply couldn't let herself go down this road again.

In the shower she heard a phone ring and listened as Steve told Burnett they would be back in a couple of hours. He took a shower after her, and thirty minutes later, they got into a hotel elevator, one she had no memory of coming up in.

Had he carried her? She hated not knowing something. Hated knowing she'd been that vulnerable.

Once they arrived in the crowded lobby, he led her into the hotel's restaurant.

A complaint rested on her lips, but she remembered she'd eaten today and he hadn't. So she shut up and followed the hostess when Steve told her they needed a table for two.

He ordered a steak and baked potato and some sweet tea. She ordered French onion soup, about the one thing she could actually enjoy, and a Diet Coke.

When the waitress left with their order, Steve looked at her, still wearing an apology in his eyes. Yup, he felt guilty for things getting out of hand. But she didn't put all the blame on him. She could have stopped it. Should have stopped it.

"How's the shoulder?" he asked.

She reached up and touched where she'd been stabbed. "Completely healed," she said. Then she remembered something they'd talked about earlier. "Did you learn medicine from your mom?"

He nodded. "Sometimes she'd volunteer at different free clinics. I used to go with her on weekends. I'm a fast learner on some things."

She suspected he was a fast learner in all things. She hadn't seen it at first, but intelligence lingered in those big brown eyes. "And you don't want to be a doctor?"

"I didn't say I don't want to be a doctor."

"But you said . . . I mean I got the feeling when you talked about your parents that you didn't want to do what they wanted you to do."

"She wants me to go into medicine for humans because that's where the money is. I want to train to treat supernaturals. That's where my skills will be the most useful."

She nodded. "I see." The waitress dropped off their drinks. Della twirled a straw around her glass and watched the bubbles rise to the top. "My parents wanted me to be a doctor, too."

"And you don't want that?" he asked.

"Hell, no. I want to go into criminal justice."

"A lawyer?"

"No. I don't want to defend the law. I want to enforce it. Before I was turned, I was thinking FBI or CIA. Now I'm thinking FRU. Which is why I didn't want Burnett to know I'd screwed up."

He shook his head. "You didn't screw up."

"I got stabbed. That's pretty screwed up." She jabbed her straw into her drink.

"We were up against a whole gang of rogue vampires. The fact that we got out of there alive is a freaking miracle."

She gave the straw another race around her glass. "But you're the one who saved us. The one who came up with a plan, and then again with the werewolves."

"Yeah, but you were a little busy trying not to let that rogue were/vampire kill you in the ring. And when the weres showed up you were already stabbed and bleeding like crazy, but you still stood up."

"I didn't do shit when they came," she muttered, ashamed of herself.

"You stood up and faced them and let them know you weren't ready to be their dinner."

He looked down at his own glass for a second. "Honestly, I was totally impressed with you. The whole time, I'm freaking out inside. Hell, my knees were shaking and you were like this epitome of calm. I kept looking at you and thinking if you could do this, I could, too."

She let go of a deep breath. "I wasn't calm. I was freaking out, too."

He smiled. "Well, that's why you're so good at this, Della. You didn't seem scared. Not once. You can do this. I personally don't like the thought of you putting yourself in danger, but don't ever think you screwed up. You kicked ass in that ring."

His compliment felt like a big hug. And as she constantly told Kylie and Miranda, she wasn't much of a hugger.

Looking down at her drink again, the realization hit. She used to be a hugger, but now when anyone wrapped their warm arms around her it reminded her of how cold she was.

Suddenly, she realized when Steve had kissed her and touched her she'd forgotten she was cold. For the first time since she'd been turned, she'd felt normal again—felt . . . human. Damn that felt good.

"Thanks." She looked up briefly and hoped he understood how much she meant it, because she didn't want to have to express it any more than just offering the word.

The waitress dropped off their food. Della spooned the French onion soup into her mouth, bypassing the cheese. But as the warm, tasty broth danced on her tongue, she couldn't help but think how good Steve's blood tasted. How good his kisses were. How it felt to be touched and not think about being cold.

When she'd showered, she'd noticed a hickey between her shoulder and left breast. She was glad he'd left his mark on her. But she was equally glad it wasn't permanent. It would fade in a few days. And that's the way it should be. Because once they were back at Shadow Falls, this was over.

Done.

She simply couldn't put her heart on the chopping block again. Lee, along with her parents, had taught her how hard it was to love someone. How easy it was for them to disappoint you.

She didn't love Steve, not yet, but these last thirty-six hours had taught her how easy it would be to let herself go there. When someone was genuinely nice, your heart welcomed them inside. Add the whole good-looking thing and him being such an awesome kisser to the scenario, and her heart had a welcome mat ready to toss down, a marching band, and banners with flashy letters reading, COME ON IN.

And that was unacceptable. She couldn't fall in love with Steve. Nope. No way. As soon as they returned to Shadow Falls, she was back to being the old Della. Solo. She had Miranda, and she had Kylie. As soon as Kylie returned.

Della didn't need a guy making her feel special, making her feel beautiful, making her feel . . . human.

Steve picked up his knife and cut a piece of steak. "Oh, when I spoke with Burnett earlier this morning he mentioned that he went to see Kylie."

Della's heart swelled. "He knows where she is? Is she coming back?"

"He must know because he said he'd seen her, but he didn't say anything about her coming back. He just said to tell you that she was okay and that she asked about you."

That was Kylie, always worried about others before she worried about herself. The girl was an idiot. Well, not an idiot. She was just one of those really caring people. Sort of like the damn shape-shifter Della was having lunch with.

Della dipped her spoon into the onion soup. "Well, if he knows where she is, then I can just go and bring her back."

"Kidnap her?" he asked.

"If I have to, yeah. She belongs at Shadow Falls with Miranda and me."

Steve chuckled. "You're not serious," he said.

"The hell I'm not," Della snapped. "Kylie's coming home and that's all there is to it."

. . .

Home. Della felt it as she landed outside the fence at Shadow Falls about thirty minutes later. Funny, how the place had started to feel that way. Of course, maybe that was to be expected when she no longer belonged with her parents.

Steve landed and transformed. "We should go to the front."

"No." She pulled out her phone. "I'm calling Burnett and telling him I'm here, then I'm jumping the fence. I just want to go to my cabin and relax . . . I don't want to be interrogated right now."

She wanted to have time to regroup in her head.

Burnett answered on the second ring. "Where are you?"

"We're here. Right outside the fence on the east side of the property."

"Good. We're having dinner now. Why don't you come over? There's a surprise."

"I'm tired. Not in the mood for surprises. I just want to take a shower and relax. Can we talk tomorrow?"

"Are you okay?" His tone grew dark, concerned.

"I'm fine," she growled.

When she hung up, Steve started walking over to her. She watched the way he moved, like a lion, lithe and with purpose. He stopped right in front of her and brushed a strand of hair back behind her ear. "You know, I kind of don't want to go back. I liked it just being you and me."

She'd liked it, too. Too much.

She caught his hand and lowered it from her face.

Swallowing a lump of regret, she forced herself to say it. Part of her had hoped she wouldn't have to spell it out for him. But that was the coward's way out. And Della Tsang wasn't a coward. Plus, Steve deserved to know up front that it wasn't him. It was her.

"Look, I . . . I enjoyed this. Everything. I really did, but . . . it's over now."

He shook his head. "Why? It doesn't have to be."

"Yeah it does." Her heart suddenly grew heavy. Too heavy for her chest. "I don't . . . I'm not . . . I'm not ready for this." She waved a hand between them.

That look of apology filled his eyes again. "I told you I didn't mean for that to happen. I'm not going to pressure you to take it there. It'll happen when it's supposed to happen. I'll be patient."

She shook her head. "I don't mean just that."

Concern tightened his brows. "Then what do you mean?"

"I mean us . . . period. Us being an item, us being an 'us.' I'm not up for that."

He shook his head. "Why? I thought we got along great."

"Why isn't important. It's just the way it is. I'm not going there. I'm completely happy the way things are, happy with me . . . not being a couple." It was such a huge mistruth she could hear her swollen heart doing all sorts of erratic thumps, each one hitting against her sternum and calling her a lying bitch.

"No," he said, "I can't accept that."

"You're going to have to accept it. Because that's just the way it is, Steve. We went on a mission and we did great. We did what we were sent to do and thanks to both of us the world might be a little safer. But what happened between us needs to end. I'm not right for you."

He studied her. "Who are you right for?" he asked, sounding jealous.

"I'm not right for anyone," she said and her heart didn't race or mark that as a lie. She had loved already. Loved and lost. "It's over, Steve. Just accept it."

She started running and right before she leapt over the fence she heard him.

"We'll see about that." His words rang in her ears. A promise or a threat, she didn't know. But the idea of it being a promise chased away the biggest part of the pain she carried in her heart.

As she walked inside her cabin, she breathed in the scents of home—the smell of Miranda's fruity shampoo, and her scented candles. Della could even pick up the scent of Kylie's favorite lotion.

Standing in the living room, Della let herself feel the tiniest bit of pride that she'd completed the mission. The feeling reconfirmed that she wanted to pursue a career in catching bad guys.

Walking into her bedroom, she opened her bottom drawer and pulled out the pictures. Images of her and her family, and others of her and Lee. All captured moments with emotion. Memories that now hurt to think about.

She started to rip them all up, but then on second thought, she dropped the pictures of her family back into the drawer. Some things she couldn't give up on. But others . . .

She tore the snapshots of her and Lee into little pieces and let the tiny specks of paper rain down into the garbage. Then she went to her bed and flopped down on her back and stared at the ceiling.

We'll see about that. Steve's words echoed in her head like the lyrics of a song—a good song, one that crawled into your head and replayed itself over and over.

She closed her eyes. Life might have thrown her some punches this last year, but Della Tsang didn't go down easy. She was just going to punch back.

Unbreakable

BREAKING NEWS

Missing plane spotted in Jasper Mountain Range

According to a statement from Sheriff Ted Carter, wreckage of a Cessna 210, believed to be the same one flown by Dr. Edward Tallman, was spotted in the Jasper Mountain Range. A SAR (Search and Rescue) team was called in when twenty minutes after takeoff the plane fell off radar yesterday at 4:20. Two helicopters from Mountain Rescue Association (MRA) searched the perimeter of the area yesterday but didn't spot the downed plane until this morning. Due to low clouds and high winds, visibility of the crash site was poor and they were unable to spot any signs of survivors. Flying with Dr. Tallman were his wife, Amy, their two teenage children, Mindy and Chase, as well as a family friend, Tami Collins.

Emergency ground crews have been put on call, but are waiting for a break in the weather. A spokeswoman was quoted saying that they know it's imperative to get to the site as soon as possible, but the safety of their crew must be considered.

It was speculated that Dr. Tallman and his family may have flown into Jasper to take part in a genetic study, however no local research facility reports any of the Tallmans' participation. Meanwhile, friends of the Tallman family and the parents of Tami Collins are in Jasper praying the news will be good once Search and Rescue teams are on the ground.

Chapter One

ONE DAY EARLIER: SATURDAY, OCTOBER 31, 10:30 A.M.

Chase Tallman watched as the bright-eyed, bloodthirsty lab tech tied a large elastic band around the middle of his arm hoping to expose a few of Chase's veins.

"There's a good one," the woman said as she passed two fingers over the crook of his arm where a blue vein now bulged out. "You have great veins," she said, sounding sincere.

Her hands were cold. Extra cold, making a chill run up his arm.

"Just a little stick and we'll be done." She smiled at him and reached over to pick up the needle with the large tube attached, taking the plastic tip off the syringe. Shit! How much blood did the woman need?

He freaking hated needles. But he didn't flinch. Fourteen was too old to flinch. He hadn't even cried when he broke his arm last summer during baseball practice. It had hurt like hell, but his coach had been the one to take him to the hospital and the last thing he'd wanted was to look weak in front of his coach.

Chase glanced around the small lab in the doctor's office that was practically hidden in some remote part of the Rockies. He wasn't exactly sure why his dad had insisted on them taking part in this research study, but it had to be pretty important for his dad to get his plane checked out and fly them up from Houston to participate.

Not that Chase liked it. Who gave up their blood for no reason? But the promise of a weekend in a cabin in the mountains, plus the plane ride, made it worth it. The fact that his sister's best friend, Tami Collins, tagged along, made it more than worth it. Hell, he'd let them stick him with needles all day for the pleasure of seeing her in her bathing suit again. Holy cow, she'd looked hot last night when she'd joined him and his sister in the hot tub.

For a second last night, he would've sworn she'd been playing footsies with him. It could have been an accident, but he hoped not. And he wished like hell he hadn't shifted away.

He liked to think she'd finally stopped looking at him as her best friend's baby brother and started looking at him like . . . a guy. A potential boyfriend kind of guy. Hell, he was less than a year younger than she and stood a good eight inches taller. Most people took him for at least sixteen.

Feeling the prick of the needle, the medical tech dug around for a vein. To distract himself from the pain, he closed his eyes and thought of Tami's dips and curves, of how her dark brown hair had looked dancing on her bare shoulders. It worked, too.

Unlike most of his friends who were into computer games and denied their fascination with the opposite sex, Chase gave up his denial. He'd rather study a pretty girl than get to the next level of Battlefield 4 any day of the week. Hell, he'd rather touch or kiss a girl than play baseball. And he really liked playing baseball.

Problem was, he was better at sports than he was at even getting close to first base with a girl. Or at least that's what Susie Muller told him last year after the eighth grade dance. But the girl had braces, how was he supposed to kiss her?

Somehow he just knew if he got the opportunity to kiss Tami, he'd be better at it. She didn't have braces and her mouth was . . . so soft looking.

Hell, he'd practiced kissing her in his fantasies a hundred times. He should be an expert by now.

"All done," the lab tech said, patting Chase's arm with one hand while she pressed a cotton swab over the tiny drop of blood oozing from the needle's prick. "Oops, I'm out of Band-Aids here. Hold this for me."

He put his finger on the ball of cotton. She reached around to get a Band-Aid out of the cabinet. He kept his finger on the piece of swab, but probably not hard enough, because a red stream of blood seeped from under the cotton ball and oozed down the crook in his arm.

"Push on it a little harder," she said, still facing the cabinet as if she knew he was bleeding. Then she turned and peeled the Band-Aid open.

As she secured a bandage over the puffy piece of cotton, he glanced up at her. When her eyes shifted upward, he almost gasped at how her eyes glowed. They had been bright green before, but now they were fluorescent lime green.

As if self-conscious, she glanced away and seemed to purposely not look back at him. Or at least it appeared that way.

"You can go," she said, taking more Band-Aids out of the cabinet and putting them on her cart.

He didn't have to be told twice. Not actually scared, because he was too old to be scared, but slightly freaked out, he rose from the chair and started out.

As he stepped out of the room, he heard his dad's deep voice boom down the hall. He looked over his shoulder. His dad stood in the doorway of another small room with a man wearing a white lab coat.

"You'll let me know the results as soon as you can, right?" his father asked.

"Of course," the man said.

What results? They were here for a research study. Weren't they?

Chase watched the two men shake hands, and then feeling as if he was eavesdropping, he turned and went in search of the waiting room to find his mom, and hopefully Tami.

"Did you cry?" his older sister, Mindy, asked as Chase walked up to where she stood with his mom and Tami.

He shot his sister a frown and would have shot her the bird if his mom hadn't been beside her. "Not as hard as you, I'm sure," he smarted back, looking at her Band-Aid. His sister, barely five feet tall, could always be a big pain in the ass, but she upped her game anytime Tami was around. Why, he didn't know. Did she secretly know that he had a crush on Tami and just wanted to make him look bad?

"Did it hurt?" Tami asked, looking from his sister to him.

"A little," Mindy answered, and tossed her dark hair over her shoulder.

"No, it didn't," Chase said.

His sister rolled her blue eyes. "Be careful or he might ask you to kiss it." She snickered.

Okay, that did it. He didn't care if his mom saw or not. He gave his sister the third finger salute accompanied by a go-screw-yourself scowl.

"Chase!" Mom reprimanded, but he ignored her. If she wanted him to behave, she was gonna have to control her firstborn who excelled at being a bitch.

His sister looked triumphant at getting Chase scolded. But he noted that Tami just grinned.

"What kind of test was it?" Tami asked, and her dark brown eyes looked back at his mom.

"Just a general research study on genetics," his mom answered.

Chase thought about his dad asking for the results. Something wasn't adding up.

"You mean, like if you guys will get cancer or something? My mom had a test to see if she would get breast cancer. She won't. Her blood work confirmed her tatas are safe," Tami said.

He almost laughed. Yet, right after hearing Tami say "breast" and "tatas," the temptation to glance at Tami's chest beneath her red sweater swept through him. However, not wanting to get caught ogling, he reached down and picked up a sports magazine and pretended to be interested in the cover. But, hands down, he'd rather have been looking at her breasts then Billy Hamilton's ugly mug. He didn't care how good the guy was at baseball.

"No, it's not for cancer," Mom said.

"Then what was it for?" Tami asked, innocently enough.

Chase glanced up, his own curiosity piqued, thinking his mom might have learned something about it by now.

"It's just a research study." Frustration sounded in his mom's voice. Though he didn't understand why she would be upset at Tami for asking the same questions he'd heard her ask his father two weeks ago. Oddly, Dad had given Mom the same vague answer as she gave Tami now.

His dad walked out from the back room, wearing his own Band-Aid. Right then, it occurred to Chase that they hadn't tested his mom. If it was really just some random research study, why hadn't they tested her as well? He almost asked, but decided his dad would answer better if they were alone.

Mom handed Dad his coat. "Thanks." He slipped it on and then leaned down to kiss her cheek. And he really had to lean, too. At six feet four, he towered above Chase's mom who was only a few inches over five feet. Nothing against Mom, but Chase had always been glad he'd inherited his dad's height gene.

"Please don't start the kissing stuff in public," Mindy said. "It's embarrassing."

Mom frowned at her. Dad grinned. "I can't help it if your mom still does it for me. You want to see a real kiss?"

"Please, no!" Mindy said seriously when their dad slipped his arm around Mom's waist and pulled her closer.

"Stop it," Mom said and giggled.

"I'd like to see it," Tami said. "I think it's sweet."

His dad laughed. "Since we had to skip breakfast for the test, are you guys ready to grab an early lunch?"

"I'm starving," Mindy said, "but Tami and I want to go to the street fair in Old James Town. It's sort of a Halloween festival. They've got rides, a haunted house, palm readers, and fortune-tellers. They even have a band playing in the town square."

And the boy who was staying in the cabin next door was going, too, Chase thought, remembering that Eric had mentioned it last night when he came over to chat while they'd been in the hot tub. Chase didn't particularly care for Eric. Or the way he'd stared at Mindy and Tami in their bathing suits. Sure, Chase had appreciated Tami, but there was a difference between appreciating and gawking. Eric had gawked. Thankfully, he'd seemed more interested in Mindy than Tami. Though Chase didn't particularly like the dude staring at his sister, either. Baxter hadn't been thrilled about it, either. Baxter, their black Lab, normally liked everyone. But he'd growled at the kid.

Chase had decided to go with the motto: If Baxter didn't like you, Chase didn't like you.

Not that Mindy seemed to mind Eric's rude stares. Heck, what did he know? Maybe girls liked to be gawked at.

Chase listened as his sister continued to sell the festival to their parents. He seriously doubted that Mindy would tell them about Eric going to the festival. His parents had a thing about Mindy not dating until she was sixteen. Mindy, however, had a thing about boys.

His mom looked at her watch. "We could stop by for an hour, but we have skiing lessons at one."

"I don't want to do the skiing lessons," Mindy whined. "We did that yesterday. Why can't you just drop us off and let us stay the day? You and Dad can pick us up after skiing. Pleeeeeasssse?"

Chase stared down at the magazine he still held, hoping his mom said no. He'd already had the perfect day planned. They'd spend four hours skiing, take Baxter for a walk at the park a mile from the cabin, and then come back and go to the hot tub. He really wanted to see if Tami rubbed her foot against his again. If she did, this time he wasn't going to move his leg.

"I . . ." His mom hesitated.

Chase glanced up. *Say no. Say no.*

"Sorry," his mom continued. "I'm not comfortable with you two alone at a street fair all day."

"Mom," Mindy whined. "I'm fifteen, not five!"

"Why don't we compromise," his dad joined in. "Take Chase with you and I think you three will be fine."

He could live with that compromise, Chase thought. He'd lose skiing, and Baxter would lose out on his walk, but going to the festival with Tami could be fun. And they could do the hot tub when they came back. Yup. Chase liked the sound of that. And what he liked more was the fact that his dad gave him the role of taking care of his sister instead of the other way around.

As much as he liked it, Mindy didn't. She rolled her eyes. "I don't want to babysit."

Chase scowled. "Didn't you hear him? I'm the one babysitting you." He almost said something about Eric being there just to get even for her bitchiness. But right before he tattled, he closed his mouth. Just because his sister was a shit didn't mean he had to be one.

"It's so unfair," Mindy snapped. "I'm older and you're always acting as if—"

"He's bigger and twice your weight," Dad said, pointing out that Mindy had inherited her height gene from Mom. "And bad things are less likely to happen with three of you together."

Mindy let out a huff of disappointment. "But—"

"It's the deal breaker as far as I'm concerned." Dad gave Mindy a stern look and then looked at their mom. "What do you say, hon? You okay if all three go?"

His mom paused. "I guess if Chase goes with you, it would be fine." She looked at Chase. "Do you mind going with your sister? Or were you set on going skiing?"

He hesitated, glancing at Mindy for a pregnant pause, hoping she appreciated that he could refuse, and all her plans would be flushed down the toilet.

Not that he would flush them. If it took putting up with Mindy to be with Tami, he'd do it in a snap. But his sister didn't have to know that. He hoped she didn't know it. The less power she held over him the better.

"Nah, I'll go," Chase finally said.

"Great," said Tami, and she actually reached over and gave his arm a soft squeeze. Her touch sent tiny currents of something really sweet through his body and had him remembering how it felt when her foot had brushed up against his. Blinking, he gazed into her face. She smiled so big that her dark brown eyes crinkled. Was she really that happy he was going?

Pulling her hand back, she looked back at his parents. "I've been wanting to have my palm read for years." She pushed her dark hair over one shoulder and he watched as it cascaded across her back. For some crazy reason he wondered if it was as soft as it appeared. "I love festivals."

Okay, so maybe it wasn't spending the day with him that had her so happy. But it didn't stop him from being thrilled at the idea of hanging with her for the next few hours—of maybe scoring a few more smiles and soft touches. Especially when tomorrow morning they would be flying home and their weekend would be over. That would mean it might be like two weeks before he saw her again. That would completely suck.

His chest felt heavy from the thought. She did that thing again with her hair, pulling it up and letting it fall on her shoulders. He studied her profile, a small nose, full lips that looked soft and always shiny. Large brown eyes, slightly slanted, with thick dark lashes.

He tucked his hands into his jeans pockets and tried to push the tug on his emotions away. While Chase really liked girls, he hated thinking of himself as one of those guys who got all sappy-eyed and started tossing around the L word. But for the life of him, it felt as if it was where he was heading. And he wasn't sure he could stop it.

He glanced back at Tami, who was still smiling. Still the most beautiful thing he'd ever laid eyes on.

He wasn't sure he wanted to stop it.

BREAKING NEWS: UPDATE

An emergency crew has decided to brave the weather and embark on a rescue mission, hoping to find survivors of the wreckage of the Cessna 210 carrying Dr. Tallman and four other passengers.

Despite the deteriorating weather conditions, the emergency rescue crew is gathering supplies and is expected to depart on the rescue mission in the next few hours. Dr. Tallman's plane fell off radar twenty minutes after leaving Jasper Regional Airport yesterday at 4 p.m. "There are five people out there who could be alive," says Search and Rescue (SAR) volunteer Tom Phillips. "Three are just teenagers. If they are alive, I'm sure they are desperate for help. If they are not, we need to bring closure to the families. It only seems right that we try to get to them as soon as possible."

Sheriff Ted Carter released this in his latest statement: "While two SAR helicopters have flown over the wreckage this morning, visibility is still low, and unfortunately no signs of life have been reported." Tom Phillips also told the media, "While under normal weather conditions the hike up the Jasper range could take up to three hours, with these weather conditions it could take twice as long."

Family and friends of the Tallmans flew in last night after being notified that the plane went missing. "I want to know my daughter is still alive. I have to believe she is," says Cary Collins, father of fifteen-year-old Tami Collins. The Faith Tabernacle church in Jasper has opened its doors to the family and is holding an open service for any of the townspeople who would like to stop in and pray for the Tallman family and Tami Collins's safe return.

Chapter Two

Chase's parents dropped them off at the corner of First Street and Walnut Avenue with instructions to meet them back at the same corner in four hours. The first thing Mindy wanted to do was go to the square where the biggest crowd hung out to listen to the band play.

Chase's stomach had other plans, and he would've loved to have snagged a hot dog from one of the concession stands. They'd passed at least three and the smell had called his name. All the blood they'd drawn for the study was probably increasing his appetite, he thought, but he didn't argue with Mindy.

Didn't argue even when he knew it wasn't the music that Mindy wanted.

She wanted to find Eric. The thought hit then that his parents had expected him to watch out for his sister. And damn it, he knew his parents would say that meant keeping her away from sixteen-year-olds who leered at her. Then again, weren't his parents being a tad ridiculous about the whole no-dating-until-sixteen rule? Hell, most of the girls in his class were already dating.

They walked the town square—snaking through the crowds, separating groups of friends—Mindy in the front and leading at a breakneck pace. She accidentally bumped into a guy wearing a black robe with a knife sticking out of his chest. And his sister, so intent in her search for a certain blond dude, didn't even notice. There must have been a costume contest happening because a good third of the attendees were dressed like creatures of the dark.

Chase offered an apologetic shrug when Mindy stormed through a group of friends, some sporting pale skin and fake fangs, others wearing werewolf masks.

You didn't want to piss off a park full of werewolves or vampires. Once or twice, he glanced at Tami at his side and she just shrugged as if she'd realized how crazed his sister was as well.

They'd made three or four treks—he'd lost count—around the square, without one glimpse of the boob-gawking Eric.

After the third time walking through the same group of creatures, who were looking pissed at his sister's lack of manners, Chase finally took her by the arm and tried to get her to see reason. "Mindy. He's not here. Let's go grab something to eat."

She frowned, obviously unhappy, and looked about ready to toss some ugly insult his way. But he kind of understood that she wasn't as upset at him as she was disappointed at being stood up by the guy she had a major crush on. He remembered hearing the jerk tell Mindy several times that he'd be at the festival and for her to please show up and find him.

"We can come back later and see if he's here," Chase offered, noting the hurt in her eyes. Hurt that he recognized as rejection. Sort of how he'd felt when Susie Muller had told him he didn't know how to kiss.

"I'm kind of hungry, too," Tami said, moving in beside him, chasing all thoughts of Susie from his mind.

The warmth of Tami's shoulder against his had him wondering if the brush was accidental or if maybe . . . just maybe, she liked touching him as much as he liked her touching him.

"Fine," his sister said, but the pain in her expression and her rejected posture had him forgetting about Tami for a second and disliking Eric even more.

If the guy stood his sister up, he'd better not show his ugly face back at the cabin before they left tomorrow, because Chase would tell him what he thought. Then he might get Baxter after his butt.

They all ordered hot dogs—two for him and one for each of the girls—with extra mustard and one order of nachos. Since his dad had slipped Chase three twenties before getting out of the car, he picked up the bill. He kind of liked paying for Tami. It made it almost feel like a date. Of course, if it were a date, she might be holding his hand and he might be trying to figure out how to sneak a kiss. But not wanting to be disappointed, he tried not to think about it too much.

They sat at an empty picnic table set out for the festival. Tami, who'd borrowed Mindy's phone because hers had lost juice, was trying to call her parents, but for some reason couldn't get the call to go through. He studied her under his lashes, noticing little things. Like the shape of her lips or the way she messed with her hair.

"We must have a bad connection here," she said and set the phone down.

She had chosen to sit beside him and not beside Mindy. Was he over-reading her every move? Or was it possible she had a thing for him, too?

A group of vampires, several of the ones they'd charged past in their search for Eric, sat at the picnic table next to them.

Mindy, as if seeing them for the first time, stared and then shuddered. She leaned down and spoke in a whisper. "They're freaky, don't you think?"

Chase looked at the group of teens. They must have lost their werewolf friends, because these were all dressed in black, probably doused with some kind of white powder to make them appear extra pale, and wore fake fangs. One of the guys had a few drops of fake blood running down his chin and one girl had what looked like bite marks on her neck.

"There has to be some costume contest going on," Chase said. Not that these guys were going to win, Chase thought. "Did you see that zombie with the skin hanging off his face? He almost looked real."

"They're still freaky," Mindy said, and cut her eyes back to the table of vampires.

"You've been reading too many novels," Chase said and took his first bite of hot dog. The spicy mustard filled his taste buds and reminded him how hungry he really was. But even starved, he stopped himself from poking the whole thing in his mouth, the way he might have done if he was just with his guy friends. The last thing he wanted to do was look like a pig in front of the girl of his dreams.

"No," Mindy said, and scooped up a chip dripping with cheese and sliced jalapeños. "It's not the books. I've been reading too many of Dad's reports."

Chase picked up his soda. "Reports?"

"His medical reports," she said. "I went by his work a couple of weeks ago and he was with a patient so I went and waited for him in his office." She leaned in and spoke quietly. "There was a file open on his desk and it was about some virus that made people crave blood. Human blood."

Tami almost choked on a nacho. "So you're saying that vampires actually exist?"

"No, I didn't say that," Mindy said. "I'm saying a virus exists that makes people crazy and they want to drink blood. You can call it anything you want."

Chase chuckled. "I think you just read it wrong."

"I didn't," Mindy said. "I mean, maybe it was about one of his patients in the loony house, but . . ."

"Dad's a nephrologist, meaning a kidney doctor, not a shrink. His patients aren't in the loony house."

Mindy took a big sip of her drink and rolled her eyes at Chase's disbelief. "Hey . . . I'm just telling you what I read."

"To be fair," Tami said, "crazy people could have bad kidneys. I don't think kidney disease is prejudiced against the mentally unstable."

Chase chuckled, and studied the girl's sassy smile. That's part of what he liked about Tami, she said some of the most unexpected things. "I guess they could," he admitted.

Tami picked up a chip and Chase realized how great it was just being here. With her. Watching her eat. He bet he could watch her clip her toenails and be happy.

"You know," Tami said. "I heard once that there are bars that actually cater to people who want to drink blood. Yuk! What kind of person would drink blood?"

"The kind that's really thirsty," a dark voice said at the end of the table.

They all turned to the voice. Eric stood there, tall, but not as tall as Chase. And blond.

His sister stared up at him with some kind of love-struck grin. "Anyone ever tell you that you look like Josh Holloway?" his sister asked.

"Yeah, all the time." Eric grinned. "I'm lost. You wanna find me?"

What? That was so lame! But Mindy smiled. Chase sneaked a peek at Tami. And while she did seem to be admiring the guy, she didn't look nearly as taken as his sister. Perhaps she preferred dark-haired guys over blonds. He could hope.

"So you made it," Eric said, his gaze locked on Mindy.

"I told you I would," his sister said, a goofy smile still plastered on her face. Holy crap, he hoped he didn't smile at Tami that way.

Eric looked over at the other table and called out a greeting to a couple of the vampires eating pizza. Then he looked back at their table and finally acknowledged Chase and Tami. Chase nodded a hello. Picking up his hot dog, he tried to push away his aversion for the guy. Like it or not, it appeared as if they would be spending the rest of the afternoon with him. But when he looked back and found Eric staring at his sister as if he'd found a present and was ready to unwrap it, Chase wasn't sure he could push his dislike—or his distrust—of the guy aside.

That was okay, he'd just have to pretend. But one thing was for sure, he wasn't going to let Eric get his sister alone. Something about this guy just smelled like trouble.

Chase didn't like trouble.

NEWS FLASH

Emergency crews head out hoping to find survivors

Three Search and Rescue (SAR) teams, as well as volunteers with the Mountain Rescue Association (MRA) trained in emergency care, started their trek up Mount Jacobs hoping to arrive at the wrecked Cessna 210 carrying Dr. Tallman's family and family friend, Tami Collins. According to Jake Steins, who has led several similar rescue missions in this area, it is still questionable if they can get to the wreckage in the current weather conditions. If all goes well, they expect to arrive at the crash site in six to eight hours.

While no signs of life have been seen by helicopters that have flown over the site, there is evidence of a recent fire. It is unknown if the fire came as a result of the crash or if survivors built a fire to ward off the cold or signal for help. The community, family, and friends are holding out hope that the passengers are simply huddling in the wreckage to escape the storm and the freezing temperatures.

"Sometimes all you can hang onto is your faith," said a friend of the Tallman family.

Chapter Three

"Sit down and join us," Mindy said and scooted over, patting the bench seat next to her.

Eric didn't hesitate to take the invitation, only the jerk took the invitation a little too far. Hell, Chase didn't think you could get a piece of sock lint between the dude and his sister.

Chase shot the guy a frown, hoping he'd get the message, but he obviously didn't understand because he proceeded to put his arm around Mindy, letting his hand dangle down her shoulder practically touching her right breast.

Thankfully, even Mindy seemed to not like it, because she leaned forward to snag another nacho, displacing his hand from her shoulder.

Not wanting to call the guy out just yet, but damn close, Chase focused on eating his hot dog. But not happy, he forgot his manners and shoved the rest of the bun and meat into his mouth.

"You want something to eat?" Mindy asked Eric, pulling the nachos toward him.

"Yeah, I'm starved," the guy said. But he didn't partake in the nachos. Instead, he looked across the table. "You gonna eat that hot dog?" he asked Chase.

With his mouth full, he didn't answer before Mindy said, "Oh, he's done. He already had one." Before he knew what she planned to do, she popped up and stole Chase's second hot dog and dropped it in front of Eric.

Chase chewed the bun and meat in his mouth with a little more gusto and stared at his sister.

She glared back.

Eric never seemed to notice the glaring match.

Before Chase could swallow and claim dibs on his lunch, the creep picked up the hot dog and practically pushed the whole damn thing in his mouth.

The guy's cheeks puffed out. Oh yeah, Chase thought, realizing why big bites looked disgusting. The gawker/hot dog stealer now had a little mustard oozing from his lips, and with his cheeks stretched out like a chipmunk, he probably couldn't even feel it.

"Are you ready to go have our palms read?" Tami asked, as if sensing the tension.

"Palms read?" Eric said, his mouth still full as he made a face. "That's stupid."

Chase leaned forward. "Then I guess we'll see you later. Come on, Mindy," he said, and when he heard his tone, he realized he sounded a bit like his dad. Deep and serious.

Tami stood up as if she completely understood and agreed with Chase's plan. Then she picked up Mindy's phone and dropped it in her pocket. "You ready?" she asked Mindy.

Mindy, however, didn't answer Tami. She'd gone back to her favorite pastime of glaring at Chase.

"Hey, I think it's stupid," Eric said, still talking around Chase's hot dog, "but I'll go along for the laughs."

"Good." Mindy cut another cold look at Chase as if warning him not to come between her and the boy she obviously thought was going to be her Prince Charming. Not that there was one thing charming about the guy.

Chase almost spoke up right then and told the guy to take a hike or go hang out with his vampire buds, but another glance at Mindy's tight-lipped, squinty-eyed glare and he knew she would raise all kinds of hell. He didn't want Tami to get mixed up in their sibling rivalry. So he shut his mouth, snagged his soda cup, and stood up.

The hot dog thief could come, but Chase wasn't going to take his eyes off him. Stealing a hot dog was one thing, but if he tried anything with Mindy, he'd have more than Chase's eyes on him.

Chase had never started a fight, but he'd finished several. People always thought bullies picked on the little guys, and they did, but being big had make him a target of some of the bullies who wanted to claim they'd taken out the tallest kid in class.

Unfortunately, it hadn't worked out for them.

Chase summed up Eric. Probably sixteen, he had a wide set of shoulders on him and probably a tad more muscle. Chase didn't care if the guy was older, or if he was built like a brick house. If he stepped out of line one more time, he'd put him in his place.

"I'm kind of scared," Tami said later while standing beside the palm reader. "You go first." She shot Chase a sweet but vulnerable smile. He was hit again by how pretty she was. Her father was American but her mom was Hawaiian, and she had the perfect blend. Her skin tone was just a tad olive and her hair was a couple shades lighter than black, and her eyes dark brown. He couldn't actually say she was his type. He didn't know if he actually had a type. But Susie Muller had also been brunette with dark eyes, not that Susie held a candle to Tami.

"Do you mind going first?" Tami asked, making Chase realize he'd just been standing there staring at her like an idiot. Probably even had that goofy smile on his face, too.

"No, that's fine."

The palm reader sat at a table with a black tablecloth, her hands folded on top. A sign on the table read: CAUTION: I WILL TELL THE TRUTH, NO MATTER HOW GOOD OR BAD.

She had jet-black hair, coal-black eyes, and she was dressed in bright orange. She reminded Chase of a gypsy. And maybe she was.

"Just two of you?" the woman asked.

"Yes," Chase answered. Because Eric thought it was stupid, Mindy had decided against getting her palm read. He could tell Tami wanted company getting hers read, and if it made her happy . . . He didn't really mind. He didn't believe in it, but for Tami he'd do it.

Chase pulled out a twenty to pay for their reading.

"I can pay for mine," Tami said. "My dad gave me money. And your dad hasn't let me pay for anything."

"Don't worry about it," Chase said, and was thankful his dad had given him ample cash. As he stuffed the change back in his jeans pocket, he cut his eyes around again to check on Mindy.

When he didn't see them his heart shot into his throat. Shit! Had he let the jerk get Mindy off by herself?

But another sweep around and he spotted them. They stood about ten feet away chatting. As they'd walked here, he'd seen Eric try to put his arm around her and she'd pulled back a bit and took his hand instead. He liked knowing that Mindy was no fool. She might like the jerk and didn't mind him holding her hand, but she wasn't going to take any shit from him, either.

Glancing back at the palm reader, the woman motioned for him to sit down. He dropped in the empty chair across from her. She motioned with her fingers for him to give her his hand. He stretched out his hand on the table.

The woman reached over and slipped her palm under the back of his hand. Her fingers were warm, almost hot. For some odd reason, he recalled the lab tech with the icy touch who'd taken his blood this morning. And for one second he remembered he'd wanted to ask his dad about what kind of study it was.

His thoughts stopped when the woman, still holding his hand, shifted in her chair. It made a spooky creaking noise, and he wondered if she'd purposefully used a chair that groaned for effect. The woman stared down and slowly ran her thumb cross his palm. Her eyes widened suddenly and she jerked her gaze up and stared at him. Right at his forehead.

She gasped slightly as if she could see something in his head.

"What?" he asked.

"Nothing." She looked back at his palm and studied it for several long, silent seconds. Was she making up some crap? Hadn't she practiced this before? *Come on, just tell me I'll live a happy life and collect your money.*

"What do you see?" Tami asked, as if too excited to wait.

"I . . . see . . ." She paused. "I see that you will have amazing powers. But if you use them for good or evil is yet to be known."

"That's kind of ominous," Tami said.

The woman looked up at Tami. "The future can always be a little frightening." Then she looked back down, and after touching his wrist with her other hand, she traced a line over his palm only halfway across his hand. "You will come to many forks in life's path. Some sooner than others. Some more painful than others. You will have to want to survive. Never . . ." Her voice grew deeper. "Never turn your back on a challenge. Fight for the right to live."

Chase frowned. The woman was a lunatic. She was talking mumbo-jumbo, but for some reason her words gave him chills. He pulled his hand away. "Fine." Glancing toward Mindy to make sure she hadn't disappeared, he then looked back at Tami.

"You still want to do this?" he asked her, not sure he liked the stuff he'd heard and not sure Tami's fortune would be any better.

"You've paid for it," the palm reader said as if there were no refunds.

"Yeah," Tami said. "I guess I shouldn't turn my back on a challenge, either." She chuckled, sounding a little nervous.

Chase stood up and moved the chair out a few inches, making it easy for Tami to get seated. Before he could move his hand, she sat down and her long, dark hair slipped over the back of his hand. His breath almost caught at how soft it felt. He wished he could leave his hand there. Enjoy the silky feel of her long strands against his knuckles. Yet suddenly afraid his touch wasn't wanted, he pulled his hand away.

The woman leaned in and slipped her hand under Tami's. Like with him, Chase saw the palm reader's eyes widen and he heard her gasp.

Okay, so that was how she played it. She pretended as if everyone's palm told bad things.

But then she pulled her hand out from under Tami's. "I'm sorry. I realize it was rude, what I said earlier. If you would like your money back, I'm fine with a refund."

NEWS FLASH: UPDATE
Emergency crew nearing the site of local plane crash

Thanks to a slight decrease in snowfall, the three teams making their way to the crash site of the Cessna 210 that was flown by Dr. Edward Tallman and carrying four other passengers is reportedly making good time. The team leader radioed that they have hopes of arriving on the mountain ledge in less than two hours. With the temperatures dropping into single digits, paramedics worry that the weather conditions alone could present a significant risk to any survivors.

It is unclear if Dr. Tallman and passengers have survival training for extreme weather conditions. Local medical teams are on standby to treat any survivors. Yet with each hour that passes, hope of finding the Tallmans and Miss Collins alive diminishes. In spite of the dire situation, family and friends of the victims remain hopeful.

"I know Edward," said a close friend of Dr. Tallman. "He's a doctor for God's sake. If at all possible, he's doing everything he can to keep his family safe."

Chapter Four

Tami looked confused. "A refund? No," she said, a little hesitant, obviously finding the woman's behavior as odd as Chase did. "I want you to finish. At least I think I do," she muttered, then glanced back at Chase.

He didn't say anything because he didn't think it should be his call, but he secretly hoped Tami said no. He hadn't liked the good-or-evil crap the woman said about him and he suspected he wouldn't like what she said about Tami.

"Are you sure?" the gypsy asked again, putting Chase on high alert.

"Yes," Tami said, now sounding determined.

The woman nodded and reached for Tami's hand again. She traced a line on Tami's palm and stopped only a fourth of an inch in. Then, blinking, she glanced away, as if to ponder some thought.

Chase saw her stare at her sign for several long seconds. She closed her eyes. She inhaled, her chest rising, then she let out the air slowly. When she opened her eyes she looked up at Tami and adjusted her shoulders. "You will have a good life. Two children. A boy and a girl."

Chase stared at the woman, thinking her whole tone and demeanor had changed. And from the frown on Tami's lips, he wasn't the only one who'd noticed it.

Tami tilted her head to the side and studied the woman. "Why do I think you're lying?"

The palm reader stiffened. She put her hand over her chest. Her large ruby ring caught the sunlight and flickered. "I speak from my heart."

"But does your heart tell the truth?" Tami asked.

She raised her chin, her mouth thinned. "I have read your fortune, now be gone with you and let me find other customers."

"What are you not telling me?" Tami asked, sounding frightened.

Chase wanted to reach over and touch her shoulder, but didn't know if she would welcome it. Then he thought, what the hell? He put his hand on her shoulder. "Let's just go," he said.

"Am I going to die or something?" Tami asked the woman.

The woman's eyes became cold, distant. "We are all going to die." She glanced out at the crowd. "See her? She's going to die." The woman motioned to the right. "That boy there. He's going to die. There is no one safe from death."

Tami, frowning, stood up and stared down at the woman. "You really suck at this."

"Just be on your way. Go!" She shooed them away like mosquitoes.

"Come on." Chase touched Tami's elbow. As they stepped a few feet away, Tami stopped and looked up at him. "Am I crazy? Didn't you think she was lying, too?"

Chase chose his words carefully. "I think she's nothing but an old biddy who doesn't know her ass from a hole in the ground."

Tami laughed and then sobered. "I don't think I'll ever have my palm read again."

"Me, either," Chase said.

Tami made a face. "I mean, all she tells me is that we're all going to die someday. Talk about obvious."

"Hey. It was better than I got. I might grow up to be evil. She might as well have said I'd be a serial killer or something. Oh, and I might or might not die. If I turn my back on a challenge I'm gonna be a goner."

Tami laughed. "You're right, she was just a crazy old lady, wasn't she?" She leaned in and bumped his shoulder with hers. A nice bump. Like he was more than just her best friend's little brother.

"Yeah," he said, and not sure if it was accidental, he shifted a little away so as not to crowd her, but he couldn't stop smiling.

Tami looked around. "Oh, crap."

"What?" he asked.

"Where's Mindy and that creep?"

Shit. For two minutes he'd forgotten about her. Chase's smile vanished and he turned to look where he'd last seen them. They were gone. Gone.

Oh, shit! He didn't trust Eric, and even less now that he knew Tami considered him a creep, too. "I'll call her." Grabbing his phone, he dialed his sister's number. It rang. In Tami's pocket.

"Oh," Tami said and pulled out the phone. "I'm sorry. She handed it to me and I just . . ."

Chase tried not to panic. Mindy had to be around. Had to.

"I'm sorry," Tami said again.

"It's not your fault. Let's just find her."

Ten minutes later he and Tami had covered three streets and hadn't found his sister. "Sometimes she makes me so mad," Chase muttered.

Tami sighed. "My brother used to make me mad, too."

Chase ran though the Tami data he had logged away in his brain. He didn't recall ever hearing about her brother, but . . .

"And now you two get along?" he asked.

"He died," Tami said.

"I'm sorry, I . . . I didn't know." He paused, not sure he should ask, but he wanted to know. He cared. "What happened?"

"Leukemia. It was almost four years ago, but I still miss him."

"Man, that sucks," Chase said. "I mean, Mindy drives me crazy sometimes, but I can't imagine not having her around."

"Yeah." After a few long moments, Tami suggested they go back to where the palm reader was in case Mindy was looking for them, too. Not having a better idea, Chase agreed. But if Mindy wasn't there, he was calling his dad.

He didn't know if it was the crazy palm reader's negative vibe playing with his mind, but he got a bad feeling. A feeling as if something really terrible was coming. As if to punctuate his point, a cold wind rolled past.

As they hurried back to where they'd last seen Mindy, he noticed Tami pulling her jacket tighter, too.

"You want my coat?" He stopped and started pulling his off.

"No, I just need to zip mine. But, thanks. That's nice." Her smile was so sweet, his chest hurt. All he could think about was how she must have felt losing her brother. He wanted to hug her.

"You're nice," she said as if wanting to clarify what she'd said.

If he wasn't so worried about his sister, he would have liked to have savored the compliment. But no, his sister had done something stupid, and he couldn't take the time to savor.

They continued walking. Chase set the pace fast, but Tami kept up. They finally got back to the area where the different street vendors had set up shop.

Still walking toward the palm reader's area, Chase heard someone call his name. His gut unclenched when he recognized Mindy's voice.

He swung around, saw her hurrying toward them, and for one second he understood his mom's saying she used when they'd arrive home a little late: "*I don't know whether to hug or hit you.*"

"Where did you go?" Mindy asked, stopping in front of them and looking indignant.

"Where did *I* go?" he asked, and now that he wasn't so worried, his anger rose. "I went looking for you. You disappeared, damn it. Dad told us to stay together."

Offering him her tight-lipped frown, she cut her eyes to Eric who stood beside her, as if telling him to shut his trap in front of her new boyfriend. "We just went to grab a soda. I thought we'd be back before you two finished getting your futures told."

"Here," Tami said and dropped Mindy's phone in her hands. "We were extra concerned because we realized I goofed and took your phone and we wouldn't be able to contact you."

That wasn't the only reason Chase was concerned, he thought. He was worried because his sister had decided to hang out with a guy who kept looking at her as if she was candy and he needed a sugar high.

"I don't need anyone worrying about me," Mindy said, sounding annoyed at Tami.

"We all need someone to worry about us," Tami said, sounding annoyed right back.

Silence descended. Angry silence. Two girls mad at each other kind of silence.

Finally, Mindy spoke up. "Let's go and get in line for the haunted house. I heard someone say it was great." She swung around on the heels of her shoes and started walking down the street. Eric followed her, but instead of looking where he was going he did nothing but stare at her ass.

"I don't like that guy!" Chase growled close to Tami's ear.

"Me, either," she said. "But let's do the haunted house and then I'll claim I started my period and we have to go home."

Chase nearly choked on his next breath. It was a good idea, but did she have to mention her period? What was that acronym Mindy tossed around for things like this? Oh, yeah, TMI. That was totally too much information.

Tami's chuckle came close to Chase's ear and he looked at her.

"What?" he asked, not understanding the humor dancing in her eyes.

"Sorry, I keep forgetting guys can't handle hearing stuff like that."

"No, I'm fine," he lied.

"Then why are you so red?" She moved a little closer, her soft shoulder lightly whispering against his bicep. Back and then forth with each step. The warmth from that light touch made his heart skip a beat. This time, he didn't shift away. He might have moved a tiny bit closer. Even though he was still mad enough to chew nails and spit out staples at his sister and her new boyfriend, this would go down as one of the best days of his life.

Which, according to the palm reader, might not be too long. *Never turn your back on a challenge.* Well, Tami was one challenge he wasn't going to turn away from.

. . .

Complete darkness descended upon them. It took a second for Chase's eyes to adjust. The first thing he did was make sure his sister and the jerk were right ahead. They were.

Without warning, a vampire, blood dripping from his fangs, pounced at them. Tami screamed, grabbed his arm, and plastered herself to his side.

Haunted houses had never done much for Chase, but after feeling Tami's body so close to his, he wondered if he could find one in Houston that ran all year long. He'd love to bring Tami to it at least once a week.

Next a guy with a chainsaw came after them. It wasn't a real chainsaw, but it sure as heck sounded like one. Tami held on tighter.

Yup, he'd just become a haunted house fan for life.

They followed the arrows, highlighting the way to walk. They dipped through a black curtain, and complete darkness swallowed them again.

Chase blinked and tried to see Mindy, who he'd sworn had gone through the curtain seconds before. He couldn't make her out. But it could just be the light. He continued to follow the tiny blue lights past a coffin with a dead guy trying to grab them.

Worried that he'd lost his sister, he hurried Tami though the next curtain. He squinted his eyes, forcing them to adjust. No Mindy.

Then he heard it. A scream. Mindy's scream.

It wasn't the fun kind of scream. "Stop it!" she yelled.

Gut instantly knotted, he grabbed Tami so as not to lose her, and followed the sound of his sister's voice. The sound led him straight toward a wall, but he discovered it was just a curtain. He swiped it back and ran inside, looking for a monster. One named Eric.

The small room filled with technical equipment had just enough light to make out shapes. Then the shapes became more visible. Eric had Mindy against a wall, his hands all over her, his mouth on hers trying to drown out her screams.

"There," Tami yelled, but Chase already had the asshole by the collar.

Wadding the asshole's shirt in his fist, Chase yanked him off his sister.

"Whoa, stop!" the guy screamed, holding up his hands.

"I think that's what my sister said!" He clenched his fist and heard Tami consoling his sister.

"It was a mix-up. I thought she was into it," Eric said.

"Liar!" a feminine voice yelled out from behind him. Not his sister, but Tami. "Mindy might have been into it for a kiss, but she never invited you to climb inside her bra! She said stop, you low-life creep."

Eric stiffened, obviously not liking being called names by a girl. "All I did was cop a feel. She was asking for it."

"You're the one asking for it!" Chase pulled back his fist and plowed it right into the guy's face, crashing against teeth and bone. It hurt like hell, but felt wonderful at the same time.

The guy went down on his ass with a loud thump. "You broke my tooth," he bit out and started to get up.

"Don't move!" Chase took a step closer and glared down at him. "You get up, I'm gonna break your nose next time."

Eric stayed down, obviously hearing the truth in Chase's voice.

Chase turned to his sister, still sniffling and wiping her eyes. "Somebody call the cops."

"No," Mindy said. "I'm okay. Thanks to you, he didn't . . . didn't get anywhere. I just want to go home. Please. Please just get me home."

His gut told him he needed to report this, but the pleading in his sister's voice had him just wanting to make it easier on her.

"Fine." Chase turned back to the piece of shit on the floor and pointed a finger at him. "If I see you before I leave, I'm gonna hit you again. And I swear when I'm done, you'll have so much blood on you, that you'll put that vampire to shame. So you'd better not go back to your cabin tonight."

NEWS FLASH: UPDATE

Search and Rescue volunteer hurt trying to reach plane crash

One of the rescue members with Search and Rescue (SAR) has fallen down a thirty-foot embankment while trying to reach the crash site of the Cessna 210—the plane that went down last night in the Jasper Mountain Range carrying four passengers and one pilot. Two emergency crew members carried the man to the site where an emergency helicopter is meeting them to transport the man to the local hospital. While the injuries are not life threatening, initial reports state that he suffered a broken leg and collarbone.

Tom Phillips, a volunteer with SAR who is more familiar with the Jasper Mountain Range, is busy trying to find a new and safer route to get to the wreckage. Meanwhile, temperatures continue to drop, making the conditions even more dangerous for any potential survivors, as well as the team trying to reach them.

Chapter Five

OCTOBER 31, 2:15 P.M.

They stormed out of the haunted house and Chase continued to rush them forward. He didn't want to chance meeting Eric again. He might just have to kill him. And he wanted to get Mindy somewhere quiet so he could make sure she was okay.

They made it almost a block to where a long picnic table sat in front of a concession stand. He motioned to the table, thinking Mindy might need to sit down. As soon as he got there he turned to her.

"Are you sure you're okay? If he . . . if he hurt you, I'll go back and find him and break his friggin' neck."

"No," Mindy said, still standing, but her voice shook a little. "He didn't do anything but . . . grope me. I'm fine."

"Crap!" Tami said. "Look at your hand, Chase. You're bleeding and your knuckles are swelling."

She caught his hand and held it. "You need some ice. I'll go get some." She took off and Chase turned back to his sister.

"I'm sorry it took me so long to find you."

"Oh gawd, Chase, it wasn't your fault. I was stupid," she said, her voice wavering a little less. "I went with him behind the curtain thinking all he'd do was kiss me, but . . ." She hesitated. "Please don't tell

Mom or Dad. I mean, it's not like something really happened. He didn't even get inside my shirt. I was just . . . so pissed that I fell for him and that I couldn't stop him. He was stronger than I was." She bit down on her lip. "Please, please don't tell. You know this would freak them out and Dad . . . Hell, Dad would kill him."

Yeah, his dad probably would kill Eric. Chase knew he wanted to. "Are you sure you're okay?"

She took a few steps closer. "Thanks to you, I am. And I've been so mean to you today. I'm sorry I was a bitch. I promise you that I'll never be a snot to you again."

Seeing Mindy acting like Mindy, the nicer Mindy, had the panic in his chest lessening. Unfortunately, the panic was probably what had stopped his hand from hurting, because it was throbbing like a mofo now.

Before he knew what Mindy intended to do, she hugged him. They hadn't hugged each other since his mom stopped making them hug to make up after a fight. Oddly, this one was nicer.

He really did love his sister, even when she was a snot.

"Thank you," she said and pulled back.

She looked around him. "Here comes Tami with the ice." She glanced down at his hand. "I'm sorry you got hurt."

"I'm fine," he lied.

She made a face, looking from Tami back to him. "Look, I know you have a thing for Tami and . . . if you tell her I said this, I'll lie and say I didn't, but . . ." She looked up again. "She kind of has a thing for you, too. I didn't approve, but after seeing you two today, I think you might be great together. So, go for it. You have my permission to date my best friend. But be nice to her."

Chase's head reeled with that piece of information.

"Here." Tami came running up with a cup of ice and some paper towels. "They didn't have any plastic baggies, so this will have to do." She pulled him over to the picnic table. "Sit down and let me put ice on it." He sat down on the bench facing her instead of the table. She stepped between his legs, and quickly started emptying ice into the paper towels.

"I'm fine. It doesn't hurt at all." It wasn't a lie this time. Hearing that Tami had a thing for him chased the pain away.

She picked up his hand and dropped the paper towel filled with ice on it. "You were awesome," she said. In the corner of his eye, he saw his sister move a few feet away as if giving them space.

He glanced up at Tami. "Not really. I should have chased his ass off a long time ago."

"Mindy wouldn't have let you. Besides, I . . . never thought watching a guy fight would be hot, but it was."

"You think I'm hot?" he asked, loving the sound of that.

She grinned. "I think you're a hero."

"So I'm not hot?"

She laughed. "You're both." She dipped her head and kissed him. It wasn't one of those that came with tongue, but it was much more than a simple peck.

And it didn't end quickly. It lasted, not long enough, but long enough for it to mean something.

When she pulled back, he looked up at her. "Are you only kissing me because I hit Eric? Because I don't want to have to hit a guy every time I want to score a kiss." He smiled at her, his heart still racing from feeling her lips against his.

"No," she said, grinning from ear to ear. "I've wanted to kiss you for a long time. And . . ." she made a funny face, "since I'm gonna die soon, I figured I'd better do it."

"In that case, do you think you should do it again?" It was a lame line. But it worked.

She kissed him again. And this one did come with a little tongue. He was nervous at first, but just like he thought, he didn't suck at it. He suddenly felt confident. He even reached up with his uninjured hand and held the back of her head.

The sound of a ringing phone broke the kiss. His sister stood about ten feet away staring and smiling as she pulled her phone out.

When she looked at the phone's screen, her eyes widened with panic. She came running up. "It's Dad. Pleeeasse tell me you didn't call him about this."

"I didn't," he told her and stood up. "He's probably just checking in."

She inhaled a breath and took the call.

"Hey, Dad," Mindy said, sounding extra cheery, but she really did sound okay. She paused. "I hate that. Yeah, we were ready to come back anyway." She looked up at Chase. "Okay, we'll meet you in twenty minutes."

She dropped the phone back in her pocket. "He's picking us up early. Something about a storm and a surgery he's been called in to do. We're going to have to leave this afternoon. Like soon, because everyone is trying to get out of town before the storm."

"I hate that," Tami said.

"Me, too," Chase said. He wasn't ready for this weekend to end. He plopped the ice he'd been using on his knuckles on the table. He moved his hand. It wasn't broken, just bruised.

Mindy stood there staring at him, looking worried again. "Promise me you aren't going to tell Mom or Dad about this."

Chase studied her frown. "Promise me that you'll be more careful from now on. And not hook up with jerks."

"I promise," Mindy said. "Now you promise. I want to hear it."

Chase shrugged. "I already promised, but to make you feel better . . . I promise I won't tell Dad or Mom." His sister came over and hugged him again.

"I love happy endings," Tami said.

As they walked back to the place they were supposed to meet his dad, they passed the palm reader. She was with someone else, holding a man's palm in her hand, probably telling him lies. Then, as if the palm reader felt them, she glanced up. Her dark black eyes followed them. But it was her expression that concerned him more. It wasn't evil. Not angry. It was sad.

Chase looked away quickly, glad Tami hadn't seen her.

He didn't believe the woman. He didn't. But he gazed back one more time and for some reason he recalled what Tami said. *I love happy endings.*

. . .

As they were walking back to meet his dad, Mindy claimed she needed to find a restroom. And because apparently girls never went to the bathroom alone, Tami went with her. Chase sat down on a bench a half a block from the facilities.

He sat there practically glowing thinking about the two kisses, and trying to decide what he needed to do next. And not just kiss her again—oh, he was definitely going to do that—but wondering what a boy was supposed to do. Did he ask her to go out with him? Ask her to go to the movies with him? A thought hit that he didn't like. His parents had been so strict about Mindy not dating until sixteen, would they feel the same way about him?

Shit! He didn't like that. And for once he could really relate to his sister's feelings.

A few minutes passed. His hand throbbed a bit along with the concern about his parents. Remembering Eric could still be around and might be stupid enough to try something, he stood up and walked toward the bathrooms, wanting to be there when they walked out.

Two girls came out of the facility but it wasn't Tami and his sister.

He stood in the same spot, scuffing his shoe on the pavement, watching the exit to the girls' restroom, trying not to worry. Chicks always took forever in the bathroom.

When another five minutes passed, he started pacing. If they didn't come out soon, he was going in. His face heated thinking about walking into a girls' restroom, but . . .

"Hey," Tami called out.

He spun around and saw them walking toward him.

"I thought you were in the bathroom?" he said, sounding a little annoyed. He instantly regretted his tone, but figured he had a right. He'd been worried.

"I saw something I wanted to buy," Tami said, and moved in close to him. "I saw it when I went to get the ice earlier."

He almost said they should have told him, but bit back the words. He didn't want Tami to think he was too controlling.

"Do you want it now or later?"

He paused a second. "It's for me?"

"Yeah," she said as if he should have figured it out.

He suddenly felt bad. He hadn't bought her anything. Not that he'd really had a chance, but . . .

"I say you open it now." Tami beamed and handed him a plastic bag.

"Yeah, open it now," Mindy said, putting her two cents in. "You'll like it."

Chase looked from Mindy to Tami. "But I didn't get you—"

"Don't be silly, open it. It's just a little thing. It's not even really for you, but . . . well, sort of."

Chase pulled a leather dog collar from the bag.

"It's for Baxter," Tami said. "But read what it says. I saw it when I was waiting for them to get ice for your hand. They had them hanging from a display case."

Chase turned the dog collar around and read the inscription: NEVER TURN YOUR BACK ON A CHALLENGE.

"Crazy, isn't it?" Tami said. "It's the same thing the fortune-teller said."

"Yeah," Chase agreed, rubbing his finger on the soft leather.

Tami made a face. "I'll bet the crazy lady saw it earlier and just used it. But . . . it's not a bad saying. And I know how much Baxter means to you."

"He does. And . . . I like the collar. Thank you. And Baxter will thank you."

She lifted up on her tiptoes. Her lips came so close to his that he could feel her soft breath. He also felt her soft breasts against his chest. And that felt really, really good.

"You're welcome," she said. Then she kissed him.

Mindy chuckled. "I hate to rain on your parade, but you two don't have time to play kissy-kissy. We need to meet Dad."

Chase frowned at his sister and tucked the collar in his coat pocket.

Then, not turning his back on a challenge, he reached over and slipped his hand into Tami's. It fit perfectly against his.

His dad drove like a bat out of hell to get to the cabin. Supposedly, he'd heard about the incoming storm while skiing and had driven Chase's mom home to start packing. "Five minutes," he said as they walked into the cabin. "There's some talk that the storm could come in earlier and I have to get home. I can't be delayed here."

His dad tossed his coat on the sofa. "Amy? You packed and ready?" he called out to Chase's mom.

"Almost," came her voice from the bedroom.

"Go," his dad said to them. "I'm serious, grab everything, drop it in your suitcases, and let's fly out of here. Four minutes. If we're late, we'll be stuck waiting for several hours for runway time and the storm could come in early."

Mindy and Tami took off to the room they shared, Chase turned to go to his. Then he realized something was wrong. Baxter hadn't met him at the door. Baxter always met him.

"Where's Baxter?" Chase muttered, looking around and checking his pocket for the dog collar Tami had given him.

"Just get your bags packed," his dad said.

Chase didn't want to piss his dad off, but instead of going to his room, he darted past his dad to find his mom.

She was rushing around the room, tossing their clothes into the open suitcase.

"Where's Baxter, Mom?" he asked.

His mom had just tossed a handful of clothes toward the bed and she froze as if the question rolled around her head. She stood there for one second and then her eyes widened with worry. "Crap!" She ran out the bedroom door.

"What?" Chase asked, running after her.

"I let him outside to potty and was standing out there watching, then your dad called to tell me how soon we had to go and I completely forgot him." She ran past his dad.

"Are we packed?" his dad asked his mom.

His mom ignored him and opened the back door and ran out on the porch. "Baxter?" she called. "Come here, boy!" When the dog didn't come running, she took off down the porch.

Chase followed and started calling his dog.

"What is it?" his dad asked, stepping out on the back porch.

"I let Baxter out and forgot about him." His mom ran from one side of the property to the other calling the dog.

Chase took off toward the woods, worried Baxter had chased a rabbit or something. The dog wasn't one to run off, but if a small animal showed up, he'd probably give chase on pure instinct.

"Chase?" his father called out. "You go pack, I'll see if I can find Baxter. You, too, Amy."

Chase wanted to argue that his dog was ten times more important than packing, but he saw the expression on his dad's face and knew he meant business.

As he walked back into the cabin, listening to his dad call out Baxter's name, Mindy ran right into him. "What's wrong? Is Baxter missing?"

"Yeah," Chase said, frowning.

"Crap!" Mindy said. "How did he get out?"

"I did it." His mom stepped in behind him. "I'm so sorry, Chase," she said, guilt lacing her voice. While Baxter was the family pet, the black Lab had picked Chase as his person the moment they'd brought him home from the shelter, where his previous owner had just dumped him off.

"It was an accident," Chase said, not wanting to blame his mom. He knew how much his mom loved Baxter, too.

"You want us to go look for him, too?" Tami asked, standing behind his sister.

"Have you two finished packing yet?" his mom asked.

"No," Mindy answered.

"Then let's all hurry up and finish and then we can look for him together."

. . .

Chase sat in the backseat, his head reclined, his eyes closed. He simply could not believe his dad was doing this. Leaving Baxter! How could he leave Chase's dog? Every now and then Tami would brush her hand against his. It felt nice, and he would have liked it if he wasn't hurting so much inside. If he wasn't so damn angry at his dad.

Suddenly, feeling as if he would burst if he didn't try one more time to convince his dad, he lifted his head up. His dad's gaze, as if knowing Chase wasn't finished fighting the battle, shot to the rearview mirror and his eyes locked on Chase's.

"Jimmy is going to find him, Chase," his dad said before Chase could say anything. "He told me he was going to look for him right after we hung up. He'll find him. You'd be amazed how good he is at . . . finding things . . . and as soon as the storm is over we'll have Baxter flown to Houston."

"Then let me stay and help this guy find him. I'll fly back with Baxter," Chase gritted out. "Please take me back and let me find my dog."

"No, I'm not going to leave you here. There's a hell of a storm coming and I want to know my family is safe."

"And what if they don't find Baxter before the storm comes in? You know your friend isn't going to look as hard as we would. He probably doesn't even like dogs. Please, let's not leave," Chase begged. "Let's all stay and find Baxter. He's part of this family."

His dad's expression tightened.

"Damn it, Dad, his first owners already abandoned him. He's going to think we did the same thing."

Chase saw his dad's hands on the wheel tighten. "I have to get home, Chase. There's a surgery I can't miss."

Every muscle in Chase's body clenched. "Would it kill you to miss a day at work? Why is your damn work more important than Baxter?"

Chase saw his father's eyes fill with a mixture of anger and empathy. "Since it's a twelve-year-old girl that's been waiting for a kidney for four years and if she doesn't get this one, she probably won't make it for the next one. I've taken care of her since she was eight. I'm a part of the transplant team and the best nephrologist they've got. I'd like to be there to make sure she gets the best care she can." He inhaled. "Look, I know you care about Baxter. I care about him, too. And I'm telling you, Jimmy will find him. Baxter is going to be fine."

A part of Chase understood his dad's dilemma with the surgery, but he could still let Chase stay. "Ask this friend of yours if I can stay with him."

His dad shook his head. "I don't trust . . . I mean, I don't know Jimmy that well."

Chase frowned. "If Baxter dies, I'll never forgive you!"

His mom turned around. "Chase, let's calm down. Your dad has complete faith in Jimmy. He's our best bet right now."

Chase didn't want to calm down. He wanted to go back to the cabin. He wanted it so badly, his gut churned.

NEWS FLASH: UPDATE

Emergency crew trying to reach plane crash site finds new route

The emergency crew trying to reach the wreckage of the plane flown by Dr. Edward Tallman with four passengers on board has decided to try a different route due to the icy terrain. The crew reports that a new route has been mapped out, and they hope to reach the wreckage within the hour.

"However," said Tom Phillips, Search and Rescue (SAR) volunteer, "if this path isn't workable, we'll have to start back to make sure we can be back to safety before nightfall."

Another SAR helicopter has flown over the site and reports no signs of life. Yet the town remains hopeful that when the team arrives at the crash site, this becomes a rescue mission and not just recovery. "But either way," says Phillips, "we have a job to do."

More updates will be made when available.

Chapter Six

Trying not to think about the girl who needed surgery, Chase prayed that the airport would tell his dad that conditions were too bad to fly. When the rental car company dropped them off at the airport, he noticed the temperature had dropped steeply. But his prayer went unanswered. And now they were in the plane, about to fly out.

His dad's phone rang. He looked back at Chase. "I'll bet that's Jimmy with good news."

Chase held his breath, hoping. Could he convince his dad to go back for the dog if they had found him?

His dad took the call, but whatever he heard the caller say must not have been good news because he wasn't smiling. "Okay, thanks. I know you will."

He stuffed his phone back in his pocket and looked back at Chase with regret.

Chase's gut clenched tighter. Had something bad already happened to Baxter?

"Jimmy hasn't found him yet, but he's still looking. He promised not to quit until he finds him."

Chase slumped back in his seat and looked out the plane's window. A few snowflakes hit the glass pane. The six-sided pattern stuck, glimmered in the sunlight, then melted, turning into a slow-moving speck of moisture.

All Chase thought about was if Baxter was getting snowed on. Or if he had gone back to the cabin and didn't understand why they were gone, just like the last family that had abandoned him.

In a few minutes, his dad had permission to take off. Tami reached over and touched his shoulder. "My gut says this guy is going to find Baxter. I really think he will."

Chase nodded and wished he could believe her—wished he could concentrate and relive their kisses and ponder all of the possibilities for them in the future. There was a lot to think about there, but instead the worry over Baxter weighed on his heart.

Looking up at his dad, he saw him glance up at the sky. Picking up his radio, he called to confirm it was safe to take off. Chase held his breath, thinking this might be his lucky break. No such luck.

His dad nodded, hung up, and told them all to turn their cell phones off. They were leaving. The storm was five hours away, his dad informed them. They would be safe.

At least that gave this Jimmy guy—someone his dad trusted with Baxter's life but not Chase's, which was not a good sign—five hours to find Baxter.

The plane took off with ease, the gray sky greeted them with a snowy mist. A few minutes later, Mindy put on her headphones and went into her music zone, but she met his eyes every now and then and he knew she was worried about Baxter as well. The heavy silence in the plane matched Chase's mood. That mood plummeted deeper when a sudden jolt shook the plane. The unexpected jarring threw Chase against the cabin wall.

"What's happening?" his mom asked, her voice heightened with panic.

"Downdraft," his father gritted out as he fought to control the plane. But the small aircraft kept falling and being yanked up and down.

The cabin filled with loud shrieks from his sister and Tami.

"I got it. I got it," his dad yelled over their screams in an attempt to put everyone at ease.

No ease came. The plane continued to fall. Fear swelled inside Chase as his dad fought the controls. The plane tilted at an angle. Tami's shoulder came against his. She grabbed his hand, her grip amazingly tight. He gripped back. Determined not to let go.

"Watch out," his mom screamed again. "The mountain! The mountain!"

Another jolt shook the plane. The wing must have clipped something. A loud crack, the shrill noise of metal being crunched, vibrated in Chase's ears. Behind that hideous noise his mom called out, "I love you guys."

That was the last thing Chase heard before everything went dark. Dark as in complete blackness. Nothingness. And because he feared what was coming, he went there willingly.

Chase was stuck. Caught. Trapped in the middle of something . . . of somewhere.

The darkness started to fade. He saw light. He saw . . . he saw his family.

"Are you okay?" he yelled out, not understanding why he felt this raw sensation that something was wrong. Not that they looked wrong.

Unlike him, they were in a tunnel. A tunnel of light. He didn't understand. Why were they there, when he was . . . here? Wherever here was.

Worry. Panic. Terror. Emotions continued to swell inside him, and somehow he knew if he could get to his family, it would be okay. He would be okay. That he wouldn't be stuck anymore. He tried to move closer to them, but something held him back. No, it didn't just hold him back. It pulled him back.

"No," he said, trying to free himself to go to them.

His mom looked up. Her mouth moved as if talking, but he couldn't hear her. Then she waved him back, as if telling him to go. Not that he had a choice.

Whoever, whatever had him, kept moving him. His family was getting smaller and smaller. Why wouldn't his mom want him to come with them? He didn't want to be alone.

In the distance, he heard barking. Baxter. Thinking of Baxter brought on another wave of unexplainable panic. Why was he worried about Baxter? He squinted to see if his dog was with his family. It didn't seem like it. But they were so small now, maybe he just couldn't see.

But the barking seemed to be closer than his parents and Mindy. He shifted his gaze, looking for the dog. When he glanced back up at his family they were nothing but tiny specks in the surrounding light.

He could still hear the barking. "Baxter?" he called. "Where are you?"

Then he remembered Baxter was lost. Lost. And the storm was coming. His heart suddenly swelled with another memory. The plane. The . . . crash.

His heart pounded against his chest.

Thump.

Thump.

Thump.

The light disappeared. Or that light did. Another light turned the inside of his eyelids red. He tried to open them, but they felt so heavy. Crusty, as if something had glued them shut.

Before he tried again, the pain hit. Pain in his arm. In his neck. His head. But amazingly, nothing else hurt. That's when it hit him. It didn't hurt because he couldn't feel anything. He couldn't feel anything below his chest. Not his legs, or his feet.

Forcing his eyes open, bits of white fell toward him. Snow. A flake fell into his eye and he blinked it away. More raw panic gripped his chest.

His parents? Mindy? Tami? He swallowed. His throat barely worked. He tried to raise his head. It hurt, but he did it anyway. "Mom? Dad?" he called, but the sound barely came out.

He blinked several times and tried to focus. All he could see was a mangled piece of metal that had once been a plane. The plane his dad loved. He called it Amy, named after Chase's mom.

"Mom?" he called again and turned his head to see if he could spot anyone. He couldn't. But then he saw the snow around the mass of mangled metal. It was red. Blood red.

He remembered the light. Seeing them in the bright tunnel. "No," he screamed and tried to get up, but he couldn't move his legs.

He dropped his head back in the pillow of snow. Hot tears rolled down his cheeks.

A wave of dizziness hit, bringing the blackness back. He embraced it.

Noise. Chase's mind registered it. Metal scraping against metal.

He saw the red again on the back of his eyelids and forced his eyes open. Snow caught on his eyelashes, or was it ice? His face felt almost frozen, sort of half-numb.

"Damn it, Tallman. This wasn't supposed to happen," the voice boomed out of nowhere.

Chase used every bit of his energy to lift his head. He saw two men standing beside the red snow and plane wreckage. One wore a white coat. The other wore black, all black: black jeans and a black coat.

"I should have never involved him in this," the man in white said, as if he was looking at . . .

Is he alive? Chase tried to speak but only air came out. Then again, he must have spoken, because the two men swung around as if he'd yelled the words.

"One of them is alive," the man in white said. They both rushed closer, their footsteps crunching on the snow.

One of them? Only one? They were dead. His dad, mom, Mindy, and . . . Tami. He remembered the light.

NEWS FLASH: UPDATE

Four confirmed dead in plane crash on Jasper Mountain Range

After a nearly six-hour trek to the crash site, the Search and Rescue (SAR) and Mountain Rescue Association (MRA) converged on the wreckage of the Cessna 210. Sheriff Ted Carter of Jasper County confirmed getting the report twenty minutes ago that four bodies have been found at the crash site of the plane flown by Dr. Edward Tallman and carrying four passengers. The friends and family of the victims already in Jasper have been notified. Identification of the bodies has yet to be made. But regrettably, the emergency crew does not anticipate finding any survivors. The crash site was worse than they had originally suspected, and it is believed that the last remaining passenger could have been thrown from the plane or is lying among the charred remains.

Sheriff Ted Carter was quoted saying, "On behalf of Jasper County, I offer my sincere condolences to the family and friends of the individuals who lost their lives today. As we continue to monitor the situation, our thoughts and prayers are with the loved ones of those who were on board."

More updates will be made when available.

Chapter Seven

Had these men really said his family was dead? Chase let his head fall back down. No, he couldn't accept that. Couldn't believe they were gone. He fought to keep his eyes open, wanting to ask again—to beg them to be wrong. To save his family. The two men appeared over him. He tried to open his mouth to speak, but nothing came out. Black spots, like fireworks, started popping off in his vision. He couldn't make out their faces, but he saw their shapes.

Then he saw . . . he saw their eyes. Glowing. Bright lime green. What the hell was wrong with his vision?

One of the men crouched down beside him, the snow crunching beneath the heels of his shoes. It was the guy in the lab coat. Chase couldn't make out his face, but he saw his eyes, still glowing, and the white coat.

"Damn it," the man said, looking up at the guy wearing black who stood over Chase. "He's a carrier. Did we bring gloves?"

"No," the other man said.

The dizziness had Chase closing his eyes, but he listened. Their voices were distant—as if on a radio in another room. He tried to pick up his right arm, but couldn't.

"We're here, kid," one of them said and Chase felt his body shift slightly as if someone was moving the snow from around him. "Damn it. If I touch him I risk activating the virus. He's in bad shape. He wouldn't be able to survive the turn."

"I disagree," the deeper voice said. "It's his only chance to survive."

"He's too weak. It'll kill him," the other voice argued.

"Probably, but he's dying anyway. Turn him and at least he has a chance. It might not be much of one, but it's the best shot he has."

He was dying. He thought hearing it would have caused him to react. He didn't. He thought of the light tunnel where he'd seen his family. He wanted to go there.

Chase opened his eyes to tell them it was okay. He couldn't speak but he stared at the blurry figures. One of the men passed something to the other.

Chase blinked the ice from his lashes and saw the man in the white lab coat holding a knife. Chase's heart thumped once in fear. Then he watched as the man turned the knife on himself. He put the knife to his palm and gripped it. Blood, one drop at a time, dripped from his clenched fist.

Chase didn't react to it because somehow it didn't seem to matter. He was dying and he was going to go to the light.

As Chase stared, the guy dropped the knife in the snow. Then he pressed his bleeding palm to Chase's arm, to an open wound he had there. The touch wasn't nearly as warm as he'd thought it would be. Then suddenly it was. It was so warm it stung.

"Hot," he tried to say, but wasn't sure he'd managed it.

A burning sensation started flowing inside him. He heard himself moan.

"Come on, kid. Hang in there. I owe your dad that much."

Chase choked on his next intake of air.

"Damn it! Don't you die on me!"

Die on me. Die on me. Die on me.

The words echoed in his head and he saw the light again. Peaceful, pure, bright but somehow soft. It didn't hurt to look at it. As a matter of fact, it was beautiful.

All of a sudden his dad and mom appeared beside him. "No," his mom said. "Go back."

"Live, son," his dad said. "Live for us."

"I don't want to," he said. "I . . . I don't want to be alone."

"Take him back, damn it!" his father roared, staring back into the tunnel of light as if someone else was there. "Please, it's not fair."

Something started pulling him away again. "No," he begged. "I like it here."

He stopped moving. He heard the bark again. Baxter.

Turning in circles, he looked for his dog. "Come here, boy. Come here."

"Chase?"

The fine voice had him swinging back around.

Tami.

She looked even more beautiful than he remembered. Her dark hair glistened with the light. Her smile lit up her face. Angelic. That's how he would describe her.

She moved to him. Her presence so sweet his chest ached.

All of a sudden she looked back over her shoulder as if someone called her. "It's my brother," she said when she turned around. "He's here. And he looks so good. He runs and can play ball like he loved to do before he got sick."

Chase tried to look over her shoulder to see him, but he couldn't. He could only see her. He let his gaze fall back on her face. On her eyes that seemed honestly happy.

But then her smiled faded. "You have to go back, Chase. Don't you remember what she said?"

"What who said?"

"You can't turn your back on a challenge, Chase. That's what the palm reader said. I bought the dog collar with the saying on it, remember? It's in your pocket. In your jacket. You have to face this challenge."

"No, I don't want to go back. I'd be alone. It would be unbearable."

"You'll be sad for a while, but not forever. It's not like it will go away, you just learn to go on and then you realize that life hasn't ended. I did it with my brother. And you'll do it, too. Go, Chase, go face the challenge."

He shook his head. "*You* were my challenge."

She grinned. "Are you kidding? I wasn't a challenge. You had me in the palm of your hand the first time I saw you playing baseball. You looked so good in the uniform." She glanced back again as if she was being called. "Go back."

"No," he said.

She looked sad. "Look, I don't know if I'm supposed to tell you this, but you can see things up here. Glimpses of the future. And I know for a fact that you're going to be okay. You're going to meet someone." She laughed. "You only *thought* I was a challenge. This other girl you'll meet is the real thing." She sighed. "Oh, Chase. You have so much life to live. And you can do it. Don't turn away from it." She looked back one more time. "I have to go. My brother is calling."

She faded. Disappeared right in front of him. The place where she'd stood held snowflakes and tiny pieces of frozen ice. Slowly it all floated to the ground.

"I'm not going back!" he muttered.

NEWS FLASH: UPDATE

All five bodies have been recovered from the crash of the
Cessna 210 in the Jasper Mountain Range

The Search and Rescue (SAR) crew found the last victim of the fatal
crash among the charred remains of the Cessna 210. Family and
friends of both the Tallmans and the Collinses are waiting for the
bodies to be released from the morgue after autopsies so they can be
taken back to Texas for burial.

Tom Phillips, Search and Rescue volunteer, was quoted saying it
was "still too early to speculate as to what caused the crash, but
weather could have played a part in the accident." Phillips added he
"could not imagine the heartbreak of the families involved."

More updates will be made when available.

Chapter Eight

Chase started to walk farther into the tunnel of light. He didn't want to be alone. To be without his father, his mother, and Mindy. She was a pain in his butt, but he loved her.

Then he heard it again. Baxter. His barking was even more persistent. He looked left, then right. Called the dog's name. "Go get Baxter," he heard his sister say. She stood next to him. "Go, Chase. Go."

The dog continued to bark.

He turned to look behind him, away from the light, and that's all it took. The power, some unknown power, pulled him back.

All the way. Back to the snow. Back to the voices. The two strange men.

Chase didn't open his eyes. Didn't want to. He hurt. Hurt everywhere. His head throbbed. His leg throbbed. His back ached like a charley horse.

Now he could feel below his chest, but it hurt so bad, he wished he couldn't. *You can't turn your back on a challenge, Chase.* He heard Tami's voice in his head and remembered what she'd said about the dog collar. Slowly moving his arm, surprised he could, he found his pocket. With eyes still closed, his fingers curled around the gift Tami had given him. He traced his thumb over the words cut into the leather.

"Told you he would make it," someone said as if they'd seen him move. "I'll stay with him, you go get us a body."

Chase's head throbbed; surely he'd misunderstood.

"Don't you think they'll just believe he got thrown from the crash? Animals got to him?"

"You're forgetting, I volunteered a time or two with the Search and Rescue team. They won't stop looking until they have the remains of all the victims. Besides, I've already called around. They have a body that fits our needs in the next county over. We'll put it under what's left of the fuel tank and light it, and they'll never know it wasn't him."

Their words echoed in his head. Okay, he must be imagining things. Head injury, he thought. Then a pain hit, as if someone had a vise grip on his rib cage. It grew so intense that he screamed out. When it finally let go, he pulled Baxter's collar up to his chest and held onto it. Then he let out a breath and tried to slip back into nothingness.

Chase smelled smoke. He felt cold. Colder than even the ice he rested on. Fever. He had a fever. He wasn't sure how long he'd been out. Five minutes, or five hours. It didn't matter, he told himself. He wasn't sure anything mattered if what he believed about his parents, sister, and Tami was true.

He didn't know what hurt the most. His body or his heart. And then suddenly he did know. His heart. He'd lost his family. Lost his dog. Lost everyone.

All of a sudden he heard footsteps coming his way. Another pain started at the top of his neck and crawled down his spine. He arched his back and moaned.

"Come on, boy. Let's get out of here."

Chase felt someone pick him up as if he weighed nothing. He opened his eyes. "Put me down," he said, the words barely a whisper.

"Sorry, son. We gotta go."

"What about the tracks?" the other man asked.

"Run some brush over them. With this weather, the team won't make it down here for another twelve to fifteen hours."

Chase was suddenly lifted from the ground. Up like he was floating. No, like he was flying. He turned his head away from the man's chest who held him close. He was about sixty feet in the air, looking down at the plane crash. The last thing he saw before he passed out again was the smoke coming from part of the wreckage.

NOVEMBER 7

Chase heard voices. He lifted his eyelids, not sure where he was. Raising his head off a pillow, he stared at the bedside table and saw the dog collar Tami had given him.

Memories started ping-ponging around his head. Tami. The plane. The crash. The light. The two men.

Grief swelled in his chest and threatened to drown him. Nothing but pride stopped him from curling up in a little ball and sobbing.

Then other vague flashes started filling his head. Time in this bed. In pain. Fever. He'd had a high fever. He recalled the man, the one who'd worn the white lab coat, the one who'd showed up at the plane crash, sitting by his side. He could almost feel him now, running cold towels over him. His words had been calming. Telling Chase that he would be okay. That the pain would end soon.

It hadn't felt like he would be okay. He'd hurt like hell.

Chase spotted a glass beside the dog collar. He remembered the man bringing him something to drink. It had tasted like some kind of berry concoction, but better than anything he'd ever tasted. When he'd finished one glass, he'd asked for more. But the man said he couldn't drink too much. Chase had growled at the man, sounding almost animal-like, not knowing where the urge had come from.

Another noise sounded outside the bedroom door. Chase pushed the memories away and sat up a bit. Suddenly, the berry smell filled his senses again. The door opened and the man carried in another glass.

Chase swallowed as his mouth watered. He sat up. He didn't ask, but the man sat down on the edge of the mattress and put the glass in Chase's hands.

He brought it to his lips and drank greedily. When he'd finished, the man took the glass from him.

"Do you remember anything?" he asked.

The momentary relief from the grief disappeared. The drowning sensation returned. "The plane crashed."

He guy nodded. "I'm sorry for your loss. Your father was a good man."

Chase recalled seeing this man in the lab when they'd gone for the test. "Are you Jimmy?"

"Yes."

Chase's gut tightened. "My dad didn't trust you to look out for me," he said without thinking.

Jimmy sighed. "We were just getting to know each other. But I've done all I can to help you. And I will continue to help you."

Chase looked around. "Why am I not in the hospital? I was in a plane crash for God's sake."

Jimmy reached out and touched Chase's arm. "Do you remember what bad shape you were in?" he asked. "Do you see any wounds on you now? Are any of your bones broken?"

Chase looked down at his arms. He had a vague memory of not being able to move his right arm, and he hadn't been able to feel his legs. Fear swirled around his chest. He yanked the covers back, exposing his legs. He bent his knees up and then lowered them back on the bed. No wounds. No broken bones. He looked up. How could . . . "What happened?"

"There's a virus. The VI virus. Your father, you, and your sister were all carriers. It's—"

"No!" Chase remembered what his sister had said about the strange virus. The virus that made people . . . made people crave blood. His gaze shot to the glass in the man's hands. Was it blood?

"No," Chase repeated. "This is crazy. I don't believe in . . ."

"Vampires?" he asked.

Chase nodded.

"How much do you know? Did your father explain?"

"No," Chase said. "My sister, she read a file. But it can't be—"

"It is. I know it's hard." He looked at Chase with empathy. "I remember when someone explained it to me the first time. It . . . felt crazy." He sighed. "It will take a while to get used to." He patted Chase's shoulder. "But you will be okay. And I'll be here to help you."

Chase's mind ran like a fan, over and over, trying to figure out if he could really trust this guy.

There was a sound at the door. "Oh, someone's wanting to see you." He got up and opened it.

Baxter stormed in, his tail thumping, his whole body wiggling with joy. He let out a low moan, then jumped up on the bed and immediately started licking Chase's face. Chase's eyes filled with tears and the dog licked them away, too.

He finally looked at the man still standing there. He cleared his face of the weakness. "You found him?" he asked.

"Yes."

"Is he okay?" Chase asked, running his hand over the dog's black fur.

"Yeah. I think he is. I was worried about him at first. All he did was bark. I had a friend look after him when I went to find the plane. I was told he barked the whole time. Never stopped. Not even for one minute. As soon as I came in with you, he went silent."

Chase remembered hearing Baxter when he'd been in that strange tunnel of light. It had been because he'd wanted to find the dog that he'd turned away. He'd heard Baxter's barks. Or he'd thought he'd heard him.

The dog whined and dropped his head on Chase's lap, licking his hand.

"I'll leave you two alone. You'll be weak for a few more days and then . . . then I'll show you a thing or two about what you can do now." Chase didn't understand, but he nodded. The man left. Chase reached over to the nightstand and picked up the dog collar. "This is for you, buddy," he said, his chest filled with grief.

He changed out the dog's collar and then buried his face in Baxter's thick fur and let a few more tears fall. "I thought I'd lost you, too.

But no." He pulled back and took the dog's face in his hand and looked into his dark eyes. "It was really you, wasn't it? You called me back. I heard you."

Somehow Chase knew it was true. Baxter had saved his life. He didn't know how he could hear the dog from the mountainside. Didn't know how he'd survived the crash. Or what the hell had happened to him, or . . . He looked at the glass with a red rim around it. Was that . . . ? Oh, hell, he still didn't know what was happening to him. He bent his legs again, remembering not being able to move them. And his arm. It had been broken. How had he healed so quickly?

Taking a deep breath, he glanced at the collar. NEVER TURN YOUR BACK ON A CHALLENGE.

Live, son, his dad's words echoed inside him. *Live for us.*

"I'll try, Dad. I'll try."

Spellbinder

Chapter One

Miranda Kane lay on the floor of her personal waiting/dressing room. Instead of meditating on the spells that she was about to be forced to perform, she committed murder.

Recently, she'd learned that killing helped calm her nerves. Not anything real, of course. It was just a game. She wouldn't step on a bug. And a Texas-sized roach, the flying kind, had been hovering in the corner of the room as if unsure her "live and let live" policy included him. It did. Every living creature had a right to life.

But watching those imaginary demonic shape-shifters clutch their chests and keel over did a girl's heart good. Especially since Perry, the blond, hot shape-shifter had broken up with her and run off to Paris.

Not only was he not calling her, he wasn't taking her calls. She didn't buy the "you deserve better" line he'd offered. Right now, he was probably French kissing some little Parisian twit.

And the fact that he was so good at French kissing just made it worse.

"Die," she seethed as she took pleasure in running her sword through the belly of the blond demon with bright eyes who reminded her of Perry. "Yes!" She punched the air in victory.

She'd been playing for two weeks, and so far, this Perry-like villain had escaped her wrath. But no longer. "Victory is mine!" she declared in a cold voice.

The swish of the door opening brought her out of the game. Since it was too late to pretend to be doing anything other than killing, she continued to watch the touchscreen on her phone. She didn't even bother straining her neck to see who was invading her privacy.

She didn't have to.

If the sweet perfume wasn't a dead giveaway, the sound of the high heels tapping on the wood floor announced her visitor. And since Miranda knew she was gonna get hell, she figured she should enjoy the win as long as she could. The dying shape-shifter slowly fell to his knees.

His light blue eyes stared up from the screen. They looked sad. In pain. And damn if she didn't feel guilty. *No. No. No. This was supposed to feel good. Not bad.*

"What are you doing?" her mom asked in a clipped tone.

"Nothing." She groaned when the shape-shifter found a magical bag of healing herbs, preventing him from taking his last breath. Before she could hit a few buttons and claim victory as her own he healed himself, bolted to his feet, and attacked.

"No!" Miranda yelled.

"No, what?"

Miranda's finger pushed the kill button and her avatar grabbed her weapon, but it was too late. The shape-shifter ran his sword right through her heart, killing her. The screen went red. Red for blood. Red for death.

Her breath caught. Her chest actually burned. Tears moistened her eyes. How appropriate. The real Perry had accomplished the very same thing.

"Since when do you waste your time playing those silly cell phone games?" her mom asked.

"I don't do it all the time." Feeling her mom's stern gaze, she got up, slid her phone into her jeans, and blinked away the beginning of tears. Her gaze shifted to the window, where only recently the sun had beamed into the room.

Now, everything felt dark. She reached for the light switch, but her mom magically turned it on.

"You know, if you used your powers a little more, you might . . ." She paused as if she regretted saying it.

Only then did Miranda meet her mom's calculating stare. Her mother's eyes, the same hazel-green color as Miranda's, were tightened in frustration.

"Are you getting nervous again?" her mom asked. "You can't. You know you always screw up when you get anxious."

No, I screw up because I'm dyslexic. I get nervous because I know I'm going to disappoint you.

After seventeen years, you'd think her mom would have pulled her head out of her butt and accepted the truth. She'd given birth to a screwup. Miranda Kane was a screwup.

"I'll do the best I can, that's all I can do." Not that Miranda's best would be good enough. It never was. Last month, she'd taken third place in the North Texas Wicca competition. It was only because of that fluke that she was in the competition today. You'd think her mom would have been proud. But nope. *Third place just means you were the second loser.* Ahh, but Miranda wasn't accustomed to being in the top twenty-five losers.

"Have you even practiced your spells at all this morning?"

"Yes." Just one and just once. She didn't know what spells came second and third—but her mom didn't need to know that.

"Why aren't you dressed?" The bright green A-line dress with a flared skirt still hung on the hook on the back wall.

She'd planned on getting dressed. Even a screwup could have good fashion sense. "I've still got thirty minutes."

"Do you know who is in the competition with you, young lady?"

Yikes. The "young lady" tag always came right before trouble. Miranda didn't want trouble. All she wanted was to go back to killing shape-shifters.

"No, I don't know," Miranda said. Nor did she give a shit. She'd been beaten by the best. Even by the not-so-best. Screwups didn't do so well in competitions. Another thing you'd have thought her mom would have learned.

"You're up against Tabitha Evans—the one you caught spying on you at Shadow Falls? You locked her in a cage?"

Miranda's mouth dropped open. "How did you know about that?"

She hadn't told her mom. If there was one thing Miranda prided herself on, it was that she wasn't a tattler.

"I know about a lot of things, young lady. Are you going to let that . . . redheaded twit show you up?"

Twit? Her mom's choice of word seemed harsh. Not for Miranda, she'd called Tabitha a twit and even worse. But for her mom, "twit" felt severe.

Not that Miranda could deny it was going to sting being beaten by Tabitha, her archenemy, but . . . there wasn't anything Miranda could do. The fact that she even had an archenemy blew her mind. She wasn't archenemy material. She honestly tried to create positive energy, put good out into the world, and hope it came back.

For that matter, Miranda didn't even have a clue why Tabitha hated her. Or why her mom hated Tabitha so much. Or Tabitha's mom. What was so dad-blasted important about cookies? Because if her memory served her right, that had been what the fallout had been about.

Miranda and Tabitha had been buddies in kindergarten. Then their moms got into some huge argument about whose turn it was to bring cookies, and the next day, Tabitha, her mom, and her cookies hadn't come to school. Gone. The girl had disappeared from her life.

It wasn't until three years ago when Miranda's mom enrolled her in the competitions that their paths had crossed again. And the girl had been a bitch from the word go.

"Are you going to let her beat you?" her mom snapped.

Did Mom have to rub it in? "I said I was going to do my best." Miranda paused. "You know what I don't understand?"

"No, let me tell you what I don't understand. You turned five goons into kangaroos with a mind-to-pinky curse, but you can't find it within yourself to complete a spell to transform a few apples into oranges."

The tightness in Miranda's throat doubled. "Maybe I was able to do the kangaroo trick because my life, as well as Della's and Kylie's, was on the line."

"And this isn't important?"

"Oh, gosh. How could I forget?" Miranda put on her worst acting abilities. "Winning is everything, right? More important than my life and the life of my friends."

"I didn't mean . . ." Her mom actually sounded remorseful.

Wow, that might be a first. Okay, not really, but sometimes she drove Miranda loony. Wanting to change the subject, Miranda asked, "Did you see Kylie and Della out front?"

"No, I haven't been out front." Her mom paused. "I didn't mean . . ."

"Forget it," Miranda said, afraid this conversation would lead to her mom going into the same ol' spiel. They came from royalty. Her father, who Miranda loved dearly when he found a few minutes to spend with her, was of English heritage and was a descendent of Merlin. Her mom, as well as her grandmother, had reigned as high priestess for several years. Miranda was expected to follow in their footsteps.

So. Not. Happening.

"It's just . . . I thought . . . I thought you'd try harder with the prize being what it is."

Miranda might have, if she knew what the prize was. Then again . . . not really. All she wanted was to be left alone to kill more shape-shifters. Was that asking too much? She moved to the window and looked out. A storm brewed. The morning sky was almost black. Flashes of lightning spidered across the sky.

A strange sensation of doom and gloom did a stroll down her backbone. Probably Tabitha sending her bad juju. The girl was a nut job. A serious nut job.

"I mean, since that boy you've got a thing for is there, I just assumed you might want to go see him. Peter?"

Miranda swung away from the storm and faced her mom. "I don't have a thing for a guy named Peter, his name is Perry and . . . Wha— what—what do you mean 'go see him'?"

Her mom's mouth thinned. "You didn't read the brochure I sent, did you?"

"What's the prize?"

"Why do I mail you stuff if—?"

"Just tell me!" Realizing she came off rude, she added, "Please."

Chapter Two

Miranda's mom huffed. "They pay your way to the next competition, which happens to be in Paris, France."

Air swelled in Miranda's lungs. "Who gets their trip paid? First, second, and third, or just first? How many of the finalists get to go?"

"There're twenty girls competing. I think it's the top five who get their way paid to Paris, but . . . you should aspire to win. Who wants to just place in the top five? You want to win."

Win? Miranda didn't give a frog's ass about winning. But going to Paris? Oh, yeah. She could hunt down her own blond, bright-eyed shape-shifter and . . . she wouldn't kill him. Maybe she could make him see reason. Maybe he'd see her and realize he was still in love with her.

Tears filled her eyes. She wanted that more than anything—wanted Perry to love her.

Her mom stared. "I'll tell you what, how about if I sweeten the deal? If you win first place, I'll pay for that rude vampire and that other strange chameleon girl to go with you."

Miranda stood in shock. Thunder boomed in the distance. She pushed away the doom and gloom feeling again and stared at her mom in disbelief. The only thing better than going to see Perry was going to see Perry with her two best friends, Kylie and Della, there for support. Miranda grabbed her mom by the arm and walked her to the door. "You should leave now."

"Why?" her mom asked.

"Because I gotta practice and get dressed. Oh, and go ahead and buy those tickets. I'm winning!"

The bell rang, announcing they had five minutes before the competition commenced. Panicked that she'd only practiced the first apples-to-oranges spell, and clueless to what the second and third spells might be, she let out a moan. But no time to whine. She bolted from the chair, slipped her feet into her green heels, and gave herself one quick final check in the mirror.

The dress fit like a glove. A tight glove. Too much breakup ice cream. She recalled Della telling her she was going to get fat and stomping her ice cream into the floor. At the time, Miranda had been super pissed, but now . . . She supposed she should tell the vamp thank you, or she'd be arriving in front of the council in her fat jeans right now.

She grabbed her brush from her purse and ran it through her long strawberry-blond hair. While she'd gotten her mom's eye color, she'd taken those red highlights from her father. As the strands fell together on her shoulders, the streaks of green, pink, and black framed her face.

Staring at her image, she recalled that in the past, the judges—nothing more than old-fashioned biddies—had made negative remarks about her hair and even docked her a few points. Miranda had thumbed her nose at their opinion and fuddy-duddy sense of style.

Now she dropped her chin to her chest in resignation. Her thumbing days were over.

At least for this competition. Because holy hell, she wanted to win. Had to win.

Their opinion could keep her from the thing she wanted more than anything. Paris with Perry. Paris with Perry, and Della and Kylie as her emotional backup.

Closing her eyes, she held out her pinky and whispered, "Hair, color of three, turn back to the color that is just boring ol' me."

Opening her eyes, breath held, praying she hadn't screwed up, she found the streaks were gone. A good sign that maybe her other spells would be just as successful. But seeing herself without her trifecta of color for the first time in two years had her breath hitching in her throat.

A crazy sensation swept over her. Who was she? Without her trademark streaks of color, without Perry, she felt hollow, lacking a sense of self.

A sad thought hit. Was she the type of girl who solely defined herself by her hair color and a boyfriend? Was she that shallow?

Needing a confidence booster, she grabbed her phone off the table to call the person who always seemed to say the right thing. The man who called her angel and never led her to believe she'd let him down. Her daddy.

But right then, another bell rang, giving them a three-minute warning. The Wicca council, standing as judges, was not tolerant of tardiness. You'd either get docked points or thrown out of the competition altogether.

Reaching back into her purse, she pulled out her necklace—her Alchemy absinthe spoon pendant, a wearable token of her Wicca heritage. The triangle-shaped emerald-green Swarovski crystal hung right below her neck and matched her dress perfectly.

"You can do this," she whispered to the stranger in the mirror and set her phone back down. "You want Perry back, right?"

When the young woman in the mirror didn't answer right away, she wanted to scream. *Now you start doubting?*

Standing straight, she cleared her mind. She did want Perry back, didn't she? The two-minute warning bell rang.

No time to self-analyze, she turned, opened her door, and stepped out. When her feet hit something warm, gooey, and disgusting, she glanced down.

"No!" She'd marched right into a big—seriously big—pile of horseshit.

Fresh manure covered her feet up to her ankles. Giggles exploded at the end of the hall.

Fury, building at the speed of light, had Miranda staring daggers at Tabitha and her sidekick, Sienna, another regular competitor.

Miranda held out her pinky, thinking pimples, thinking hooked noses, and boobs of a ninety-year-old woman—the kind of boobs old women could flash people with by pulling up their skirts. These two girls deserved floppy tits.

Then bam!

Right before she let the thought slip from her mind into her shoulder and travel down her arm to escape from her pinky, she remembered. Any spells placed on other contestants cost points.

Precious, precious points. Points Miranda couldn't afford to lose.

She dropped her arm. With the stench billowing upward, she tried breathing through her mouth. Tabitha and Sienna continued to giggle. Oh, this was sooo funny.

Not!

Miranda squared her shoulders. "Why does the perfection of this spell of yours not surprise me?" She aimed her words at Tabitha, knowing it had been her idea. "Oh, wait, I know. Because you are so full of shit!" she seethed.

The one-minute bell rang. The two girls ran out to take their places.

Miranda had less than thirty seconds to make the circle on the stage. No time to conjure up a cleansing spell, she held her head high and walked out on the stage, pretending she wasn't up to her ankles in horse crap.

Crazy idea?

Yes.

Stupid?

No.

Was she mortified?

Absolutely.

Yet logic trumped embarrassment. The judges docked points for tardiness; she'd never heard of them docking points for horse dung.

Soft music echoed from the loudspeaker as Miranda took her place. She stood ramrod straight. Murmurs of discontent echoed from all directions. The witches on both sides of her in the circle put hands over their noses. Tabitha, one person to her right, held a slight smile on her lips.

Oh, what Miranda wouldn't give to turn and make huge dollops of horse manure rain down on her.

The twelve judges sitting at the end of the stage behind a long wooden table waved their hands in front of their faces. The front-row audience of the dome-shaped auditorium squished up their noses as if the stench was just now invading their air.

What a way to start a competition. Especially one she was damned determined to win.

"Ms. Kane?" one of the judges snapped after the one beside her pointed to Miranda's shit-covered feet. The music came to an abrupt halt.

"Yes, ma'am?" Miranda answered, her voice magically projecting through the entire auditorium.

"Do you lack so much respect for this competition that you would walk on our stage . . . like that?"

"No disrespect intended," Miranda answered, praying her voice didn't crack. "I'm simply trying to honor your promptness rule. I wasn't expecting to find . . . excrement waiting outside my dressing room door."

"Are you implying that someone here did this?"

"It would appear that way," she stated, realizing her dilemma. Their next question would probably be for her to identify the person responsible for the horseshit.

Miranda was not a tattler. Nope.

"I am tired of these childish games," a different judge spoke up and she held out her finger, giving it a good wiggle. The dung on Miranda's shoes and on the floor vanished.

"Who is responsible for this act?" the witch asked. "They will pay for this with a ten-point deduction."

Just ten? Surely, equine dung came with a higher consequence? "I . . . I'm afraid I didn't see the spell being placed." That was the truth.

"Do you suspect someone guilty of this crime?" another judge spoke up.

Miranda could feel Tabitha's and Sienna's gazes on her. Were they afraid? They should be. "I . . . I can't really say."

"Can't or won't?" the woman questioned.

Miranda's gaze shifted to the audience, where she saw her mom sitting in the second row. She was nodding her head as if telling Miranda to spill her guts.

Her hesitation provoked another judge to speak up. "This is silly. Your silence will cost you ten points. Now tell us and let's get moving."

Just tell them, a voice whispered inside her head. The two witches deserved it, but to do so went against her moral compass.

She opened her mouth to do just that, but when she did, she saw who sat behind her mom. Kylie, a light blonde who was . . . as perfect on the outside as she was on the inside. Sweet as apple pie. And Della, with her almost-black hair and dark eyes, eyes that barely slanted upward, that hinted at her half-Asian heritage. No one would call Della sweet. Not to her face anyway. And yes, in truth, Della could be a tad standoffish, and feisty, but it was mostly an act. Miranda couldn't have a more loyal friend. Both of them were . . . her support team. Her best friends. Two girls she looked up to, admired.

What would they do?

The answer resounded back with clarity.

Chapter Three

Miranda would stand her moral ground. "I will take the deduction in points," she said, decision made, but her fury again rising.

"So be it," another judge said and slammed her gavel down on the wooden French farm table.

Miranda refused to look at Tabitha for fear she'd lose it and send her own horseshit spell the girl's way.

Not only was the witch getting off without being punished, Miranda was being punished for her actions.

Not that she was throwing in the towel on winning. It simply meant she would have to work harder. It meant she'd have to pull off each and every spell without one hiccup.

Could she do it?

A tiny drop of sweat collected between Miranda's boobs.

"Sienna Banker." The name of the eighteenth contestant was called. The order in which they were to perform was decided by random drawings. That meant the only ones left were Miranda and Tabitha.

It only added to Miranda's pressure.

She stood on wobbly knees, watching the B with an itch move in front of the table. The girl extended her hand, her pinky twitching. The spell spilled from her lips. "Apples to apples . . ."

Miranda purposely tried to not listen to the spell.

Part of her problem in competitions was simply repeating bad spells. She'd managed to change the apple into an orange twice in her dressing room. She had the spell down, she didn't need to screw with it.

"Oh, orange of mine," the girl continued.

No. No. No. Do not listen. Miranda cupped her hands at her sides and mentally hummed the "Yankee Doodle" song. She'd picked up that song and the act of humming when nervous from her dad. Her gaze cut to the audience for a second. Not that she expected him to be out there. For some reason, even when he was in town, he never attended the competitions.

Applause erupted from the audience.

Miranda stood stoic at the girl's success. She wished no one failure, but their victory added to her problem. Another drop of sweat crawled down her cleavage.

Suddenly, a dark mood, the same one that had appeared when she'd studied the storm, whispered across Miranda's soul. She shot Tabitha a frown.

The girl stood frowning in return, looking uncomfortable in her own skin. Was Tabitha doing this to Miranda? She didn't appear to be casting a mood spell.

But it had to be her, didn't it?

"Tabitha Evans," the judge spoke up.

Friggin' great. Miranda was going to be last. Swallowing down a lump of fear, she mentally went back to humming. *Yankee Doodle went to . . .*

Tabitha stepped up to the table where a fresh apple had just been placed. She repeated a few words, twitched her pinky, and a perfectly round, juicy-looking orange appeared.

Her orange was removed. Another apple took center table.

"Miranda Kane." Her name set a gang of butterflies loose in her stomach.

She stepped up to the table, now closer to the audience. Her mom's face stood out. Then Kylie's and Della's. *You two are going to Paris with me.*

Raising her arm, she recited her spell. "Apple, oh apple, fruit of the tree. Grant me this spell, I place upon thee. An apple no more, an orange you shall be."

When the piece of fruit didn't transform immediately, murmurs of defeat could be heard from the crowd. Time held its breath.

A second before accepting her failure, a light cloud of magical fog appeared hovering over the table. The apple disappeared and an orange, a bright, perfectly round orange, proudly took its place.

A light applause echoed from the crowd. The tickle of victory filled her chest. One down, two to go.

Given a five-minute break before the second part of the competition, Miranda ignored the increasing sense of lurking danger and darted off the stage. She refused to let Tabitha's silly hex distract her. Determined, she hurried back to her room to study the competition brochure and hopefully discover what the next spell entailed. If she worked quickly, she might even fit in one practice.

Face it. If she wanted to win, she could use a little practice.

She shut her door, ran to the small table where the brochure had been left unread. The small print seemed to try to push in her brain at the same time. Damn dyslexia. Closing her eyes, she tried to concentrate. *One line at a time. One line at a time.*

Opening her eyes, she moved down to the second paragraph and ran her finger under the line she needed to read: *The second spell will be altering . . .*

The door to her dressing room shot open, slamming against the wall. Turning, she glared at the intruder, certain it would be her mom, probably to yell at her about the horseshit.

Not her mom. But the horseshit maker herself.

"Stop it!" Tabitha seethed.

"Stop what?" Miranda asked.

"You know what," she accused in a serious voice. She walked off, slamming the door so hard Miranda's eardrums flinched.

"No, I don't know, bitch," Miranda muttered in a sneer. Then, determined to focus on the competition, she pushed all curiosity about Tabitha's little tantrum into a mental vault, and stared back at the brochure.

The second spell will be altering live DNA. Each contestant must transform a feline into another animal—the animal of the contestant's choice.

A smile lit up Miranda face. What had she done for karma to smile down on her like this? Of course, she could only hope the judges meant it when they said the animal was the contestant's choice. Odds were, most of the witches would take the conventional route and go with a dog or rabbit.

She bit down on her lip and did a little victory dance. She'd never been accused of being conventional. It was then she saw her reflection in the mirror. No streaks in her hair. She looked content. Maybe those streaks didn't define her after all. Did that mean Perry didn't define her either? There was only one way to find out. Go to Paris. Find answers.

She looked back at the brochure. Confidence made the air taste sweeter. She was no stranger to altering DNA. This happened to be the spell she'd once attempted, failed at miserably, but had finally conquered.

All that practicing, week after week, had left that spell tattooed on her brain. She could only hope she got this feline turned and turned back before trouble arose. But again, the judges docked you for not completing a spell, not for being skunked.

The three-minute warning bell dinged. She moved to leave. Only this time, she looked down and up before she stepped out. Noting the hallway was crap-free, with poise giving her steps some pep, she headed back to the stage.

Miranda found her place with the other girls forming a circle center stage. Flanked by a set of identical twins, whom she'd run across in several competitions, she offered them each a nod. Candy and Sandy Gleason were tall blondes who'd both won more competitions than they lost.

One of the judges stood up to address the crowd. "No animals will be harmed in the competition. All felines have been blessed, and a superior spell has been placed on them so in ten minutes, no matter what their state of being is, they will be turned back into cats."

Miranda had expected nothing less from the council, especially since two years ago, the Wicca council had been sued by the Wicca-affiliated Animal Rights Association because a frog had accidentally been left as a prince longer than he'd agreed.

Miranda looked up and saw Tabitha standing directly across from her. The girl scowled. Miranda ignored her and the lurking feeling of danger Tabitha had obviously brought on.

Sienna's name was called first. Miranda sighed with relief. The only thing she hated more than going last was going first.

A large black cat appeared on the table. It raised its paw and let out a slow meow. Sienna closed her eyes, raised her hand, her pinky twitching. She started her spell. "Cat to dog. Man's best friend . . ."

Miranda purposely stopped listening, not wanting her words to influence her spell. The cat vanished . . . or half-vanished. The creature standing proudly was part gray poodle part black feline.

Murmurs erupted in the audience. The judges started whispering amongst themselves. The voice of the group stood up. "You have accomplished your task, but with defects. You get only fifty percent of your points."

Sienna nodded, lifted her pinky, and changed her creature back into the cat. When the girl moved back into the circle, Miranda saw the sheen of disappointment in her eyes. Miranda didn't particularly like Sienna, but having been in her shoes so many times, she felt her pain.

Ten more girls were called forward to cast their spell. Only three got the whole one hundred points. Six had simply failed altogether. Miranda felt the blow for each and every one of them, too.

Hence one of the reasons Miranda hated competitions. Winning felt good, watching others not win always stung a little.

"Miranda Kane."

Hearing her name fill the silent auditorium had her earlier confidence leaking from her pores. She stepped forward. Taking a deep breath that filled her chest to the brim, she held out her arm and began . . . "Cat, oh feline friend of mine, find your true colors of black and white, turn to creature that lurks at night—one that no one dares to anger thee, or skunked they will be." One twitch of the pinky and the thought ran amuck in her head. *It's in the bag. In the bag.*

The cloud of magic surrounded the black cat. Then faded. Miranda's breath hitched when she saw what she'd done. *Oh, shit!*

Chapter Four

There, on the table, sat a burlap bag. In it, something wiggled and rolled. Soft growling noises came from the cloth sack.

Voices of confusion arose. Stepping forward, praying her only screwup had been invoking the bag, Miranda loosened the string. The room fell quiet. Not even the air stirred. A black pointed nose appeared, and then the beautiful black-and-white skunk emerged in all his glory. It pranced the length of the table and then back. Then turning away from the judges, it raised its tail.

Soft laughter pushed away the silence.

"Change it back. Now!" one of the council insisted.

Reciting the reverse spell, the skunk returned to feline form. Miranda waited to hear if her bag would cost her any points. With her ten-point deduction for not tattling, she really needed to ace this one.

The unhappy-looking judges whispered amongst themselves.

Even the air Miranda breathed quivered with nervousness.

Finally, the head priestess leaned forward and locked gazes with Miranda. "You accomplished your task, and while the bag was extra, we vote not to deduct points."

Miranda held her exhilaration in check, but heard a loud victory whistle coming from the audience. Her gaze cut to the crowd and she saw Della standing up, one fist pumped in the air, and a huge best-friend smile on her face. Kylie sat beside her, tugging at her shirttail, as if trying to let her know that cheering wasn't common practice at Wicca competitions.

"Please, no outbursts," said the ol' biddy judge, staring into the audience.

Silence filled the room. Miranda, not at all upset at Della, bit her lip to stop from smiling. But Della had just earned herself a big hug. Sure, the vamp claimed she didn't like hugs, but Miranda knew better.

"Tabitha Evans," a judge announced, moving the competition along.

The name of her nemesis brought Miranda back to the present.

Tabitha shot Miranda a scowl as she moved forward. Right then, it occurred to Miranda what Tabitha might have meant by "Stop it." Did she think Miranda was creating the mood spell? If so, that meant that Tabitha hadn't set it. Was real shit, not just horse crap, about to hit the fan?

No, Miranda seriously doubted it.

On the wave of that thought came another trickle of danger and impending doom. Cutting her eyes around at the other girls, she tried to see if any of them wore a mask of guilt. Was one of the other competitors doing this? But if this was a true mood spell, why wasn't everyone reacting?

Sure, mood spells could be cast on individuals, but it took a pretty strong spell to target it like that. And if targeted, then why her and Tabitha? And if it wasn't a mood spell, but actually Miranda's gift of forewarning, then why was Tabitha reading it as well?

Miranda's ability of forecasting trouble, inherited from her father's family, wasn't that common. Ha, wouldn't it totally suck to find out that Tabitha was some distant cousin?

Actually, more sucky, would be if the foreboding were real. Her gaze shifted to the audience and to Della and Kylie. If trouble plopped its butt down on her, at least she'd have help. Man, she'd lucked out getting those two best friends.

Tabitha began to speak. Her words rang loud and with confidence. "Feline of black, feline are you, change now to resemble Pepé Le Pew."

Miranda frowned. She didn't have a copyright on skunk transformation, but why her archenemy cared to mimic Miranda's spell was disconcerting.

The condensation of the spell descended from the ceiling. It swirled around the feline, stopped, and then started again. When it evaporated, a skunk . . . well, a skunk with tall, skinny feline legs, centered the table.

Tabitha's sigh of discontent came just before the murmurs of the audience.

The judges leaned toward each other to compare notes. When they settled back in their seats, the spokeswoman stood and addressed Tabitha. "You will only receive seventy percent of your points. Let this be a lesson to you to use your own spell and not borrow the creativeness of others."

Miranda should have been happy about the girl's comeuppance, but nope. Screwing up in front of your peers and an audience was bad enough. One didn't need to be chastised as well.

Ten minutes later, the second round of competition was over. Only the top ten finalists would move forward. The judges read out their tallies. Miranda's stomach knotted when she heard she fell into fifth place and the four ahead of her held perfect scores.

Normally, she'd have been thrilled, but it meant Miranda would have to get 100 percent on her next spell and everyone else would have to be docked points, to take first place. For once she was channeling her mother, and not accepting anything but a complete win.

Miranda had barely gotten to her dressing room for her four-minute reprieve, when a loud knock sounded at her door. Was it Tabitha again? What was it with that girl?

She ran to the door and swung it open. "What the hell is wrong with . . . you?" She spit out the last word, even though she'd been mistaken on the identity of the knocker.

Or knockers.

Both Kylie and Della stood perched at the door.

"Nothing is wrong with me," Della smarted back. "You, on the other hand, have got problems! You should have handed them that girl's head on a platter."

Miranda pushed her sassy remark aside and went right in for a hug. "This is for cheering for me." She tightened her embrace. "Gawd, I've missed you. How are things at home?"

Della wiggled out of Miranda's hold. "The same."

Della had gone back home last week due to her father being arrested for the murder of his sister. She swore her father wasn't guilty, and it appeared as if it was his twin brother, who was more than likely a rogue vampire, who'd really done the killing. With the help of the FRU, they were trying to solve the cold case.

Miranda couldn't blame Della for going home, but no one could blame Miranda for wanting her to get her butt back. Shadow Falls wasn't the same without her.

"Thank you both so much for coming." Miranda hugged Kylie next.

When she pulled back, the three-minute warning bell rang.

"Shit," Miranda muttered.

"You're doing great," Kylie the optimist said.

"I have to," she said. "I don't have time to explain it in detail, but the top five finalists get their way paid to the next competition and it's in Paris."

"Paris?" Kylie said. "Wow. And that just happens to be where—"

"Perry is. I know," Miranda said, and looked at Della. "I'm trying really hard to win so I can go shake some sense into him. He'll take one look at me and realize how much he loves me." So she did want him back, she realized.

"Okay," Kylie said, but she didn't sound overly confident.

"Screw Perry," Della said. "Do you know who's here?"

Miranda scowled and ignored the vamp's comment. "And the best part is . . . and this is really good, guys . . ." She paused to add drama. "If I win first place, you two get to come with me. Mom's agreed to pay."

Kylie and Della stood there dumbstruck.

"Isn't that great?" she asked.

Della started shaking her head, and Miranda spoke up again. "Duh, have you forgotten, Steve's in Paris, too." Steve being Della's almost boyfriend.

"But—"

"Just for a few days," Miranda added.

Della frowned. "I can't run off to Paris. I've got to help my dad."

"Please," Miranda pleaded. "I need you two there. You are my champions. I'll screw it up without you two."

The one-minute bell rang. "I gotta go. Just think about it. You can't let me down. You can't."

Miranda rushed out and stood in the circle of ten . . . and felt it immediately. Her palms itched with nerves. Not just from the competition or the sense of trouble. Though those both added to her level of anxiety. But now, accompanying that unease, was the sensation of being singled out—studied.

Searching the crowd, she spotted her mom, and even Della and Kylie settling back into their seats. None of them were causing her this discomfort. She let her gaze shift around, when all of a sudden, she saw a curtain to a doorway to the back auditorium flutter closed. Instantly, the feeling faded. Someone had been watching her. Could it be the same person casting the mood spell?

She probably should have mentioned that to Kylie and Della, but her mind hadn't gone there.

Inhaling, Miranda realized that Tabitha—frowning—stood beside her. Was Tabitha feeling any of this? The temptation to lean in and whisper the question bit hard.

But then a judge stood to address the crowd. Miranda pushed past the unease to listen. The last spell had purposely been left out of the brochure—a test of their spontaneity. Miranda sucked at spontaneity.

"Today, we have decided to test the contestants' ability to call upon one of the elemental powers."

Miranda's breath caught. *Not fire. Not fire. Please not fire.* The one thing she sucked at more than spontaneity was . . .

"Fire." The high priestess held up her hand and a flame came out of her fingertips.

Heavyhearted, Miranda considered walking off the stage. Her inability to control this particular elemental power had left a mark on her, or rather it had left a mark on her father.

She'd been eight and mortified when her attempt to light a candle had created a fireball running amuck around the house. Running until it found her father's backside. The poor man hadn't been able to sit down for a week. Not that he had punished her. He'd simply laughed, saying his mooning days were over. Unlike her mom, he never seemed to care that she wasn't perfect.

Looking around again, she questioned her reasons for putting herself through the embarrassment of trying and failing.

The answer came back. For Perry.

"Our first contestant is . . . Tabitha Evans."

Miranda heard air leave the girl's lungs as she walked up to the front of the stage.

A fireplace magically appeared on her left, and on the right was a stand with a small candle perched on top. "Each shall light the candle, then move the flame to the fireplace." The judge's explanation was exactly what Miranda had feared. What if her fire strayed from the given path?

"Each contestant will be allowed three tries to complete her spell. Points will be deducted for each failed attempt," the judge continued. "For safety's sake, a magical bubble will be placed around each performing contestant."

Miranda's panic eased. The only person she could hurt playing with fire this time was herself. That she could risk.

"Fire, oh heat, I ask of ye . . ." Tabitha lit the candle right away, but her tiny ball of flame kept losing its power and fading to smoke. On the third try she did it. The second, third, and fourth girls didn't make it at all. Candy got it in two tries and her twin did it in one. Sienna took two. The next two girls failed. Then it became apparent that she was going to be last. Again.

Waiting for her name to be called, her heart raced. Even with the magic bubble, the room's temperature rose. The sensation of being the target of someone's direct stare picked up again. She wanted to glare at the audience to see who had her under such intense scrutiny, but she needed to focus. Focus on fire.

"Miranda Kane." Her name rang loud in her ears. Too loud.

She moved forward. The magic bubble, invisible with the exception of a light blue tint, started to enclose her. The sounds became muffled. Even her own thoughts seemed too loud. Her first impulse was to escape while she had a chance. Air hitched in her throat. Her palms grew damp with sweat.

Right before she felt the invisible walls seal together, an odd wash of calm hit her chest.

You can do this. You can! She thought of seeing Perry. Of having Della and Kylie at her side.

She extended her hand. "Spark of flame, dance of heat, light this wick, then follow me." Her thoughts became jumbled. She wiggled her pinky.

Nothing happened. The candle's wick remained unlit.

Desperation rose inside her. She felt the audience's anticipation of her failure. She started to lower her arm and ask for her second attempt, when a surge of calm, of clarity, rose inside her again.

Her breath caught as the tranquility filled her lungs. The realization hit. This . . . whatever it was, had not come from within her. Someone . . . someone was manipulating her powers.

She went to push the aid away, but too late. The wick of the candle sparked to life. The flame rose from the candle and grew to a perfect orb of fire. It floated in midair, waiting for orders.

Was this her spell, or the work of the foreign source?

"Go." A simple hand motion sent the fire into the fireplace and the kindling embraced the heat and a fire with blue flames built inside the hearth.

The bubble around her slowly started to ebb away like fog. The applause echoed louder. Her gaze shot to the audience. Who had done this? She turned to direct the council to this mishap in their rules, but before the words left her lips, screams echoed behind her.

Swinging around, she saw the huge orb of fire soaring from the back of the stage. Had she done this? Oh, shit, she probably had.

The circle of blue-and-red flames flew forward toward the line of her competitors.

No! Miranda refused to let her stupidity hurt anyone else.

Without thought, she rushed forward, calling the flame toward her with an inward plea. *If you are gonna burn anyone's ass, it's gonna be mine this time.* The sphere hung in place for a second. Then, spitting out embers, it began rotating, flames flickering from the circle. It must have heard her plea.

With fire racing toward her, she swept her arms out and over her head and asked with all her soul for the magic to reseal the protective bubble. The invisible barriers rose around her, trapping her and the orb of fire in their own prison.

The heat in the enclosure stung her skin to the point of pain. Gray smoke thickened the air and burned her lungs.

Screams from outside of her confinement filled her ears. *"Help her! Somebody help her."*

The invisible bubble shook from the attempted spells slamming into the wall. The spellbound bubble couldn't be breached.

"Somebody do something."

They couldn't save her.

It was up to Miranda. All up to her.

With the orb of fire hovering right above her, she raised her hand, calling forth the element of water. Her words had no more left her lips when she felt her knees give. Everything went black.

Chapter Five

"Breathe! You hear me? Breathe, damn it!"

Miranda felt someone fold her into their arms—a male someone, by the feel of muscles and the spicy male scent.

Perry?

Forcing her eyes open, she became trapped in a blue gaze. Not Perry's blue gaze. Falling around her and her mystery guy were what looked like gray snowflakes, mixed with a soft rain.

Nice. Kind of . . . well, not really.

What the heck?

"You're going to be okay," Blue Eyes said.

Wait. She knew those eyes.

She blinked. She knew that face.

"You okay?" the deep voice asked.

She knew that voice.

"Talk to me," he said.

Held so close, she felt his words vibrate in his chest, as she breathed in a scent that was purely male. Yes, she knew him.

Shawn? Shawn Hanson.

But that seemed to be all she knew. Where was she? And how . . . ?

Reality jerked her from her stupor. She recalled the competition and the orb of fire. She'd screwed up.

She sat up. He let her go, but kept one arm around her shoulders.

Embarrassment consumed her.

"Was anyone hurt?" She forced the words from her raw throat.

"No. Thanks to you," Shawn said. "But you might want to stop it from raining," he said and winked.

Oh, yeah, she'd called upon the element of water to save her. And that gray snow wasn't snow, but ash. Had it worked? Had she saved herself or had . . . ?

She shifted a pinky to stop the rain. Still feeling like a fish out of water, even though she was soaked, she looked around. At the foot of the stage gathered the crowd of about three hundred. Closer, standing on the stage, were another thirty or so faces peering at her—probably laughing on the inside at her mistake.

She spotted her mom, looking fretful. In the mix of people, Della and Kylie stood a few feet away. Kylie's aura was bright, as it got when she went into protective mode. Had Kylie saved her? Her gaze shifted to Della. Perhaps even Della with her vampire strength had helped in the rescue. Then she noted Della's "told-you-so" smile. Why was . . . ? Oh, heck, Miranda knew why.

Ever since Perry had taken off for Paris, the vamp had been pushing her to go out with Shawn. Now the question waiting to be answered was why Shawn was here.

She started to get up. Shawn bolted to his feet and reached down to help her. The words, *I can do it* rested on her tongue. But she bit them back.

His warm hand slipped into hers and she felt it. The spark of attraction. She'd carried a torch for him—the older brother of one of her friends—since she was twelve and he was fourteen.

In the corner of her eye, she saw Della grin and wave a hand under her nose as if she was picking up on the pheromones.

And dad-blast it, it was true. She had the hots for Shawn, but he wasn't . . . Perry. She couldn't open herself up to Shawn until . . . until she knew how things really stood between her and Perry.

On her feet, she saw the council gathering in one corner of the stage. Freaking great. No doubt they were about to chastise her for causing such chaos. Her gaze went back to her mom. The thought of her being humiliated—again—at Miranda's failure stung like a paper cut right across the heart.

Then another deep cut sliced into her heart. She wasn't going to Paris. She wouldn't see Perry.

A knot of emotion rose in her throat.

All of a sudden, a loud bam sounded. Miranda's gaze, along with everyone else's, went to the auditorium door that had been slammed open. Three men dressed in dark suits came storming inside. A gasp echoed in the building.

Leading the group into the large room was a tall, dark man who owned any room he walked into—no matter what the size. Burnett James. Burnett, super vampire and part owner of Shadow Falls Camp, was also an agent with the Fallen Research Unit (FRU), which was basically the FBI of supernaturals. He didn't slow down until he and the other men stopped right in front of her and Shawn.

What was Burnett doing here?

Did her screwup warrant the FRU showing up? Then she noted the vampire's stern expression. Oh, hell, she was in deep doo-doo now.

Burnett wasted no time taking control of the situation, ordering people back, and insisting no one leave until his people had had a chance to interview them.

After swallowing her shock at seeing him, she found her voice. "What are you—?"

He held up one finger and sent her a look that demanded silence. She didn't argue. Kylie and Della might feel comfortable enough to butt heads with the badass vamp, but Miranda . . . not so much.

She could still remember the fury in his eyes when she'd accidentally turned him into a kangaroo.

"We'll speak in private," he stated.

Private? Oh, shit! Had her spell seriously gone so wonky that it required the FRU's presence?

She forced herself to speak again. "I have a dressing room."

Nodding, he gave orders for the other agents to start interviewing the audience. Though why, Miranda didn't have a clue. He already had the guilty party in custody. Her.

He motioned for Miranda to lead the way and then with a slight wave, he indicated that Shawn, Della, and Kylie were to follow. Not so private after all, huh? Nothing like getting your ass chewed out in front of people.

With five people in the dressing room, it felt small, and she worried there wasn't enough air in there for everyone. And considering her state of mind, she needed a lot of oxygen. Taking a gulp now, she almost felt light-headed.

"Are you really okay?" Burnett asked as soon as the door to the dressing room clicked shut. While the question insinuated he cared, his tone rang rock hard and had her palms itching again.

"I'm . . . fine . . ." Finally she couldn't stand it anymore. "I'm sorry," she said. "I mean, I stopped it before it hurt anyone, right?" She glanced at Shawn, praying he hadn't lied to her earlier. "You said I did. Did you lie to me?"

"No." Shawn looked at her oddly. "Wait, do you think . . . You didn't cause that fireball, Miranda."

"I didn't?" Air, old air, gushed out of her lungs.

"No," Shawn said. "You were still entrapped in the bubble when it appeared. Your spell was contained. But you sure as hell stopped it from hurting anyone else."

Relief washed over her and she smiled—a weak one, but a smile. "I thought . . . I mean, I'd just finished my spell and I thought . . ." *I screwed up again.*

"She was freaking amazing," Della spouted out. "You should have seen her, Burnett. Before Kylie or I could get on the stage, she had that monster-ass fireball trapped in that invisible bubble, waving her arms around, as if daring it to come any closer. Then she made it rain and that ball burst into cinders. And then she fell to her knees like in that epic movie, *Gone to the Breeze,* I think that was the name of it, where the heroine yells out, 'I shall never go hungry again.'"

"*Gone with the Wind,*" Miranda corrected, then stood dumbstruck hearing Della's description of the events.

"Breeze, wind, same thing," Della said.

Kylie spoke up as if reading Miranda's mind. "Della's right. You were amazing."

"I agree," Shawn said, and his blue eyes landed on her with warmth. Warmth. Lots of warmth. What was he doing here anyway?

"Now isn't the time for praise." Burnett studied Shawn. "Do you know who might have done this?"

"No," Shawn spoke up. "Whoever placed the spell didn't leave an imprint. It's the same as the scene from yesterday."

But they did, Miranda thought, remembering the foreboding she'd picked up on. Then she reheard what Shawn had said.

"What other scene?" Miranda asked. "What are you talking about?"

Burnett spoke up. "You might as well know. Two girls were murdered."

"That's horrible, but how does that . . . what does that have to do with this?"

"They were both supposed to participate in this competition."

"What?" Miranda asked. "Who?"

Burnett frowned. "Roni Force and Cindy Bryant."

"Oh, my God. I know them. We're not close, but . . . I've met them both. Why hasn't anyone mentioned it here?"

"We've kept it out of the media while we did the initial investigation."

Miranda's brain still wasn't wrapping around this. "But . . . why would anyone want to kill them?"

"That's what we're trying to find out. We didn't see a connection between the two murders until we realized this morning that they were both supposed to compete today. I sent Shawn here while I chased down some other leads. But after what happened, it seems that it has something to do with all this."

"All this? This what?" Miranda asked.

"The competition."

"But why . . . I mean . . ."

Burnett ran a hand through his dark hair. The strands seemed to fall right back as if even his hair feared disappointing him. He gazed at Shawn and then back at Miranda. "According to him, this is the second biggest contest. The finalists in this contest will compete to reign as high priestess. Correct?"

"Yes, but I just don't see anyone . . . killing off the competition." But no sooner had the words left her mouth, she knew better. "Okay, maybe you have a point."

Just because she didn't live, eat, and breathe the idea of rising in the ranks, didn't mean others didn't. For that matter, more than the contestants wanted to win, there were the contestants' moms. Wicca-competition moms made soccer moms seem like candy stripers.

Right then, the door to her dressing room whooshed open. Speaking of soccer moms, her mother stormed in. "You did it! You did it!" She grabbed Miranda up for a hug. "They just announced the winners. You finally put those little bitches in their places."

Miranda pulled back. Her mind spun. She'd won. She was going to Paris. Kylie and Della could come with her—if she could get them to agree to it.

"We're going to win, Miranda. I'll do anything to make sure you win!"

Burnett stared at her mom. As if . . .

"Don't say that, Mom."

"Why not? It's true. You finally stood up to your potential. You're going to be high priestess. I feel it in my bones. This is the day I've been living for."

Burnett cleared his throat. "Excuse me, Ms. Kane. But can you give us a few more minutes . . . alone?"

She looked slightly insulted. "Sure, but hurry. The press wants to interview and photograph my daughter." She left with as much commotion as she'd arrived with. The door slammed shut.

Silence fell on them. Miranda looked at Burnett. "Please don't tell me you suspect . . ."

"No." Burnett held out his hands. "Don't worry. I'm not particularly fond of your mom, but I don't see her as a potential suspect. That said, do you have any idea who would do this?"

"What about the girl that put horseshit in front of your door?" Della said. "I smelled it when she did it," she added, looking at Burnett. "I swear, if Kylie hadn't held me back, I'd have pulled her off the stage and opened a can of whoop ass."

"What?" Burnett asked, looking at Della for explanation.

Kylie took a step closer. "And she's the one who was spying on you at Shadow Falls, too, right?"

"I'm lost here!" Burnett said. "Who is she? And when was she spying on you at the camp?"

"A long time ago." Miranda shook her head. "It was nothing."

"Piece of cake," Della said. "Miranda put her in a cage for a while and then Kylie told her she couldn't keep her, so Miranda released her."

Burnett shook his head. His gaze and frown shot back to Miranda. "Could Tabitha be responsible for this?"

Miranda shrugged under his intense gaze, but forced herself to speak her mind. "Tabitha is crazy, but . . . I mean, dropping shit at someone's door is one thing. Killing . . . I don't think she'd do that."

"Well, someone did it, and until we know for sure, you need to stay on guard. Your winning the competition could mean you're the next target."

"Next target for what?" she asked and then her heart pounded when she realized what he meant. She was the next target for murder.

Thoughts ran amok in her mind. *Murder. Murder.*

"Wait. I felt it," she finally spit out.

"Felt what?" Burnett asked.

"A foreboding. Danger."

Burnett looked at Shawn. "You didn't feel it?"

"No. Predictions of danger is a special gift. It doesn't run in my family."

Burnett looked back at Miranda. "Do you know who sent you this message?"

"No one sent it. It's like ESP. I just picked up on it. But if I feel it again, I'll recognize the source as the same one."

Burnett shook his head. "So you felt this warning and you didn't do anything?"

She didn't like how that sounded, but he did have a point. "Well, I . . . I thought it was a mood spell, but then . . ."

"Then what?" Burnett asked impatiently.

"I thought Tabitha was doing it, and then . . . Tabitha was acting crazy. She told me to stop it, like I was the one putting the spell on her."

"So you think you both felt the warning?" Burnett looked confused.

"Not likely," Shawn said. "As I said, the gift generally runs in a family. And it's not that common."

Burnett let go of a deep breath and focused back on Miranda. "So what were you trying to say?"

"I . . . don't know. I mean, I sort of thought what you said, that we both were reading it, but Shawn's right. That isn't likely. So I'm just trying to make sense of it."

Burnett's phone dinged with a text. He looked at it and then back at Miranda. "When you make sense of it, make sure you let me know." Then his gaze shot back to Shawn. "I need to go do some interviews of the Wicca council. Keep an eye on her. And don't go out there for interviews or photos until I'm back."

Shawn's eyes filled with unease. "But what if her mom comes back in and . . ."

"Handle her," Burnett said.

"Didn't you see her?" Shawn asked. "She can't be handled."

"Don't worry, I'll protect you," Della said with sarcasm.

Chapter Six

As soon as Burnett left, Miranda dropped down into a chair and stared at her two best friends standing next to Shawn. "I can't believe this."

She took a deep breath and tried to take it all in.

Two girls were dead.

She'd won. She'd freaking won the competition.

Which, according to Burnett, made her a target. She'd possibly just made someone's hit list. Not good. Not good at all.

But it also meant she was going to Paris.

Going to see Perry.

And Della and Kylie could come with her.

Just before she found some pleasure in that thought, another one hit.

She didn't deserve to win. Right before the bubble had closed she'd gotten zapped with some kind of juju. And whoever did it had to have some mega power, because no one seemed to notice.

She ran her fingers through her hair. "Crap!"

"Crap what?" Della asked. "You mean your hair? You lost your colors. I almost didn't recognize you."

"I think it looks good," Kylie offered.

"It looks boring," Della said. "Miranda's not boring."

"She's not boring," Shawn said.

"No, not crap about my hair. Crap . . . I'm gonna have to recuse myself from the contest."

"Why?" Kylie asked.

Miranda hated saying it. "Because . . . because someone helped me. Someone powerful helped me." Her gaze shifted to Kylie, a chameleon who could shift into any kind of supernatural. "Oh, gawd, I know you love me, but you shouldn't have done that."

Kylie bit down on her lip. "I do love you, but I didn't do anything."

"You . . . you didn't send me power?"

"No."

"Now me, on the other hand," Della said. "If I could have, I'd have sent you a bucket load of power."

Miranda just sat there. "Then who would have done it?"

"Your mom, maybe?" Kylie offered. "We know how much she wanted you to win."

"No." Miranda shook her head. "She's a rule follower. Hates cheaters."

All of a sudden, Miranda felt Shawn's gaze on her. She looked at him. His Adam's apple bobbed up and down. Guilt was hard to swallow. She stood up. "You?"

When he didn't immediately deny it, she knew she was right. "Why would you do that?"

"I . . . I didn't . . ." He paused, then ran a hand through his thick, blond curls.

Miranda looked at Della. "Is he lying?"

Della tilted her head to the side to listen to Shawn's heartbeat with her ultrasensitive vampire hearing. "Do bears shit in the woods?"

Miranda gazed back at Shawn. "Yes. They do!"

He held up his hands. "No, I didn't send you power."

"Now, he's telling the truth," Della said, looking puzzled.

"I offered you some calm. That's all." He raked a hand over his face. "You looked panicked and I just . . . I didn't even mean to do it. I saw you and it just happened. And it was just a breath of calm." He inhaled and his oh-so-blue gaze seemed to ask for forgiveness, even when he didn't say the words. "You pulled off the spell . . . you did that all on your own."

"Yeah, but . . ." Miranda stood there befuddled. Shawn knew if he got caught the council would have come down on his ass. Why would his instincts push him to . . . why did he care if she botched it and made an idiot out of herself? And why did . . . why did knowing he cared make her lungs accept air a little better? Finally, she spoke. "It's against the rules."

"So is putting horseshit in front of another contestant's door," Shawn said, his tone firm and wide shoulders widening. "You took a ten-point deduction to protect someone who didn't deserve protecting. And guess what the deduction is for someone offering calm? Ten. So you're even."

"I like how this guy thinks," Della said.

So did Miranda. She liked a lot more than just how he thought, too. As in the tall firm body, blond curls, and blue eyes. He looked like a swimsuit model, who should be photographed on a beach, holding a surfboard at his side.

She could still remember how it felt to be in his arms. Safe. His scent had been . . . yummy—fresh and kind of like the seashore. But she didn't want to go there. There was another scent she craved. One of a certain shape-shifter. A certain shape-shifter who'd turned his back on her.

"Oh, hell," Shawn muttered. "Do you know what this means?"

"What?" Miranda asked and Della and Kylie stared at him, too.

"As Burnett said, winning puts your life in more danger. And if what I did really helped you, then . . . it's partly my fault." He placed his hands behind his neck and squeezed. "You're right. You need to recuse yourself. I'll tell the council what I did." He started to walk out.

The idea of him getting into trouble for helping her didn't sit well.

"No." She caught him. The touch sent another jolt of attraction through her and she pulled her hand away. "I can just say someone did it."

The look in his eyes brought home the fact that the reason he was doing this was to protect her. And that little insight led her to another one. "If I recuse myself from the contest, someone else will win."

"Yes," Shawn said as if confused.

"So by me walking out, it would likely save me, but put someone else's life in danger."

Shawn frowned. "And if you don't, it's your life that could be in danger. And it would be my fault. If someone else wins, it's not my fault."

"No, then it would be mine. Because if something happened to someone else, then . . . I would know it would have been me if I hadn't pulled out." She shook her head. "I can't do that. I can't just say I don't want to be killed and let it be someone else."

"Better than you being dead," Della said and Kylie seemed to agree. Shawn's frown came on strong. "Exactly—"

"No!" Miranda set a hand on her hip and glared at her best friends. "I know you two. Neither one of you would step aside to save yourself. You're too brave."

Neither of them could deny it.

"The hell with being brave," Shawn snapped. "Two girls have already died."

"Then you three just have to make sure that doesn't happen to me," Miranda snapped back. "Face it, whoever would take my place wouldn't have you guys to protect her."

Burnett texted Della and Kylie and asked them to help take the names of everyone in the crowd since some of them were dead set on leaving. That left Miranda and Shawn alone. She didn't know what to say, so she said nothing. She dropped into a chair. Shawn pulled another one over.

She considered grabbing her phone and going back to killing shape-shifters, but the desire to do that had waned. Still, she pulled her phone out of her pocket and feigned interest in the screen. Tension filled the small space and made even breathing uncomfortable. And loud. She could hear him take in air and tried not to make any sound herself when she drew in oxygen.

When her cell rang, thankful for the interruption, she answered it before even checking to see the identity of the caller.

"Hello," she said.

"Hi, angel."

His voice, that's all it took and she could feel his arms around her, smell his familiar cologne. "Hi, Daddy."

"I heard you've been playing with fire again," he said. "Is that why my buttocks were itching?"

"I didn't do it," she said, feeling her chest grow heavy even when she heard the tease in his voice.

"I'm joking. Your mom told me you saved the day. I just wanted to call and make sure my little girl's okay."

"I am," she said and wondered what her mom had told her dad. Especially since her dad had never been in favor of the competitions.

"I won, Dad," she said, wanting him to be proud of her, even if she wasn't completely sure she deserved the win.

"You've always been a winner to me," he said, his tone making it clear that he still didn't approve of the contests. "But I'm proud of you. Gotta go now."

She hung up, and realized Shawn was studying her. "My dad," she said.

He nodded and then went back to staring at his own phone. And breathing.

The silence felt awkward. And after about twenty minutes, she couldn't stand it.

"Why did you do it?" she asked. "Why did you help me?"

He didn't glance up. "I told you. You were panicked."

"I'm sure a few of the other girls were nervous as well."

"I don't know the other girls." He continued to stare at his feet.

"You don't know me all that well either."

He looked up, his blue eyes intense. "Yes, I do."

She shook her head. "Not really. I was your sister's friend for a few years."

"You were my sister's friend who had a crush on me."

She frowned. "How do you know that?"

He smiled, and damn if that smile wasn't a heart stopper. "A guy knows."

She rolled her eyes. "Fine, but that still doesn't mean you know me. You never gave me the time of day."

He arched one brow and half smiled. "I knew exactly what you looked like in that lime-green bikini you used to wear when you came to swim with Ellen in our pool. I knew when you laughed, your hazel eyes brightened to a light green. I knew you ate ketchup on your scrambled eggs. I knew you had PE fifth period when I was a senior. I would sometimes walk through the gym just to get a glimpse of you in shorts and a tank top. And then there was our kiss?"

Miranda stared, his words slowly filling her brain. "You . . . Wait. What . . . ? We never kissed."

He grinned. "So you really didn't know it was me?"

"I don't know who you kissed, but we never—"

"So you've never kissed anyone when you didn't know who they were? Like on a balcony one night during a full moon?"

"What . . . ?" Holy shit! There had been the New Year's Eve masquerade party she'd gone to when she was fifteen. A guy dressed like Zorro had found her on the balcony seconds before midnight, and when the bell rang, he'd . . . he'd pulled her into his arms and kissed her like . . . she'd ever been kissed before.

"You were Zorro?"

"Ah, so you do remember." A confident smile lit up his face. "That said, if your memory is blurry, I could remind you." His gaze dropped to her lips.

She shook her head. "But . . . I mean why . . . why didn't you tell me who you were? What kind of guy kisses a girl like that and runs?"

He shrugged. "The kind who'd been caught by his dad admiring you sunbathing and got the back of his head slapped because I was sixteen and you were fourteen." He glanced down for a second and then looked up. "You didn't look fourteen in that bikini."

"I was fifteen when you kissed me."

"Yeah, but I was seventeen and about to go away to college. And that didn't feel so right either."

Angry for reasons she wasn't even sure of, she snagged her phone and started scanning Twitter.

He let the silence linger for only a few minutes. "Why did you call a couple weeks ago to see if I was okay and then not call back when I asked you to?"

"Because I'm confused." She spoke the truth without realizing that it might require an explanation.

"About what?"

She hesitated and stared down at her phone. It just didn't feel right talking to him about this.

"About Perry?" he asked.

She looked up, shocked that he . . . "How do you know about him?"

He leaned his chair back on two legs. "I met him a while back when Burnett had used him as a lookout for a case. He seemed like a nice guy."

"He is," Miranda said.

He dropped the chair back down on all fours. "I admit I liked him less when I found out that you and he were . . . an item. But I heard he left, and that he sort of broke it off."

She glanced back at her phone as if she'd stumbled across something interesting, but in truth it was an avoidance tactic.

"We're just taking a break," she said, hoping that didn't sound as lame to Shawn as it had to her when Perry had said it.

"I see," he said.

She looked at him again. Did that mean he understood? Because if he did, would he please explain it to her?

Their gazes met and held.

Or they did until voices started booming on the other side of the door.

Chapter Seven

"I said no, Ms. Kane. She'll not be interviewed or photographed until I've checked out the media!" Burnett's baritone voice penetrated the door.

Miranda's heart went out to him. Sure, he was accustomed to dealing with rogues and serial killers, but he'd never dealt with her mom. And she was a whole other animal.

"Why?" her mom asked. "Someone pulled a prank with that fireball. Granted, it was dangerous, but why so much precaution?"

"Because I care about your daughter," Burnett answered.

"Can I at least see her?" Her mom's high-pitched voice rose.

"I would never keep a mother from her child," Burnett seethed and slung open the door. It banged against the wall, causing Miranda to jump.

Her mom stormed in, and on her heels was a bright-eyed Burnett, looking ready to kill. Thank goodness Miranda knew his moral ethics prevented him from murder. Then again, this was her mom, who could skew moral ethics with her headstrong personality.

"This man is ruining your victory!" her mom spouted out. "You deserve your five minutes of fame!"

"It's okay," Miranda said. She didn't need fame—she wasn't even sure she wanted fame, period—but this was what her mom lived for. "I won, that's what matters." She hugged her mom, hoping to calm her and prevent Burnett from wringing her neck. Arms still wrapped around her mom, she spotted Kylie and Della standing in the doorway.

Kylie smiled with concern. Della looked half pissed. The vamp didn't like Miranda's mom. Not that Della's parents were all that much better.

The clearing of a throat had Miranda dropping her arms from around her mother. "Sorry, Ms. Kane," Shawn said as he stood from his chair. "I'm about to really upset you."

Oh, great! Now Shawn wasn't afraid of her mother. Miranda eyed Shawn with warning. *What was he up to?*

He met her eyes briefly and then turned to her mother. "You see, your daughter needs to recuse herself from this competition."

Miranda's jaw dropped open. "We already talked about this."

"Are you insane?" her mom snapped.

Miranda ignored her mom and stared daggers at the blond warlock.

He wiped his face with a palm then took a step back from her mom. Fear flashed in his eyes. And rightfully so.

Shawn glanced back at Miranda. "Yeah, we talked, and I disagreed with you."

Miranda dropped a hand on her hip. "You didn't say you disagreed with me."

"I didn't say I agreed with you either."

She felt a bit speechless. "As if that matters. I don't need you to agree with me." Miranda shook her head and then glanced back at Burnett. "I'm not recusing myself from the competition. It will just put someone else in danger."

"That's a hell no! My daughter will not recuse herself," her mom added and came to stand by Miranda as if to create a solid front. Then she turned and looked at Miranda. "Wait. Why would it put someone else in danger?"

Before Miranda could address her mom's question, Shawn countered with, "Then I'll have to confess to the council."

"Confess what?" Burnett asked.

"You will not!" Miranda said, and her hot tone now sounded a bit like her mom.

"Confess what?" Her mom repeated Burnett's inquiry.

"Your daughter got some outside help with the competition."

"My daughter does not cheat!" Her mom started moving toward Shawn.

Miranda caught her arm and held on for dear life. Her mom did Pilates and aerobics three times a week, so it wasn't easy.

Burnett shot between Shawn and her mom as if fearing for his junior agent's life. About time Burnett realized what he was dealing with.

"What are you saying?" Burnett asked Shawn, holding out a hand in case her mom got free.

"I sent her a surge of calm."

"You? You sent it?" her mom seethed and yanked out of Miranda's hold.

"Yes," Shawn said.

Her mom cut her eyes back to Miranda. "Did you ask him to send that to you?"

"No," she and Shawn said at the same time.

"Good!" Her mom stretched out her hand and pointed her pinky.

"No." Burnett moved closer to her mother and ever so gently lowered her arm. "Can we please calm down and let me figure out what's going on?"

"Winning this competition puts your daughter's life at risk." Shawn moved around Burnett.

"Why would it put her life at risk?" she asked, and when Shawn didn't answer, she turned her head and glared at Burnett. Miranda knew that look. It was the same one her mom shot her dad before she turned him into a baboon.

"You," she said, her voice tight with anger. "You had better start talking before I render you mute."

Damn it! *This was just going to get worse.*

Burnett told her the whole story about the two girls who'd been murdered. Miranda's mom, her face lacking color, dropped down into a chair. Miranda went and stood beside her.

Her mom looked up at her and then reached over and took Miranda's hand.

"Do you know who . . . who is doing this?"

"Not yet," Burnett said. "The problem is that it doesn't necessarily have to be the finalists here in the U.S. I'm told there will be twenty finalists from all over the world. I'll be contacting them or their families to confirm nothing has happened to them."

"The thing is, Miranda has a reason to recuse herself," Shawn spoke up. "Right now it appears the killer is taking out contestants. Right?" He focused on Burnett.

"It appears—"

Shawn didn't let him finish before starting up again. "So if she drops out now, the chances are she won't be in danger. She won't have to go to Paris," he continued, driving home his point.

A point she didn't appreciate. "No," Miranda snapped. "I'm going to Paris."

Her mom looked up. "Not if your life is in danger, you aren't."

Miranda heard the words, but couldn't believe them. Winning, or rather, Miranda making high priestess, meant everything to her mom. Miranda's chest squeezed and she felt a knot rise in her throat. For the first time in years, Miranda felt loved. And for some crazy reason, the emotion tightening her throat and making her chest ache made the thought of disappointing her mom almost unbearable.

"I'll be okay." She pushed the words out. "Burnett will protect me."

"But, baby, if something happened to you, I . . . I wouldn't know what to do."

"Nothing is going to happen. He won't let it," Miranda insisted and waved a hand toward Burnett.

Everyone turned and looked at Burnett as if for confirmation.

He sighed. "If I thought by dropping out you would be out of danger, I would have already gotten your name off the list. You see, we just found out that one of the girls who was murdered had dropped out of the competition three days ago. And since I'm going to be going to France, I would rather you be near me than here."

"I'm pretty sure I'm going, too," Kylie spoke up, looking directly at

Miranda's mom. "I won't let anything happen to her." Kylie's blue gaze shifted from her mother to Miranda. Warmth filled Miranda's lungs. Nothing like best friends.

"She's a protector," Miranda spoke up. "More powerful than anyone when someone she loves is in danger. So you see, it's going to be fine." She glanced at Della. "You're going, too, right? Mom's paying for it." Miranda looked at her mom for confirmation. Her mom nodded, then Miranda refocused on Della.

"I . . ." Della's frown gave Miranda her answer and she didn't like it.

"I just really want—"

"Yes, she will be going." Burnett took a step forward.

Della turned her confused gaze on the big bad vampire and shook her head. "With what's going on here with my dad, I don't think . . ."

"You need to—"

Della shook her head and spoke again. "I'm sure between you and Kylie, you can—"

"Hear me out," Burnett said with a growl. "A lead in the case you're working just popped up in DeVille, France. You're going to want to go."

"What lead?" Della snapped. Her eyes widened with interest. "Chase?"

Miranda knew the case that Della was working was about her father's murder conviction—the eighteen-year-old murder of his own sister. And the person who might have info on it was Chase, another super vampire, who had saved Della's life by blending his blood with hers when she went through the second turn. Supposedly, the blending of blood had bonded the two together. But then Della found out he'd been lying to her and had connections to her father's brother who was a possible rogue vamp, who the FRU, and Della, believed to be the real murderer.

"Is it Chase?" Della insisted when Burnett didn't answer immediately.

He nodded. "I got word about an hour ago. He was traveling with a guy of Asian descent."

"Wait," Kylie spoke up. "You don't think these two cases are connected, do you?"

"Not that we can see right now," Burnett said. "But I agree, it's almost too much of a coincidence."

Della's chest expanded and her eyes brightened with emotion, though what emotion, Miranda couldn't say.

Della glanced back at Miranda. "Looks like I'll be going."

Two days later, the cool afternoon wind whipped Miranda's hair around her face. She stood on a small patch of grass and stared up at the Eiffel Tower. Kylie and Della stood beside her. Her two best friends in the world, but even their presence wasn't offering the comfort she longed for.

And hanging back about a hundred feet was the blond warlock. Miranda could feel his gaze on her. She hadn't spoken to him since the competition. It still pissed her off that he'd gone against her wishes and threatened to get her thrown out.

They had arrived in Paris that morning. Her mom wasn't supposed to arrive for two more days. Miranda was jetlagged and emotionally exhausted. Out of precaution, Burnett had taken them to an apartment, not the designated hotel where all the contestants were to stay. As silly as it sounded, Miranda has been relieved that the apartment building didn't have gargoyles. She hated gargoyles and just walking over here, she'd shuddered at the sight of several glaring down at her from the neighboring buildings' eaves.

They had crashed for about six hours. But upon waking up, Miranda had begged Burnett to let them go out.

In his normal overly protective fashion, Burnett refused. Miranda had been about to protest, but Della beat her to the punch. She insisted they hadn't come all the way to Paris to stare at an apartment's white walls. The vamp had complained since they'd landed in France that Burnett wasn't letting her take off to DeVille to work on her own investigation. Burnett relented with one condition: they'd take a tagalong. Hence, Shawn, following them like a lost puppy. She wished he'd stop staring at her. The temptation to zap blinders on him tickled her pinky.

Miranda wasn't even sure what she wanted to do. Oh, hell, she did know. She wanted to go see Perry, but she just wasn't sure it was the right thing.

She'd bit her tongue a hundred times to stop herself from asking Burnett if Perry knew she was coming. But if he knew, it would break her heart because he hadn't come to see her yet. Did he not miss her at all? Did he not care anymore? Were all the things he'd told her these last six months lies? How could he just stop caring?

The damp cold seemed to sneak beneath Miranda's pale green jacket and her heart ached a little more. Reaching up, she touched her spoon-pendant necklace then pulled the coat around her a little tighter.

"Oh!" Della seethed. "I just stepped in dog crap. Isn't there like a poop police?"

"Can't you just enjoy Paris?" Miranda snapped.

"Look who's talking, you can't look at any of the buildings because the gargoyles scare you."

"So I'm afraid of gargoyles. Did you know some of them are actually demons?" Miranda snapped back with sass and regretted confiding her fear with them.

Looking away, she went back to staring up at one of Paris's biggest attractions. After several long moments, she felt Della's and Kylie's gazes on her as if waiting for her to say something. Deciding to at least try to be compliant for once, she offered, "It's a big tower."

"Why the hell are we here?" Della asked. "We all know what you want to do."

Miranda knew exactly what Della meant, but it pissed her off that Della herself didn't want the same thing. Perry hadn't come alone to Paris. With him was Steve, Della's sort-of ex.

How could Della not be aching to see Steve? Had Della given up on Steve the way Perry had given up on her?

"Yeah," Miranda smarted back. "Let's go to the Louvre. Seeing some chubby-cheeked lady with a fake smile is more exciting."

"Get your head out of your ass," Della snapped. "If you want to find Perry just say so and let's get it over with."

Miranda shot the vamp a cold glare. "I don't know if I want to see him."

"Please," Della said. "I'd bet my best bra that's the reason you won. Just to come here to see him."

"What?" Miranda asked. "You want me to say I have to see Perry so you can see Steve? Why don't you just grow some fangs and admit you want to see him?"

Della's eyes grew bright with anger—probably the fangs slur pissed her off—but the vamp was always throwing witch insults at Miranda. Or maybe it wasn't the vamp criticism, but her friend was as miserable about Steve as Miranda was about Perry. Miranda almost felt guilty.

"If I wanted to see Steve, I would be there now! I'm not the coward," Della snapped and her tone pushed Miranda's guilt back. "You pinky-twitching little twit."

The last comment validated Miranda's anger and she rolled her eyes, waiting for Kylie to tell Della to cool it. Kylie was the mediator, the peacekeeper. When she didn't do her job, Miranda turned her eyes on blondie. "Aren't you going to tell her to behave?"

Kylie made a funny face. "Nah, I thought I'd let you two just kill each other and get it over with. It's been a long time coming."

"Can I? Can I kill her?" Della smarted off again. "Please. I know! What if I feed her to the gargoyles?"

"Not funny!" Miranda frowned and looked away from her friends. A part of her knew she was being a bitch, but damn it, she was hurting too much to be anything else. Right then, she felt it. The ominous feeling she'd gotten when she'd been on stage.

"It's back," she said and looked around.

"What?" Della asked.

"Trouble. Trouble's back."

"Define trouble," Della said.

"The kind that brings fireballs." Miranda looked around, left and right, and there, behind a group of Asian tourists, she spotted a mane of red hair. Tabitha stood fifty feet away staring up at the Eiffel Tower. Did that mean she was conjuring it?

"We've got company." Della lifted her nose in the air.

"I know. I already see her," Miranda said, and when she turned back to Della, she spotted two other familiar faces. The twins, Candy and Sandy Gleason, about three hundred feet away caught in the middle of another group of Eiffel Tower admirers.

"Where?" Della snapped.

"Tabitha's there and then—"

"No," Kylie said and raised her face to sniff the air. "She means vampire. There're several close by and they reek of old human blood."

"Yeah, but they're still probably nicer than Tabitha." From the corner of Miranda's eye, she saw a blurry figure swoop past, and it flew around the six Asians with their cell phone cameras focused on the tower.

Miranda watched in horror as the figure swooped down on Tabitha.

"There," Miranda screamed and took off.

Forget being the first to spot the vamp or the first to run, Kylie and Della surged forward, followed by Shawn, and the three of them passed her in a fraction of a second.

Hating her lack of speed, Miranda stopped and watched in horror as the scraggily looking vampire stopped behind Tabitha, reached one hand around her chest, and pressed his other hand on the side of her face. She'd seen it in the movies, the scary-looking position that made it easy to twist and break someone's neck. Fear rose in Tabitha's blue eyes. The same fear clutched Miranda's stomach.

Chapter Eight

Archenemy or not, her heart ached for Tabitha. Regretting her snarky comments about the girl, she recalled preschool when she and Tabitha shared a love of the same cookies, the same nursery rhymes, and anything princess related.

"Stop him!" Miranda screamed. She raised her hand to throw a spell.

"Let her go," Kylie said, her voice a deep rumble as Miranda's spell went on hold. Kylie, the protector, could work more magic than she.

The greasy, dark-haired vamp laughed as if nothing was going to stop him. His dirty clothes and overall appearance marked him as rogue.

The yellow-toothed smile of confidence just meant he didn't have a clue he was up against a protector and a super vampire. He pressed his hand roughly into Tabitha's cheek, but before he could get any rougher, Kylie caught his arm. With little effort, she slung him up and over her head and he landed with a dark thud on the cold ground. Della shot forward in case he tried to get up.

Screams rose from the crowd of tourists and they scurried about like rats without a maze. Then it started raining vampires. Two, three, four. Della and Shawn charged, each taking on two. Kylie took on three.

Miranda's gaze flipped from one fight to the other, then landed on

Tabitha. The girl dropped to her knees and ungracefully lost the contents of her stomach. Miranda got about twenty feet from the girl when the feeling of danger increased. Warning chills ran down her spine. She glanced up and saw the cannon-sized fireball barreling from the sky. Barreling right at Tabitha.

Knowing Della, Shawn, and Kylie were too busy dealing with rogue vamps to see the fireball, Miranda raised her hand, wiggled her pinky, and shrunk the size of the ball to a dime. It hit the ground about two feet from Tabitha. The girl screamed and stood up as if to run.

Shifting her gaze around to see if any more trouble had arisen, Miranda spotted Shawn, now fighting three vamps with a glowing sword. She'd heard about honor swords given to a few warlocks who were gifted with strong integrity and an abundance of magic.

When the fourth vamp came up against Shawn, Miranda decided he could use some help. Holding out her arm, trying to think of a spell that wouldn't be noted by humans, she saw a large, black-and-tan German shepherd and two French bulldogs. "Got this," she muttered. "Attack him." Right as her pinky twitched, she realized her mistake. The last detail she'd held in her dyslexic mind had been Della's comment about all the poop, not the dogs.

In horror, she watched as piles of dog excrement rose from the grassy knoll and were slung at the fourth vamp.

"Oh no," she muttered.

Before she could fix it, a fog, thicker than smoke, rose from the ground. The heavy cloud painted everything a whitish gray and made it impossible to see a foot in front of her.

"Miranda?" Shawn's voice rose in the mist, but it sounded distant.

"I'm here," Miranda answered, and just like that, someone grabbed her. An image of the dirty vamp that had almost broken Tabitha's neck filled her mind. Instinct had her raising her knee to hit the soft spot between his legs, while her mind raced for a curse.

"Damn." She heard someone grunt the word. It took her about a second to recognize that moan as Shawn's.

"Oops," she muttered.

Then, like magic—of course magic—the fog evaporated. The thick cloud became only a pale veil of mist. She saw Shawn cupping his privates and embarrassment wiggled its way into her chest.

"Where the hell did they go?" Della snapped, looking first at Kylie and then turning to look at Miranda and Shawn.

It took a few moments for Miranda to realize who was gone. The vamps. Including the one she'd attacked with dog poop.

"Oh, lordy." She really hated her dyslexic goofs sometimes. But on second thought . . . this might not be one of those times. The rogue vamp who would now go through his life being attacked by any nearby piles of poop deserved it. Didn't he?

Then it hit that the fog had been a ploy for the vampires to escape. But vamps couldn't make fog. Witches and warlocks, and perhaps a chameleon in witch mode, could create fog.

"I don't know where they went," Shawn growled. Miranda cut him a quick look. Pain still hardened his expression, and he had one fist pressed low on his waist.

His gaze shifted to Miranda and she mouthed the words, *I'm sorry.*

Only concern marred his expression as he nodded. Then, taking a step away, he pulled out his phone and she heard him say Burnett's name.

Remembering the fireball, she realized someone else besides the vampires was gone. Breath held, she did a visual search around the park.

"Where's Tabitha?" Miranda voiced her concern and did a full circle hoping to spot the red-haired witch.

"She was right there," Kylie said.

Finally, Miranda spotted her about a hundred feet away. The girl sat on the ground, still clutching her middle, her head down.

Miranda started over.

A low sound reached Miranda's ears as she got closer to Tabitha. The girl hummed. The tune hit a familiar melody in Miranda's head. "Yankee Doodle." The same tune she hummed to help deal with stress. An odd nervous habit she'd picked up from her dad.

Had Tabitha picked the habit up from Miranda when they were in preschool? Miranda wasn't sure, but where else would Tabitha have gotten it?

"It's okay," Miranda said when she got closer.

With spittle on her chin, the redheaded witch glanced up. Fury filled her eyes. "You. I should have known you were behind this."

"I wasn't—"

"What happened?" A voice rang out to Miranda's right. Sienna ran up and dropped to the ground and threw her arms around Tabitha for a quick hug.

"She happened," Tabitha seethed, pushing out of the hug and looking up at Miranda.

"Bullshit!" Della appeared at her side with Kylie. "You might not have noticed, but Miranda shrank a fireball that was targeted at your ass." Della looked at Miranda. "You should have let it take her out. The world would have been a better place."

Tabitha started to raise her hand. Miranda jumped in front of Della. She'd just saved Tabitha's life, but no way would she let the girl do any harm to one of her best friends.

Della pushed Miranda aside and let out a deep hiss. "You even think of twitching that pinky at me and I'll break it off and feed it to some unlucky Parisian frog. I'm not nearly as good-natured as my friend here."

Tabitha, not as dumb as she acted, dropped her hand, but she wasn't completely backing down. "I'm reporting this to that FRU agent."

"Who, me?" Shawn asked, appearing at Miranda's side. "If you—"

"Or do you mean me?" Another deep voice sounded as a quick shadowy flash stopped right beside Shawn. Miranda didn't have to see the owner of the voice to know it was Burnett.

"Or perhaps you could explain why you two went against my orders and left the hotel." He directed his question to Sienna and Tabitha.

"We're not prisoners," Sienna snapped.

"No, you're not. But someone wants you dead." Burnett's tone was deep and angry. "Would you rather be dead?"

When Sienna didn't answer, Burnett added, "Does anyone want to tell me what happened here?"

"I think she's trying to kill me," Tabitha said, glaring at Miranda.

"Why would I want to kill you?" Miranda snapped back.

"Would you quit acting as if you don't know?" Tabitha snapped and got to her feet.

"Know what?" Miranda blasted back and felt Kylie take her by the arm as if to calm her.

Tabitha didn't answer, and started walking away.

"Stop her," Burnett said to Shawn. "Everyone goes back to the apartment until I figure out what's up." He turned to another agent. "Start collecting cameras from the crowd. Take them to the office and start downloading them, tell everyone they can pick them up in a few hours."

Would you quit acting as if you don't know? Miranda kept hearing Tabitha's parting comment. She started to walk with Shawn, wanting answers from Tabitha, but Burnett caught her by her arm. "No. Now's not the time for female drama."

Miranda stopped, but frowned in the redheaded witch's direction. Why did she get the feeling that there was more to Tabitha's little show than just female drama? What could have happened almost fourteen years ago between their moms that could still be worth fighting over?

Four hours later, on her first night in Paris, Miranda sat beside Kylie on the apartment's sofa. Della had been released to go to DeVille with another agent. Before she left, Miranda had apologized for being a bitch. Della had half-smiled and said she'd already forgiven her. Miranda had insisted on a hug, and of course, Della relented, but made it a short one.

That was the thing about the vamp: she might get mad in a flicker of a second, but she was almost as quick to forgive. And Miranda knew that beneath her friend's prickly attitude was a heart of gold.

Sienna and Tabitha sat on the love seat. Tabitha hadn't stopped frowning at Miranda, and it took everything she had not to jump up and demand the girl explain her parting comment from earlier.

Burnett had confiscated all the cameras from the tourists and downloaded the images and video to a laptop. After interviewing, or rather interrogating everyone, he'd connected a projector and they were watching the attack via photos and video on the white wall.

Shawn narrated the images as they flashed. "Here, you can see the fireball. And here's where Miranda shrunk it down to the size of a pea." Shawn's gaze shifted to Tabitha.

When surprise filled her eyes, Miranda knew that Tabitha really hadn't known she'd saved her butt. And if the tightness in the redhead's expression was any indication, she didn't like knowing it.

Miranda looked at the clock on the wall, wishing this would end so she could find out exactly what Tabitha was so pissed about. What was it that Miranda was supposed to know and didn't? The bad blood between them had gone on too long. It was time for answers.

"Okay," Burnett said, pausing the projector. "It seems apparent that Tabitha was the intended victim."

"What? Why do you think that?" Tabitha asked, fear sounding in her voice.

Kylie leaned forward. "The first vampire grabbed you and it appears you were the fireball's target."

"But . . . but . . ." Tabitha started sputtering. "I mean . . . I thought you believed it was someone trying to take out the competition."

"We do," Burnett spoke up.

"Then why didn't they go after Miranda or Sienna?"

"That's what we're trying to figure out," he said.

Burnett sat on a straight-backed chair and turned his gaze to Shawn. "Now, about the fireball stunt, would—?"

"Spell," Sienna interrupted.

Burnett turned to look at the girl. His expression said he wasn't all that fond of her. "Excuse me?"

"We don't perform stunts. We do spells."

He nodded, discontent flashing in his eyes. "Would someone have to be in the vicinity to perform this . . . spell?" He directed his question toward Shawn, but glanced around at Miranda and the other two witches as well.

"It's not impossible to do it from a distance, but it is improbable," Miranda answered.

Shawn nodded at Burnett as if agreeing with her. Sienna and Tabitha did the same.

"So, chances are, the person responsible for the fireball was caught on camera?" Burnett looked at the image on the wall and it was a picture of Sienna.

"I suppose," Shawn said.

"Why are we just discussing the fireball? It was a vampire that almost broke Tabitha's neck," Sienna said as if offended he accused her kind.

"I'm not forgetting," Burnett said. "But I'm pretty sure the vampires were hired help, the real villain is one of your own kind. Perhaps even someone in the competition."

"Wait," Sienna blurted out. "Are you saying *we* are suspects?"

Chapter Nine

Burnett looked at Sienna really hard, and the tilt to his head told Miranda he was about to question the girl and listen to her heartbeat for lies. Did Burnett suspect Sienna of being behind this? Miranda didn't know the witch well enough to make that call.

"Does that disturb you?" Burnett asked.

"Yes, it disturbs me," she said with sass. "Tabitha is my friend. I wouldn't hurt her."

"Were you two together today?"

"No," Sienna said. "I was meeting my parents for dinner when I saw the commotion."

"So, you didn't cause the commotion?"

"Sienna wouldn't do that," Tabitha insisted.

Sienna frowned. "But he has to hear that from me, don't you?"

Burnett didn't pretend. "Yes."

"No, I didn't try to kill Tabitha. And I resent that you think I did."

Miranda tried to read Burnett to see if he caught the girl lying, but Burnett's expression didn't give anything away. Then, remembering Kylie's ability to turn vampire, she looked at her with the question in her eyes.

Kylie nodded, telling her that Sienna was telling the truth.

Sienna's gaze shot to Miranda. "Why aren't you asking *her* questions?

Is it because she goes to your school, and you don't want one of your precious students to be guilty?"

"I'm precious?" Miranda said, sending the girl a fake smile. "Thank you for that compliment."

Burnett let out a low growl. "It's true. My relationship with Miranda Kane prevents me from being suspicious of her. However, evidence guides me in the same direction."

"What evidence?" Sienna asked.

Burnett didn't appreciate being questioned, and his expression said so. "Why would she have saved Tabitha if she was the one attempting to kill her? Any more questions?" he asked in a clipped tone that demanded respect.

Sienna didn't have a comeback.

Neither did Miranda. But probably for different reasons. It felt good—heart gooey, need-a-hug kind of good—knowing that Burnett believed in her. The temptation to jump up and embrace him hit hard. Embrace him like she would her dad. Her dad, whom she'd barely seen these last few months.

It hit her then. Hit her harder than it had earlier. She missed her dad. His work had always kept him on the road, but since she'd signed on full-time to Shadow Falls, it felt as if she barely saw him at all.

Kylie, with her chameleon shifting abilities, must have turned Fae, because she seemed to read Miranda's mood and she leaned over and whispered, "It's gonna be okay." Her shoulder lightly pressed against Miranda's and a sweet calm flowed from her touch. Yup, she was Fae, all right. Only a Fae's touch could ease a heartache.

Burnett turned back to Shawn. "Play the last video."

They all watched another video taken by a tourist who never knew his vacation images would be used in an investigation. This one, however, had a different angle, and showed something the others hadn't.

The poop attack.

Miranda fell back into the leather cushions wishing she could disappear.

"What the hell was that?" Burnett said and replayed it again.

The camera caught the vamp being hit with four or five piles of excrement.

"I never saw that," Shawn said. "I was too busy fighting."

"Me neither," Kylie added, and then she must have picked up on Miranda's emotion because she looked at her.

Miranda nodded ever so slightly.

Burnett looked at Miranda. She wanted so badly to lie—admitting she goobered a spell in front of Shawn, not to mention Tabitha and Sienna, sucked—but her conscience wouldn't let her.

"I saw Shawn had his hands full, and I wanted to help."

"By slinging shit at the vampire?" Sienna asked.

"It worked," Shawn added before Miranda started to explain her screwup. His blue eyes shifted from Sienna to Miranda, and he smiled. Tenderly. Sweetly. "Thank you."

Oh, hell! As nuts as it sounded, it almost felt as if he knew she'd screwed up and was trying to save her from the embarrassment.

Burnett ran a hand through his hair as if worried. "Did you cancel the spell?"

"No, he was trying to kill us."

Burnett chuckled. "Hell, I guess he deserves it." He looked back down at the computer and projector. "Let's go through all of this again and look for anything else unusual. Remember, chances are, the person who sent the fireball is somewhere on one of these cameras."

Watching them all again brought on some flashes of memory for Miranda. When the show ended, she closed her eyes and let her own mental video play on the backs of her eyelids. And it brought on an insight. "You know who I saw there, and I haven't seen in any of the video or photos?"

"Who?" Burnett and Shawn asked at the same time.

"The twins, Candy and Sandy. I saw them in the mix of the crowd."

Burnett turned to Shawn. "I thought you said they were at the hotel?"

"I spoke with Candy when we got back and she said they hadn't left."

Burnett looked back at Miranda. "Are you sure?"

Miranda saw the images again in her mind then she refocused on Burnett. "Yeah. I'm positive."

"You're accusing Sandy and Candy of doing this?" Tabitha asked, her tone jam-packed with sarcasm.

"I didn't accuse them of anything. I said I saw them there."

"Well, I didn't see them." Sienna dropped back on the love seat and crossed her arms over her chest. A tiny smile appeared in her eyes as if she got pleasure from disagreeing with Miranda.

"Did you see them?" Sienna asked Tabitha.

"No," Tabitha said, but with a lot less animosity. Who knew Sienna was a bigger bitch than Tabitha?

"You?" Sienna pointed the question to Kylie. "Did you see the twins?"

"No, but I wasn't looking for them." Anger flashed in Kylie's eyes. "But if Miranda says she saw them, she did." There was something deep and protective in her friend's voice. Sienna ignored it.

Tabitha looked at Shawn. "I suppose you were too busy admiring Miranda to have seen them."

Shawn's frown came on fast. "I was sent to watch out for her."

"Like you don't have a thing for her," Tabitha said. "I saw how you stared at her at the competition, and how you fawned over her when she passed out. Even tonight, you're looking at her like she's a piece of candy and you're a diabetic."

"My feelings for Ms. Kane outside of this case are none of your business." His tone demanded her respect.

"And I'm not candy," Miranda spit out without thinking. Then she wanted to shrink into the sofa cushions. Were Shawn's feelings for her that noticeable? As crazy as it sounded, it made her both uncomfortable and . . . happy. Then, in a twitch of a pinky, she realized she hadn't thought about Perry in the last few hours. Did that mean anything? Had she come all the way to Paris to finally accept his decision—to give their relationship space? Oh, that sucked on so many levels.

And that insight brought on a couple of even more contradicting emotions: relief and guilt.

Relief that she was finally moving in the right direction—meaning emotionally moving away from Perry—and guilt because . . . because she was emotionally moving away from Perry. How could she shift away from him when she loved him? Was it because down deep she still held a thing for Shawn?

Burnett stood up and looked at Shawn and Kylie. "You two hold down the fort here. I think I'll have a little chat with the twins." He started out, but turned and looked back, his gaze shifting to Miranda and then to Sienna and Tabitha. "I hope I don't have to remind you three that you can't leave here. We escaped this incident without having to ship anyone's body back to the U.S., let's not give whoever is doing this another shot at it."

"But you just said that Tabitha was the intended victim," Sienna said.

"For that attempt," Burnett said. "He's already killed two of the girls who were high contenders to make this round of the contest. From where I stand, it appears you are all intended victims. And until I know differently, you will do as I say. Like it or not!"

He left in a flash, a cloud of anxiety lingering in his wake.

A cloud that brought on silence. A silence shattered by the ringing of Miranda's phone. She reached for the cell, hoping it would be her dad, but nope.

She looked at Kylie and whispered, "Oh, crap. It's my mom. If I tell her what happened, she's gonna freak."

Her mom hadn't freaked, probably because Miranda hadn't told her. Well, she'd told her a little, but downplayed the whole thing to make it sound like nothing more than a little inconvenience. *And a little attempted murder.*

"Seriously, it was just a few misbehaving vampires." Miranda stood, wanting to find a private place to chat. Before she got away, Kylie reached over and squeezed her hand, offering a touch of calm. Obviously, she could read Miranda's emotions.

"Does Burnett know?" her mom asked as Miranda stepped into the small kitchen. The door swished closed behind her.

"Yes, he's looking into it." Her "you just lied" alarm didn't completely go off. Downplaying something wasn't completely lying. Besides, her mom was thousands of miles away and wasn't going to be here for a couple days. No reason to get her all panicky.

There was a pause.

"Is Dad home?" Miranda asked, remembering how she'd suddenly missed him earlier.

"No, he was asked to work another week in England."

"He seems to be working more and more lately." Miranda tried to keep her frustration from her voice.

"Yeah. He's a workaholic." A slight note of discontent sounded in her mom's voice. Her mom had never complained about her dad's schedule, she'd accepted it. As a matter of fact, she'd heard her mom tell people that she wasn't sure she could live with a man full-time.

Her parents had never had what you could call a normal relationship. But they seemed happy. For the first time, Miranda worried perhaps her mom was getting lonely. Not that her mom was the type to get lonely. She had the social calendar of a celebrity. If anything, before Miranda had left to go to school at Shadow Falls, she'd often felt she was interfering with her mom's busy schedule.

"So, he's not going to come to Paris?" Miranda's question met silence. "It would only take a few hours to get here by train. Mom?"

"Uh, no. Your dad's not into competitions. You know that, dear."

"Yeah, but I've never been up for high priestess before." Not that this was her dad's dream. Her mom was the one pushing for Miranda to climb the Wicca ladder of success. "Or in France. I just thought he might . . . you know, make an exception." Another pause. "Maybe you could call him and ask. We haven't had any family time in months."

"You're right. We should go skiing in Colorado. Right after Christmas. I think it's his year to work on Christmas day. But I'll mention it when I speak with him."

Her dad, along with a friend, owned several boutique hotels across the U.S. Her mom had never wanted to live out of a hotel room, and other than a couple of times a year, they never stayed at one of her dad's properties.

"Maybe if I call and ask him to come to Paris, he'll do it," Miranda said, feeling secure in her relationship with her father. It was her mom that Miranda had always felt she disappointed.

"It will only make him feel bad if he has to tell you no. Let's not make him feel bad, okay?"

Miranda had heard that line before. When she first realized that most fathers didn't travel so much for their jobs, she complained that her dad wasn't going to be around for a holiday. *It's just a day,* her mother told her, *we can celebrate Christmas or Easter any day.* And they did. Always.

Her family life had never been traditional, but when she considered her friends with more traditional family lives, friends whose parents divorced, and even sued each other for custody of the kids, Miranda decided nontraditional wasn't all that bad.

Sure, her parents argued. Her mom would turn her poor dad into a baboon or a rat, but she always changed him back, and after a few days of not speaking to each other, they always made up. More importantly, Miranda sensed they were happy.

"When is your plane landing in Paris?" Miranda asked in lieu of agreeing to not calling her dad. She missed him, darn it. What would it hurt to call him and ask him to come?

She had never really considered herself a daddy's girl, but realizing someone might be trying to kill you had this girl wanting her first hero.

"I'm not sure. I'll have to check my ticket."

"Okay," Miranda said, and looked back to make sure the door was closed. Now that she had her daddy issues resolved, she decided it was time to tackle a different issue altogether.

"Mom, can I ask you something?"

"Why . . . sure," she replied, yet her tone sounded unsure. "But if this is about sex, let me sit down first. And if you're going to tell me you're pregnant I'm gonna need to fix a drink." Silence spilled into the line while Miranda tried to wrap her head around her mom's response. "Oh, gawd, do I need a drink?"

"No. It's not about sex and I'm not pregnant." Miranda recalled that Della's parents were always accusing her of such things. Rolling her eyes, she sat down at the small kitchen table. "Why would you even think that?"

"Is it about that boy, Peter?"

"Perry, not Peter, and no, it is not about him."

"Okay, then I should be able to handle it standing up and sober."

Miranda inwardly sighed. Who knew her mom was such a drama queen? "What happened between you and Tabitha's mom fourteen years ago?" Miranda heard her mom's deep breath.

"What? Is Mary Esther there?"

Miranda figured Mary Esther was Tabitha's mom. And it seemed odd that her mom would refer to her by her first name. "No."

"So her little twit said something, huh? Ignore her."

"Ignore what? Mom, what happened? Why do I feel as if everyone knows something that I don't?"

All of a sudden, Miranda remembered what she had started to suspect. She and Tabitha shared the premonition gift. Shit! Did that mean . . . ?

Miranda mentally pulled up a vision of Tabitha's mom. The woman had similar features to her mom and was about the same height, and the same body shape. "Mom, are you and Mary Esther related?"

"Why would you ask that?" Her mom's voice inched up to the panic stage.

"Because Tabitha and I share some talents that are mostly common in bloodlines. Tell me. Is Mary Esther like my aunt or something? Is Tabitha my cousin?"

"I can't talk about this now," her mom snapped, and hung up.

Chapter Ten

The kitchen door swung open behind Miranda. Still in a kind of shock, she looked back, half expecting it to be Tabitha. She was wrong.

"How bad was it?" Kylie asked.

It took Miranda a second to realize Kylie was referring to her telling her mom about the whole mess at the Eiffel Tower. "Not too bad. I sugarcoated it. But . . ." Miranda paused to consider how to put this. "But I think . . . I mean, it sounds crazy, but I think Tabitha and I are cousins. I think our moms are sisters."

"Whoa, how did you find that out?"

"I asked. Not that she admitted it, but . . . remember Tabitha and I share the gift of premonition. That usually runs in families. And when I was young, we ended up going to the same day care. My mom and her mom had this big fight and Tabitha got pulled from the school. Mom told me all the fuss was about the cookies."

"Cookies?" Kylie asked and grinned. "And you believed her."

"Hey, I was three. Cookies were a big deal." Miranda stood up. "I didn't see Tabitha again until Mom started forcing me to go to competitions. And right off the bat, she hated me. I couldn't figure it out. But just now I realized how her mom and my mom are similar. About the same height, same body shape, hair color. I mean, it would make sense, right?"

"I guess," Kylie said. "Did your mom deny it?"

"No. But she got all panicky and said she couldn't talk about it, then hung up."

"Has she ever mentioned a sister?"

"No, she said she was an only child. And seeing that she's so into herself, I never doubted it." Miranda sighed.

"What about your grandparents?"

"They died when I was really young. I barely remember them."

"Hey, do you think that's what Tabitha meant when she said for you to stop acting as if you didn't know?"

"Yeah, that's what I think."

"You know what?" Kylie said. "Now that I consider it, you and Tabitha sort of look alike. I mean, she has red hair and blue eyes, but if you just compare facial features, you two could be sisters."

Miranda nodded and looked at the door. Maybe it was time for her and Tabitha to have a talk.

The talk didn't happen. By the time she left the kitchen, Sienna and Tabitha had locked themselves into one of the three bedrooms. Miranda had knocked. Sienna had answered. When Miranda said she wanted to talk to Tabitha, Sienna informed her that Tabitha was resting and didn't want to be disturbed.

Now, two hours later, past midnight, Miranda lay in bed staring at the ceiling, listening to Kylie sleep, and trying not to listen to her own heart break.

It broke over missing Perry. And over her confusion about what she felt for Shawn. It broke over missing her dad. It broke over feeling as if her mother was keeping secrets.

And in a little way it broke over knowing someone might be out to kill her.

Funny how being on someone's hit list hurt less than the other issues. Maybe it was because Miranda really hadn't wrapped her head around it yet.

Right then Miranda heard footsteps outside her door. *Who could that be?*

Throwing back the covers, Miranda tugged on her pink cotton nightshirt, reading the word *princess* written across the front. Giving it a glance, she decided it wasn't indecent, and went and opened the door.

No one was in the hall, but a light flashed from the kitchen doorway as if someone opened the refrigerator. She moved her sock feet down the wood floor to see who was raiding the fridge.

As she inched past the door to another bedroom, the one where Tabitha and Sienna had taken refuge, she heard someone talking. She stopped, half considering knocking and insisting Tabitha come out and talk. But then she heard Sienna say, "Look, Mom, I can't do anything about it. That FRU agent says I have to stay here. Fine, call him and tell him you're picking me up and I'll go."

Was Tabitha asleep? Or was she the one in the kitchen?

Right before stepping into the doorway, she realized it might be Shawn. Oh, damn! There was a good chance it was Shawn. And considering the time, he could be . . . well, half naked. Did she want to have a late-night encounter with a partially clothed Shawn?

Her heart did a couple of somersaults. The answer was both a yes and a no. She considered turning around, but decided to just take a peek and make sure it wasn't Tabitha before running. It had nothing to do with her trying to envision Shawn half naked.

Moving her head past the door frame, she peered inside. Not a half-naked Shawn. Not that she could see the face. Yet the person who had their head buried in the fridge wore a light blue nightgown. Not Shawn.

The person stood up, and red hair swung down her back.

It was time—time for her and Tabitha to have that talk.

"Hey." Miranda stepped into the room.

Tabitha, obviously startled, yelped, swung around, and hurled a condiment bottle at her.

Miranda ducked. The bottle whizzed over her head and smacked against something.

She turned around. The bottle had landed on a half-naked Shawn—a very nice-looking half-naked Shawn. Wearing only a pair of boxers, he held a bottle in his hand. Across his bare and gorgeous chest was a spray of red goo.

Ketchup.

"Sorry," Tabitha offered and then let out a sudden snicker. "I . . . she startled me." She pressed a hand over her lips.

Miranda couldn't help it. She chuckled as well.

Shawn glanced down at his chest, moved into the kitchen a few steps, and placed the opened bottle on the table. He looked up, and his blue eyes settled on Miranda. His warm gaze swept down and up her body. Hadn't she deemed this nightshirt decent? Why did she suddenly feel half naked herself?

"I'm glad I could entertain you two," he said in a sleepy voice and walked out.

Miranda watched him leave, noting he looked as good going as he did coming. Then she wanted to cover her eyes thinking she shouldn't have noticed.

"It's nothing." Shawn's voice echoed from the hall. "Just ketchup." Footsteps continued, two sets. One leading away and one coming closer.

Kylie appeared in the door frame. "Everything okay?"

"Yeah," Miranda said. "I surprised Tabitha, and she . . . threw a bottle of ketchup. It hit Shawn."

"Oh." Kylie leaned back on her heels and looked down the hall as if watching Shawn go. When she turned back a smile was on her lips. "Did he get mad?"

"Just a little annoyed." Miranda grinned. Then she tilted her head to the side, cutting her eyes at Tabitha, hoping Kylie would understand that she wanted to talk to the redhead.

Kylie must have gotten the message. "Okay, I'll go back to bed." She walked away, leaving Miranda and Tabitha alone.

Miranda turned and faced Tabitha. Her hair hung loose, and without any makeup, she looked younger . . . and . . . familiar. Suddenly, Miranda could see what Kylie had mentioned earlier. She and Tabitha did sort of look alike.

Were they cousins? If so, how sad was it that they'd been kept apart all this time. And for what? An argument between sisters?

Tension seemed to rise from the tile floor and crowd the room.

"Why did you do it?" Tabitha asked.

"Do what?" Miranda shifted on her feet.

"Save my life. Why?"

Miranda considered the question and then shrugged. "It wasn't as if I thought about it. I saw the fireball and just did it."

"Are you sorry you did it?" Tabitha asked.

"No," Miranda said and tried to find a way to figure out if she was right about them being related.

Tabitha frowned. "Then you are a better person than I am, because I don't know if I'd have done it for you."

"Nice to know," Miranda replied, trying not to be too offended, but how could she not? The girl would have let the fireball fry her butt.

"You hate me that much?" Miranda asked.

"I hate your mother that much." Tabitha clutched her fists at her sides.

"Why? Just because your mom hates my mom, you hate her?" Miranda asked. "Don't you think—"

"That's only part of it." Tightness deepened her tone.

Miranda tried to make sense of what Tabitha was saying, and finally gave up. "What's the other part? What happened between them?"

Tabitha just stared. "You really don't know, do you?"

"I think I do," Miranda said and when Tabitha didn't chime in, Miranda decided to say it. "It's apparent that we share talents, so that would make us blood."

Tabitha nodded, slowly, her expression one of pain as if admitting it hurt. "Sucks, doesn't it?"

Miranda rolled her eyes. The girl could just kiss her grits! Miranda wasn't all that crazy about being related to her either.

"So our mothers . . . they were sisters, right?" Miranda asked.

"What?" Astonishment flashed in Tabitha's eyes. "You really don't know, do you?"

"Know . . . what?" Miranda asked. When all Tabitha did was gape at her, Miranda added, "Holy hell! Just tell me."

She would have loved to fake it, pretend she knew the secret. Frankly, Miranda didn't like feeling ignorant, but her need for answers wiped out the embarrassment.

Tabitha shook her head as if in pity. "How could you not have figured it out? Are you stupid?"

Chapter Eleven

Stupid? Oh, Miranda did not like that word!

"Well, Miss Smarty Pants, why don't you just fill me in!" Miranda seethed. She cupped her hands at her sides to keep from wiggling her pinky at the girl to give her pimples.

"They aren't sisters. We are!"

Miranda's breath caught. She remembered what Kylie had said. *Now that I consider it, you and Tabitha sort of look alike. I mean, she has red hair and blue eyes, but if you just compare facial features, you two could be sisters.* Her mind started spinning. "How . . . how could that be possible?"

"Your slut of a mother had sex with my dad, that's how!"

"My mom's not—"

"Please! Figure it out, or do you suck at math, too? I'm five months older than you."

"Whoa! Stop!" Miranda held up her hand, her pinky itching to send some nasty spell Tabitha's way. "First, my mother's not a slut and second . . ." She didn't have a second. Yes, she did. "My parents have been married since—"

"They aren't married! He's married to my mom! She was pregnant with me when your mom threw herself at my dad."

"No," Miranda said, realizing how stupid this all was. "My dad's name is Kane and yours is—"

"Yeah, I know he also goes by Austin Kane, and your mom had her name changed to Kane. Hence, you are a Kane. But his real name is Austin Evans. I know because I've seen his birth certificate. He was born in England. My mother is Irish. They met and married there."

"No," Miranda snapped. "You're lying. This is like a mean trick, or something."

Kylie appeared in the doorway behind Tabitha. No doubt the arguing had roused her again. "What's wrong?" Kylie asked.

Tabitha ignored Kylie. "This is no trick! Don't be a fool." Tabitha's voice rose with anger. "What does he tell you when he leaves? That he's working? Because that's what he tells me. Of course, unlike you, I'm not foolish enough to believe it."

Everything in Miranda's life suddenly felt like a lie. She felt like a fool. "If you're lying to me, I swear I'll . . ."

"You'll what? Turn me into a skunk, like you did to your friend's cat? Or are you going for a kangaroo, this time? Not that it matters. Because I'm not lying. And I can see in your eyes that you already know I'm not. Accept it, Miranda. Your mother is a slut and you're nothing more than a bastard child."

Fury rose through Miranda. She clutched her fists. She wanted nothing more than to twitch her pinky and turn the twit into something nasty—something worse than a skunk. And she would have if there wasn't doubt eating away at her heart. As much as she hated to admit it, there was truth in this witch's words.

"You don't know if it's true," Kylie said as she followed Miranda back to the bedroom a few minutes after Tabitha took off to hers. "It could just be a lie."

"Do you think so?" Miranda wanted to believe it. Wanted it so badly that her heart trembled. But damn it, it made sense. Her dad's work schedule, her mom hating Tabitha's mom. It had never been about cookies. Did that mean . . . ? No, she couldn't believe the part about her mom being a slut. She could not believe her mom would be happy being the other woman. Then again, there was the fact that Tabitha was five months older than Miranda. *Oh, hell, maybe my mom is a slut!* Tears stung her eyes.

She snatched her phone from the bedside table. "I'm gonna find out."

She went to contacts. Found the word "Daddy." Her finger hovered right over the word. Those tears that had stung her sinuses now filled her eyes and she felt the warm drops roll down her cheeks. How could he have lied to her all this time? How could her mom accept his lies? How could Miranda love the man and know so little about him?

"How do I ask him?" She looked up at Kylie, blinking away the blurry wetness.

"I . . . don't know. Just ask."

"And say what? Hey, Dad, do you have another family you haven't told me about?"

Kylie, sensing her emotion, dropped down beside her and hugged her tight. "It's going to be okay."

"No, it's not," Miranda said, even as the calm emotion flowed from her friend's touch, but it wasn't enough to stop the knot of pain throbbing inside her. "Tabitha's right, I'm a fool not to have figured this out. He's only home a couple of weeks a month."

"Look, I know how you feel. It's hard to realize that our parents aren't the people we grew up thinking they are. I learned my dad was really just my stepdad, and he was boinking his intern who was only a few years older than me. My mom had been lying to me about who my dad was, and keeping me from my real grandparents. But believe me when I tell you that while it hurts realizing they aren't the perfect people we want them to be, it doesn't mean they don't love you. If anything, learning the truth has helped my relationship with both my mom and my stepdad."

Miranda wiped her eyes. "Having an affair is one thing, but having another family is . . . is . . . How can that ever be okay? If what Tabitha says is true, I didn't even know my own father's real name." A moan left her lips. Even to her own ears, it sounded pathetic, but she couldn't help it.

She felt pathetic.

Glancing down at her phone, she touched the word "Daddy."

"Do you want me to leave?" Kylie stood up.

"I don't care," Miranda said. "I'll tell you everything anyway." She always did. She and Della were her sounding boards—sometimes she didn't even know how she felt about things until she talked to them.

She put the phone to her ear, and held her breath waiting for the phone to ring. Her heart started to race with the first ring. She looked up at her friend. "Shit! What am I going to say to him?"

Kylie simply made a face as if to say she didn't have an answer. "Maybe you aren't ready to talk to him yet."

As tempting as it was to hang up, Miranda didn't. Turned out, she didn't have to. On the fifth ring, the call went to her dad's voice mail.

A big wave of relief washed over her. Kylie was right. She wasn't ready to tackle this. Not with her dad at least. But there was one parent she was accustomed to arguing with. One that was possibly a home wrecker.

She hung up and immediately started to call her mom, but then quickly changed her mind.

Tossing her cell down on the bed, she reached for a pillow to hug. As crazy as it was, her first thought was that she wanted Perry. To have him hold her. To hear him tell her it would be okay. His touch, his tenderness, his kisses, they always made her feel okay. Even more than Kylie and Della, Perry had felt like her soul mate. Now her soul mate was gone and he hadn't even bothered to call her. Hadn't even come to see her and she was here in Paris.

Rolling onto her side, she looked up at Kylie, who stared down at her with empathy.

"I used to think I was the lucky one," Miranda said. "Your home life was crazy and then Della's dad being accused of murder. Sure, my mom can be a bitch about me not being high priestess material, but I thought at least I didn't have the crazy kind of problems you two did. Now I realize I'm not the lucky one, I'm just the stupid one who didn't see it."

"You are not stupid!" Kylie dropped back down on the bed. "You trusted them. Trusting people you love doesn't make you stupid. I know, because I trusted my parents all those years, and they were hiding stuff, too."

Miranda closed her eyes, hoping to hide the tears she felt forming. "I trusted Perry, too."

Kylie put her hand on Miranda's shoulder. Warmth and peace flowed from her touch. "Love makes us vulnerable," Kylie said. "But to live without it makes us miserable."

"I'm miserable now," Miranda said.

"I know, but it will pass. I promise."

Miranda just lay there with her eyes closed, her arms wrapped so tightly around a pillow that even it longed to breathe. As a few more tears slipped from her closed eyes, she craved the numbness of sleep.

Miranda found some reprieve with slumber, but only for a bit when something caused a big shift in her mattress. Shooting up, thoughts of rogue vampires chasing away the calm of sleep, she saw a figure sitting on the end of her bed and knew she was only partially right. Vampire, yes. Rogue, no.

"Hey," Della said and Miranda spotted a look of defeat in her eyes.

"You're back," Kylie said, sounding sleepy, and leaning up on her elbow.

"Did you find your uncle?" Miranda asked.

"No," Della said, a frown pulling her lips. "It appears he had come and gone by the time I arrived. But you want to know something crazy? I could swear I got a weak scent of Chase when I got close to this building."

"You think he was here?" Kylie asked.

"No, I'm sure it's just someone with similar DNA."

"Sorry," Miranda and Kylie said at the same time.

"It's okay," Della said without a lot of confidence. "I'm not giving up. I can't. But enough about me. Let's talk about you." Della tilted her head to the side and studied Miranda. "You look upset. Is everything okay?"

Knowing that lying to a vampire was useless, Miranda shook her head and tears formed in her eyes. "No, it's not okay. My daddy has another family. Tabitha is my half-sister."

"No shit!" Della said. "Wait, Tabitha, is she the horse-crap bitch?" Della asked.

Miranda nodded. "My whole life is a lie."

"Wow, that does suck." Della made an odd face and glanced at Kylie and then back to Miranda. "Yikes . . . uh . . . this might not be a good time, but I found something else while I was away."

"What?" Miranda asked, hoping she sounded more interested than she felt. Down deep, all she wanted was to go back to sleep.

Della's gaze shifted back to Miranda. "A huge pterodactyl with bright blue eyes."

Miranda's breath caught. "You . . . you saw Perry."

Della nodded. "Yup."

Tears prickled Miranda's eyes. "Did he even ask about me? Wait!" She threw up her hands as if to block any words. "Don't answer that. I don't care." She pulled her knees to her chest. "To me, he doesn't exist anymore. He's a nonissue. Not important. Doesn't matter."

"Actually . . . it does matter. You see, we have a little problem." Della frowned. "And it's not exactly little. It's about six feet tall and weighs in at—"

"What?" Miranda asked. "I'm too tired to handle riddles. Just tell me."

"All righty . . . it's Perry . . . he kind of followed me here."

"Kind of?" Miranda asked.

"Okay, he followed me."

"He's here?" Miranda jumped up and stood on the bed. "Here? Now?"

"Yup." Della glanced up at Miranda, who was bouncing up and down on the mattress in excitement. "In the living room. He wants to see you. He's been away a few days and didn't know you were here. Do you want me to chase him off? I'll probably have to hurt him because he was pretty adamant about seeing you. But for you, I'll do it."

"No." Her mind spun. "I need clothes." She jumped off the bed and yanked open her suitcase, which was on top of the dresser. She tossed clothes over her shoulder, looking for her perfect blouse and jeans. The ones she knew Perry liked. The ones she packed especially to wear when she saw him.

Her heart thumped with excitement. Her skin felt supersensitive.

After almost four weeks, she was finally going to see him.

As crazy as it seemed, she recalled the game of killing the blue-eyed shape-shifter. Then she remembered that in the end, that shape-shifter lived but had killed her. Stabbed her, right in the heart.

Like it or not, she knew Perry still had that power to hurt her.

Chapter Twelve

As Miranda stepped out of the bedroom, she heard voices. Even with her heart on the chopping block, her palms itched and the air tasted sweeter as she took the last steps to the doorway.

Perry was here. He wanted to see her.

The sweetness faded when the first thing she saw was Shawn, still half naked, his arms crossed and a frown dominating his expression. His gaze shot to her. "You don't have to see him if you don't want to," he said, his tone deep. Was that a touch of hurt she heard in his tone?

She looked across the room and her heart leapt at the sight of the shape-shifter. He wore jeans—they appeared a little tighter than he normally wore—and a green long-sleeved polo shirt. His hair, blond with a few loose locks, looked a little mussed the way it did after he'd flown or maybe after one of their make-out sessions. His eyes were their normal bright azure, and those baby blues were on her. Staring, drawing her closer. Emotion flashed in those liquid pools of color and she felt as if that emotion echoed inside of her.

"Do you want him to leave?" Shawn asked again, and he uncrossed his arms, showcasing his bare chest, but damn if she already hadn't forgotten the half-naked warlock was even in the room.

Miranda glanced back at him, and she hated knowing this might hurt him, but she couldn't, wouldn't send Perry away.

"No. It's fine. I want to see him."

She saw the way Shawn's eyes reflected disappointment.

When she looked back at Perry, his eyes were brighter.

"Now that we've got that settled," he said. His deep, familiar voice sounded like music to her ears and his tight focus stayed on Shawn. Inhaling deeply, as if fighting some other impulse, he glanced back to her. "Would you like to take a walk with me, so we might have some privacy?"

The emphasis he put on the word "privacy" seemed to mean something. Had he already picked up on Shawn's interest in her? If so, was Perry about to morph into some superbeast and try to teach the warlock a lesson?

Standing frozen, feeling a bit overwhelmed, she just stared.

Perry repeated, "A walk? It's a nice night."

The word "yes" danced on her lips, when Shawn spoke up again. "Sorry. She can't leave the apartment. I'm in charge of her care."

She turned to Shawn, slightly annoyed. "A quick walk. We won't be long."

"No." His frown deepened. "Sorry, Burnett's orders were clear. No one leaves."

"Burnett trusts me," Perry said, his tone deepening with anger as his eyes grew brighter with the same emotion. For a second she feared he would shift and start trouble. He didn't.

"Perhaps," Shawn said. "Even as misguided as that may be, it's not you he's worried about. She might be in danger and I'm the agent hired to make sure nothing happens to her."

"As if I would let anything happen to her?" Perry countered.

Shawn's gaze flipped back to Miranda. She shook her head slightly, pleading for him not to do this. He seemed to understand, because she saw his wide chest expand as if taking in a pound of oxygen.

"You can have the privacy of the living room." He turned and walked back into the hall leading to the third bedroom.

She watched Shawn go—feeling his unhappiness—before turning back to Perry. The shape-shifter's gaze was on her, but brighter—anger always did that to him.

They stared at each other for several minutes. Emotions ran

though her chest like wild horses. She'd missed him so damn much. She loved him. She was so angry at him. How could he put her through all this?

As that hurt swelled up in her heart, it bumped into the other recent painful realization about her dad.

"Hey," Perry said.

"Hey," she repeated and took a few steps closer. But it wasn't as close as she wanted. She wanted his arms around her. His lips against hers. She wanted him to make everything that hurt inside her go away. He could do that.

He had in the past. But never had that hurt been caused by him.

His gaze shifted to the door where Shawn had disappeared. "So . . . ?"

"So what?" she asked, not wanting to explain anything about Shawn, not even sure she should. There really wasn't anything to explain.

"You look . . . nice." His voice softened.

And then she softened, too. She nodded and took another step closer.

"Your hair . . . You decided not to streak it anymore."

"You don't like it?" she asked.

He studied her. "I like you. I don't care what color your hair is." He took the next few steps—closing the distance between them.

His scent, like fresh outdoor air, filled her senses and she took a deep breath, greedy for more. Her hands ached to reach for him, but her pride made that move difficult. Mentally, emotionally, she'd been reaching for him for four weeks. He'd pushed her away. He hadn't even called her.

Slowly, he lifted a hand and brushed a strand of hair from her cheek.

His touch sent a powerful bolt of emotion to her chest. It took everything she had not to fall against him.

"I've missed you so damn much," he said.

Me, too! "Really?" she asked. "Normally, I think you call people when you miss them." She wasn't sure where she got the backbone to say that, but suddenly she realized she deserved to know.

He lowered his hand and head. For several beats of silence he stared at the floor and didn't move. Finally he lifted his gaze again. "I was afraid."

"Of what?"

"That if I talked to you, I would have said screw the school and come running back to you."

"Back to the girl you broke up with? That seems odd." Her sinuses stung and she felt tears forming.

"Don't you get it, Miranda? I broke up with you because I wasn't sure that I could ever control my power, and if I couldn't then . . . I'd never be able to live a normal life, not in the human world. And I know your plans for your life, you've told me them a hundred times." A sad shade of blue touched his eyes. "Those plans don't include hiding or hiding a husband. I wouldn't fit in your world. I'd hold you back. You deserve to have what you want."

"Says who? Who decides what I deserve? I thought that was my decision?" A few tears fell. "Do you want to know something? I never thought I deserved better than you . . . not until you broke my heart. Do you know how miserable I've been waiting on you to call? I took up killing shape-shifters."

His eyes widened.

"A game!" she said, rolling her eyes. "But I don't even like games. Especially killing games."

He nodded then glanced down again. "I'm sorry. Maybe breaking up was wrong, but—"

"Maybe?" she said, seething. How could he stand here and not see how hurt she'd been? How could he feel any justification in what he'd done? Was this what she was going to get from her dad, too? Some lame excuse for screwing up and hurting others?

"Oh, I can't believe you!" For the first time she understood her mom's inability to resist turning her dad into a baboon when he infuriated her. Her pinky begged to be used and she gripped her hands to hold back the temptation.

Perry stood there, looking too good, looking sad and frustrated at the same time. "Is this your way of trying to tell me that *this* is exactly what it looks like?"

"*This,* what?" she asked.

"This . . . him." Perry waved toward the hall where Shawn had disappeared. "Mr. I'm-Too-Sexy-For-My-Shirt guy!"

His remark pushed several emotions back and anger took the lead. "What do you think it is?" she asked.

His frown deepened. "I can tell when a guy is interested in a girl."

"I'm surprised. Because you totally suck at telling when a girl is interested in a guy."

"What? Are you saying you're not interested in him or that you are?"

"I'm saying you suck at knowing. You sure as heck didn't realize how I felt about you when you . . . broke it off and broke my heart. If you did, you wouldn't have done it. Wouldn't have hurt me like this."

He took a step closer, his eyes stared right into hers and her heart clutched. "I didn't mean to hurt you."

"Well, you did."

He tucked his hands into his jeans and took another step. So close that when she glanced up, all she could see was his face. He lowered his head just an inch and his forehead touched the top of hers. Now she could only see his lips. So close. Crazy how many nerve endings one could feel from a casual touch of foreheads.

"I'm sorry." His head shifted. His nose brushed against hers. His lips came to the edge of her mouth. Brushing her cheek ever so lightly, a whisper away from her mouth. "I missed you. Missed you so damn much."

Her heart thumped in her chest, so loud, she was certain he could hear it. She wanted his mouth on hers so badly, but should she . . . Should she even want it after he'd put her through hell?

Did this wanting mean she forgave him? Yes. A little. Maybe. Oh, hell, she wasn't even sure.

"I'm coming home in a couple of weeks." His words came so low and so close to her lips, she could almost taste him.

And she wanted to taste him. She'd missed his kisses, his warm mouth, his tongue against hers. His hands touching her in intimate places. Her knees felt weak. And she wanted more. She wanted him.

So attentive to his mouth, and the desires running through her, it took her a second to hear the words he'd said.

Her breath caught. "You are? You're coming home?"

He nodded. And each slight shift of his head brought his lips to her cheek. The nearness made her dizzy.

Recalling why he'd come here, why he broke up with her, she cut her eyes up at him. "So did they help you?"

"Have I turned into a lion and mauled the guy in the next room yet?" A touch of mirth sparked in his eyes.

"No," she said and while she got his humor she realized the old Perry might have done just that. He had a hard time dealing with emotions.

"Do you know how much I want to maul him?" he asked.

"Probably as much as I wanted to kick your butt for breaking up with me." She got a little more resolve then. As badly as she wanted to wrap her arms around him and tell him everything was okay, she didn't.

It wasn't okay. You couldn't hurt someone like that and just expect them to forgive you. Well, not immediately. Time. Maybe in time.

"Do you still love me?" he asked. The side of his face pressed against her temple.

She considered how to answer that. "I do." She couldn't lie. "But I'm still hurt. And all that hurt is mixed up with the love and I'm confused."

"Then I guess I have some making up to do when I get back."

She nodded and let herself feel his closeness. It felt wonderful. Too wonderful. And she felt too weak to fight it off. "You should probably . . . I'm tired. And tomorrow I have to . . ."

"I'm going to be there tomorrow at your competition."

"Tomorrow is just the practice. The real competition is on Wednesday. But it's not open to the public."

"Then I'll sneak in," he said.

Being a shape-shifter, he could do that.

"I'll be there," he said.

All of a sudden she wasn't sure if she was ready for him to leave. She swallowed. "I'll call tomorrow and see if I can have them put your name on the list. You won't have to sneak in."

"Good," he said and his body brushed a little nearer. So close her breasts came against his wide chest. "Can I kiss you?" he whispered. "Just one. One little kiss."

Air left her lips. The exhale sounded like a sigh.

"I'll take that as a yes." He smiled and then that smile and those wonderful lips met hers.

She wasn't even sure who ended the kiss. If it was her, or him. Probably her, because the magic of it had started to fade and the hurt that he'd caused slowly rose to the surface.

He reached up and put a palm on each of her cheeks. His forehead lowered ever so slightly and he studied her eyes.

"I'm so sorry I hurt you," he said. "And I know you don't believe me, but I did it because I do care. And I'm going to do everything in my power to fix this."

She inhaled and words slipped out before she could stop them. "I'm not sure you can fix this."

"Watch me," he said with determination.

She didn't say anything. Part of her wanted to believe him. Okay, most of her wanted to believe him. But the hurt from her heart, and not just the Perry hurt, but Daddy hurt, swelled up inside her.

"What else is wrong?" he asked, his gaze soft, caring, and all-knowing.

She swallowed, felt the knot in her throat, and didn't think she could talk. He always did that. It was as if he could read her by looking into her eyes.

"Are you worried about the case? I'm not going to let anyone hurt you, if that's what it is." He used his thumb to brush a tear from beneath her lashes. "Della told me all about the threat. I'm sure Burnett is all over it, and now I am, too."

She shook her head. "It's not just that."

"What else?"

"Do you remember Tabitha, the girl—"

"The one you went to preschool with and caught spying on you at Shadow Falls?"

Miranda nodded, a swell of emotion tightening her chest when she realized he remembered. How many guys remembered the little details of their girlfriend's life?

"She's my half-sister."

"Damn," Perry said. "So your dad had an affair with her mom when your mother was pregnant?"

Miranda had to swallow before she could tell him the truth. Or at least, the truth Tabitha had told her. "She's older." She took a step back and swiped at a few tears lingering on her cheek. "She says that her mom and my dad were married. That my mom is . . . the one who had the affair."

"Oh." He frowned. "Have you asked your parents?"

"I called my dad, but he didn't answer, and I didn't leave a message. I didn't know how to ask him." She swallowed another painful lump down her throat. "My mom is on her way here."

"Is your dad coming?" Perry asked.

She shook her head. "He never was into the competitions." That's when she realized the reasons for that. "I wonder if this is why? Did he know Tabitha was going to be competing in the same competitions as me?"

Perry stood there as if in thought. "I'm gonna say something and I'm not sure it's going to help, but it might." He frowned. "As bad as your situation is, at least he was in both of your lives. Both my mom and dad left me, Miranda. And while I tell myself that it doesn't matter, at times . . . like these past four weeks, missing you and feeling so lonely, it felt like it matters. So I don't care how imperfect your parents are, it could be worse. You father, or even both your parents could have chosen not to be there at all."

He inched close again and put his arms around her. She leaned her head to his chest and they just stood there. His arms around her. Her chest against his chest.

They didn't move, or they didn't until the front door to the apartment shot open. Perry swung her behind him to face the intruder. A deep protective growl rang out.

Chapter Thirteen

Miranda felt the tingling current of concern surge through Perry's back as he turned to the door. An electrical buzz radiated from him, telling her he was preparing to shift into something fierce. She wasn't however, ready to let him do all the work to protect them. She lifted her hand, pinky ready.

"When did you get back?" the deep voice asked and tension shattered.

Miranda recognized Burnett's voice and lowered her pinky.

"This evening," Perry answered, frustration sounding in his tone and his eyes brightened. "I would have been here sooner had I known you all were here."

Burnett nodded. "I called and spoke with your instructor, Mr. DeLeon. We decided it could wait until you were back from your assignment."

"I would have liked to have been included in that decision." Perry's shoulders tensed.

"You are here now, that's what matters," Burnett replied. He moved closer and pressed a hand on Perry's shoulder. "It's good to see you. I've missed your presence at Shadow Falls."

She sensed some of Perry's tension lessen. The relationship between Burnett and Perry had always been close. Not everyone knew it, but when Perry had gone into his first home, Burnett, already a teen, had been there as well. So in a way, Burnett was like an older brother to Perry. It had been because of Burnett that Perry had come to Shadow Falls.

"I've missed being there," Perry said as he shuffled his feet slightly. "Did Mr. DeLeon tell you my news?"

Burnett smiled. "Of course he did. I'm proud of your progress."

Miranda suddenly felt bad that she hadn't had more interest in his accomplishments. But maybe she'd have been more invested if he hadn't used those accomplishments as a meter to decide if they would stay together.

Miranda suddenly remembered where Burnett had gone this evening. "Did you speak with the twins?"

He nodded. Footsteps echoed down the hall. Kylie and Della walked into the room. Kylie walked right up to Perry and gave him a tight hug. "I've missed you."

"Same here," Perry said and embraced her back.

Suddenly, Shawn showed up—with his shirt on this time. His gaze shifted to Miranda, and she spotted the disappointment in his eyes again. She glanced away, unsure why she felt guilt, but she did. Just a touch.

As soon as Perry spotted Shawn, he dropped his arms from around Kylie. His smile turned upside down and he shifted closer to Miranda.

"Who are the twins?" Perry questioned.

"Fellow contestants in the competition," Burnett offered. "They claimed to have been at the hotel during the last attack, but Miranda spotted them on the scene."

"And?" Miranda asked.

"They admitted to being there. Said they initially lied because they were afraid of going against my advice not to leave the hotel."

"And were they lying again?" Della asked.

"No," Burnett said, "they were speaking the truth. That or their hearts can lie."

"So you are looking at one of the contestants for doing this?" Perry asked.

"Or someone who has something to gain from a person's win."

"So it could be friends or family of a contestant," Perry said and Burnett nodded. "Are you considering it could be one of the contestants from another country?"

"There have been no threats to any of the contestants other than those from the U.S.," Burnett said. "Tomorrow morning I plan to call a meeting with the parents of our competitors. Hopefully, that will give us some insight."

"I don't think my mom will be here yet," Miranda added.

Burnett glanced at her. "She's already here. She arrived a few hours after we did yesterday."

"No, I spoke with her and . . ." Miranda recalled how her mom had talked around the question of when she was arriving. Why would she lie to her? What the hell was she hiding?

"And what?" Burnett asked.

Instantly realizing this might give Burnett the wrong impression—as if her mom might be connected to the murders—she had to kick her brain into high gear to find an answer.

"I just assumed she hadn't left yet." It wasn't a lie. Not a complete one, so hopefully her heart rate wouldn't put Burnett on alert. The fact that it alarmed Miranda was another matter altogether.

Thirty minutes later, Miranda, Kylie, and Della climbed into the one full-sized bed in the bedroom. They rested shoulder to shoulder—with Miranda in the middle. Not that the arrangement was all that strange—many nights at the cabin they'd all piled into Della's full-sized bed.

But being in Paris, it felt . . . different.

"Lights off or on?" Kylie asked.

"Off," Miranda said.

Kylie shifted and the room went black. Then she settled back on the mattress.

Burnett had insisted that they all needed to get some rest before the sun rose. Perry hadn't tried to kiss her good-bye, but she sensed he'd been considering it. Her tiny step away from him must have told him she didn't like the idea.

She'd already let him kiss her once and she wasn't sure it had been a good idea. So instead of trying to kiss her, he'd run the back of his hand down her forearm. His touch held so much emotional current, it had hurt.

It still hurt, but her mind wasn't stuck on the Perry issue alone. She was still wondering about her mother and the reason she might have let Miranda believe she hadn't arrived in Paris yet. It had to be about Tabitha and her mom, didn't it?

Miranda closed her eyes. Thinking of her mom as a slut, the other woman, was only slightly better than thinking of her as a murderer. Didn't her mom have more pride than that?

"Do you not want to talk about it?" Kylie asked.

Miranda, knowing she was talking to her, pushed her head deeper into the pillow. "About what?"

"Please!" Della snapped. "You are so cram-packed with crap it's oozing out your ears. And I'm so close to you, it's grossing me out. Just spill it, witch."

Emotion tightened Miranda's throat and she turned her head slightly to stare through the dark room at the crude vamp. "Spill what?"

"Two things," Della said. "Why did you lie to Burnett? And what happened with you and Mr. Perry?"

Miranda's breath caught. "Did it come off as a lie?"

Kylie shifted again and the light came on. "Not exactly."

"We just know you," Della offered. "When you're trying to cover up something, you always shuffle your feet like a cat trying to cover up a deposit in his litter box." She paused. "So what's up?"

"Why is it that you think I'm supposed to share everything with you and you never tell us anything?"

"It's too late to argue," Kylie said. "If you don't want to talk, we're just gonna sleep."

When no one spoke up, the light went off. The mattress shifted as Kylie got comfortable again.

"What have I not told you?" Della hissed into the darkness and shifted onto her side, propping herself up on her elbow.

"Steve," Miranda said. "Or are you gonna pretend like you didn't see him?"

"Yeah, that's what I'm pretending, so leave it alone."

"Do you still love Chase?" Miranda asked.

"I don't want to. I don't want to feel anything for him. He lied. Over and over again."

"But . . . ?" Miranda asked as Kylie sat up and rested against the bed's headboard again. This time, however, she didn't turn on the light.

"It's the bond thing," Della said. "It must be. I don't feel . . . right. Like part of me is missing."

"Love feels a little like that," Kylie said. "I'll bet I've called Lucas six times since we've been here."

"Lucas hasn't deceived you," Della said, hurt sounding in her voice.

"Yeah, he did. He was going to get engaged behind my back. So he sort of did deceive me," Kylie said. "But you forgive because you love them."

"Maybe she doesn't love Chase, but she loves Steve," Miranda said and looked at Della. "Could that be a possibility?"

"I don't know." Della ran her hands through her hair. "At this point, I'm not sure I want to love anyone. I hate feeling my happiness depends on someone else." She went to the window and pulled back the curtain and stared out into the night.

"I know the feeling," Miranda said with a sigh.

Della turned around and looked at her. "So you and Perry didn't jump back on the merry-go-round of love?"

"He kissed me," Miranda said.

"And what kind of kiss was it?" Della asked.

"Good. And bad. I'm still so mad. It's like I can't turn the mad off. I know I love him, but I still want to hurt him for what he did to me."

"Maybe you should. Give him an ass kicking."

"No," Kylie said. "Your anger will go away. It just fades."

"Maybe it doesn't happen like that with everyone," Della said. "You are just the sweet, forgiving type."

"I'm not that sweet," Kylie said. "I hate it when you act like I'm a goody-two-shoes."

Miranda and Della looked at each other and then back at the chameleon. "When the shoe fits," Miranda said and offered Kylie a sympathetic smile. "But we wouldn't change you if we could."

"Too sweet." Della pointed to Kylie, then moved her finger to Miranda. "Too flighty." And then pointed at herself. "Too pissy. We're quite a team." Della giggled and dropped back on the bed. "I feel as if we should be sitting at our kitchen table with Diet Cokes."

"That's a good idea." Miranda zapped them three Cokes. They all leaned back on the bed's headboard and the sound of the three cans being popped open sounded in the dark room.

"So what's up with your mom?" Kylie asked Miranda.

"I don't know. She didn't tell me she was here. She sorta let me believe she wasn't. And there has to be a reason."

"What reason?" Della asked.

"I don't know. I just sugarcoated my answer to Burnett because I didn't want him to think she had anything to do with the murders."

Della shook her head and sipped from her can. "Your mom's a bitch, but I don't think she'd kill anyone any more than I think my dad would." Della downed a big sip of soda.

"Thank you," Miranda said. "Except for the bitch part." She frowned. "It probably has to do with Tabitha and her mom. Maybe they met somewhere to hash it out."

"That would be fun to watch," Della said.

Miranda rolled her eyes at the vamp.

"No, it wouldn't," Kylie said and shot Della a warning look. Then her gaze went back to Miranda. "Why don't you try to call her?"

"I think I need to see her in person." Miranda let her gaze shift to the window. "Is that the sun rising?" she asked. "Tell me it's not morning yet."

"It's not morning yet," Della said. "See, I like you enough to lie to you."

Miranda rolled her eyes.

"What time do you have to be at practice?" Kylie asked.

"Noon." She moaned and leaned back on the headboard, exhausted.

"Then why don't we try to sleep? You're gonna need it. You have to win and become a high priestess."

"Yeah," she said and handed Kylie her Coke to put on the bedside table. Then she wiggled her butt until she slid down on the mattress.

"Don't you want to win?" Kylie asked. Both her friends sat up, looking down at her.

"I didn't think I did, but now . . . Yes, I want to win." She admitted something, not only to them, but to herself. "I want to win so bad I can taste it. I never wanted to say it, because I didn't think it was possible. But now . . ."

"What?" Della asked.

"The Perry thing and now this whole Tabitha thing, both of them hurt, and it's stealing away my joy."

"Maybe it's not as bad as you think," Kylie said. "Tabitha could be wrong about things. You won't know until you talk with your parents."

"Yeah," Miranda said, but in her heart she knew it was true. She just didn't know how she was ever going to forgive her parents for all the lies.

She closed her eyes and then opened them and glanced from Kylie to Della. "I love you. You two are like sisters I never . . . Damn!" She hit her fists on the mattress.

"What?" Kylie asked.

"Tabitha's my sister. My sister is sleeping in the next room over."

Della stared at her and her brows tightened. "You . . . you knew that already." Della glanced at Kylie. "Is she losing it?"

"No, I'm not losing it," Miranda snapped in a sleepy voice. "It just hadn't sunk in all the way. I mean, all my life I begged my mom and dad to make me a sister. Sometimes I felt all alone and I didn't even have to be alone, because I already had a sister." Miranda paused. "And she hates me."

"If it makes you feel better, sometimes my sister hates me." Della butt-scooted farther down on the mattress. Her shoulder met Miranda's.

"I guess." Miranda let her eyes close and waited for sleep. The last thought whispering across her worried mind was the kiss. The soft and painful kiss she'd gotten from Perry. And then another kiss entered her brain, the kiss she'd gotten years ago at a masquerade party.

"I'm so messed up, guys."

Voices. Miranda heard them and pulled the pillow over her head. Sunshine still snuck in the tiny slits of her closed eyes. Her mind raced to orient her. She wasn't at her cabin.

She remembered.

Paris.

Perry.

Rogue vampires.

Lying parents.

A sister.

A practice competition.

Ugh. She buried her head deeper into the pillow.

She heard the bedroom door swish open.

"Miranda?"

She expected to hear Kylie or Della urging her to wake up. The last person's voice she expected to hear was . . .

She tossed the pillow off her head and sat up. Her gaze met his blue eyes, and emotion tightened her gut. She hadn't been ready to speak to him on the phone last night, she certainly didn't feel up to a face-to-face with him.

But it looked as if she didn't have a choice.

"Daddy?"

Chapter Fourteen

Miranda's chest filled with pain. She had to swallow, twice, to keep the tears from climbing up her throat.

"What . . . are you doing here?" She looked up at him, seeing him differently for the first time. Seeing him as someone else's dad. It hit then. Tabitha had gotten more from her father than she had. Her half-sister inherited his red hair. And his blue eyes. While Miranda was stuck with hazel eyes and blond hair with only red highlights.

"I thought you didn't do competitions?" The words came out with sarcasm and a ton of hurt. He was her daddy. She didn't want to share him, but she had been . . . sharing him. She just hadn't known it.

He reached up and rubbed the back of his neck. He always did that when he was nervous. But about what? Then she quickly became aware of his gaze shifting to her and then back to the wall.

He knew.

He knew she knew.

Had Tabitha told him?

"I know this is hard." His words were tight, and filled with what sounded like regret. A little too late for that, wasn't it?

She pulled her knees up to her chest and hugged them. What kind of explanation could he offer? She couldn't think of one that made this acceptable. And yet he was here to try. Didn't that mean something?

It might, but emotionally right now she couldn't feel any reprieve. Lies. Everything she'd thought about her family had been a lie.

"Your mother called me," he said. "Then Tabitha called."

That achiness in her chest exploded and flowed into all her limbs. Tears filled her eyes.

"So it's all true?" she asked.

His hand swiped down his face, almost as if buying a few seconds to think, seconds that he didn't have to look at her.

Did he consider her a mistake?

"I don't know what all you know, but . . ." He paused and seemed to notice the tears streaming down her face. "Don't cry. It kills me to see you cry."

"Is it true?" she demanded and when he didn't immediately answer, she spelled out what she meant. "Is Tabitha my sister?"

"Yes." He looked back at the wall.

She blinked and more hot tears rolled down her cheek. "Are you married to her mom, and not to my mom?"

He glanced back at her. His gaze, his posture, everything about him looked heavy as if the guilt weighed him down. But she wouldn't let herself feel sorry for him.

"Yes," he said. "But . . . it's not like it sounds."

She ignored his remark and tossed out another question. "Did my mom know? Did she know you were married when you met her?"

She didn't know why she needed that answer, but she did. Perhaps, she needed to know how much to blame her mom for this. If she had known, then . . .

"Miranda, I know this sounds terrible, but—"

"Did you lie to my mom?" She spit the question out again.

He inhaled. "Yes, in the beginning I lied to her. But it's not like you think."

"What's not like I think, Daddy? I don't even know your real name. How could you do this to me? To us? Mom and me?"

He hung his head and didn't move. Finally, he looked up. "Divorce was almost impossible to get in Ireland, Miranda. Mary Esther and I had separated. I was considering fighting to get the divorce, but . . .

Her grandfather turned my uncle against me. My uncle was in charge of my trust fund."

He shuffled his feet. "Back then, I was nothing more than a spoiled rich kid. I'd lived off my family's money. If I had pursued a divorce, all of my inheritance would have been lost to me. In the beginning I was willing to sacrifice it, but then I learned Mary Ester was pregnant. While I might have been spoiled, I did not want to turn my back on my child. While I loved your mother with all my heart, I was actually planning on walking away from her, because I felt she deserved better. The day I was going to break up with her, your mother announced her own news. She was pregnant with you. Then I was nothing more than a stupid kid, with two children to support. I couldn't reject what was my only source of income, which was my trust fund. I told your mom the truth. It took a while, but she forgave me for lying and accepted what I could offer."

"So you just lived with both wives? How gross and sick is that? I seriously think I'm going to throw up."

Shock widened his eyes. "I do not live with Mary Esther as her husband. Yes, I have a place next door to her. For the most part, I support her, and Tabitha. I am as big a part of Tabitha's life as I am yours. And I know your mom hates that, but I can no more turn my back on Tabitha than I could you. Mary Esther was a mistake, but Tabitha is still my child."

And what am I? The question sat on the tip of her tongue, but she couldn't ask it. *A bastard child?*

"I love your mother, Miranda. I know this life has not been easy for her, and I regret that. While there is no legal paper calling her my wife, she is the love of my life. Together we made you. We are a family. I love you. We love you."

"Then why the lies? Why not tell me? Why not give me your real name?"

"In the beginning it was to protect my trust fund, if my uncle had found out I wasn't . . . living as Mary Esther's husband, he would have happily cut me off. Then when he died four years ago, I actually wanted to come clean, to have you two girls meet and get to know each other.

But your mother and Mary Esther had too many grudges. It became easier to live the lie than to come clean. I never meant to hurt you."

Miranda swiped the tears from her face. "Well, you failed. Failed miserably. This, the lies, the secrets, it hurts."

"I can see that, and don't for one minute think it isn't killing me. I want to fix it. That's what I'm here to do. You both are such neat people. I'm so proud of both of you. This afternoon after the practice, we are all getting together. I know it's hard and I regret not doing it earlier, but I want you and Tabitha to get along, to love each other."

"She hates me." Then Miranda realized something else. "Did she know this whole time? Did you tell Tabitha and not me?"

"No. A few years ago, she overheard her mother and me arguing. She figured it out. Like you, she's pretty disappointed in me. You two are my world. My reason for living. I want to fix this."

She looked at the man whom she'd loved all her life. Her first hero, the man who called her "angel." The patient father who'd taught her to ride a bike, to tie her shoelaces. He'd even taught her her first spell. Every pore and cell in her body loved this man, and yet it hurt so badly she wished she didn't.

Wished she didn't love him this much.

She swallowed and lifted her chin. Without trying to hide her hurt, she told him what she'd told Perry.

"I'm not completely certain you can fix this." And damn, it hurt to say that.

"Do you feel anything?" Burnett asked Miranda as he walked into her dressing room a few minutes before practice. The competition and practice were being held in an old auditorium that had once been a library— complete with gargoyles. Like everything in Paris, it felt old. It was old. Kind of gave her the creeps.

"Miranda?" Burnett said her name.

Oh, yeah . . . Did she feel anything? Hell yeah. Emotions did jumping jacks in her gut. After her dad had left, Kylie and Della had come and let her cry on their shoulders. If not for them, she was pretty sure she'd still be facedown in her bed wallowing in self-pity. As it was, her eyes were puffy from crying. She dreaded the meeting that was going to take place after the practice. Dreaded it with a passion. And part of that dread was facing her mom. She didn't know why, but she knew it was going to hurt.

Perhaps her mom felt the same thing. It would explain why she hadn't already visited Miranda.

"Do you feel anything?" he repeated, as if impatient that she hadn't instantly replied.

The answer echoed back. She felt as if her heart had been used as a pit bull's play toy. Then someone had found the damaged organ and stuck it back in her chest, but it wasn't working.

Not that Burnett wanted to know this. He was concerned about whoever it was trying to knock off the competition. He wanted to know if she felt any doom and gloom premonitions.

"No, not yet."

"Do you have your cell with you?" he asked.

She nodded.

"Good. Take it with you. If you feel anything, anything at all, call me, right then. I don't care if you're in the middle of practice and have to piss off one of those prima donna highfalutin witches out there. You call me. Got it?"

Miranda couldn't help but wonder if he'd told Tabitha the same thing. Probably. Thankfully, Tabitha had already left the apartment when her dad . . . correction . . . their dad . . . had shown up. Facing her was going to be as hard as facing her mom. Hadn't she called Tabitha a liar last night?

Burnett started to walk out and then turned. She looked up at him. His scowl faded. "You okay?"

She nodded.

He swung back to the door, but darted back around with vampire speed. "I have a feeling if Holiday were here, she'd give you a comforting hug. She'd probably be able to know exactly why you look so sad.

Maybe you'd even confide in her. I'm not nearly as good at the coun-
seling sh—stuff as she is. As a matter of fact, I kind of suck at it. But
if you need to talk, I can listen. I have a few minutes now."

As tempting as it was, she was afraid if she talked she'd start crying
again. She shook her head.

He looked almost relieved, and turned around.

A small hiccup of emotion left her throat. He looked back again.
His expression was uncertain and almost painful. "You need a hug?"

She ran into his arms like a scared child. Hugging wasn't Burnett's
favorite pastime, and the fact that he'd offered meant the world. As
tough and hard as this man could be, he cared. Cared deeply. Holiday
and his daughter, Hannah, were two very lucky ladies.

He patted Miranda on the back. The slow tapping of his right hand
felt awkward. His posture tense. Sensing he was uncomfortable, she
pulled back.

He studied her. "Did that help?"

"Yes." She smiled with emotion.

He nodded. "Is this about Perry and—?"

"No."

He tilted his head to the side and frowned as if he'd heard the lie.

"Okay, maybe a little. But it's only part of it." But since he'd brought
the subject up, she asked. "Is Perry here?" He had told Miranda he was
coming, but less than a month ago he'd told her he would never walk
away. And he had.

Her ability to trust him had been damaged. Maybe the shape-shifter
had changed his mind again.

"Yes, he's here. I don't think I could have kept him away."

She nodded and Burnett raised his brows. For some reason she suspected he was recalling Shawn's half-assed confession of being interested in her.

Burnett continued to stare. "Is this . . . the tears, somehow about
your dad's visit this morning?"

She nodded.

"Anything I can do to help?" he asked.

"You did."

"I did?" he asked, confused.

"The hug," she said, swallowing the lump in her throat.

"Oh." Then suspicion tightened his brow. "But this . . . problem isn't anything I need to know about, is it?"

"It's not about the murders," she assured him, sensing that was what Burnett meant.

"Okay," he said, hearing her truth. "But like I said, if you want to talk, I suck at giving advice about personal issues, but I'll be happy to listen."

"Thank you," she said and couldn't stop herself. She hugged him again.

As she released him, he moved toward the door, but sent back one parting comment. "Remember, any sense of danger, even if it's tiny, contact me immediately."

Miranda stood in the circle of twenty competitors—constantly aware of Tabitha standing four girls down on Miranda's right. She didn't look at her. But every few minutes, Miranda could feel the girl's gaze on her.

Did her half-sister really hate her? For one crazy moment, Miranda tried to see this from Tabitha's point of view. It would be easy for Tabitha to blame Miranda and her mom for destroying her cozy little family. If not for the conception of Miranda, perhaps her mother and father would have made the marriage work.

Damn, if Miranda couldn't see how it would be easy for Tabitha to hate her. And her mom. Who wanted to share your father with an off-spring of "the other woman"?

Trying to concentrate on the council's words, she stood frozen in one spot. She felt several other gazes zeroing in on her from the audience. Scanning the spectators, she found the onlookers. Her mom sat in the first row. Alone. The seat beside her . . . empty. Where was her dad? Rumor was there had been an accident on one of the major streets and it had delayed several of the attendees.

Miranda noted the worry and fret tightening her mom's expression. Was her mom dreading the meeting after the practice?

Join the crowd, Mom!

In the back of the audience, she spotted a blond shape-shifter. He watched her with the intense stare of a bodyguard. His protectiveness would have been appreciated if he hadn't dropped her like a hot potato and let her fry in misery. And she didn't care why he'd broken up with her, it still had been so wrong!

In the opposite corner of the room stood Shawn. He smiled. The slight nod of his head seemed to say he had her back. Her gaze eased back to Perry and she saw him glaring at Shawn. Okay, that felt awkward.

She focused on the high priestess speaking. She appeared French, her accent made her sound almost lyrical, but her pronunciation was spot-on.

The practice consisted of how the competition would go down. They weren't told what the spells would be, but there were hints that they would return to one of the four elements. Miranda sent up a prayer that it wouldn't be fire. Especially with her father here. His scars on his buttocks would no doubt itch if she started playing with fire again.

The memory of his teasing throughout the years scraped across her mind, and somehow it seemed tainted. Or at least different now that she knew his secrets. Tears stung her eyes and she wondered if all her memories would feel like a lie.

The sound of the heavy auditorium doors opening echoed in the large space. A crowd of around fourteen came bustling in. Miranda spotted her dad and Mary Esther, Tabitha's mom, walking beside him. They almost got to her mother's row.

Her mom looked back and scowled. Oh friggin' great! Were Mary Esther and her mom about to cause a scene?

Dread and embarrassment ran through her. No one wanted their dirty laundry played out in front of a crowd. Her feet itched to hightail it out of there, but then the strong sense of danger chased away all thoughts of being humiliated.

She heard Burnett's order: *If you feel anything, anything at all, call me.* She reached in her pocket to pull out her phone and spotted Tabitha doing the same thing. Both with cell phones in hand, their gazes clashed.

Obviously, Burnett had given Tabitha the same orders. She felt exactly what Miranda did.

Some bad shit was about to go down.

Fog, thick as mud, fell from the auditorium's rafters. And nothing but screams followed.

Chapter Fifteen

"Miranda?" a voice, a deep male voice, called her name.

It took less than a second to recognize it was Shawn. Blinded and disoriented by the fog, she called out, "Here. I'm here."

"Get away from me!" Another shrill voice echoed above the other screams.

"Tabitha?" Miranda called. Something was happening to her half-sister.

"Stop!" Tabitha screamed again. "Help!" Her plea seemed to fade in the distance.

"Tabitha! Where are you?" Miranda called out, but only the screams of others filled the thick mist.

The next thing Miranda knew something from above wrapped around her forearms and lifted her up. Up to the rafters, up away from the fog.

She glanced to the ceiling at the same time the large tan bird the size of a horse with a hooked beak glanced down. Its familiar light blue eyes met hers. Perry. Her next breath came easier, then she remembered.

"Find Tabitha," she yelled at him.

"Can't see shit," she heard him say.

She glanced down. The menacing-looking fog continued to rise from the floor and drew closer like fingers trying to pull them in.

Perry flapped his wings. "I got you. Relax."

Her breath caught when he swooped down, down into the thick white cloud, and she was again blinded by/the dense mist. Blinking, she saw what looked like a tunnel of light ahead.

A second glance and she realized it was the entrance to the auditorium. The doors were open. Perry swooped down lower to clear the exit and she could hear people scurrying out like rats. Her feet hit a few heads of the escaping crowd. "Sorry. Sorry."

She pulled her knees up. Moving like the wind, with her in tow, Perry shot through the exit, his talons holding her tight, but not too tight. Perry would never hurt her.

Seconds after clearing the door, her breath caught as Perry took her up. All the way up, higher than the top of the auditorium. She saw him cocking his head one way and then the other as if searching for a place to land.

Then with the dark sky glaring down at them, and distant thunder roaring, he began his descent to the roof's edge, just a few feet from an evil-looking gargoyle. "Not here," she said, but he obviously didn't hear her.

"You okay?" His beak moved. Then his gaze shifted toward the streets below. "Damn."

"What?" she asked.

"Stay here," Perry ordered.

Like she could leave! Then his wings widened as if . . .

"No," she screamed, feeling as if the statue stared at her. "Don't leave me."

He leapt off the ledge. Air from his wings flapping stirred her hair.

He got only a few feet away when she saw electric bubbles exploding around him and he turned into a small black crow. Where the hell was he going? Why was he leaving her . . . here?

She was ten stories up, and sharing a space with a huge, nasty-looking concrete beast. Wasn't this just like her childhood nightmares?

Then she remembered Tabitha.

"Come back," she screamed. Her mouth hung open as she pulled in big gulps of oxygen and watched the crow grow smaller, abandoning her once again.

A strike of lightning hit the roof, shaking the building and sending another wave of panic over her. Glancing down at the people below, she considered screaming, but sensed her voice would go unheard. Heart racing, realizing she still clutched her phone, she went to finish dialing Burnett. She lacked one number to complete the call when a scary-sounding chuckle sounded and the cold wet air hitched in her lungs.

Her gaze shot to the gargoyle. She shook her head, forcing herself to breathe. "You aren't real," she said.

"Yes, I am."

Chills whispered down her back, the only thing that kept her from taking a dive off the ledge was that the voice hadn't come from the beast. Slowly turning her head, she came face-to-face with a rogue vampire—a rogue vampire smelling way too pungently of dog poop.

"Oh, damn!" Before Miranda could react, or even think of a spell, the vamp charged. Her phone fell to the roof with a clatter. He caught her around her waist, pulled her back against his front, and leapt off the building.

Free-falling, the ground rushing up to her, her thoughts went to dying. Was she ready? No. So much she wanted to do. Why did it have to end?

Then the vamp started flying, the wind slapping her hair into her face, stinging her cheeks. His arm cut into her middle, making it almost impossible to feed her lungs air. But she welcomed the pain in lieu of death.

"Wiggle that little finger or even think about using your stupid magic on me again, and I will rip out your jugular and paint Paris red with your blood."

To make his point, he pressed his sharp canines to the curve of her throat.

Miranda hadn't dared move her pinky, but she spent the few very long seconds in flight coming up with spells that she would throw at the foul-smelling bloodsucker as soon as they landed.

Her heart clutched when her abductor started descending. He swooped down into a castle's courtyard and through some concrete arches. She prepared herself to fight, but her feet had barely hit the concrete when a heavy door opened and she was tossed into a pit of darkness. A darkness so black, so thick, that it brought on instant isolation.

Before she even hit the bottom, a clanking sound echoed behind her, telling her she was locked in.

Landing on her knees, her hands scraped into the rocky ground. She moaned as the sharp gravel cut into the fleshy part of her palms. Tears stung her eyes. The coppery smell of blood singed her senses.

Fear tasted like metal on her tongue and the dank smell of wet earth filled her nose. Where was she?

Crawling to her feet, she held her hands out to feel her way in the blackness. She went to twitch her pinky to bring light, but nothing happened. She did it again. The same results slapped her in the face. Why wasn't her magic working?

Beneath the smell of aged dirt, she caught the scent of sage, burning bark, and then something really foul—the scent of death. Decay.

Tears filled her eyes as horror turned her stomach rock hard. At first she considered she was locked up with a corpse, but then logic intervened. She'd smelled the combination of scents before, a black spell, a curse to prevent any other magic from working.

She slid her feet, an inch at a time, in hopes of not falling again. The sound of her breathing seemed too loud. Then she heard it, a slight moan. She wasn't alone. Someone was in here with her. But was he/she friend or foe?

Fear told her to be quiet. Logic forced one word to the tip of her tongue. "Hello?"

She stood in the dark silence, breathing in scents that were keeping her from using her powers. Tilting her head to the side, she listened to make sure she hadn't been mistaken.

Only a dead silence filled her ears. Her stomach knotted. Part of her wanted to fall to the ground and sob. Part of her thought of Kylie and Della and how strong they were and how she longed to be more like them.

She took another step and heard it again—a slight intake of air. Swallowing the knot of fear down her throat, she stiffened her backbone.

"Is someone else in here?" Her words seemed to echo and terror again spidered down her spine.

Chapter Sixteen

"What do you want with me?" the voice answered.

Miranda recognized the voice.

"Tabitha? Is that you? It's me, Miranda."

"Are you doing this to me? Are you—"

"No, I'm in here, too." She inhaled. "A dirty vamp, one that was at the Eiffel Tower, he grabbed me, brought me here, and tossed me in."

"Me, too." Her voice shook as if she'd been crying.

Miranda didn't take any points off for that. Her cheeks were still damp with her own tears. "Where are we, do you know?"

"I think it's a dungeon," Tabitha said.

Miranda slowly started inching toward the voice. "Keep talking so I can find you."

"It looked like a castle from above," her half-sister said.

"Yeah, I saw that, too." Miranda's foot hit something. Something that didn't feel like a rock. She knelt down and touched the object, quickly recognizing it as a foot. With a boot on it. Had Tabitha been wearing boots?

"Is that you?" Miranda asked.

"Is what me?"

Tabitha's words send a wave of panic through Miranda and she bolted back, tripped over her own feet, and landed on her butt.

She scrambled to get up, to get farther away from the foot she'd just touched.

One step.

Two.

Tabitha's thin voice rang out, "Miranda, what happened?"

Trying not to hyperventilate, she spit out the question, "Did I just touch you?"

"Nooo," Tabitha said, sounding confused.

A whimper escaped Miranda's lips. "Then I just touched someone else's foot."

"What? Are you saying . . . that someone else is in here?" Her voice sounded winded.

Miranda swallowed. "Yeah." She brushed off her fingertips as if to wipe away the touch.

"Who are you?" Tabitha demanded.

No answer came back.

"Are they dead?" Tabitha asked.

Dread hit Miranda like heavy smoke. "I . . . I don't know."

"Were they cold?"

"I just touched a foot . . . with a shoe on it." The thought of touching death had her rubbing her hands on her jeans.

"I hate this. I want to go home." Tabitha started crying.

"Me, too," Miranda said, but then realized panicking wasn't going to help. "Don't cry. Talk so I can find you."

"I'm here. Against a wall. What do you want me to say?"

"Count," Miranda said and started moving again.

"One. Two. Three." Tabitha's voice sounded closer and closer with each step. Meanwhile Miranda tried to keep her orientation so that when she found the courage she could go back and check on the foot.

Or rather the body connected to the foot.

Oh, God. She hoped there was a body connected to the foot. Her breath hitched in her throat.

"Is this you?" she asked, her shoe hitting something.

"Yeah," Tabitha answered, her voice shaky.

Miranda moved a few more inches until she felt the wall and then she turned and sat down beside her half-sister who immediately started sniffling again. "Don't cry."

"Don't tell me what to do. I'm locked in the dark with a dead person. And probably a ghost. Oh shit, I hate ghosts."

"We don't know if there's a ghost," Miranda said. But right then she figured out what this place might be. Spooky music ran through her mind. Chances were this place wasn't just a dungeon, but part of the catacombs. Old mines for limestone used to build Paris thousands of years ago. Alone that wouldn't have been so bad, but then the mines had been used as a place to toss the dead.

Tabitha was right. They probably had ghosts down here.

"Stop making this worse than it is," Miranda said and told herself the same thing. "We don't even know if . . . if they are dead. And we need to figure a way out of here."

"They haven't spoken and I've been in here for a good twenty minutes."

"Well, maybe they're unconscious?" Miranda said. "Why don't we hold our breath and listen to see if anyone else is breathing."

"Okay," Tabitha answered.

Miranda heard her sister inhale and she did the same.

Silence filled the blackness and not a sound entered their prison.

"They're dead!" Tabitha squealed.

But right then, Miranda heard it. "Shh. Listen."

"To what?"

"Be quiet." Miranda tilted her head and locked the air in her lungs. She heard it again. Too far away to be Tabitha. A short, light sound of someone drawing in a shallow breath. "Did you hear it? Someone is breathing."

"But why aren't they talking?"

"Like I said, because they're unconscious. Maybe I should check on them," Miranda said. "I just wish . . ."

"Wish what?" Tabitha asked.

"I wish I could see what I was doing. Wish I could see if . . . the door I was thrown in is the only way out." She had no idea what the catacombs looked like. *Did these mines have back doors?* Miranda blinked and tried to make out shapes in the blackness. But nothing came. She touched the wall, it felt like dirt. Was this just one big room, or was it like a tunnel? "I tried to make light."

"There's a black spell curse, I can smell it," Tabitha said.

"I know. I smelled it, too."

"So we can't do anything. We just stay here until we . . . until we fall unconscious, too. And die. We're gonna die here."

"No!" Miranda snapped. "We do something. I'm not just gonna give up." She inhaled and tried to think of what to do. Silence filled the space, time passing in slow, dark seconds.

Tabitha shifted and then spoke up again. "I can't die," she said, her voice sounding tight again. "I saw Daddy this morning and I told him I hated him. I can't let that be the last thing I said to him."

Miranda found her sister's hand and squeezed it. "We're not going to die. Burnett, Kylie, and Della are looking for us. They'll find us. But for the record, I don't think . . . I think our dad knows you really don't hate him."

"I'm just so mad at him," Tabitha said.

"Me, too," Miranda confessed.

"Did you see him, too?" Tabitha asked.

Miranda nodded and then realized Tabitha couldn't see her. "Yeah."

"What did he say to you?"

Miranda paused, unsure if she should tell Tabitha what he said about loving Miranda's mother. It would probably only hurt Tabitha. "He tried to explain things."

"Did he tell you that he loves your mother, because that's what he told me and that's when I told him I hated him." She hiccupped. "But I don't hate him. I hate your mom."

Miranda swallowed, unsure now was the time to talk about this, but she supposed there would never really be a right time. "He told me that he and your mom were separated when he met my mother."

"But he was still a married man, and she had no right—"

"He told me that my mother didn't know he was . . . married. Not at first."

She heard her sister take in a deep gulp of air. "It's still not right. It hurts."

"I know," Miranda said. "It hurts me, too."

Then Miranda heard the slight inhale of air again from across the room. She wondered how long this person had been down here. Alone.

At least she and Tabitha had each other.

She closed her eyes and tried to come up with a plan to help them escape. She knew Burnett, Della, Kylie, and probably even Perry and Shawn were all looking for them, but that didn't mean she and Tabitha could just sit and wait. "Who the hell is doing this?" she muttered.

Tabitha must have shifted, but the subtle sound echoed. "I don't know for sure, but . . ."

"But what?" Miranda demanded.

"They took both me and Sienna. But they didn't throw Sienna down here."

"What are you saying? You think Sienna is doing this?"

"No, but I think . . . her mom might be." A light gulp filled the silence. "Right before they threw me in here, I could swear I heard Sienna's mom tell the other vampire to bring her inside."

Miranda exhaled. "Well, Burnett was going to have a meeting after the practice with the parents. He'll figure it out. He's good at that."

A long silence filled the space. "You seem to have a lot of faith in him," Tabitha said.

"Yeah, I do. He's . . . like family." She closed her eyes a second. "Wait," Miranda said as a realization hit. "We're family. We're half-sisters."

"Duh," Tabitha said.

Miranda rolled her eyes. "Can we not hate each other right now?"

"I didn't say I hated you," Tabitha said. "I hate—"

"Forget it. Look, what I was gonna say is that maybe the black spell is strong enough to stop one person's magic, but if . . . if we share enough of the same DNA we can try to do blood magic. Maybe with the two of our powers together we can undo the black spell."

"You're right," Tabitha said. "I remember Candy and Sandy did a performance once at a contest. But . . . they are twins, and we're just half-sisters."

"We won't know unless we try," Miranda insisted.

"Okay. Do you remember how they did it?" Tabitha asked.

"Sort of," Miranda said. "They held hands and chanted and said they meditated on the same thing."

"So what are we going to try to do?"

"Some light would be nice. Then I'll see if I can help our friend here."

"Okay," she said. "What's the chant?"

Miranda let her brain work. "How about . . . out with dark, in with bright, together we ask for blessed light."

Tabitha repeated it and then said, "Sounds good."

Miranda started the chant and gave her half-sister's hand a squeeze. Tabitha joined in. They said it once, twice, then three times.

"It's not working," Tabitha said.

"Maybe we're doing something wrong." Miranda tried to remember everything the twins had said about blood spells.

"Maybe we're not meditating right," Miranda said. "Are you practicing visualization?"

"Yes," Tabitha said.

"What are you visualizing?" Miranda asked.

"A flashlight," her half-sister said.

"Oh, I was going with a candle."

"Why a candle?" Tabitha asked. "This is the twenty-first century."

"Because it felt . . . Never mind, you're right. Let's try it again."

Just before they started the chant again, a moan escaped. Tabitha jumped closer to the Miranda. "I hate this."

"Come on," Miranda said. "We're wasting time."

They tried again, repeating the spell twice. Three times. Four. Right before she was about to give up, the smell of the herbs grew stronger as if someone knew their spell was being tested.

Tabitha moaned. "It's not—"

"Don't stop!" Miranda said and clutched her sister's hand tighter. Then all of a sudden the sound of something thudding to the ground sounded. When it did, the pungent smell grew ten times stronger.

"What was that?" Tabitha asked, her hold still tight on Miranda's hand.

"Maybe a flashlight?" Miranda got on her hands and knees. Feeling her way and moving slowly.

"If it was a flashlight why wasn't it lit?"

"Maybe the powers that be thought the least we could do was to turn it on. Come on, let's see if we can find it."

She heard her sister scrambling around. Tabitha's sigh echoed in the sheer darkness. "Someone has strengthened the black spell. Do you smell that?"

"Yeah, but I still think we succeeded at this one." Miranda's words seemed to be swallowed up by the murkiness.

"It probably wasn't a flashlight," Tabitha whined.

Miranda knew she was being an optimist, but sometimes that's all one had. "You don't know that. Keep looking."

"Hey," Tabitha said. "I think . . . You were right!"

A circular light beamed on the ceiling.

"We did it." The sensation of power filled Miranda's chest, even when she knew this might be all they got.

Tabitha shifted the light. Miranda followed the beam. "There are tunnels," her sister said. "Maybe there's a way out."

"Yeah," Miranda said, and continued to watch as her sister slowly shifted the light. The circular beam stopped on a young man—dressed in jeans and a T-shirt. He lay so still that Miranda worried he was dead. That the intake of air they'd heard had been his last.

Finally, his chest shifted ever so slightly. "He's alive," Miranda said.

Both Miranda and Tabitha stood up.

"I know." Tabitha backed away. Miranda edged closer. With each step, the smell of blood got stronger. And this time, it wasn't her blood.

"Shine it on his face," Miranda said, and when she took another step, the orb of light slipped up above the neck of their fellow prisoner. She squinted at the individual—at his forehead—something all supernaturals did to identity another species.

The pattern finally emerged.

"He's vampire." Tabitha caught Miranda by the arm and tugged her backward. "He's probably one of them. Don't get close to him. He . . . he might attack."

"If he was one of them, why would they have locked him up?" Miranda tugged the flashlight from Tabitha's hand and shifted it down his torso. There on his light blue shirt was a big bloodstain. His shirt looked ripped. Had he been stabbed or was he shot?

"Look, he's been hurt," Miranda said and looked back at her sister. "He's not one of them."

"That doesn't mean he's nice. Even if he's not one of them, he's probably hungry and if he wakes up . . . he . . . he'll want blood. I say let's take our light, follow the tunnel, and get as far from him as possible. Maybe we can even find our way out." She took the flashlight back and pointed in the opposite direction.

Miranda's gaze stayed on the dark spot where the nearly dead vampire lay. With the beam of light, even not pointed at him, she could still see the shape. She heard him moan again, a little louder, as if he was somehow aware of the light.

"Don't get too close. He'll smell your blood," Tabitha bit out. "And you know what he'll do."

Tabitha's warning had merit. Miranda had heard horror stories of others killed trying to help stray and injured vampires. And yet what if that was Della, or Burnett, or any one of the vampires at Shadow Falls? What if someone let them die?

"Come on, there's a pathway over here," her half-sister said and gave her another tug. "Let's get away from him before he wakes up and kills us both." Tabitha took her hand and squeezed. "Maybe the black curse isn't as strong deeper into the tunnel."

"No." Miranda dropped her sister's hand. "We can't just leave him to die. We have to help him."

"Are you freaking nuts?" Tabitha asked. "The only way to help him is to give him blood."

"I know," Miranda said.

"Well, we kind of need ours!" she spit out.

"We don't need all of it." Miranda remembered how in the beginning the idea of donating blood to the vampire bank had repulsed her. Then Kylie had agreed to do it and Miranda went along.

Funny how all her time at Shadow Falls had almost made her forget how prejudiced the outside world could be. "My friend Kylie says that people donate blood to blood banks all the time. Giving it to vampires is the same thing."

"That's different." Tabitha caught her by the arm. "Look, I know you got that vampire girlfriend, and you live at that school where everyone gets along, but this is the real world. You don't know if he's rogue and—"

"He doesn't deserve to die."

Tabitha put the light under her chin, creating some eerie shadows on her face and she glared at Miranda. "I can't believe you. He's a vampire."

Miranda glared right back. "I can't believe my sister is a bigot."

"I'm not!" Tabitha snapped and sounded genuinely offended. "I don't dislike vampires. But if it's my life or his, or my half-sister's, well, I choose us. He could be rogue, and if you give him a little blood, he might . . . just want more."

"Look, I know it might be dangerous, but I can't just let him die."

"You didn't do that to him. You aren't responsible."

"I am if I leave without trying to help. You can leave if you want. And as soon as he's better, we'll try to find you."

Tabitha shook her head. "You are gonna die. He's going to be bloodthirsty and you are going to get all the blood sucked out of you. Then he'll probably rip you open and eat your liver. I hear they like livers."

"No," Miranda said, but her stomach quivered.

"No, you're not going to die or no, they don't like livers?"

"No, I'm not going to die," Miranda said, thinking she recalled Della mentioning livers being a prime body part. Then, feeling her pulse pumping to the tune of fear, she watched Tabitha stomp off. With the flashlight.

Hey, that was her flashlight, too, Miranda thought.

She stood there, part of her screaming to run after her sister—but she couldn't. She wouldn't be able to live with herself knowing she'd let someone die. Someone who could be as good as Burnett, or Della.

In only seconds, the shadows seemed to move closer and complete darkness fell on her. Her heart thumped against her breastbone. She could hear Tabitha's footfalls moving away. Growing quieter, until she couldn't hear anything. Alone.

The sound of someone taking a deep breath echoed and seemed to argue with her last thought. Okay, not alone.

Stiffening her backbone, she turned back to where she knew the injured vampire lay. "Please don't prove her right. I kind of like my liver."

Chapter Seventeen

Miranda took one step. Then the darkness seemingly attacking her from all angles started to fade. She swung around and saw the orb of light moving back toward her.

Tabitha? The light came closer. Her footsteps sounded. Then her shape became visual. She kept walking and didn't stop until they stood face-to-face.

"You lied," Miranda said, emotion in her throat.

"About what?" Tabitha asked, a frown on her lips.

"At the apartment when I told you I'd saved your life. You said you wouldn't save mine."

"I haven't saved you," she said. "We're still stuck down here, possibly with a rogue vampire, and a black curse hanging over our heads."

Miranda smiled. "Yeah, but you came back. That means—"

"Maybe I just didn't want to be alone."

Miranda heard the lie in her sister's voice. "That or you actually care a little bit."

"Fine," Tabitha said. "I care. But if I die, or you die, I'm never going to forgive you for this."

"We're not going to die," Miranda said, and with the warm fuzzy feeling spilling from her heart, she suddenly believed it.

Her sister shined the flashlight at the vampire, then took a deep breath and met Miranda's eyes. "I'm really not a bigot. I can't stand it when people judge other people. It's just . . . vampires scare me a little."

"I know," Miranda said. "They used to scare me, too. But believe me, I couldn't have a better friend than Della." She reached over and touched Tabitha's arm. "Thank you. For coming back."

Tabitha nodded. "So how do we do it?"

"I've got a plan." Miranda rubbed her injured hand and then squeezed it to see if she could get it to bleed again. She didn't say it was a good plan. Would it work? She didn't really know. The only way she'd donated blood was with a needle and a bag. "When they threw me in here I cut my palm a little. I think if I . . . if I just put my hand there, he'll smell blood and . . . bite."

Tabitha's eyes went wide with panic. "If he hurts you or won't stop, I'll . . . I'll hit him with the flashlight. Hard. Really hard."

She almost told Tabitha if he wouldn't stop, to run like hell. Oh God, was she putting Tabitha's life on the line to do something . . . stupid? Another moan left the vampire's lips. No, Miranda's heart told her they were doing the right thing. She had to believe it.

Besides, if the black curse didn't lift, they could really use another person to help out—someone strong like a vampire.

She moved closer to the crumpled figure. "Shine the light on my hand." Looking at her hand, she pushed on the fleshy part of the palm until she saw some blood ooze out. Then she dropped on her knees. She tasted fear on her tongue, but put her hand close to the vampire's mouth.

His eyes popped open. He reached up, grabbed her arm, and latched onto her wrist where her veins were the closest.

"Ouch," Miranda said as she felt his teeth sink into skin.

"Should I hit him?" Tabitha screamed. "Should I hit him?"

"No!" Miranda stared at the vamp as he drank from her. "Look, buddy, this is just a snack, not a feast, okay? Just a taste until you can heal yourself, got it?"

"Should I hit him?" Tabitha repeated. "Should I hit him now?"

Miranda shook her head. "I'll give him a little more."

She counted to ten, started feeling a tad weak, and panicked. She took a deep breath and then said, "Okay, enough." She tried to pull away but his fingers latched around her arm with a death grip.

"Hey!" Tabitha leaned over and shined the light right into the vamp's eyes. "She said enough. Let go of her or I swear I'll put a lump on this side of your head the same size as the one you've got right here." She tapped his forehead with the flashlight.

The vamp blinked, his eyes tightened and grew even brighter, but his hold on her arm suddenly lightened. Slowly, he pulled his teeth out.

Miranda drew her arm back then plopped her butt on the ground. The vamp dropped his head back and closed his eyes.

"Who are you?" he asked in a French accent.

Tabitha shined the light right in his eyes, but he kept them closed. "We are badass witches and if you try anything funky, we'll put some voodoo on your ass and you won't know what hit you."

He lifted his head again, opened one eye, and looked at Tabitha. "You don't look badass."

"Looks can be deceiving," Miranda said, and when she felt a damp warm stream of blood running down her wrist, she clamped her hand over the bite to stop the bleeding. "Why don't you tell us who you are?"

He didn't open his eyes, but he answered. "I am Anthony. Anthony Bastin."

After a few seconds of silence, he opened his eyes and stared at Miranda. "Is it not polite to offer your name when you are given one?"

"Hey, bucko," Tabitha snapped. "We just saved your life, so how about a little respect."

His gaze cut to Tabitha. "You are right, I apologize." He licked his lips and stared at them for a second. "You two are part of the competition. The ones for high priestess, right?"

"How do you know about that?" Miranda asked.

"I work at the auditorium where the competition was being held. Two nights ago, I caught the rogues sneaking around." His gaze went back to Tabitha. "They overpowered me . . . and brought me here. Of course, it was five to one. Or the outcome would have been different."

"Right," Tabitha said and rolled her eyes.

The vamp stared at her.

"Do you think you can walk?" Miranda asked. "I think we should see if this tunnel leads anywhere."

He tried to sit up, grunted, and then slumped back. "Give me a few more minutes. The blood will help me heal, but it can take time."

"Okay, but not too much," Miranda said and looked up at the heavy metal door that led outside. Outside where their captors were.

"Just a couple of minutes," he said.

In seconds, the vampire's breathing slowed. "I think he's asleep," Tabitha whispered and shifted the light a little closer to see Anthony's face.

Miranda looked at him. His firm jaw and chiseled features hinted at his French heritage. "We'll give him five minutes and then we have to move, even if we have to carry him."

Tabitha eased the orb of light down the masculine torso, highlighting a toned chest and a flat stomach. "You know, he'd be kind of cute if he wasn't so dirty."

"Yeah," Miranda admitted, not that she was the tiniest bit interested. She'd always been drawn more to blonds. Her mind went to Perry. Then it twisted to her younger years and her crush on Shawn.

"Do you think he needs more blood?" Tabitha asked.

"He might," Miranda said. "I guess I could give him a little more."

"You've already given him some. If he needs more, I'll . . . do it."

Miranda smiled. "That's generous of you. Are you feeling guilty, or do you think he's that good-looking?"

Tabitha chuckled. "He is cute. But you shouldn't talk. You're in love with a shape-shifter. Everyone knows that shape-shifters are . . . difficult."

Miranda cut her eyes to Tabitha. "How do you know about that?"

"I heard rumors," she said. "And I heard you two talking last night."

"Not all shape-shifters are bad any more than all vampires," Miranda said. "Or witches for that matter. Plus, it's rude to eavesdrop."

Tabitha didn't answer for a few minutes, then she said, "I was curious." She got quiet again. "Are you gonna take him back, or go with the hot FRU agent?"

Miranda closed her eyes for a second. "I think it's been five minutes." She looked back at the sleeping vamp.

"Fine, don't tell me. I just thought we'd kind of . . . never mind."

Bonded. Miranda knew what she was going to say. "I don't know what I'm going to do. Perry broke up with me."

"The shape-shifter?" she asked.

"Yeah." Miranda rubbed her finger over the bite wounds to see if they had stopped bleeding. "He said I deserved better than him and that he was doing it for me."

"Why would he say that? Is something wrong with him?" Tabitha asked.

"He's powerful, very powerful, and he had a hard time controlling his shifts in public. He didn't think he could live a normal life."

"You said he didn't think . . . is he better now?"

"Yeah, he came here to a school and they seem to be helping him."

"Then what's the problem?"

"He didn't even call me. I didn't want to break up." She breathed in. "It hurt. And now . . . now I don't know if I can just take him back. What if later on he decides he's still not good enough?"

"Then drop his butt and go with the warlock. Sienna wasn't lying when she said he stared at you that whole time."

Miranda leaned back against the mud wall. "I like Shawn, but . . . I need to figure out what I feel about Perry. And . . . ."

"What?" Tabitha asked.

"I don't know. It just feels complicated." *Even more complicated since I discovered the truth about my parents.*

They both sat there, nothing but the sound of breathing filling the space. "Do you have a boyfriend?" Miranda asked.

"I did, but he went off to California to college last year. He said we wouldn't break up, but then it just . . . I don't know. It started to feel weird. He stopped calling so much and when he did it just felt off. I'm pretty sure he was dating someone else. So I wrote him a letter and told him it was over."

"Sorry," Miranda said.

"Me, too," Tabitha said. "At first I was hurt but then it just felt like the right thing. I don't think I really loved him. Or if I did, I stopped loving him. Mom says I'm young and that I shouldn't commit myself to anyone." She sighed. "I think she regrets marrying my dad." Tabitha exhaled and stared into the darkness for several seconds. "What's sad is that I think my mom still loves him. Always has."

"It's a mess," Miranda said, hurting for Tabitha. "What do you think Dad was going to say when he got us all together?"

Tabitha shifted. "I think he wants us all to get along. But I'm telling you, my mom and your mom will never be buddies."

"But we can," Miranda said.

"Yeah, if we live through this." Tabitha hugged her knees closer and frowned.

"We will." Miranda stood up. "Let's wake up sleeping beauty and see if he can walk now. I don't know what the chances are that there's a way out of here, but we gotta try."

They got a couple hundred feet, both she and Tabitha holding Anthony by the waist, an arm around each of their shoulders, helping him walk. It wasn't easy. The vampire was heavier than he looked.

"You two just go on," Anthony finally said, his voice sounding weak. "If you find a way out, send someone back for me."

"No," Miranda and Tabitha said at the same time.

"Look, I'm too weak, I'm slowing you down." He pulled away from them, leaned against the wall, and slid down, until his butt hit the dirt floor.

"Not if you had more blood," Tabitha said. "You can have some of mine."

He looked up at her and made a funny face. "Aren't you afraid I'll eat your liver?"

Tabitha made a funny face right back. Miranda chuckled.

Tabitha huffed. "You weren't unconscious? You were faking it."

"Faking what? That I'd been knifed? I was not faking. I was in and out of consciousness. Every few minutes I'd hear you two talking."

Tabitha stared down at him, and slipped one hand on her hip. "And you couldn't do the polite thing and let us know you were awake. And you French people say Americans are rude."

He cut his eyes up at her sister. "Oh, yes, how ill-mannered of me. Never mind that I was on my deathbed. I should have used my last strength to warn you that I was not dead yet."

Tabitha frowned. "Fine. Maybe you couldn't help it," she snapped. "And now you know I was afraid of you, but I'm not afraid anymore. See!" She stuck her wrist in front of his mouth. "Bite me," she said, in almost a teasing tone.

He cut his warm brown eyes up at her. "You do not have to do that." He pushed her arm away, but his eyes glowed as if he had smelled her blood.

"I know I don't," Tabitha said. "But my sister here is too much of a soft heart. She won't leave you. So I'm not doing it for you, I'm doing it to help us escape. So just go ahead. Drink a little." She pushed her hand in front of his face.

"She means it," Miranda said. "If you can get your strength back, you might be able to help us get out of here."

He reached up and wrapped his hand around her arm. Then he ran his finger across her vein. He inhaled and then looked up again. "You sure?"

"I said I was, didn't I?" Tabitha said and she dropped down to the ground beside him. He reached up and pulled her arm to his mouth. She flinched when his teeth sank into her wrist.

"Not too much," Miranda said when she saw him feeding as if starved.

He immediately released Tabitha. When he pulled back, his gaze cut up to her, a drip of blood was on his lip and he licked it off. "Sorry," he said and put a hand over his face, almost as if embarrassed.

"You okay?" Tabitha asked.

"Yes." He let his hand drop from his face. His eyes stayed closed for a few beats of silence, then he looked up at her sister. "Thank you."

What about me? Miranda bit her tongue, then bit back a smile, sensing something blooming between these two.

"You're welcome," Tabitha said. "Did it help?"

"I think so," he answered. "Give me two minutes and we will know for sure."

A loud clank sounded behind them. It sound like someone had opened the metal door. But the sound hadn't come from the same direction they had, but through the tunnel.

"I don't think we have a few minutes," Miranda said, fear sounding in her voice. Tabitha jumped up and reached for Anthony.

"You two run back where we were, I'll try to stop them." He stood up, looking stronger.

"No," Tabitha said. "We fight together."

Anthony moved in front of Miranda and her sister.

Footsteps, fast footsteps, echoed around them.

Anthony lifted his face and took in a deep breath as if to catch the scent of the people coming toward them. "Vampire," he muttered, and took a few more steps in front of them. "Stop!" Anthony warned when a shadowy figure emerged.

"I'm not here to cause harm," the male voice spoke.

It was still too dark to see the newcomer's face, but the voice rang all kinds of bells. Bells that played a familiar tune. She knew this person.

He took a few more steps. Tabitha shined the light at him.

Miranda gaped. "What are you doing here?"

Chapter Eighteen

Chase Tallman, Della's Chase, stood in the catacombs. He nodded at Miranda. "I heard you were in trouble."

"You know him?" Anthony asked and his eyes, a bright protective yellow, turned to her.

"Yes."

"Do you trust him?" Anthony asked.

"I don't know." Miranda recalled how much this guy had hurt Della and remembered he worked for the Vampire Council, a group even the FRU didn't trust.

"Come on," Chase said and took another step. "We don't have a lot of time."

Anthony let out a deep warning growl. "Don't come any closer."

Chase stopped and glanced at Miranda. "Whatever you think of me, you know I'm not the bad guy here. In just a few minutes, they're going to be coming to collect you all for dinner. And I don't think they plan on you three sitting at the table."

"Are you part of their gang?" Tabitha asked.

"No." Chase's expression spoke of his impatience. "I'm here to help Miranda. She's close to someone I care about and if something happens to her . . ." He stopped talking, frowned, and stared back at Miranda. "Do you really think I would hurt you?"

No, Miranda realized, she didn't, but something wasn't making sense and finally she realized what it was. "But you came here before I even won the competition. So you didn't come here for me."

"True." He nodded. "I came here for another reason, but I'm here now. You have to trust me." He cut his eyes off to one corner. "And this place gives me the creeps, so can we leave . . . now!"

She recalled that Chase, like Della, could sense spirits. And suddenly Miranda wanted out of here. She looked at Tabitha and then Anthony. "I trust him . . . not to hurt us." Her gaze shifted back to Chase. "But I'm gonna kick your ass for hurting Della. If you know anything about her father's case . . ."

"I'm trying to fix that." He appeared insulted. "Now come on." He waved his hand for them to move forward. "There's a way out of here."

They had only taken a few steps when she heard clanking sounds coming from the direction they'd left. Then voices echoed in the distance.

It must be dinnertime, Miranda thought and her stomach turned rock hard.

"Friggin' hell," Chase said. "Let's run."

"Wait." Miranda took a deep breath and found hope in the fact that the black curse didn't smell so strong. "We might be able to help." She reached for her sister's hand and chanted.

"Protect us now. Keep us safe. Build us a barrier of ironclad stakes."

A loud bang sounded and Miranda saw the bars appear. The voices in the distance rang closer.

"Not bad," Chase said. "But that's not going to hold them for long. Let's get out of here now. There's another door at the end of this tunnel."

They took off. Chase ran behind them, as if to protect them if the rogue vamps got through the gate.

Tabitha still held the flashlight, and they ran hard, the thumping of their feet pounding the hard dirt mingling with the voices of the rogues. Voices that seemed to grow closer.

The tunnel curved to the right, then the left. Ahead, Miranda saw the blackness fading to a gray. The exit must be close. She prayed it was, because now she could hear the footsteps of those behind them.

All of a sudden a loud clang rang out, and the gray ahead went pitch black again.

"Shit!" Chase seethed. "Someone closed the door."

"Faster," Anthony said and Miranda felt him breathing down her neck.

"There." He snatched the flashlight from her sister and pointed it up to the metal latch. "Can you two throw up another gate and give me a few minutes?"

Miranda didn't even take the time to answer, she grabbed Tabitha's hand, and they repeated the chant together. Behind her she heard Chase struggling with the heavy metal door.

The clattering of steel falling into place filled the air and not a second too soon, for the crowd of eight vampires turned the corner at the same time.

"We are so good," Tabitha said.

They were good, Miranda thought, but as Chase had said earlier, the gate wouldn't stop these rogues, just slow them down. Miranda looked back at Chase. Both he and Anthony worked to get the thing opened. And it wasn't happening fast.

Miranda grabbed Tabitha and moved a few feet back. The dirty vamps growled and they all grabbed ahold of the bars and started pulling. The eerie screech of metal bending filled the air.

"It's not going to hold long," she called out.

"Then put up another one," Chase yelled. "We've almost got it."

Right then one of the bars gave. Not even thinking of what she was about to do, Miranda twitched her pinky at the vamp. And there where the vamp had been was a kangaroo. A pink one. And then a couple of large pimples appeared on the animal's snout.

The vamp started jumping up and down, craning his pink nose to look down at himself. All the other vamps released the bars and stared in horror.

Tabitha burst out laughing, and then, holding her own pinky up, said, "Who's next?"

"No one is!" Miranda didn't recognize the voice, but her eyes lifted up, and she recognized the woman from a few of the competitions she'd attended.

Sienna's mother. And she didn't appear happy. Dressed in some hideous-looking dress, she reminded Miranda of Cruella de Vil in the cartoon *101 Dalmatians*.

"Why are you doing this?" Tabitha asked her.

The woman glanced at Tabitha. "You think you are the only ones who can put up bars?" She twitched her finger and suddenly behind them appeared another iron gate, separating them from Anthony and Chase.

And right then the smell, the stench of a black curse filled the air. She heard Chase let out a curse.

Tabitha, suddenly looking more angry than scared, took a step closer to the gate. "Does Sienna know her mother is a murderer?"

The woman glared at Tabitha. "I'm doing this for my daughter." Then she glanced back at the vamps. "You let me down," she sneered. "I told you to kill them."

"We were going to, but why waste their blood?" one of the vamps snapped. "We were going to feed off them in our celebration."

"Then call this day a celebration and feed on them now!" She raised her hand as if to remove the bars Tabitha and Miranda had brought forth.

So Miranda put up another one. And removed the bars behind them.   .

Light suddenly spilled into the darkness. Miranda glanced back and saw Chase and Anthony push open the iron door to the outside. Sunlight spilled into the darkness in soft rays.

"Let's go," Chase yelled and shot forward along with Anthony.

Miranda felt Chase grab her and saw Anthony snatch up Tabitha. Then all four of them flew out of the opening in the ground.

With almost the speed of light, Chase set her on her feet.

He ran over to the iron door to the catacombs and shut it. The loud clank sounded and still in a bit of panic, Miranda jumped.

They were safe. *Safe. Safe.* She repeated the word in her head.

"They won't be getting out anytime soon." Chase turned back to

Miranda and then raised his nose. "And . . . here comes the cavalry. Which means, I'd better go."

Cavalry? She suddenly understood. Burnett and the others. She knew they would come for her.

"No," Miranda said. "You can't treat Della this way. You can't let her father pay for—"

He shot closer to her. "I'm not. I'm going to fix this. Tell Della I will be in touch as soon as I have answers. Tell her . . . I send my love."

Then he was gone. A blur racing across the sky.

"I want to know what he ate for breakfast," Anthony said, no doubt awed by Chase's speed and strength.

All of a sudden the metal door on the ground leading to the catacombs creaked open.

Miranda jumped back; Anthony moved forward.

Out of the ground came a beam of light. Miranda blinked and saw Kylie.

She glowed like she always did when she was in protective mode.

Beside Kylie appeared a fierce-looking bird from the Dark Ages. His blue eyes met Miranda's briefly and he flapped his wings as if in warning to Anthony. Then flashed two other vampires. Two Miranda loved: Burnett and Della.

Miranda saw Della lift her head up in the air as if testing for scents.

Burnett, his eyes glowing the same lime green as Della's, shot forward. "Friend or foe?" he asked Miranda, staring at Anthony.

"Friend," Miranda said.

Della moved closer and lifted her face into the air again. "Was . . ."

"Yes," Miranda said and tears filled her eyes. "Chase was here. He saved us."

Della, looking confused, took off, no doubt hoping to find Chase.

Burnett moved in. "Are you okay?"

Miranda nodded and she couldn't stop grinning, but she couldn't stop crying either.

"But I need a hug," she said and grabbed Burnett.

. . .

"This is ridiculous," Tabitha said, sitting beside Miranda at the supernatural doctor's office. "We told him we were okay. We don't need treatment!"

By *him,* Miranda knew her sister meant Burnett. He'd insisted on taking them in to be checked. Anthony, too. The good-looking French vampire just happened to be in with the doctor now.

She looked over at Burnett and Perry, along with Kylie, Della, and Shawn standing right outside the waiting room. Della had returned only a few seconds after she'd taken off. Chase had gotten away. Miranda had passed on Chase's message. Della hadn't been happy, but something in her eyes told Miranda that Chase wasn't the only one who still cared.

Tabitha clutched her hands together and moaned, bringing Miranda back to the present. "He's the most stubborn and—"

"Lovable," Miranda said, glancing back at Burnett. "He's amazing. They all are," she said, and felt emotion tightening her throat again. She didn't know why she suddenly was so weepy. Maybe getting kidnapped and almost becoming some rogue's dinner was her breaking point.

Tabitha stopped talking and followed Miranda's gaze. "He doesn't like me. None of them do."

"They just don't know you," Miranda said. "And you did the horse-crap spell on me. They're very protective."

She heard Tabitha sigh. "You act like they're family."

Miranda smiled. "They are."

"What does that make me?" Tabitha asked, almost sounding jealous.

Miranda looked at her. "Family, too." She smiled and noted how matted her sister's hair was. "You look terrible. You got mud—"

"You should see yourself," Tabitha said and chuckled. She reached over and squeezed Miranda's hand. "I'm glad we didn't die."

"Me, too," Miranda said.

"You know, I realize it was mostly that other vampire . . . Chase, who helped us, but I think we saved ourselves, too."

Miranda nodded, liking her sister's point of view. "We did save ourselves, too."

"I'll bet our dad and moms are worried," Tabitha said.

"Yeah," Miranda agreed.

The door of the examining room opened and Anthony walked out and looked at them.

But he mostly had eyes for Tabitha.

"Next," he said.

"I'll go," Tabitha said and she leaned close. "Maybe you should go talk to Perry, he keeps looking at you."

Miranda sighed. She'd noticed Perry staring. Normally, she could read him and at least kind of know what he was thinking. Not now. He almost looked scared to talk to her. Did he think she blamed him for leaving her on the roof?

How could he think that?

She'd heard someone say that it was because of Perry that they'd been found. He'd left Miranda on the building after he'd seen a vampire flying away with Tabitha. He'd gone to help her, not knowing the other vamp had been around. Unfortunately, he'd lost sight of the vamp and Tabitha about a half mile from the castle. But that had been when Chase had spotted him flying overhead and followed in his direction at a vampire's speed. So it was because of Perry that Chase knew where to find them.

Tabitha walked back into the doctor's office. Anthony dropped down in the chair next to Miranda.

"I know you are the one who first wanted to save me," he said. "I owe you a big thank you." His French accent was kind of nice. Even sexy if you were into accents.

She looked at him. "It was just a little blood. I donate to the blood bank at Shadow Falls." She looked down at the two tiny marks on her wrist where Anthony's teeth had sank into her skin. "But it's not a direct deposit like it was with you."

"You and your sister are good people."

"Thank you," Miranda said.

"Tell me, is your sister . . . how do you say . . ." He paused. "Sorry, my English is not too good."

Miranda smiled. "It's better than my French." She sighed. "And Tabitha doesn't have a boyfriend," Miranda said, knowing what he wanted to ask. "But we're leaving to go back to the U.S. in two days."

"Well, lucky for me, I have an uncle who lives in Texas. Is this not where you two are from?"

Miranda smiled. "Yup."

All of a sudden, voices rose outside of the waiting room. Miranda looked and saw her mom, dad, and Tabitha's mom all barreling inside. Her mom was yelling at Burnett, Tabitha's mom was yelling at her mom, and her dad stood there running his hand through his hair as if the two women were more than he could handle.

Miranda looked at Anthony and frowned. "Here's a lesson in English for you. Ever heard of the saying, the shit just hit the fan?"

"I do not think so. What does this expression mean?"

"Just watch and see," Miranda said. "Just watch and see."

The doctor had given all of them a clean bill of health, but insisted they all needed a day of rest.

Thankfully, that meant Burnett sent her dad, mom, and Tabitha mom's away. The talk her father had wanted to have with everyone had to be postponed. Not that Miranda or Tabitha minded. They went back to the apartment and crashed together in the bedroom where Tabitha and Sienna had slept the night before.

Several hours later, Miranda woke up and found Tabitha sitting up, just staring at the wall.

"You okay?" Miranda asked.

"Yeah. I just . . . I feel sorry for Sienna," Tabitha said.

"Me, too." Miranda rolled over and looked at her half-sister.

"Do you think her mom will ever get out of prison?"

"I doubt it," Miranda said. "She killed Roni Force and Cindy Bryant. And she'd have killed us if Chase and the others hadn't gotten to us. And just to make sure her daughter was high priestess."

"I know. It's just . . . I keep thinking about how Sienna feels. She can't help it that her mother is a lunatic."

Miranda nodded, thinking of her own parents' sins. "I guess no one should feel guilty about what their parents do."

From Tabitha's expression, she knew exactly what Miranda meant. She leaned back on the bed and stared up at the ceiling. "I still think they could have told us, or done things differently."

"Me, too," Miranda agreed. "It's so screwed up."

"It's love," Tabitha said. "Love screws with your head and your heart."

Miranda considered how she felt about Perry. It felt sort of screwed-up, too.

"But . . ." Tabitha continued. "I still love our dad and my mom."

"Me, too. They're our parents. We have to love them."

Tabitha rolled to her side and put her face in her hand. "Do you think we look alike?"

"Everyone says we do," Miranda answered.

"I like that," Tabitha said.

"Me, too." Something shifted at the window and caught Miranda's gaze. A bird sat on the sill, looking inside. It was raining and the bird's feathers were ruffled. The animal looked cold and pathetic. It looked lost.

"I think that's Perry," Tabitha said. "He's been out there since I woke up." Her sister got out of bed. "Why don't I leave and let you two talk?"

The idea made her nervous, but it was time. Miranda nodded. "Thanks."

Tabitha got to the door and then turned around. "I won't eavesdrop this time."

Miranda smiled. "I appreciate that."

Tabitha turned to leave then stopped and glanced back over her shoulder. "You'll tell me what happens, right? Now that . . . that we're okay with being sisters."

"Yeah," Miranda said, knowing she and Tabitha were going to be okay. They were sisters and while the circumstances felt wrong, it felt right, too.

If only everything felt that way, she thought, and glanced back at Perry.

Chapter Nineteen

Perry flew in as soon as she opened the window. Wings out, he landed on the bed. In mere seconds he'd returned to human form. He still looked cold and pathetic. His hair was damp; his pale yellow T-shirt clung to him. His eyes were clouded with guilt.

"I'm sorry," he said before she could open her mouth.

"Perry, you didn't—"

"I left you up there. I didn't know there were more rogues around. I swear, I'd die before I let anyone—"

"Stop," Miranda demanded. "You didn't do anything wrong."

"If I hadn't left you, he wouldn't have gotten you. You wouldn't have had to endure any of that." He sat up. "You could have died, and—"

"Stop! If you hadn't left me when you did, my sister would be dead. I didn't know I had a sister for all these years and if I'd lost her now, I would . . . I couldn't have stood that. I'm not mad at you. I owe you."

She went and sat down beside him, then hugged him. "Thank you."

She felt him bury his face in her hair. The embrace of gratitude slowly changed to something more. Something soft and romantic.

Closing her eyes, she savored his scent, the safe feel of his arms around her.

"I love you," he said, pulling her a little closer.

She recalled Tabitha's words. *Love screws with your head and your heart.*

Pulling back, she gazed up into his eyes. She knew he ached to hear her say everything was okay, but God help her, she was afraid. Afraid to give herself to the emotion when . . . when she could see how love had messed up her entire family.

He sighed as if her silence spoke louder than words. "I won't give up."

She nodded and for some reason she liked hearing that. Maybe all she needed was time. Then she leaned back against him and just let him hold her. For now, wasn't that enough?

The next day, around noon, Miranda stood in a circle of five witches in the large auditorium, bracketed between the two twins. Her palms were sweating. Sienna had dropped out of the competition, so the council had flown in the runner-up.

Tabitha had come to see her in her dressing room right before the competition started. Her words rang in Miranda's ear. *As long as one of us wins, I'll be happy.* Tabitha had hugged her and wished her good luck. The honesty in her sister's eyes told Miranda her sister meant it.

The meeting her dad had been intent on having yesterday had taken place this morning. It had been short and sweet. Their father had basically repeated what he'd told her earlier, and asked both girls' forgiveness for handling things poorly.

Miranda's mom had sat quietly, tears in her eyes, the whole time. Mary Esther, sitting in the opposite corner with her daughter, had looked hurt. Hearing her husband confess his love to Miranda's mom must have been hard. The same look was reflected in Tabitha's eyes. Yup, love could really screw people up.

Afterward, the two moms agreed to at least try to be civil to each other. It was more than Miranda expected. Especially from Mary Esther. Tabitha was right, it seemed clear that the woman still cared about their father.

After the meeting, they had all come to the auditorium together. Miranda hadn't said much to either of her parents. Not that it stopped her mom from visiting Miranda before Tabitha had showed up.

Her mom had hugged her, told her how proud she was of her, and that she was certain Miranda would win this competition. *"It's in your blood."* She had raised Miranda's chin and looked her right in the eyes. *"You realize this is it. You'll be eighteen in a few months. You can't enter this competition again. Win this for your mama."*

As her mom started out, Miranda asked, *"Did you know?"*

"Know what?" her mom asked.

"Know Dad was married?"

She blinked, and then answered. *"Not at first."*

"Don't lie to me," Miranda said, noting the guilt in her mom's eyes.

Her mom frowned. *"I was suspicious, but I didn't know for sure."* She sighed. *"I guess I should have been more inquisitive."*

"Yeah," Miranda answered.

"Sometimes it's easier to see only what you want to see," her mom had continued with sadness in her eyes.

"Tabitha Evans," the reigning high priestess called out. Hearing her sister's name pulled Miranda out of her thoughts and back to the present—back to the competition. She and her sister were the last two to perform in the U.S. part of the competition. Miranda watched with pride as her sister stepped up and moved the flame from the fireplace to the candle, earning herself the complete hundred points for the spell.

Tabitha and Miranda were tied before this last challenge. If Miranda got the entire hundred points, the council would use the score from the last competition to break the tie. And since she'd beaten Tabitha, the tie would rule in Miranda's favor.

All she had to do was to complete this last little spell without a hitch, and she would be high priestess. Then she'd have to do one more competition with the other foreign contestants. But even if she flunked that round, she'd still be high priestess for the U.S. She'd have made her mother one happy woman. She would have finally made her mother proud.

"Miranda Kane." The speaker of the council called her name.

Miranda moved to the front and gazed at the audience. Perry stood in the back watching her. A soft smile in his eyes—patience in his expression.

Shawn stood by Burnett. She didn't have a clue what she was going to do about him. But seeing his warm gaze just made her feel worse.

Shifting her focus up to the front of the crowd, she saw her mom, her eyes so full of hope and pride, and holding tight to her father's hand. Mary Esther sat three seats away. Alone. The seat next to her was empty.

Shifting ever so slightly, Miranda cut her eyes to Tabitha. Her half-sister stared into the audience. Her expression the same as it had been during the meeting—disillusioned. Was she thinking about her mom?

"You can begin," the announcer's voice rang loud. Taking a deep breath, unsure she could do this, Miranda extended her hand. "Fire to flame. Smaller but the same. I move thee to the wick in the Goddess's name."

The spark rose from the fire, a perfect little spark, red with tiny streaks of blue. It moved slowly to the candle and hung above it for several seconds. Finally it lowered. The warm glow touched the wick and . . . vanished. A small puff of smoke snaked up to the ceiling, taking with it Miranda's dreams. Her mother's dreams.

She heard the crowd moan in disappointment. While it might have been impossible, she could swear she had heard the sound of her mom's soft sad sigh. Her dream for her daughter gone.

"Our winner, Tabitha Evans," the council announced and the sound of the applause rang too loudly in Miranda's ears. A feeling she'd known too often filled her chest and twisted her stomach. The one associated with losing. The one she'd felt so often, having to face the disappointment in her mother's eyes.

Head held high, refusing to show emotion, she walked over to her half-sister. Tabitha stood in blissful shock. Miranda hugged her. Tight. "Congratulations."

Taking a deep breath, and trying not to look at her mom, Miranda darted to her dressing room. Her chest felt heavy. She'd let her mom down. Let her down so badly.

"Miranda?" she heard someone call her name. She didn't stop. Moving faster, she longed for solitude. She made it inside of her small dressing room, took one deep gulp of oxygen, and then another. The door behind her swished open, slamming against the wall.

Miranda turned, expecting to see her mom, dreading the discontent she'd see in her mother's eyes, but it wasn't her mom perched in the doorway.

Tabitha, her cheeks bright, anger in her eyes, stood in the doorway. "You purposefully lost to me, didn't you?"

Miranda rolled her eyes. "Please. I wanted this as bad as you did. For me. For my mom. You know how much my mom wanted this. You won fair and square. And don't gloat about it. Just leave." She gripped her hands into tight fists.

"I don't believe you," her half-sister said.

"Well, what do you want me to do? Take a lie detector test? Sign me up!"

"Tabitha," Mary Esther's voice called out. "You need to give a speech."

"Go," Miranda said and gave Tabitha a nudge out the door. "Go before my mother shows up and our moms get into another fight."

"Are you sure?" Tabitha asked. "You didn't do this on purpose?"

"I'm sure." She gave her sister a quick hug. "Now go, before I get jealous and give you pimples or something."

Tabitha grinned and then took off. And that's when Miranda saw Della and Kylie standing there in the hall. Their expressions showed they knew.

Miranda waited until her sister had turned the corner and couldn't hear. Crossing the hall, she faced her two best friends. "Never tell a soul. Promise me."

They looked at each other and then said in unison, "Promise."

"But why?" Kylie asked. "You've wanted this. I know you wanted this. Your mom groomed you for this all your life. Making your mom proud meant so much to you. Why throw it away?"

Miranda put her hand over her lips as tears slipped from her lashes. Then she wiped them away. As much as it stung, she'd done the right thing.

"Tabitha deserves it."

"More than you?" Della snapped. "How the hell did you come up with that theory? I swear, I do not understand nice people."

Miranda took in another deep breath. "My dad loves my mom. Not hers. And Mary Esther had him first. That's wrong."

"That sucks. And I don't think that's a good enough reason," Della said. "The sins of the mother are not supposed to climb down the generation ladder."

"Well, they do," Miranda said. "And yes, it sucks." She held out her arms. "So much so I . . . Can I have a hug?" They both walked into Miranda's embrace.

And there in Paris, her dream of making high priestess forever vanished, Miranda knew that as uncertain as some things were in life—things like love—she would always have her two best friends.

Fierce

◆

Chapter One

Fredericka Lakota slipped the polished hammered wolf pendant on the silver chain, and hung it up. Stepping back, she . . . frowned. She was a better artist in her head than she was in the flesh. But wasn't that appropriate? She was better at everything in her head—even a better person—than she was in life, too.

Not a good person, but better than most people considered her. But people were like jewelry, the quality depended on what you were made of. She hadn't come from great stock.

Not that she wasn't pure-blooded werewolf. Any supernatural could tell that by looking at her pattern. But her parents had been rogue. Or at least her father had, she'd never known her mother.

She stepped back and looked at her ten jewelry sets. At the bottom of the black velvet display case she'd made was her logo painted in silver script: Ricka Lakota Designs.

Ricka because Fredericka was too long. In time, she supposed the nickname wouldn't bother her.

Was her work good enough to show in a gallery?

In the morning she'd take her entire collection into Fallen, where after viewing her work, Brandon Hart, the owner of the new gallery in Fallen, would either invite her to sell her wares in the new business, or she'd be told to take a hike.

He planned to pick ten individuals' works to display in his gallery.

However, he'd warned her in an e-mail that he'd already had two other jewelry artists make appointments and only wanted one.

She didn't know shit about Brandon Hart—she guessed he was human. Was he even qualified to judge her work? What if he didn't like it? Or didn't like her? She wasn't what anyone would call likable. *Raised a rogue, always a rogue.* So many supernaturals believed it. And she'd given up trying to prove people wrong.

All of a sudden she heard footsteps. The workshop located behind Holiday James' cabin was off the beaten path. Fredericka didn't get a lot of company, which was exactly why she liked it. The only one who'd seen her work was Holiday, who also happened to be the owner of the school. Which was another reason the interview frightened Fredericka.

Moving to the opened window, she pulled air through her nose to see who trotted through the woods toward her. Instead of picking up a scent first, she heard the rush of waterfalls. What the heck? She'd woken up in the middle of the night hearing it, too.

Then catching the scent, Fredericka hurried over to the chair where her long-sleeved shirt lay and slipped it on over her tank top.

She'd barely gotten the shirt on when Kylie, a chameleon, the rarest species of supernatural, knocked. "Fredericka?"

The door swished open. Fredericka shot in front of the display. Her shirt slipped off her shoulder but she snagged it back before Kylie's gaze went there. "What?"

"Holiday sent me," Kylie said. "Someone's at the office to see you."

"You must have misunderstood." Fredericka stepped forward, hoping the girl would step out. No such luck.

"I don't think so." Kylie made an apologetic face.

Oh, please, no one had come to see Fredericka. Case in point, she'd been here six months and hadn't had one visitor. On Parents' Day she always found a place to hide out. The last thing she wanted was for her peers to start feeling sorry for her. That was worse than them judging her.

Kylie remained in the doorway. "Holiday said she tried to call you, but you didn't answer. She texted me and asked me to see if you were here."

Fredericka pulled her cell phone from her back pocket. It was out of battery again.

"Then let's go," Fredericka said, certain Kylie had misunderstood the reason Fredericka was being summoned, but eager to get the girl out of her private haven.

Fredericka gave another wave toward the door. Kylie leaned to the right.

"Wow! Did you make those?" The girl moved around Fredericka. She touched a necklace. Fredericka almost told her to keep her paws to herself.

"Ricka Lakota Designs," Kylie read then looked back. "Ricka. I like that. Is that your nickname?"

"No." Fredericka emotionally flinched. And after hearing the name from someone's lips, she knew her next order of business was to change her logo.

"Can we go?" She motioned to the door for the second time.

"Sorry." Kylie backed out.

Fredericka locked the door. Kylie waited to walk with her. Any other person would have skedaddled, especially after Fredericka had been so curt. But Kylie wasn't just anyone.

Not only was she the rarest of supernaturals, who could go invisible—and yeah, Fredericka had actually seen her do it—but unlike so many of those here, she was the type who tried to see good in everyone. The poor thing had to look long and hard before she spotted any in Fredericka. Especially considering they'd had a rocky start. Like boulder-size rocky.

Kylie had taken the one guy Fredericka had thought she loved. Key word, *thought*. Not that Fredericka held it against Kylie now. Lucas had been the one pursuing the relationship. Fredericka had come to see that.

They started down the path. The cool breeze, scented with wet earth, whispered through the trees and brought with it the sound of rushing water again.

Fredericka stopped and glanced back in the woods. "Do you hear that?"

Kylie glanced over her shoulder. "Hear what?"

"The water."

Kylie's eyes widened as if Fredericka had asked something weird. "You hear the falls?"

"Yeah. Why? Is that bad or something?"

"No, it's just . . ."

"Just what?" Fredericka asked.

"Usually, when you hear the falls, it's calling you."

"Why would it call me?" Fredericka asked.

"Normally, it's when the death angels are trying to communicate with you."

"Oh, I have nothing to say to them."

"I don't think they call you to the falls to punish you," she said, reading Fredericka's fear.

Fredericka's shoulders tightened. She didn't like being read. And she sure as hell didn't want to be called. "Well, if they want me, they'll have to text me." And she hoped like hell they didn't. The death angels were spirits who held supernaturals responsible for their actions. Fredericka had more than her share of negative checkmarks on her conduct card.

Kylie shrugged and they continued on. Before they even got past Holiday's cabin, the girl spoke again. "Why don't you want anyone to see your work? It's amazing. I'd give anything to have talent like that."

Call it stupid, but the compliment fell like soft rain on Fredericka. "How about I swap you my jewelry-making talent for the ability to go invisible?"

Kylie laughed. "It's not nearly as cool as it seems."

"You aren't gonna convince me," Fredericka said.

"Seriously," Kylie said. "That necklace was gorgeous."

"Thanks. I guess I'll know for sure tomorrow."

"What's happening tomorrow?" Kylie sounded genuinely interested.

Fredericka didn't have a clue why she did it, but she told her about the interview.

"Oh, you are so gonna get it!"

"I hope so," Fredericka said, and got a buzz of excitement talking about it. Right then, she realized the reason she might not have told anyone about her work was because she didn't have friends. Or at least, she didn't have girlfriends. She hung out with the guys. And face it, those guys weren't interested in her jewelry making.

Not that she needed anyone to be interested. She simply got along better with boys. Girls could be bitches.

For a while, a rumor spread around the school that she was gay. But nope. She was totally into the opposite sex. In particular, Cary.

Almost if Kylie read her mind, she asked, "So how are things with you and Mr. Cannon?

"Good," Fredericka said, but they'd be so much better when school was out. Cary Cannon, a full were, taught history at the Academy. Only two years older than she, the guy took her breath away the first time she'd laid eyes on him. Smart and sexy. She'd never been a history fan until now.

He'd acknowledged his attraction to her, but insisted they only be friends until she graduated. The wait was killing her. Meanwhile, they met every day after school, and she'd listen to him talk about all his trips to see historic places—Paris, Rome, Egypt. If it had history, Cary had been there or wanted to go there. Someday she hoped to go with him, too.

"How good?" Kylie smiled in that way girls did when they wanted you to tell them a secret.

"We're just friends," Fredericka said.

"Well, think how good it will be when you move it to that next stage. You two will know everything about each other."

"Yeah." It hit her that while she'd gotten to know a lot about Cary, he didn't know much about her. Not his fault. She wasn't exactly forthcoming.

She'd almost told him yesterday about her jewelry, but had chickened out. He wasn't like the male were students. But face it, the man got excited about pyramids, about Notre Dame. Her biggest fear was that he'd think her passion for jewelry was silly. And that was the last way she wanted him to see her.

"This is where I drop off," Kylie said when they got to the main path, obviously going back to her cabin. Her smile came off so real and it made Fredericka wish that she could be like other girls and have close friends. The way Kylie was with her witch and vampire roommates.

"I want to hear how things go tomorrow. Good luck."

Fredericka nodded, then instantly realized the downside of having shared her secret. If her work didn't get accepted, everyone would know she'd failed. Why hadn't she just kept her mouth shut?

Fredericka took off, her pace faster than it had been in the morning. With a full moon coming soon, her strength grew greater daily.

"Hey." Kylie's call had Fredericka glancing over her shoulder. "You may want to mention to Holiday about hearing the falls."

"Yeah," Fredericka said, but she wouldn't. She wanted to forget about that.

As she got closer to the office, she wondered exactly what it was that Holiday wanted, because no one could be here to see her. But when she stepped on the front porch, she caught the trace of another were. A familiar trace.

She curled her hands into fists.

What the hell did Marissa Canzoni want? Her gaze shot back to the trail. She didn't have to face this. Her feet were poised to swing around, when she remembered she'd stopped running from her problems a long time ago.

Bracing herself for whatever shit Marissa had dug up and the emotional backlash that seeing her would bring, she walked into Holiday's office.

"Ricka." Marissa nodded as Fredericka walked in. "Look at you. All grown up." Thankfully, the woman didn't appear to be about to put on some front, like jumping up and hugging her. There was no affection between them. Not that Fredericka hated her. She'd been the nicest in the long line of her father's bitches who he'd expected to take care of Fredericka the first ten years of her life. Her father would bring them into his home, sleep with them, make house with them for a month, maybe two, and then disappear for weeks at a time. Work, he called it.

But Fredericka always wondered if deep down he'd simply been trying to get away from her. How could he not resent her? Her mother
had died giving Fredericka life. Nothing like growing up knowing
you'd killed your own mother—especially when you saw the grief in
your father's eyes each time he looked at you and said, "You look just
like her."

Some of her dad's women really hated Fredericka. Like Donique,
who'd left those damn scars on Fredericka's arm. Like Shelbie, whose
cruel words left scars on Fredericka's heart. Or Karine, who simply
neglected to feed her. Marissa had simply tolerated Fredericka. A far
cry from feeling loved, but who needed to feel loved, as long as you
weren't abused, called terrible names, or left hungry.

"Hello, Marissa." Fredericka moved in and sat down on the sofa in
Holiday's office. "What brings you here?" she asked, and tried not to
look at Holiday—not wanting to give the fae an opportunity to read
her emotions.

"It's your father," Marissa said. "I'm sorry, but he was killed last
week."

It felt as though her words floated around the room for several seconds before Fredericka could take them in. Even then, Fredericka sat
there, not letting one pinch of emotion sneak out. It wasn't the an-
nouncement of his death that took a bite out of her heart, but rather
the time of his passing. She had always felt better believing he'd been
dead these last eight years. Better than believing he'd purposely abandoned her with a pack of rogue weres.

Thankfully, Lucas Parker's dad had taken pity on her and assigned
one of his pack matrons to watch over her. Not that there had been
any love there either, but the woman had never dared mistreat her, for
fear of Mr. Parker's retaliation.

"I, uhh, had a few things to give you." Marissa held an envelope but
reached into her purse and handed Fredericka a small strip of photos.
The pictures felt thin, aged. Fredericka didn't look at them—didn't
have to.

She knew exactly what they were. She'd been five and her father
had taken her to a mall where there had been one of those photo booths.

He'd put his money in and they'd made funny faces as the camera took their pictures. It was one of her favorite memories and it had been captured on film.

Fredericka's breath hitched in her lungs. Just holding those images threatened to unearth her vulnerability and lack of self-worth she fought so diligently to deny.

"He loved you, Ricka. I know he didn't show it all the time, but he carried those four photos with him forever. He never carried one photo of me, or the other women he called his own. And when he came to me these last eight years, he would always ask me, "Do you think she's happier, there?"

Loved? He'd abandoned her.

Strangely, the most Fredericka had ever felt loved by the man was when she saw him kill Donique after she showed him the burns on her arm. But that had done a number on Fredericka, too. And she'd never told him any of the things his next bitches did to her. Then their deaths would have been on her, just like Donique's, like her own mother's.

"Thank you for letting me know." Fredericka stood and shot out.

She heard Holiday call her back, but no way in hell would she turn around.

No way in hell would she cry either! She wouldn't. Folding the pictures, she tucked them in her pocket and ran back to the workshop, determined to make another display board. One where the nickname her father had given her wouldn't appear. If she never heard that name again, it would be too soon.

As her feet hit the hard cold earth, her thoughts echoed from her head to her heart. He'd been alive. All this time, he'd been alive. All of those birthdays, Christmases, when others clung to their families, she'd been alone. He could have been there.

"Rest in hell, Daddy," she muttered.

She got to the workshop and dug into her pockets for the key. First the right pocket, beneath the photos. It wasn't there. Then the left. It wasn't there either. What the hell had she done with it?

She considered just breaking down the door, but that door didn't belong to her. Holiday and Burnett had entrusted her with the shop. Destroying it would have been unacceptable.

She searched the ground, thinking she might have dropped it. Even got on her hands and knees. The position tugged at her inner wolf and she longed for the full moon that was less than a week away. A time when her spirit felt free of the emotional ties of the human world.

That's when she heard it again. The rush of water cascading down. It grew louder and louder.

"Come get the key," a voice echoed from the sound.

She looked down the trail. *The death angels* had taken it? What right did they have to take something that didn't belong to them? She stood up, her fear of the death angels shattered. Nothing but fury motivated her now.

Did they want to condemn her for how she'd turned out? Hold her responsible for her inability to trust, to let people close? For occasionally shooting life the middle finger? Where were they when she'd been young?

The anger and a shitload of resentment had her running down the path, ready to offer a little comeuppance to anyone who dared to judge her.

Chapter Two

The sound of the falls grew louder and louder. Fredericka veered off the path and let her ears and her own hostility guide her. Pushing through thick brush and low-hanging trees, thorns clung to her jeans and occasionally caught hold of her long hair. She kept hearing Marissa's words. *He loved you, Ricka.*

Lie. Lie. Lie!

The rumble of the falls vibrated the ground. Suddenly the forest ended and she came to an abrupt halt. The falls stood twenty feet from her. Water roared and rushed down into a pond that looked so serene she wanted to toss a rock at it.

Tiny drops of water danced in the verdantly scented air. The trees, the plant life, they all looked . . . fresh. Fresh like spring, but it wasn't spring. It couldn't be real.

Then she felt it . . . an aura that she could only define as hope. Like how she felt when she was just beginning a jewelry project, when the thrill of making a new piece hit. Before she was blindsided by her own limitations.

A shadow moved behind the wall of water. She could swear it motioned her inside.

She didn't trust it, but just to prove she wasn't a coward, she stepped into the pond. Her breath caught when she moved but the water didn't.

She pushed on, walked through the wall of white cascading water. The wet coldness prickled her skin. Her hair hung limp past her shoulders, and water dripped from the dark strands. The person, or spirit, whatever it had been that had waved her inside, wasn't anywhere to be seen. A serene quietness invaded the space.

"What do you want with me?" she yelled, hoping to prove she wasn't afraid—or maybe that her fury outweighed her fear. Either way, she was here. Let them throw her sins at her like stones. She'd take it, and then she'd throw them back and remind them she hadn't asked to be like this. The world had shaped and molded her into who she was.

She moved up to the rock floor, stood there and sensed the brewing of a perfect storm; the calm of this place coming face-to-face with the emotional turbulence raging inside her. *He had not loved her!*

The folded pictures in her pocket felt heavy like a rock.

Slipping them out, never looking at them, she ripped them into shreds.

"You want to blame someone? Blame him!"

She dropped down on her butt. Her chest ached. The hairline fractures in her heart gave way to become real cracks. Then she felt them—the tears she'd vowed not to cry. Looking at the tiny pieces of photographs in her hand, she caught one glimpse of her daddy's smile. She threw the shredded photos into the water, wanting them and the pain to go away. To stay away.

The still water started moving in circles, slow at first, then faster. Fredericka's breath hitched in her lungs. The wake of the water brought all the bits of papers into a little cyclone. Round and round they went until piece by piece, like a jigsaw puzzle, all those tiny bits of images came back together.

She blinked, not believing it.

Then the ebb and flow of the water brought the strip of four images back to her. Left them at her feet.

Through tears, she saw the two smiling faces staring up at her. Her father and her at their happiest moment.

Stunned and completely leery of the power it took to undo her destruction, she scooted back away from the images.

Sobs, sad little hiccups suddenly filled the alcove of rock. It took several seconds to realize that noise came from her.

A shift, a movement behind the wall of water brought her wet eyes up. Then a shape moved through the liquid divide.

Ready to kick ass and ask questions later, she got up onto her haunches. But the person emerging was the last person Fredericka would hurt. She dropped back on her butt and looked up at Holiday.

"Kylie said it was calling you," Holiday said.

"I don't want to talk about this." Fredericka found just an ounce of strength to pull herself together.

The redheaded fae came and sat down beside her.

"I won't push you to talk about anything, but . . . I need to tell you that you have an envelope with what looks like a couple of letters in it, waiting for you in my office. And I just want to make sure that you're okay. You were so upset and I—"

"I'm fine. I always am." For the first time, Fredericka looked around. As serene as the outside of the falls was, inside was even more beautiful. The sun came through the falls and cast flickering rainbows on the cavern walls. Colors danced and meshed and melded together.

"What is this place?" Fredericka asked.

Holiday looked at her. "You have Native American blood in you, don't you?"

"Yes. Why?" Fredericka asked.

"The Native Americans used the falls for spiritual ceremonies. They considered it a private place. Very few people are called to visit. It's believed that some descendants of those Native Americans are among the few who are called."

"What do they want with me?"

"It's different for every person, but . . . coming brings peace, or . . . prepares us for difficult times. It's like a spiritual hug."

"I have my quota of difficult times. And I don't do a lot of hugging." Fredericka stood up and took a step to leave.

"You forgot this." Holiday held out the strip of images.

Fredericka's gaze shifted to the photos of her father holding her, laughing. "I don't want them. I've torn them up once."

Holiday stared at her a little confused, then looked down at the photos.

"It put them back together." Fredericka motioned to the water and half expected the woman to accuse of her lying. She didn't. "Does weird shit like that happen here all the time?"

"Sometimes."

"Too freaky for me." Fredericka turned to leave again.

"Fredericka?" Holiday called. When she turned around, Holiday had a slight frown on her face. "You should know that . . . that sometimes coming here brings on some special gifts."

"It's not my birthday. So no thank you."

"That doesn't seem to matter," the fae said.

Fredericka hesitated to ask. "What kind of gifts?"

"It's different for everyone, but . . . a very common one is . . . is being able to communicate with spirits."

"No." *Make that a hell no!* "Tell them to keep their gifts, and their hugs. I just want to be left alone." Fredericka ran off.

She went back to the workshop, only to remember she'd lost the key. Recalling the death angels had lied to her and said they'd had it, she was tempted to just break the door down. She stopped herself a second before she barreled her shoulder through the entrance. Just because she felt emotionally destroyed didn't give her the right to destroy property that didn't belong to her.

Her emotions still spiraling, her phone dinged with a text.

She looked at it, and muttered a curse. She'd forgotten she was supposed to meet Cary. She considered texting him back and claiming she had a headache. But no. If there was a time she needed a friend it was now. She started toward his classroom where they always met. Her heart ached and her head searched for a way to tell him what had happened. As she neared his office she envisioned his arms around her. So shoot her, she wanted . . . needed a hug. Not by a death angel but by a friend, a boyfriend, or at least a potential one.

Cary was in the little office in the back of the classroom on his laptop. He looked up with a big smile on his face. His emotions were so opposite of hers that it felt awkward. Or would be when she spilled her guts.

"You aren't going to believe this." Passion sparkled in his green eyes.

"What?" she asked, pushing her issues aside, guessing his excitement was something about history. And for the first time, she resented it just a little.

"Remember I told you that there were about five of my friends who wanted to go to Europe for six weeks but it was canceled because it was going to be too expensive? Well one girl has found a group deal and now it's back on for the summer."

"This summer?" she asked, trying not to sound devastated, but wasn't this summer supposed to be about them? She waited, wondering if he was going to say: *And I want you to come with me.* It would be hard financially, but maybe if she got the gig at the gallery and sold . . .

"The flight leaves the day after school is out, so I won't even have to miss work. Isn't that fantastic?"

She nodded. "Yeah, that's . . . I thought we were going to spend some time together this summer."

"We will when I get back," he said.

She pulled in air, pushing her resentment away, and nodded. This was Cary's passion, the last thing she wanted was to become a clingy girlfriend who resented his hobbies and wanted his world to only focus on her.

Just because he wasn't as excited as she was about moving their relationship forward, didn't mean anything. Well, it did, and it stung, but it wasn't a deal breaker.

Was it?

"Look at the pictures of the place she's found for us to stay." He pointed to his screen.

She sat down in the second chair and stared at the images of the apartment, trying to get the pictures of her dad out of her mind. Blinking again, she focused on the screen. It was just an apartment, nothing special, but she still said, "That's nice."

"Are you wet?" he asked, staring at her hair.

She nodded.

"How did you . . . ?"

Her mind raced, her heart still breaking. Could she tell Cary? She wanted to, but where to start? "I . . . was working in the workshop when Kylie came and got me. Holiday had . . ."

"Workshop?" he asked. "Doing what?"

"I design and make jewelry," she said, but the thrill of what she did felt buried beneath the grief. Hidden beneath the memories of her past. Painful recollections that she wanted to disown.

He looked confused. "You string beads?"

Ouch! "No. I . . . some of them might have beads, but I do it with metal and wire. I weld pieces and I use silver a lot."

"Oh." He looked confused. "So what does that have to do with you being wet?"

"I . . . was just starting at the beginning."

"The beginning of what?"

"Of what happened." Her chest tightened. Why did she feel insignificant right now? As if what she had to say wasn't important.

"What happened?" He looked at her hair. "It's not raining."

"No, I . . . went to the falls."

"The falls?" he asked. "That freaky place on the property?"

She nodded and wished this was easier.

"Why would you go there?"

"I was . . ." *called,* but she didn't want to say it. It wasn't important. And suddenly what was important bubbled to the surface and she swallowed to keep her tears back. "My dad died."

Cary's eyes widened. "I'm sorry. But wasn't . . . ?" He raked a hand through his hair. "I thought your dad was already dead?"

She had halfway thought that, too, but she couldn't remember telling him. "No."

"But you said something about growing up with Lucas's pack, so I just thought that meant your parents were dead."

"No," she said. And for some crazy reason her mind and heart gathered up all the details she knew about his parents. They lived in Dallas. His dad was a professor. His mom was a part-time nurse. He had one sister and she was going to college to be an accountant. That's when it hit. She knew these things not because he'd told her, but because she'd asked.

He hadn't asked.

He continued to stare at her. "But you aren't close to him, are you?"

Her sinuses stung. "I haven't seen him in eight years." She swallowed that pain and it lumped together with all the other knots of regret.

"So I guess it's not . . . that big of a deal, huh?"

His words just sort of hung in the air, heavy. She tried to push back how hurtful those words sounded, but like the lump in her throat, it wasn't moving.

She shot up from the chair. "It's a bigger deal than going to Europe for six weeks." The words almost unleashed her tears.

He stood, anger brightening his eyes. Then it faded. "I . . . I didn't mean . . ." He brushed a few damp strands of hair off her cheek, then pulled her against his shoulder. She went, and didn't realize how cold she was until she came against his warmth. The warmth of a were. She longed to have his arms around her. To feel comforted, to know someone cared.

"I know you're upset. I forgive you for lashing out."

He forgives me?

He.

Forgives.

Me?

She pulled back. "I don't . . . need to be forgiven, Cary. You do."

"What?" His eyes brightened again.

She shook her head and the reality of what they'd had these past few months—and what they hadn't had—sank in.

"Forget it," she said. "Forget this." She waved a hand between them. "Forget us." She turned to leave.

He caught her by her arm. The one with scars, and his grip was just the slightest bit too tight.

"Don't act childish," he said.

She felt her own eyes grow bright. "Childish?" She wanted to call him a self-absorbed, history-loving dog and to tell him to mind his paws, but she didn't. Because that would have proved him right.

With pride, the kind that came with being a were—a were who already had shame to hide—she lifted her chin and met his eyes directly. "I tell you my dad died and you say it's not a big deal? I came here needing . . . something, support or just understanding, but you obviously don't know how to offer that." She inhaled. "See you in class on Monday, Mr. Cannon."

Chapter Three

The next morning Fredericka parked in front of the soon-to-be gallery. After she'd left Cary's last night, she'd decided against coming today. She'd wanted to curl up in a little ball and forget everything. Her heart and spirit were just too broken, but at a quarter to nine this morning, her spirit raised its ugly head and refused to give up without at least trying.

Fredericka Lakota wasn't a quitter.

She ran to the office to get another key from Holiday then ran to gather her things. When she grabbed the display board and saw her nickname, her heart took another dip. She almost didn't bring it. Then because the black backdrop gave her work a more professional flare, she grabbed it anyway. She wasn't going in half-ass. Screw the pain! If she let it overtake her, she'd drown in it.

If she was going—and she was—she was going in to win this, to convince Brandon Hart that she deserved a spot in his gallery.

Now, staring at the old house on Main Street, she noted the place looked a little run-down. Or maybe not so run-down as abandoned. The lawn needed cutting and the property needed something to make it look inviting, or maybe commercial. Several of the older homes on the street had been turned into shops, but this place still looked like a residence—an empty residence.

According to the flyer Holiday had given her, he planned on opening in two weeks. The guy had better get his ass in gear.

She cut her engine off. Her phone dinged with a text. At least the dang thing was still working. Reaching onto the seat where she'd left it, she read the message.

I'm sorry. Come see me, please. It was from Cary.

Her chest tightened. Should she give the guy another chance?

Her gut said no. Her heart said yes. But was her heart just lonely? Oh, hell, now wasn't the time to think about that.

Getting out of the school's car Holiday had been so kind as to loan to her, she reached into the backseat to pull out the small suitcase on wheels that held her display board and jewelry. Feeling nervous, she walked up to the porch. The sound of suitcase wheels bumping and rolling behind her seemed too loud, as if the whole world held its breath with her.

A cold breeze stirred her hair as she stepped up onto the porch. The door, left slightly ajar, creaked, reminding her of the sound effects for some scary movie. She inched closer. Should she knock or just walk in? Now a bit closer, she peered inside. Several glass display cases had been set up and the walls were lined with shelves—a perfect place to exhibit art. But she didn't see Brandon Hart. Then again, she was early.

She considered going back and sitting in the car, but then after a second glance around the room she spotted a woman looking out the back window. How had she missed her? Could Brandon be a woman?

Fredericka stuck her head in a little. "Hello?"

The woman, around thirty years of age, with long sandy-blond hair, turned around so fast her hair spun in the air. Surprise widened her bright green eyes.

"I'm sorry. I'm Fredericka. I . . . was supposed to meet Brandon Hart here at ten? The door was open."

The woman stood silently for several long, uncomfortable seconds before she found her voice. "That's my brother. He . . . he's in the backyard working on his art."

"Should I come back in fifteen minutes?" Fredericka asked.

"No. Come in. I'm . . . Linda."

Fredericka picked up her case and eased in, looking around as she moved. In the corner of one room were eight wind chimes hanging from the ceiling. One of the artists', Fredericka assumed.

The chimes started moving and the soft ringing sounds filled the room.

For all the gallery lacked on the outside, the inside looked good. Fresh paint brightened the walls and the floor had been polished. The shelves against the wall appeared new. The refurbishing smells hung in the air, stinging Fredericka's sinuses.

"Should I set up my stuff for him to see?" Fredericka motioned to the top of one of the glass display cases.

"Sure." Linda twisted her hands together as if nervous, which didn't make sense, since Fredericka was the one about to be judged.

A rhythmic thud came from the backyard. She couldn't help but wonder what kind of art Brandon did and if that was him making that noise. But not wanting to come off as nosy, she pulled out her black display board and fit the small hooks into the board, then started pulling out her jewelry. As her gaze passed over the name scrawled across the bottom, she pushed the hurt aside.

While the sounds outside continued, the house grew too quiet. An awkward kind of silence thickened the air. "Your brother said he was interviewing other jewelry artists. I'm hoping he'll appreciate my work."

When Linda didn't answer, Fredericka looked around. The woman was gone. But damn, she moved soundlessly. With Fredericka's were hearing she didn't miss much. Fighting a chill, the wind chimes started up again. The sound was almost sad.

She hung her last necklace—even rearranged the placement of one pair of earrings. Looking around to make sure Linda hadn't returned, Fredericka inched closer to the window, wanting a peek at the man who would judge her. Her breath caught when she saw the sculpture. The wooden horse stood at least six feet tall. Carved to perfection, each dip and valley on the animal showed bone and muscle.

Then her gaze shifted to the second very nice piece of art. Only this one was flesh and blood. Standing with his back to her, the dark-haired artist wore jeans, and the faded blue denim nicely fit the lower half of his body, showcasing his own perfection.

Equally nice was the shirtless upper part of his body. He pulled the axe out of the large piece of tree trunk and brought it down again.

She admired the way his body moved, muscles rolling under light olive skin. This time however, when he pulled the axe out of the wood and swung the tool up, she saw it. The side of his torso.

Air locked in her chest as she studied his scars.

Burn marks.

She knew, because she'd stared at her own too long. He shifted his stance, and gave her a view of his profile. He bore a scar on the left side of his cheek, then another one on the left side of his forehead. They weren't as bad as the one on his side, not puckered, just a slight discoloration, and the skin looked pulled a little tight.

All of a sudden, as if he sensed someone watching, he swung around. His eyes, blue, bright blue like a summer sky, met hers. His gaze and his frown became so intense, she felt trapped.

He snatched up a shirt hanging over a patio table and she recalled doing the same thing yesterday when she'd heard Kylie coming to the workshop.

She should have looked away, offering him a bit of privacy, but she couldn't. Instead, she watched him slip his arms into the shirt and tackle one button at a time.

One.

Two.

Three.

He was covering that beautiful chest.

But good God, she shouldn't be watching. Especially when he watched her watch.

It wasn't until that last button was secured that she snapped out of it. She turned and stared instead at his art. But her gaze didn't stay there. She glanced back at him.

There was just something . . . raw and feral about this guy. And it both fascinated and scared her. That was a first. She'd never found herself the least bit fascinated, or scared, of a human.

Or was he even . . . human?

Right then he snagged a baseball cap off the table and slipped it on, covering his forehead, and covering the pattern only supernaturals could see to identify species. With a definite frown in place and his shoulders tight as if in defense mode, he hurried inside. His pace, his intensity reminded her of a . . . wolf.

One about to attack. And she was his prey.

"Can . . . I . . . help you?" His voice came out deep and masculine, his frustration clear in his clipped tone. He gave the door a good swing behind him and it slammed with a whack.

She jumped. "I . . . I'm Fredericka Lakota." Her voice shook, and her skin felt supersensitive, like just before a shift. What was it about this guy?

Then a better question hit. What was this guy? She lifted her gaze up to his forehead again. The hat covered it. She inhaled, trying to pick up on his scent. She got human, but . . . maybe something else.

He stood there for a second, his expression shifting away from anger. He gave the bib of his hat a good tug. "I'm sorry, I . . . completely forgot about the appointment. I do that when I'm starting a new piece."

"No problem. I do that, too."

He glanced at the display board standing up on his table. He eased in, offering her only the right side of his face, no doubt to keep his scars out of her line of vision.

"I'm guessing this is yours?" He motioned to her display.

"Yes." As soon as his gaze shifted from her eyes, hers shifted back to his face, trying to see under his cap's bib to catch a glimpse of his pattern. She even leaned in a bit.

He unexpectedly shifted his gaze back to her and caught her staring.

She glanced away, too quickly, and damn it she knew he thought she was looking at his scar. She almost wanted to explain, but what could she say, *I was just checking to see if you were human*? Yeah, that would go over like a fart in church.

"These are silver, right?" he asked, glancing away, but not before she saw emotion touch his eyes. She wouldn't call it embarrassment, but it was something close. That feeling one got when they were exposed and wished they weren't.

And damn it, but she knew that feeling so well.

"Are they silver?" he repeated.

"Yes," she answered, flustered.

"You like wolves?" he said, quickly cutting his eyes up to her face. Was he trying to read her pattern? Before she could tell, he focused back on the jewelry.

"Sort of," she said, now more curious.

"You use a kiln?" He didn't look at her now. For some reason that stung.

"No, a torch."

He nodded. "So . . . how much are you pricing these for?"

"I'm thinking ninety for the chain and pendant, or the whole set with the earrings for a hundred and ten." She waited for him to tell her it was too much. That she simply gave herself way too much credit.

"You need to charge more," he said.

Stunned, she could barely find her voice. "You think people will pay more?"

He shifted his eyes to her without moving his face. "I think you're worth more than that."

A breeze of pure joy whispered through her. He liked her work. On the inside she did a happy dance. On the outside she stood completely still, an odd kind of energy buzzing through her.

"Can you do custom designs if someone wants it?"

She hadn't considered it, but she could. She nodded.

"Is this all the stock you have?"

"Right now, but I could do at least three more sets before the store opens." That was pushing it, but damn it, she wanted this.

"Okay."

Okay what? "Does this mean I get the gallery space?"

He hesitated. Fredericka's heart stopped. Everyone at the school had plans, career choices, college choices. Fredericka only had her art. Was it too much to want it to mean more than just a passing hobby?

"You haven't seen the contract yet," he said.

"I'm sure it will be fine." She felt herself smiling, something she didn't do a lot of.

He turned his head to look at her. She caught a quick glimpse of his scar again, before he turned back. Her thoughts shifted from curiosity to empathy. How would she feel if she couldn't hide her scars? If they were out there for the world to see? She'd have become a hermit. But maybe her scars were deeper than his—tied to shame and . . . murder.

Either way, her admiration for Brandon Hart inched up.

With half his face turned away from her, he looked from her jewelry to her. "You . . . you'll have to man the store at least two days a week."

"Weekends okay?" she asked.

He stood there as if thinking. "You work somewhere else?"

"No, I . . . I'm finishing up school."

"College?" he asked.

"High school."

"How old are you?"

"How old are you?" she countered.

He frowned ever so slightly. "I'm not applying for a job."

"Maybe I'm just curious," she said. And she was, and not just about his age. But about his scars and . . . even more about his species. Was she wrong that his scent actually had some trace of supernatural in him? If he'd take off that darn hat, she'd be able to know.

He stood there waiting as if expecting her to give in and tell him her age. She didn't budge. The silence hung heavy. Then he caved. "I'm twenty."

She nodded. "I'll be eighteen next month. I got a late start in school."

"Can you do some half days during the week?"

"I might be able to swing it." Hopefully she could convince Holiday.

"Ten percent of sales goes to help pay for the upkeep of the gallery."

"Sounds fair." Her lips twitched and she realized she was still smiling.

He was still staring at her smile.

She found herself wishing he would smile. Wishing she knew his story. Hoping his story of how he'd gotten those scars wasn't anywhere as devastating as hers.

"Follow me, Ricka, and I'll get you the contract." He started down the hall.

"Fredericka," she said, her smile fading.

"You don't look like a Fredericka. I like Ricka."

"But I don't," she said, her tone serious.

He paused and looked over his right shoulder at her. "Why?"

Because the man who called me that just died last week. Because that name reminds me of the good, the bad, and the evil that came with it. "What if I called you Bran?"

"Deal." He turned and commenced down the hall.

"What deal?" She stared at his shoulders, held tight and proud. She liked how he carried himself.

"You call me anything you want, and I'll do the same, Ricka."

"Okay, asshole," she said before she could stop herself.

He laughed.

She started to tell him she hadn't meant it to be funny, but realized she was smiling. It was his laugh. It sounded almost musical. She found herself wishing she'd seen his face when he'd done it. Damn this guy was a mystery.

She stepped a little closer, hoping to catch his scent again. Her gaze locked on the dark brown curls that hung just a little long and brushed against the collar of his light blue shirt. Practically mesmerized at how soft his hair looked, she didn't realize he'd stopped. Or she didn't until she walked right into him.

Her breasts came against his shoulder blades, and her hand automatically came around his waist. A spark of something sweet hit when their bodies came in contact. The kind of sweetness that made her feel small against his large frame. The kind that made her wish she'd put on a little makeup, and done something special with her hair.

Her breath caught. Attraction. But holy hell, she was attracted to a human. Or at least someone who was mostly a human.

"Sorry." She stepped back, but not before she heard his breath catch or before she took in a nose full of air. He smelled like raw wood, like outdoors, he smelled . . . good.

He moved into a small office, pulled a contract out of a drawer, then dropped into a chair. His butt had barely landed when he swiveled the chair to the left, giving her his right side. Did he do it automatically? Or was he more self-conscious because he thought she'd been staring at his scars?

He pushed the paper and a pen to her. She dropped into the chair and pulled the paper closer to read it. It was simple and short.

She signed it. And filled out the request for information. And when she looked up she realized she was smiling again. *I think you're worth more than that.*

His earlier words moved around in her head, leaving a trail of something sweet in their wake. Was it sad that it had meant so much?

Probably, but she'd take it.

He ran his fingers over the edge of the desk. "I guess I'll see you in two weeks."

Two weeks seemed like a short time for her to get three more jewelry sets made, but it suddenly seemed like too long of a time before . . . before seeing him again. Before peeling off the layers of Brandon Hart and discovering his secrets. And for some unknown reason, she really wanted to know his secrets.

She heard the seconds tick by on some clock close by. And with every tick marking time, the more awkward it became. Him. Her. Staring at each other.

Her phone dinged with another incoming text. She remembered Cary, but he didn't feel so important right now.

"I look forward to working with you," Brandon said and that sounded like a send-off.

She nodded, got up, got all the way to the door, then couldn't help it. She looked back. This time he was the one caught staring. At her butt.

He lifted his gaze, and a touch of boy guilt—the look good guys got when they were caught checking you out—flashed in his eyes. He continued to gaze into her eyes, but he still kept his left cheek turned just so she wouldn't see his scar. Somehow she wanted to convince him he didn't have to hide from her.

"You need something else?" he asked.

Yeah, answers. Lots of answers.

She should leave. Go while the getting was good. But damn it. Instead, she turned completely around and faced him. "Could you use some help getting the place ready?"

He picked up the pen, clicked it once, and hesitated. "I . . . I don't have the funds to pay right now."

"I didn't ask you to pay me."

He still hesitated and clicked the pen one more time.

Afraid he was going to turn her down, she spoke up. "I'll see you tomorrow around ten." She took off feeling the buzz of excitement and clueless as to where she'd gotten the gumption to push, but somehow proud that she had.

As she stepped out of the hall, she heard the musical sound of the chimes playing.

Moving quickly, she collected her jewelry, storing it in the suitcase, fearing he was going to come out and shoot down her plan.

Finished in less than a minute, she picked up her case. The chimes were still playing. Glancing over at them, she saw them moving back and forth, yet a cold stillness seemed to fill the room. She cut her eyes up to the ceiling, thinking a vent must be pushing in cold air, but there wasn't any vent. There wasn't any air flowing, but the chimes shifted gently and played a song.

As she moved closer to the door, she looked back over her shoulder toward the hall leading to the other side of the house, half expecting to see his sister. She wasn't there, but her were sixth sense said someone was watching.

"Bye," she called out as she walked out the door.

"Later," she heard him say.

She got into Holiday's silver Honda, still feeling as if someone watched.

Starting the car, she put it in reverse. Her tires crunched on the gravel and she backed out of the driveway. She was putting the car in drive when she spotted Linda, Brandon's sister, standing at the side of the house staring down at the small unkempt flower bed. Fredericka waved but Linda didn't see her. She started forward, right as a cop car pulled into the house's driveway.

She inched away slowly, slow enough to see the two uniformed cops walk up to Brandon's door and knock. Slow enough to see him open the door. Slow enough to see his devastated expression.

Was Brandon Hart in some kind of trouble?

Chapter Four

"I got it." Fredericka walked into the office to drop off the car keys before she went to work on her jewelry.

"I knew you would." Holiday smiled.

Fredericka inhaled, not wanting to think about yesterday—about Marissa, her father, or even Cary. But from the moment she'd pulled into the parking lot, the joy she'd found at the gallery had been leaking out of her. And the pain that was her past was slowly filling her soul.

For years, she'd kept that pain buried; why did it have to rear its ugly head? Especially now, when she'd finally taken a step to building her own way in this world.

"Have you ever met Brandon Hart, the guy opening the gallery?" Fredericka dropped down in the chair.

Holiday shook her head. "No. From what I heard, he just got into town about a month ago. Why?"

"It's just . . ." She didn't want to tell Holiday she found him fascinating, because Holiday knew she'd also found Cary fascinating. "Brandon's scent was . . . human, but maybe not all human."

Holiday appeared to be surprised, and sat back in her chair. "What did his pattern tell you?"

"He wore a baseball cap." Fredericka almost told her about the cops showing up, but was afraid Holiday would have concerns about her working with him. And Fredericka's gut said that Brandon wasn't bad. There were all sorts of reasons the cops could have shown up.

She just couldn't think of one right now.

"I agreed to help him do some things around the gallery tomorrow. Is there any way, if it's not too much trouble, I could use the car again?" Fredericka hated asking for favors. But if things went well, maybe she could afford to buy her own car soon.

"Sure." Holiday glanced down at her desk.

Fredericka saw what she was looking at, too. A manila envelope. The one Marissa had brought with her. And just like that the pain from yesterday bubbled up inside and crowded out what was left of her recent joy.

When Holiday looked up, Fredericka shook her head. "I don't want it."

"But . . ."

"There are no buts! He left me. I was ten years old. He left with the rogue pack—no explanation, no good-bye. I woke up one day and he wasn't there. For weeks, I waited for him to come back." Tears filled her eyes, but she swallowed to keep them at bay. "When he didn't, I told myself he was dead. It was easier. So as far as I'm concerned he died a long time ago."

"I'm sorry," she said softly and Fredericka cringed at the pity she saw in the fae's eyes. "But I'm sure you have questions. And the answers might be in here."

"Maybe I don't care about the answers. It's not going to change anything."

"Or maybe you're just not ready. I'll keep this right here." She picked up the envelope and put it in a drawer, almost as if realizing the sight of it caused Fredericka pain. "When you're ready, you come to me."

Fredericka stood up. She doubted she would ever be ready. She'd already grieved for her dad once, she shouldn't have to do it again. And yet she was, wasn't she? At least part of her was.

Except when she was at the gallery, it had been . . . easy not to think about it. Brandon Hart and the mystery that surrounded him was just the diversion she needed. Ten o'clock tomorrow couldn't come fast enough.

Until then she'd have to rely on her art to offer a small reprieve. Thankfully, she didn't have any time to waste before diving headfirst into that bit of escape. She had three jewelry sets to make.

Fredericka, wanting to get a jumpstart on the three sets of jewelry, had started her sketch for her next design when her phone dinged with a text. She flinched thinking it would be from Cary again. What the hell was she going to say to him? Hadn't she already said it? Wasn't her parting comment about seeing him in class on Monday enough to let him know she was done thinking of him as anything but her teacher?

The text wasn't from him. Instead it was from Kylie.

> Holiday told me you got the place in the gallery. Super excited
> for you.

Fredericka smiled. And again she considered how she'd missed out on things by not having girlfriends. Someone to share secrets with. Someone who gave a damn. Maybe someday she'd be able to do that. To let others close.

You string beads? Cary's words about her jewelry making filled her head. She knew it was partly just about being a guy, but when she considered all the other hurtful things he'd said, it seemed more like a jerk thing than a guy thing.

I think you're worth more than that. Brandon's words echoed behind Cary's. Brandon was for sure all guy—an image of him cutting wood filled her head—yet he'd managed to say something nice—something that boosted her confidence instead of knocking it down a notch. The fact that he was an artist might have given him an edge, but . . . Footsteps echoed in the distance.

She moved to the window she always left cracked open for just this purpose. Those footsteps were familiar. Damn. Lifting her face up to catch any scents, she identified the intruder.

A few seconds later a knock came at the workshop door. Since when did Cary come looking for her?

"Come in." She turned away and put the pen on her paper, pretending to be sketching.

He moved in beside her. But she kept her focus on the sketch and even shaded in one part.

"You didn't answer my texts," he said.

"No, I . . . I had my interview at the gallery."

"What gallery?"

The one that wants to sell my strung beads. "I'm going to be showing and selling my work in a new gallery in Fallen. The owner wants me to have three more jewelry sets before we open. So if you don't mind I really need to—"

"You don't have time to hear me apologize?" he asked, sounding somber.

She looked at him for the first time. He looked apologetic. And he looked good—more like a guy she liked and less like a teacher. He wore jeans, and a light blue T-shirt that hugged his broad shoulders. His green eyes held a touch of remorse.

"For a quick one," she said, remembering that just yesterday she'd had her head filled with dreams of what they would have soon. Funny how the loss of that dream hadn't cost her that much.

"What I said about your dad came out all wrong. Forgive me?"

She inhaled and when she was about to exonerate him, she stopped herself. "It's not just what you said, Cary. It's that . . . I think I'm a lot more into you than you are me. And that doesn't feel right."

"Is this about my trip to Europe? I had planned that trip before you and I ever liked each other. I know it got canceled but still—"

"It's about everything," she said.

"What's everything?" He reached up to brush a strand of her hair off her cheek. His touch was sweet, but for some reason she recalled a stronger sweetness earlier—when she'd bumped into Brandon.

"What do you know about me?" she asked.

"What do you mean?"

"Just that, Cary. What do you know about me?"

He paused and she could tell he was searching for something he could tell her. But he came up empty. "You don't talk about yourself."

"Neither do you. Well, not about the personal stuff. But I asked questions. I know where you were born, about your parents and your sister. I know you like mustard on your hot dogs."

"That's not fair," he said.

"What's not fair?" She held her chin up.

"I've purposely kept my distance, trying to . . . If I got to know more about you I'd want . . ." He leaned in. "This." He kissed her. She didn't respond at first, but then she did—wanting to experience the magic of it. To feel like somebody's girl. It had been so long since she'd been kissed.

Then she felt it. The soft purr of a male were. He wanted her. Wanted more than just a kiss. That should make her feel good, and it did, just not as much as she thought it would. She pulled back.

"Don't give up on us," he said.

She looked at him. On the tip of her tongue were the words, *I won't.* But those weren't the words that slipped out. "I don't think there is an 'us.'"

Right then she knew the reason, too. The mystery that awaited her in Brandon Hart. Oh, hell, was she nuts? Cary was full were and a perfect mate for her. For all she knew, Brandon could just be human.

And getting emotionally involved with a human would be crazy. Even thinking about it was crazy considering she didn't even know if he liked her. Just because she'd caught Brandon eyeing her butt didn't mean anything.

"Don't play games," he said, his eyes growing bright with anger. Then he grabbed her arm, the one with scars, and his hand buried into her flesh.

"I don't play games. Now leave, or do I have to escort you out?" And she would have.

He walked out, but something warned her that she hadn't heard the last from him. Obviously, Cary Cannon didn't like not getting his way. Too bad.

She'd let people bully her for the first ten years of her life—she had the scars to prove it—but no one, *no one* manhandled her now.

At ten the next morning Fredericka pulled up in front of the soon-to-be gallery ready to work. Ready to uncover some answers about Brandon Hart. Ready to find something else besides her past to consume her and gnaw away at her sanity.

She'd spent half the night remembering her father, grieving for a man who had thought so little of her that he'd left her with people he barely knew. And then spent the other half angry that she had to do it all over again. That she still cared.

But I'm sure you have questions. And the answers might be in here. Holiday's words played in her head like a broken record. While temptation pulled at her head and heart, she couldn't think of one reason her father might give that would make abandoning her okay. Not one.

So why subject herself to the pain of even reading it?

Taking a deep breath, and pushing her thoughts from her issues, she focused on the house—the soon-to-be gallery. Trying to come up with ideas to make it . . . more inviting. Some paint. Maybe a bright color. A sign. Yes, he needed a sign hanging from the eaves. The flower beds needed to be replanted.

In the morning sun, the house looked sleepy, as if it hadn't woken up yet. No lights on. The blinds were still closed. Was he waiting on her? Was he even awake?

Still holding onto the steering wheel, she imagined him in bed, shirtless. Her heart started to race, and she gave herself a mental kick in the butt. Letting the crazy attraction blossom was all kinds of wrong. On top of him probably being human, she'd be working with him. Any kind of a relationship outside of a common friendship would complicate things.

And her life was complicated enough.

She got out of the car, slipped her phone into her back pocket, and went to start her day. The cool air brushed her hair back and she remembered that in four days the moon would be full and she could find solace in her run in the woods. Whatever problems weighed on her heart at a full moon, they became lighter when she shifted and could just let her inner wolf run and romp in the night. It was almost like having a great dream, it made for a little escape that hung on for a few days.

The door stood slightly ajar as it had yesterday. She leaned close and peered inside, half expecting to see his sister again. She wasn't around. The chimes hanging from the ceiling, in what looked like it had once been the dining room, played a soft song as if welcoming her inside.

She knocked.

"Coming," a deep voice said, and she recognized it to be Brandon's. She took in a breath, a tiny bit of excitement flowing through her, hoping he wasn't wearing his hat today. And god help her, but kind of hoping he wasn't wearing his shirt either.

Just friends!

But as he cut the corner from the hall to the office, she saw him. He wore a dark green T-shirt and a baseball hat.

But his frown caught most of her attention. That and the fact that he was already turning so she couldn't see his scars.

"Good morning," she said, and while she was three feet from him, she could smell him and his freshly showered aroma. Teasing her senses were the scents of a guy's spicy soap, shampoo, and minty toothpaste. But he still held his natural scent of wood and outdoors—and the slightest hint of some kind of paranormal. She just couldn't put her finger on it.

As crazy as it sounded, she wanted to bury her face in his neck and that smell. She wanted to taste the mint on his breath. No doubt, the upcoming lunar change was heightening her awareness of the opposite sex. Heck, if she could just make it past the full moon, she might not even find him all that alluring.

She could hope.

Then it hit her that yesterday she hadn't been the least bit lured by Cary's scent or even his kiss.

"Is it good?" he asked and Brandon's frown tightened.

"Not a morning person?" And she did it again. Smiled. What was it about this man that made her want to be happy? It hit then. It wasn't just about being happy, it was about wanting to see him happy. Was it the scars? Did she just assume he was as haunted as her on the inside? Or was it the sadness in his eyes that reminded her of what she saw when she looked in the mirror?

Was Brandon Hart damaged?

"I'm generally fine with morning, if I've slept."

I didn't sleep either. "Something keeping you up?" she asked and as crazy as it sounded she wanted him to confide in her.

"Yeah." He shrugged and looked around, his gaze landing on the chimes still playing soft music.

Her gaze went back to him. She liked the way his hair, appearing still a little damp, curled up on the ends. What she didn't like was that he purposely kept his left side away from her line of view.

"Worried about the opening?" she asked.

"I need caffeine."

Okay, so he didn't want to explain why he hadn't slept. He was obviously keeping his guard up, didn't want her getting too close, and that should be a message for her to do the same thing.

Should be. But damn it, here again, she'd never been good with "shoulds." It seemed her natural instinct was to go against "shoulds"—as if some part of her longed to be a rebel.

Chapter Five

Fredericka followed him into the opposite side of the house that held the office. She ended up in a kitchen, painted bright yellow with red accents. It didn't look like a guy's kitchen. She remembered Brandon's sister. Did she live here?

He stopped at the counter and glanced back at her with the good side of his face. She almost asked about his sister, when he spoke up.

"Would you like some coffee?"

"Never acquired a taste for it. But I've always loved the smell of it."

He poured himself a cup. And turned a little more than halfway, still hiding. The fact that he knew exactly how far he could turn his face toward her, allowing her to see both his eyes, but the scar under his cheekbone close to his ear remained out of sight, didn't get past her.

Their gazes locked and in the bright blue of his eyes she saw a bit of exhaustion there. Oddly, the same feeling echoed inside of her. The silence grew awkward really quickly.

"I was thinking of all that needs to be done out front. Would you like some suggestions?"

"Sure." He sipped from his cup. The steam rose up and gathered under his cap.

She recounted to him her ideas: the paint, the garden, the sign. He listened and sipped his coffee. "I had plans for all of that except painting. Not sure I have time for that."

"You would if I help."

"You paint?" he asked.

"Yeah." She ignored her phone that dinged with a text.

"You need to get that?" he asked.

"I'll check it later," she said, fearing it was from Cary. He'd sent her one text early this morning about wanting to talk to her. But she'd said all she had to say to the guy.

"Come with me, I'll show you something." He led her through a door into a garage. The smell of fresh paint hit her.

On a workbench she saw it. The sign. It read, FALLEN GALLERY. It was painted in yellow and black, and had some red accents. Kind of like the kitchen, only a little less bright. It looked both artistic and classy. She looked at him and smiled.

"That's exactly what I had in mind. Why don't we paint the porch the same yellow? Then we can plant the gardens with some flowers that have a little yellow and reds. You'll also need a sign that lists the hours. And maybe put a nice bench on the front porch. You know, for the man's man who isn't into art and is just waiting on his wife or girl-friend."

He stood there staring at her and sipping from his cup. The temperature in the garage seemed at least ten degrees below that in the house and his coffee sent up steam. When he still didn't speak she got worried.

Had she sounded too eager? Was she overstepping her bounds by making too many suggestions? Showing too much enthusiasm?

"You don't think real men are into art?" he asked, but there was almost a teasing to his tone.

"No, I just mean the macho types, who don't give a flip about walking through a gallery."

He lifted one brow and the smile, while not on his lips, was in his eyes. "So you don't think men who are into art are macho?"

"I didn't say that," she said, not sure how to react. Was he flirting?

Did she want him to be flirting? Oh, yes, she did. But was it really a good thing? Her gaze lifted to his forehead covered by his hat, but afraid he'd think she was gaping at his scars, she quickly looked away.

"Would you like to ride into town with me and help pick out the paint and flowers?"

"I would love to."

He nodded. "Wait right here. I'll get you a helmet." He walked out, leaving her in the garage.

"A helmet?" Her words seemed to hang in the cold, empty room. Then she looked around and saw the red motorcycle parked beside the silver Malibu. She'd never been on a motorcycle. But she'd seen plenty of women with their arms wrapped around some hot guy as he drove right into the wind. She'd always envied those women. They had someone to hold onto. There had been times in life when she would have liked to have someone like that.

She stared at the motorcycle and realized how close they would have to be to each other. A soft thrill ran through her, but so did a little tickle of fear.

"Here you go." He walked back in with two helmets in his hands, still only offering her the unscarred side of his face. His hat was gone, but he'd replaced it with a blue-and-black bandana and his dark hair flipped up around the cloth. Over his T-shirt he wore a dark brown leather jacket. It looked faded, worn, and warm. Right then, chills prickled her arm.

Running her hands up her arms, over the long-sleeved shirt, she looked down at the helmets.

He held one out. She took it, without thinking. Then he put his on. Turning around, he reached over to the wall and pulled down another leather jacket that hung on a hook.

"The wind can make it feel a lot colder than it is." He held the black jacket out.

She gazed back at the bike. Envisioned them on it, her body pressed against his, her arms around his waist. She didn't anticipate she'd be cold.

Warning bells rang in her head as anticipation whispered down her body.

"How . . . how are we going to bring back the paint?"

"We aren't. We'll just buy it and have it delivered."

"We . . . we could just take the car." She glanced at the Malibu.

"It's . . . not mine. It's my sister's." His gaze went to the door leading back into the house and held there for several seconds.

"I could drive," she offered. "The car . . . it's out front."

He studied her, still holding out the black jacket. "Have you ever ridden on a bike?"

She shook her head.

"You afraid?" There was a touch of challenge in his voice.

"No," she said, but she recognized the one word as a lie. Just not for the reasons he accused her of.

"Then let's go." He casually tossed the jacket over his shoulder and then threw one leg over the bike, and looked back at her. "Climb on."

For some reason, his two words sounded like a dare. Her heart raced. She could tell him no. She could. But instead, she slipped the helmet on and fastened it.

And with her body buzzing with anticipation, she walked over to him. He held out the jacket.

She took it. Their fingers touched, and a jolt of awareness shot up her arm. He watched her put it on and zip it. It was big, but felt good, warm. And the scent that rolled off it was uniquely his.

"Just slip in behind me." The helmet covered his scars completely. Their eyes met again. He smiled.

And it was as breathtaking as she'd imagined it. She smiled back.

"Hop on," he said.

She did as he requested, but allowed a couple of inches between their bodies.

"Hold on to my waist," he said, his voice low.

She inhaled and cupped her hands on each side of his waist. The leather beneath her palms felt cool. But what she mostly felt was him beneath the material, his lean waist. She remembered seeing him without his shirt.

Her pulse increased, the air in her lungs hitched. And she could swear she heard him let out a gulp of air as if he'd felt it, too.

"See the motor?" He pointed back with his right hand.

"Yes," she managed to say, but her voice came out a little high.

"It's hot. Don't let your legs touch it. Keep your feet on the foot pegs. You see them?"

"Yes." She put her feet up on them.

He hit something attached to his handlebars and the garage door opened. He started the engine. The bike jolted forward and brought her against him. Her breasts pushed against his shoulder blades.

She couldn't help but wonder if he hadn't done that on purpose. But she couldn't get mad at him. It felt wonderful to be that close.

He reached down and pulled one of her hands from his waist to wrap around his middle. "You need to hold tight."

Her forearm pressed against his stomach. She felt his hard abs, and then she felt him breath. Hesitantly, she moved her other arm around him as well.

She stared at Brandon's back, covered in the worn material, and his scent along with the smell of leather flavored the air.

"Just hold on," he said. The roar of the motor filled her ears. She automatically tightened her arms around him. Then he took off.

The wind caught the long strands of her hair, whipping it around her. The roar of the bike stirred her senses.

When he turned, the bike leaned closer to the ground. She clung to him a little tighter; the bike carried their weight as if they were one. Oddly, she realized how Brandon's body temperature was almost equal to her own. And weres ran higher than humans. Was it possible that he was . . . part were?

He turned his head to the side. "You okay?"

"Yes," she said, and realized she was smiling. "This is fun."

"I know." The vibrations of the engine filled her entire body and reminded her of the purr of a male were when close to a potential mate. No matter how hard she fought it, she felt her own body tighten with awareness.

They rode for a good fifteen minutes. And it wasn't just to a store. He drove past town on some scenic drive, where the trees clung to the fall color. He maneuvered the bike around winding roads and he didn't stop until he came to a lake where the red and orange leaves reflected on the still water.

When he cut off the engine, he dropped his legs down to hold up the bike. He didn't talk, just stared out at the view. She stayed completely still, her arms still around his waist.

"It's beautiful," she finally said. She wasn't just talking about the scenery. But the moment. The sense of freedom from the ride. The warmth of his back against her chest. The sensation of having someone to cling to.

"I know. Peaceful, isn't it?"

"Yeah." She recalled the falls, and how this natural beauty was reminiscent of that, yet it lacked the odd sense of power. Still, somehow, being here with him made this place just as impressive.

He glanced back at her over his shoulder. "I hope you didn't mind the ride."

"No. I enjoyed it."

"Good." He paused. Only the sounds of nature could be heard. A duck called out. A fish splashed, sending a few ripples in the water, and he looked back at the lake. "Where are you from, Ricka?"

She flinched when he called her by her nickname, but she answered, "A real Texan. Lived mostly in the Dallas area. You?" she asked.

"Born in Houston, but lived most of my life in Los Angeles."

It felt a little odd having a conversation with someone when you couldn't see their face. A sad thought hit. Because of his scars he was more comfortable this way.

"What brought you to Fallen?" she asked.

"My sister," he said and she felt him tighten as if for some reason the thought had caused him stress. After a few more beats of silence he asked, "How long have you made jewelry?"

"About two years. I went to a Renaissance festival, saw someone doing it, and I practically stayed there all day just watching." She paused and then asked, "How many awards have you won with your work?"

"How do you know I've won awards?" he asked, sounding humble. When she didn't answer right away he asked, "You didn't Google me, did you?"

"No, I saw your horse sculpture, remember? It's amazing. You had to have won awards. But . . . now that you mention it, I'll probably Google you when I leave here."

He laughed. "I've won about twelve. And I did Google you."

"You did?"

"Yeah." He paused again. "Didn't find a thing. I find that a little strange," he said. "Why is that?"

Chapter Six

"Is it strange?" Fredericka asked.

"Yeah. No Twitter accounts or Facebook friends?"

No friends. "I'm not into it," she lied.

There was another pause and she wanted to redirect the conversation. "What made you get into wood sculpture?"

"Kind of the same as you. I saw another artist do it. I'd always liked art, but when I saw his work, I knew that was the medium I wanted to work in." Another fish splashed and some birds called as they flew about them. "I guess we should go shopping now," he said.

"Probably," she answered.

The drive back was just as impressive as the one there. As they retraced their path, she realized that unlike Cary, Brandon was curious about her. A few minutes later, he parked the bike at the hardware store. She let go of him for the first time since they'd left the gallery, and she kind of didn't want to.

He climbed off, and she did the same. As she unstrapped her helmet, she waited to see him do his. Would she finally be able to see his pattern?

But as he pulled the helmet off, the bandana stayed in place. And once again he was back to giving her only the right side of his face.

They started in. As odd as it sounded, she missed his touch. And when he put his hand on the middle of her back, she wondered if he hadn't felt the same way. Especially when his soft touch sent warm shivers up her spine.

The closest entrance was the gardening area.

"Why don't you go look for the type of flowers you think would work? I want to go talk to the manager to make sure they can deliver by tomorrow."

"Okay." She took a few steps then she turned around to watch him walk away. He took a few more steps then he glanced back at her. Their eyes met and they both smiled. Warmth and something wonderful filled Fredericka's chest.

Then embarrassed, she went to look for the right flowers. She'd just turned down an aisle when she heard someone, a female someone call out, "Brandon, is that you?"

Shifting to where she could peer through the pansies, and not be seen spying, she saw a woman walk up to Brandon. She looked around thirty and wore her light blond hair in a ponytail.

"Katie," Brandon said.

The first thing Fredericka noted was that he didn't turn his scarred side of his face away from the woman. The second thing she noticed was how Brandon glanced back to see if she was still there.

"Yeah," Brandon said, and again looked to where she'd been standing a few seconds earlier.

"I got your call." She gave him a quick hug.

A crazy thought hit. Was this woman his girlfriend? She looked a little old for him, but maybe he liked older women.

"Sorry, I was out of town Thursday and Friday. Did you need anything?" She frowned. "Oh, my. Do we know anything else?"

Anything else about what?

"No. Still nothing. The sheriff came by, but had nothing new."

Curiosity piqued and she tilted her head to make sure not to miss anything.

"I'm sorry," the woman said.

Sorry about what?

"Yeah." Brandon gave the aisle another glance. "The reason I called is that I . . . hired one of your students and I just . . . well, I kind of wanted a character witness."

Student? Was he talking about her? Fredericka felt her shoulders tighten when she realized she hadn't told Brandon what school she attended, but her address had listed the school. He must have assumed she went to Fallen High School.

"A Ricka Lakota," Brandon said.

Air hitched in Fredericka's throat. She shouldn't blame him for wanting to check her out before hiring her, but oddly it felt like an insult. Hadn't she been judged enough in life?

"I don't have a student by that name," the woman said.

"She's a senior," Brandon replied.

"Sorry." Katie shook her head.

"Is there another school around here?" he asked.

"Parker High, but it's about twenty-five miles away. Oh, wait." The woman made a face. "There that's school for troubled kids. Shadow something? You don't think she's from there, do you? I mean, I've seen a few of those kids around town, and let's just say they make me nervous."

Trepidation filled Fredericka's stomach.

"I'm sure I just misunderstood," Brandon said, but something in his voice told her he knew he hadn't.

And what was he planning on doing about it? Dread started unraveling the newfound happiness she'd found these last few hours.

"Did you find the right flowers?" Brandon asked as he came and stood beside her.

"Yeah, I think these yellow ones and those red ones. They'll die if we get a freeze, but how often does it freeze here?"

"Not that often," he said. "You want to go check out the paint?"

"Yeah." She looked at him, still giving her the unscarred side of his face, when he hadn't felt compelled to hide from Katie. And she heard it in his tone, that slight difference as if he no longer trusted her.

That hurt.

But it shouldn't, she told herself. She'd been judged all her life. Just not from the human world. Why would they be any different?

They selected the paint, bought some tools to get ready to paint, paid for everything, and set up the delivery for the next day. Brandon hardly spoke to her. And she noted that he never hid his scars from the salesclerk.

With the small bag containing the wire brush and scraper in his hands, and obviously with Katie's warning in his head, Brandon led the way out of the store.

While unstrapping the helmets, he asked, "Do you take art in school?"

Fredericka tensed. "Why don't you just ask the question, instead of dancing around it?"

He looked up, forgetting for one second about his scars, and then shifted. "Ask what question?"

She stiffened her shoulders and decided to just put it out there. "I heard what that woman, Katie, said to you."

He blinked, looking a little confused, but not at all embarrassed. "How could you have heard, you weren't around."

"I don't know, maybe your voices carried, the point is that I heard it."

He stood there for several seconds just staring. "Okay." After a few more long seconds he asked, "What school do you go to?"

She lifted her chin, refusing to appear ashamed. "Shadow Falls Camp. And for the record I never kept that from you. On the contract, it's listed along with my address. It's not my fault that you assumed incorrectly. And it's not my fault that some people like to judge others before knowing the facts."

His eyes tightened. "I'm assuming you are talking about the comment Katie made about the school."

"You assume correctly," she said.

He stood there, a beat of silence too long. "Okay. What are the facts? What kind of school is it?"

Fredericka remembered hearing Holiday set one of the local residents straight about the school and she repeated almost verbatim what she'd said. "It's a camp and school for the gifted. Teens who are a bit different, but need a place to grow. Since the camp started over four years ago, there hasn't been one arrest of a student. I doubt that Fallen High School can claim the same."

He continued to just stand there. "Have you ever been arrested?"

His question stung. "Have you?"

He tensed. "I'm hiring you."

"Yeah, and I'm working for you, and I even saw the cops show up at your place. But I guess I'm not so fast to judge people." She tilted her head back. "But to answer your question, no, I have never been arrested." Her sins had never been reported to local police. And even if they had, she wasn't sure the courts would have held her as responsible as she herself did.

He inhaled. "The cops weren't there about me." His shoulders dropped. "I'm sorry. I think." He frowned.

"You think?" she asked. She'd never heard anyone apologize and take it back in the same breath.

"Yeah, I think. I mean, I'm hiring you. I have a right to ask questions."

"And I'm working for you, so do I not have the same rights?" she asked. And before he answered, and before she considered what she was doing, she tossed the question out that bothered her the most. "Why do you hide your scars from me, but you didn't from Katie, or the salesclerks?"

He frowned and freed the first helmet, then handed it to her. His gaze met hers and he didn't turn his cheek this time.

"Maybe I care more about how you see me than how they do?"

His words had her frustration evaporating. And she realized instantly what a hypocrite she was.

"I'm sorry," she said.

"Don't be." She heard it in his voice. He hated pity as much as she did.

"No, that's not what I meant." She paused. "I meant . . . I shouldn't call you out for hiding your scars when . . . I'm . . ." She pulled her jacket off and tugged her unbuttoned shirt that she always wore over a tank top off her shoulder and down her arm. "When you're not the only one hiding."

His gaze widened when he saw the tightly pulled marks the size of a teaspoon that ran up her forearm. She knew the exact shape and size, because it had been a heated teaspoon that had made the marks.

He opened his mouth to say something, but then shut it. He shook his head, his eyes filled with empathy. "I'm sorry."

"Don't be." She repeated his own words and then pulled her shirt up and slipped the warm leather jacket back on. The realization hit then. She'd never willingly shown anyone her scars. Was it because he had them, too? What exactly was the lure she felt for this guy?

A car pulled into the lot and parked right across from them. Brandon glanced at the car and then looked at her. "Can we talk about this . . ."

"Later." She finished for him and nodded.

He put on his helmet and she started to do the same when she heard footsteps approaching from behind her. Her next intake of air brought with it a were scent. The air locked in her lungs as she recognized the trace.

"Fredericka, what are you doing?"

Chapter Seven

Fredericka turned and looked at Cary, now standing right behind her. He stared at the motorcycle helmet she held in her hand, then he looked up at Brandon. His gaze shot to his forehead hidden beneath the helmet.

She knew he wanted to see his pattern, and probably considered it rude for him to be hiding it. Then she saw him lift his head slightly to take a big nose full of air, hoping his scent would tell him Brandon's species.

From the puzzled look in the teacher's eyes, she knew he found it as puzzling as she did. Tension built so fast that Fredericka's mind rushed to find a way to put a stop to what could be a huge disaster.

"Mr. Cannon, this is Brandon," she spoke quickly. "Brandon Hart, he owns the gallery. I'm helping him get the gallery fixed up for the opening." Fredericka's gaze went to Brandon, who looked as puzzled at Cary. "This is Cary Cannon, he's my history teacher."

Brandon's expression softened with the introduction. "Nice to meet you, sir." He extended his hand.

Cary ignored Brandon's hand, and his gaze shifted back to her. She saw his eyes start to brighten.

"How is driving around on a motorcycle helping with the gallery?" Cary asked.

Fredericka sensed Brandon's concern as he dropped his hand. Her own shoulders tightened and she felt her hackles start to rise. Trying not to let emotion brighten her eyes, she blinked and took in a deep breath.

"We were picking out paint," she said. "And we were leaving," she added. "So if you will excuse us." She started putting on the helmet.

"Can I speak with you a second?" Cary caught her elbow. His hold was a bit too tight. She felt her eyes grow warmer, a telltale sign that her eyes were lightening.

In the corner of her eye, she saw Brandon's gaze go to Cary's hand grasping her elbow. Not wanting any trouble, she looked at Brandon, praying her eyes were not so bright he'd notice. "Excuse me one second."

She started walking away, and Cary didn't remove his hand. She got a few feet away, turned her back toward Brandon, and then seethed. "Let go of me."

He did, but his frown said he disliked her tone. Thankfully, she didn't give a frack about what he liked or disliked.

"What is he?" he asked.

"My boss," she offered, knowing what he really asked, but too pissed to answer.

"You know what I mean."

She had to take a few gulps of air to calm herself enough to explain. "I got just what you got." Meaning his scent.

"And yet you are hanging out with him?"

"I work with him at the gallery." The fact that she wanted a completely different kind of relationship wasn't any of Cary's damn business.

"I think Holiday would be very disappointed in you," he growled.

"Holiday knows where I am!"

"Then dare I say I'm disappointed in you. Since when do you go around flaunting yourself to the likes of him?"

Her mouth dropped open. "First, I'm not flaunting myself. Second, if I was flaunting myself it's my prerogative. So take your attitude and stick it where the sun doesn't shine."

"What about us?" he growled.

"How many times do I have to tell you that there isn't an 'us.' There never was an us. Just an idea of us. And I no longer like that idea! And frankly neither did you when you made plans to leave first thing this summer."

"You are dumping me for him?"

"No, I told you that you and I weren't going to make it before I ever interviewed at the gallery."

"But you aren't denying that you and he are more than employer and employee?"

"I don't have to deny anything to you."

"Fine, but you'll regret this," he snapped, his threat clear in his tone.

She looked at his bright eyes. "What's that supposed to mean?"

"Holiday and Burnett trust me. If I go to them with problems about someone, don't you think they'll listen?"

She immediately understood what he was saying. "What problems? I haven't done anything!"

"But who do you think they'd trust more, me or one of their free-loading students?" he said. "So why don't you just come back with me?"

"Why don't you go to hell! I'm pretty sure there's a special spot for you there." She didn't know what made her angrier: the blackmail threat, or his freeloading comment. Because damn him, she wasn't free-loading. She'd already spoken to Holiday about paying her back.

She swung around and left Cary.

She walked over to Brandon who stood watching them, concern tightening his expression. Aware her eyes were probably a pissed-off orange, she glanced away, keeping her eyes away from his gaze. She could hear her heart thumping in her ears and she recognized the emotions making it race. And it wasn't just anger.

Fear.

If I go to them with problems about someone, don't you think they'll listen? As much as she wished it wasn't so, Cary was right. Holiday and Burnett would believe Cary over her. How could they not? She was, after all, the daughter of a rogue.

"Let's go," she said, glancing down and busying her hands by putting on the helmet.

Brandon hesitated one second. "Fine, but it's another thing I'm going to need an explanation about." He crawled onto the bike and she crawled on behind him.

She wrapped her arms around Brandon and leaned in. "Cary Cannon is an asshole. How's that for an explanation?"

"I figured that out all by myself," Brandon said, as he started the motor and drove off.

She felt Cary's glare on them all the way out of the parking lot.

Fredericka held on tight during the ride. When he pulled up in front of the gallery, another car was parked in front.

"Damn it. We've got company," Brandon muttered. A frown sounded in his voice, and she felt his muscles tense beneath her hands. She wasn't sure if he was annoyed because he'd have to delay their conversation or because he didn't like the person waiting in the silver Saturn parked in front of the mailbox.

Or maybe both.

However, for Fredericka it gave her just a few more minutes to decide how to answer Brandon's questions about Cary.

The garage door opened and Brandon pulled in.

"I'll be right back." He took his helmet off. His bandana stayed in place. "If you don't mind, go on in and I'll be in shortly." He frowned. "It's an old boyfriend of my sister's."

"Sure." She watched him walk out, but couldn't help wondering why his sister didn't take care of her own boyfriend issues. Or maybe that was just what brothers were for. She wouldn't know, never having had one.

Having already gotten caught eavesdropping, she escaped into the house. Her first step inside made her realize again how pretty the yellows and reds made the kitchen. But as warm as the colors were, the room was cold.

She walked into what would be the gallery part of the house. An odd quietness seemed to echo within the rooms. She realized what it was, or wasn't. Her gaze moved to the wind chimes. Dead still.

Pulling her coat tighter, her mind focused on how she was going to explain Cary's possessive attitude, she moved to the window facing the backyard. Her breath caught when she saw the new piece of art that Brandon was working on.

It wasn't finished, only about half of the large piece of wood was carved. But there was no mistaking what it was.

A wolf.

Chapter Eight

"Damn it's cold in here."

Fredericka nearly jumped when she heard Brandon. She'd been so shocked at his wolf sculpture that she hadn't even heard him walk inside.

"You're carving a wolf?" She turned.

"Yeah," he said and she noted he was looking right at her, no longer hiding the scars. But the bandana still hid his forehead.

"Why?"

He shrugged and moved to stand beside her. "I've had a fascination with them. Got it from my grandmother."

Inhaling again, she checked to see if there wasn't a hint of were in his scent.

It was there, wasn't it? Or was she just hoping?

"Why did she like them?" she asked, feeling his warmth from his shoulder beside her. Warmth like a were? It had to be were, didn't it?

"She was an odd duck." He stared out the window. "You going to tell me about this teacher?"

She closed her eyes and all of a sudden she decided to go with the truth. She glanced at Brandon. "I used to like him. We never . . . I mean . . ." She glanced back out the window. "Because he's my teacher we decided to wait until I graduated to let our feelings go anywhere. But . . . I recently realized that he and I aren't really a good match."

"You mean with him being an asshole?" he asked.

She grinned, and looked up at him again. His eyes were so blue she wanted to just lose herself in there. And it wasn't until now that she realized how tall Brandon was. He stood a good six inches over her five-eight frame.

Very few guys made her feel feminine. And yet somehow he managed to do it.

"Yeah." Then she recalled Cary's threat and her smile faded.

"What are you going to do?" He lifted one of his brows.

"About what?"

"I mean about his trying to blackmail you?"

She shook her head. "How did you . . . ? You were too far away to hear what he was saying."

"Guess your voices carried," he said, repeating her earlier words back at her. "I've always had extra keen hearing."

What else did he always have? She was a breath away from asking, or from reaching up and pulling off his bandana.

"How did you get your scars?" he asked.

Her breath caught and thoughts of seeing his pattern flew out the window. She should have known that by showing him her scars that he would ask. And yet exposing her physical scars was nothing compared to exposing her emotional ones.

When she didn't answer, he started speaking.

"My mom was an alcoholic. She'd sober up for a year or two and then go back to it. Back and forth."

It only took a second for his tone to completely pull her in. She listened with her heart, because somehow she sensed how hard this was for him to say.

"When she'd get bad, I'd go live with my grandmother—sometimes I'd stay for six months or more, until my mom would sober up. Then my grandmother died when I was eight, and I started going to stay with my dad during her bad times. That's what she called them, too. Her bad times."

He paused to look out the window. "I was fifteen, back at home with my mom again. I already had my driver's permit. She came to pick me up from football practice. She was drunk off her ass again. I told her to let me drive. She wouldn't. She got all mad and for a reason I'll never understand I let her talk me into just giving in."

He closed his eyes for a second. She reached over and laced her fingers through his. Their hands came together like pieces of a puzzle that belonged side by side.

"She missed a turn, and ran into a tree. She wasn't wearing her seat belt. She was thrown out of the car and died immediately. I was knocked unconscious. The car caught fire. A cop saw the accident and pulled me out."

The words "I'm sorry" were on the tip of her tongue, but she didn't say them, because even though she was, they weren't enough. She just squeezed his hand.

And after swallowing the emotion down her throat, knowing she owed him the same thing, she started talking.

"My mom died giving birth to me. It was just my dad and me. He was . . . I suppose you could say he lived on the wrong side of the law. But I guess I loved him because . . . he was all I had. We were always on the run. He'd have his girlfriends watch me. I was five. This girlfriend was . . . on something. I don't know what kind of drug, but she'd take it and get mean. She . . . believed in the adage: 'Spare the rod, spoil the child.' Only . . . her rod was a heated spoon."

"Oh, hell!" he said and he turned her around and pulled her into him. Her head came to the wonderful spot on a guy's shoulder. Between his warmth, his scent, and having his arms around her, the pain in her chest lessened.

She stood there just holding him, and letting him hold her. It suddenly dawned on her that the eerie silence she'd found in the house earlier had vanished. The wind chimes, the ones that seemed to play by themselves, were back to making music.

Finally, she pulled back just a little and rested her chin on his chest and looked up at him.

"We're a pretty pathetic pair, aren't we?" she asked, teasingly.

He shook his head. "No," he said, completely serious. "We're amazing. Look what we came through."

Her chest tightened with his declaration. "You yes, but . . . don't give me that much credit. You don't know me all that well." And when he found out . . .

He leaned his head down. His forehead rested on hers. "Something tells me that you don't give yourself nearly as much credit as you deserve."

Their eyes met and held and she was positive he was going to kiss her, or would have if her phone didn't ding with a text.

Suddenly the moment felt awkward. She pulled away and snatched her phone from her back pocket.

The text was from Holiday. Its message was short.

Can you be back here by four? Need car. Holiday.

Fredericka wasn't sure how she knew, but she did. Cary was behind this. He'd already started initiating her punishment.

"Problem?" Brandon asked.

"Uh, no, not really," she said, deciding not to pull Brandon into this. "I just have to be back in . . ." she looked at the time, "in two hours." She pushed back her concern. "Why don't we start scraping off the paint on the porch? I'll come back tomorrow afternoon and we can start painting then."

"You really don't have to do that," he said.

"Hey, I offered, remember?"

He smiled. "Okay. I'll get the tools. You go figure out what all you think should be painted. Oh, and I'll order us a pizza. I mean, if you like pizza? I'm starved."

"Yeah, that sounds good."

When he walked out, she looked back at her phone. Holiday's text still showed on the screen. A feeling hit that she'd better come up with a plan, or Cary would try to ruin everything: her work at the gallery and whatever type of relationship was blossoming between her and Brandon. Hell, he could get her kicked out of Shadow Falls.

Yup, she'd better come up with a plan. And fast.

* * *

By the time pizza arrived they'd finished prepping the bottom half of the porch to paint. Brandon and she ate sitting on the concrete steps, and they chatted about the ideas for the gallery, about art, about the weather. It almost seemed as if they'd both had enough of hard discussions and agreed to keep it light.

Light was good.

Light was comfortable.

When they'd finished off the large meat-lovers' pizza and each drank two glasses of sweet iced tea, Brandon went and pulled two ladders from the garage for them to start getting the top half of the porch ready to paint.

Fredericka noticed that for the most part, he no longer hid his scars from her. But something told her he was still very aware of them. And it made her extra careful not to focus on them. Even though her eyes kept wanting to go to his forehead where the bandana seemed to slip down on his brow.

The last thing she wanted was for him to think she found him unpleasant to look at. Because it was quite the opposite.

He only wore a T-shirt and jeans. And she'd enjoyed working at his side, watching him work. Watching him move. Watching his muscles shift like liquid beneath his skin. And a few times she felt him watching her and all she could think about was the kiss the text had interrupted.

Part of her worried the reason it hadn't happened was because like her, Brandon was concerned about them having a relationship while she sort of worked for him.

He set up the ladders on opposite sides of the porch. "Be careful, these ladders are old and wobbly."

"I'm sure they're fine." She grabbed her wire brush and started climbing. Brandon did the same. They worked side by side, comfortable. Not talking. But it wasn't an awkward kind of silence. The sound of their wire brushes raking across the wood was pleasant. Every now and then they'd crawl down and reposition their ladders. After a while, she set her brush down on the top of the ladder and reached in her back pocket for her phone to check the time.

Brandon glanced at her.

"I should be heading out in a few minutes," she said.

"Already? Time flies when you're having fun."

"Yeah," she said. And she meant it. She'd had fun. "I'm gonna get that last little spot," she said and slipped her phone back into her pocket and climbed one more step.

She was almost to the top when she felt the ladder start to lean. A squeal left her lips as the ladder went one way and she went the other.

Somehow, and she didn't have a clue how, Brandon managed to get down his ladder and position himself beneath her. She free-fell for about five feet and then he caught her.

"Gotcha," he said, his blue gaze staring down at her with concern.

Breath held, she became aware of being in his arms. Held close and solid, not even a wobble in his stance. Considering she wasn't one of those hundred-pound petite gals, it was amazing he could even hold her up. Brandon was strong. Stronger than your average human. And his hearing was keener. His temperature warmer.

He had to be . . .

She blinked and that's when she realized he'd lost his bandana. Instantly unfocusing her eyes, she stared at his forehead to get the answer to the question she'd longed to know since she first laid eyes on him.

What was Brandon Hart?

Chapter Nine

She stared at the answer.

Human, mostly human, with were and a smaller percentage of fae.

"You okay?" Brandon asked.

Was her off-focus stare at his pattern confusing him? Did that mean he didn't know what he was?

Considering he was about 75 percent human, she supposed it was possible. She'd never lived among mixed breeds to know what they knew or didn't know. But it was true that some kids at the camp hadn't known when they arrived.

So, she supposed, it was possible that Brandon was completely unaware that he wasn't all human.

"Are you okay?" he repeated.

"Yes, I . . . I'm just stunned a little. You . . . moved really fast."

"I've always been fast on my feet," he said, still cradling her against him.

She couldn't remember the last time anyone actually held her. And it appeared he wasn't even straining to do it.

"Strong, too," she muttered.

"What?" he asked.

"I said . . . you can put me down."

He smiled. "Or not."

"You're going to hold me all day?"

"It wouldn't be a hardship." His smiled faded. "But I'm not sure it would be wise, huh?" He set her down.

Perhaps, she should have let what he said go, but the words spilled from her lips. "Because I kind of work with you?" she asked.

"Yeah. It might be . . . awkward." He ran a hand through his hair. "We should probably think it through, before . . . jumping into anything."

She inhaled, unsure what to say. "I guess I should . . ." she motioned to her car, "get going."

He nodded. She turned to go.

"Ricka," he said her name. Or her nickname, and oddly, hearing it didn't feel so bad this time.

She faced him.

"Are you going to be okay with that teacher?"

She nodded, not really sure, but still so high on his touch that she didn't want to think about it. "Everything new can feel a little awkward."

He smiled, but his blue eyes still looked torn. "I know." He took a step closer and reached up and brushed a few strands of hair off her face. Then he leaned down and his lips touched hers. His scent, like the outdoors, filled her senses. And he tasted like . . . like pizza, and a little like sweet tea. His tongue slipped so easily into her mouth, and she felt herself lean into him.

Then, way before she was ready, he pulled back. He ran a palm down his face; she ran her tongue over her bottom lip.

He sighed. "Okay, I probably shouldn't have done that."

She smiled. "I'm glad you did. I . . . liked it."

He exhaled. "Me, too. That's the problem."

Grinning, she met his eyes. "Maybe it's not that big of a problem. Why don't we talk about it tomorrow? I'll come over after school. We can paint."

He nodded. Right then a phone rang inside his house.

"Tomorrow," he said and reached over and squeezed her hand before running inside for the phone.

· · ·

Still smiling, she got into the car and wished it was already tomorrow. Starting the engine, she pulled out of the drive. She looked at the house as she pulled away. And that's when she saw her.

Brandon's sister, Linda, stood at the side of the house, in front of a flower bed, the same one Fredericka had seen her at yesterday when she'd pulled away.

Had his sister seen Brandon kiss her? For that matter, had she been home all day while Fredericka and Brandon painted?

Fredericka waved, worried his sister might not approve of her. The woman waved back. Suddenly, leaving without even speaking seemed rude. She pulled the car over to the side of the street and put the car in park. She got out of the vehicle, prepared to just offer a quick hello and good-bye. But when she stepped up onto the curb and looked up at the side of the house, the woman was gone.

Vanished.

Fredericka stopped and just stood there, a cold breeze sent goose bumps up her back. She started to get back in her car when she heard, or maybe just felt something behind her.

She swung around, but nothing was there.

Nothing but a dead cold that had her catching her breath.

"What does a ghost feel like?" Fredericka blurted out when she first walked into Holiday's office. Fredericka hadn't been able to shake the eerie feeling she got standing outside Brandon's house.

Holiday looked up, surprised, as if she hadn't heard Fredericka walk in. "What happened?"

Fredericka set the keys down on the camp leader's desk and dropped down into a chair. "I met Brandon Hart's sister the first day I went to be interviewed. She . . . was quiet and disappeared and then . . . it happened again today."

"Are you talking about this woman?" Holiday slid the Sunday newspaper across her desk.

The picture of a woman, blond, her hair hanging down around her shoulders and a smile on her face, stared up at Fredericka. "Yes, that's her." Fredericka read the first line.

Missing Fallen resident feared dead.

She gasped.

Holiday frowned and reached over and put her hand on Fredericka's, still resting on the paper. "You've seen her?"

Fredericka nodded and glanced up. Calm flowed into her from Holiday's touch and yet the realization that she had seen a ghost, actually seen her, spoke to her, brought on a fresh wave of panic. "So she's really . . . ?"

Holiday nodded.

"Damn!" Fredericka closed her eyes and concentrated on breathing and not freaking out. But how could she not freak out? She'd seen a ghost. Not just once but three times.

Holiday must have sensed her rising panic, because she put her other hand on top of Fredericka's. "It's okay."

Fredericka opened her eyes. "What's okay about this? Name one thing that's okay about this."

"I know it's scary, Fredericka, but just think, you will be able to help her and her brother."

"How?" Fredericka asked.

"Linda Hart needs to cross over. Usually they stay here for a reason. And her brother needs answers." The fae lifted one brow. "Everyone needs answers."

Even in her panicked state, Fredericka knew Holiday was referencing back to the envelope containing letters from her dad. As if Fredericka didn't already have enough crap to worry about at this moment.

Holiday sighed. "Does she know she's dead?"

"How would I know? I didn't know she was a ghost so it's not as if it came up in conversation."

Holiday just smiled as if she had patience to spare. Something Fredericka completely lacked right now.

"Does she show signs of being injured?" the camp leader asked. "Does she have wounds?"

"No. She . . . looked fine." Fredericka thought a minute. "She did look dressed for summer and not winter."

Holiday nodded. "According to the paper she went missing six months ago. So that would make sense."

Suddenly, Fredericka recalled seeing the police come to Brandon's door. "They don't think her brother did it, do they?"

"No." Holiday looked down at the paper. "It says here that he didn't come into town until a few months ago." She leaned back, moving her hands from Fredericka's. "Have you gotten a look at his pattern?"

Fredericka nodded and remembered that before she'd seen Linda again, it had been a subject she'd longed to discuss with the fae. "He's around seventy-five percent human. He has were and then a smaller amount of fae."

"Is he aware of this?"

"That's what I wanted to ask you. I mean, he's never said anything about being anything. But he has some of the were abilities. He has the sensitive hearing and is fast and strong. And I know it came from his grandmother because he mentioned she liked wolves. Is it possible that he still doesn't know?"

"Very possible. Were blood is one of the most likely to go unnoticed. Anything less than half were and they usually don't turn with the moon and their abilities ebb and flow with lunar cycles. A lot of humans who believe in the full-moon craziness are actually part were and don't know it. Other than slightly elevated body temperatures, for some there are no obvious outward signs."

Fredericka took a gulp of air and remembered how warm it felt to be close to him.

Holiday leaned in a bit. "You don't think his grandmother told him anything?"

Fredericka shrugged. "He called her an odd duck."

Holiday picked up a pen. "So maybe she told the family, but no one really believed her."

Fredericka just nodded. "So I shouldn't tell him?"

"No." Holiday frowned. "However, it's believed that just being around someone who shares the same type heritage will trigger a mixed breed into awareness. And if he was told by his grandmother, it's very possible that he may see some truth in it."

"Would that be so bad?" she asked.

Holiday hesitated. "It could be." She rolled the pen in her hand as her frown deepened. "Which basically means that your working for him could bring about some complications. I know this means a lot to you, but are you sure that this is worth it?"

"Of course it is!" Fredericka answered quickly. "This is my dream. Please."

"I . . ." Holiday set the pen down and hesitated as if contemplating. "I don't want to rob you of your dream, Fredericka. But Mr. Cannon came by earlier and said he was concerned about you."

Fredericka stiffened. So she'd been right. Cary had already started initiating her punishment. Her first impulse was to tell Holiday of Cary's threat. But why? She'd believe him over the word of a rogue's daughter every time.

"He explained that you just haven't been yourself and your studies are slacking. I know hearing about your dad has probably upset you. I just don't want you taking on more than you can handle."

"I can handle it," Fredericka snapped, and she would, just as soon as she figured out how to handle Cary. "And I told Brandon I would help him paint after school tomorrow."

The concerned look didn't fade from Holiday's eyes. Had Cary told her that he thought Fredericka was interested in Brandon?

Holiday nodded. "I wouldn't recommend getting too friendly with him."

"I'll be fine."

"Even with the spirit?" Holiday asked.

"Yeah," Fredericka said, but the thought sent another shot of panic to her gut. "But that problem will go away, right? They cross over."

"With your help," Holiday said.

Oh, crap. "What . . . exactly do I have to do?"

Chapter Ten

Fredericka spent the rest of the afternoon working on her new pieces of jewelry and trying not to panic about getting information from Brandon's sister on how she died. Then after she had that information, she'd have to figure out how to share it without informing anyone that she was talking to dead people.

How the hell did Holiday and the others who had this so-called gift manage to do this without completely losing it? If Fredericka was a little closer to Kylie, she'd go to her and ask some questions and maybe even for some advice. But Fredericka didn't know her that well. She wasn't close to anyone. Not really.

Right then she recalled how close she'd felt to Brandon.

I wouldn't recommend getting too friendly with him. Holiday's warning played in her head.

Fredericka would bet that meant no kissing. It was too late for that, wasn't it?

And if he tried again . . . ? Oh, hell. She knew she didn't want to stop it.

She'd just finished putting away her tools, when her phone rang. Frowning, she snatched it up, thinking it might be Cary.

But the number wasn't his. Or at least not his cell phone. Oh, hell, had he bought a burner phone so she couldn't prove he was blackmailing her?

"Hello," she said, ready to give Cary hell.

"Ricka?"

She recognized Brandon's voice immediately but wasn't expecting it. "Hi."

"You busy?" he asked.

"No." She remembered she'd left her number on the contract. "Just putting away my tools. I'm almost finished with the next pair of earrings."

"I just finished working, too." A beat of silence hung long before he continued. "I . . . was concerned about that teacher. He's not going to cause you any trouble, is he? If you need me to talk to someone, I will."

"No, I'm fine," she lied. Other than a warning, there hadn't been any consequences. And she'd be extra careful from here on out to record all her homework, so he couldn't claim she wasn't doing it.

"That's not the only reason I called," he said.

"It isn't?" she asked, and prayed it wasn't to tell her he'd decided she and he weren't going to work.

"No, I . . . just wanted to say that I had a great time today and I already wish it was tomorrow."

"Me, too." She smiled, and for the first time, all the negative feelings about dealing with the dead faded and she felt . . . happy. Frederika Lakota was happy. And considering how long it had been since she'd really felt this, it was kind of amazing. She dropped down into the chair and pulled her knees up to her chest.

"I tried telling myself that we needed to put a stop to it. And it might be the smart thing to do, but I don't want to do the smart thing right now."

"What could be so bad?" she asked and ran her finger over a threadbare spot on her knee.

"Well, we could break up and then you wouldn't want to work here."

"First I'd like to think we're both mature enough to handle anything, and second . . . you should never go into something thinking it will end."

"That's almost exactly what I told myself," he said and she could swear she heard a mattress sigh. Was he in bed? While it shouldn't matter where he was, in a silly way she liked thinking of him in bed.

Maybe even shirtless.

"It's crazy, I feel this strange kind of connection with you. And it's not just our . . ."

"Scars," she finished for him and she recalled what Holiday had said about a mixed blood recognizing themselves in another of their kind.

"Yes. I mean, there's the fact that we're both artists, but it seems even more than that."

"I feel it, too," she said and she was surprised at how her voice sounded wispy.

"Good, I feel a little less crazy." There was a pause. "Tell me something about yourself." His voice sounded a little lazy.

"You already know a lot," she said, instantly worrying that when he knew everything about her, he'd decide she was too . . . damaged.

"Tell me more," he said.

"I'd rather not." She leaned her forehead down onto her knee. The happiness living and breathing in her chest felt vulnerable.

"It can't all be bad," he said.

"Yeah, it can," she said.

A silence filled the line. "Where's your dad now?"

She swallowed. "He's dead."

"How old were you?"

She felt that ache she'd been fighting the last few days swell up in her chest. "It happened a little more than a week ago."

"Damn. I'm sorry. That has to be tough."

"I hadn't seen him in eight years." Her throat tightened. "He wasn't what you would call a great dad."

"It doesn't matter. He was still your dad." He inhaled and she heard him roll over again. Definitely on a mattress. "It took me a long time to realize that. I mean, my mom wouldn't have ever won a mother-of-the-year award, but I still loved her, even when I hated her. And I grieved for her. At first it pissed me off. I felt as if by grieving I was allowing her another way of hurting me. It's not so. You have to grieve."

Fredericka heard his words and she wondered how he could know just what to say.

Right then she recalled Cary's callous remarks about her father's death and tears filled her eyes.

"Thank you," she said.

"For what?"

"Saying the right thing." She brushed a few tears from her eyes.

"You okay?" he asked, as if he could tell she was crying.

"Yeah." She took in a shaky breath. "Sorry."

"Don't be. You want to hear me bitch about something? Maybe it will make you feel better."

"Go for it," she said and chuckled just a bit.

He laughed, but something about the sound said he was serious. "My sister."

Fredericka glanced down at the newspaper still on the workbench. She'd brought it with her from Holiday's office. She'd read the whole thing before she'd gotten to work.

When he didn't say anything else, she spoke up. "I read about it this afternoon." She paused. "What do you think happened to her?"

"What do I think happened? I think that asshole of a boyfriend happened. But I can't prove it. I can't even prove she's dead, but I know she is. If they could just find her body then . . . then maybe they could hang that guy high."

"I'm sorry," she said.

"Me, too." There was a long pause. "She was only my half-sister. My dad was married to someone else before he knocked up my mom. Linda was ten years older than me. She used to tell me, 'Don't you sass me, I changed your diaper.' We never lived together but we saw each other three or four times a year. But when I was in the hospital after the accident, she came to see me every day."

Tears filled Fredericka's eyes. And just like that she wasn't afraid of seeing a ghost. She wanted to see her. Wanted to find a way to help both his sister and Brandon.

"I'd come to see her when she'd just moved here," Brandon continued. "We were looking for a place for her to buy and we found this house. It was more money than she had. I'd just gotten paid for two big pieces I'd done, so I agreed to help her with the idea that when I got four or five pieces to show, she could open the front two rooms into a gallery.

"You want to hear something crazy?" he asked.

"Sure," she said.

"I sometimes feel her. It's as if she's here." She heard him inhale. "Have you seen the chimes hanging up in the front room?"

"Yeah." Chills ran down Fredericka's spine, remembering the ghostly sound of those chimes. And then she recalled going into the house to the absence of that sound when Brandon had gone to speak to . . . Oh, shit. Brandon had said the guy waiting in the car had been one of Linda's old boyfriends. Was it the same boyfriend Brandon suspected of killing her? Was that why they had gone dead silent? Was Linda trying to tell her something?

"They were hers." Grief sounded in Brandon's voice and she ached for him. "She made them. She used to say she wasn't really an artist, but she was. She needed to believe in herself. I hung them right after I got that room finished. Not to sell, but . . . because I just wanted some of her in the shop. But sometimes when they ring, there's not a bit of air flowing in the house."

The next day, Fredericka walked into history class, her last for the day. Afterward, she was heading to the gallery. When she saw Cary standing by his desk, offering her a slight smirk, she pushed back her fury. She didn't do it because it was the right thing to do; she did it because if she was going to outfox and stop the jerk from causing her trouble, she was going to have to have all her wits. And when livid, one was often witless.

Cary met her gaze again, briefly, and she saw it. He wasn't finished punishing her.

Game on, Fredericka thought. All she had to do was figure out what he planned on doing and put up a roadblock. It wasn't even all that hard to do—just start thinking like an asshole, because that's exactly what he was.

He moved in front of the class. As he did she wondered how she could have ever thought he was someone she wanted in her life.

"Okay, everyone, pass up the twenty questions you were to answer. And I'm not going to lie to you. These will count for a big part of your grade." Something about the way he said it sent a warning bell through her.

Fredericka looked down at her paper. She'd spent two hours last night on her homework, making sure she hadn't missed one question. No way in hell was she going to let him accuse her of not doing her work.

"Here." Della—a vampire and one of Kylie's roommates—who sat behind her, handed up her homework along with the other three students' behind her. Fredericka hesitated and then she purposely didn't put hers in the stack when she passed them up.

Only after Cary had collected all the papers in the front row and set them on his desk, did Fredericka raise her hand. "I'm sorry, I forgot to put mine in the stack."

She stood up, and then turned to Miranda, the student sitting in the next row. She held out her paper to the witch. "Oh, did I complete them all?" she asked as if worried.

The witch leaned in.

"Weren't there twenty questions?" Fredericka asked.

"Yeah," Miranda nodded and glanced up from the paper.

"Good," Fredericka said and then moved up and in front of the entire class, she put her paper on top of the others.

Cary stared at her, another flicker of anger bright in his eyes. His face even got a little red. He knew exactly what she was doing. Covering her ass. But she'd let him know. She didn't give a damn what he knew, or how much it pissed him off, as long as he wasn't able to tell any more lies about her.

Forty minutes later, a bell rang announcing the end of class. Fredericka, her books already stacked, was the first to stand up.

"Fredericka," Cary said, over the bell. "I need to speak with you a second."

The temptation to just walk out hit her, and hit hard. But she knew he'd use it against her. Standing there, listening to the shuffle of students leaving, she was left to face him.

Chapter Eleven

"Where were you running off to?" Cary asked Fredericka, as soon as the classroom door closed.

She wanted to tell him to mind his own damn business, but that might add fuel to his fire. So instead she just lied. "Nowhere in particular."

"Then why don't you stay and help me grade some papers?"

She stiffened her shoulders. "Sorry, I'd rather not."

His eyes turned a lighter shade of blue. Disturbing blue. "You really don't want to piss me off," he said, his tone so threatening she almost flinched.

"I'm not trying to piss you off, Cary. But what was almost between us is over. Let it go."

"It's over when I say it's over!" He took a step closer. "And you're damn lucky I'm even interested. Do you think I don't know that you were raised rogue?"

"And you're a prime example that even someone from a good background can grow up to be an asshole." She turned and walked out. Not giving him the privilege of knowing he had the power to hurt her. But his words echoed in her head and landed with a thump on her heart; at times she questioned her own self-worth.

• • •

That hurt stayed with Fredericka until Brandon opened the door and met her with a smile. A smile that said welcome. That said he was happy to see her. A smile that said he didn't judge her.

And just like that, the heavy weight in her heart faded to almost nothing.

"Come here," he said.

For a second she thought he was going to kiss her. And she would have let him, too.

He caught her hand and led her into the gallery. "I want you to see my project. I woke up and couldn't sleep, so I worked." They walked through the first two rooms to the back door and then stepped outside.

Fredericka's breath caught at the site of the wolf sculpture on the patio. "That's beautiful," she told him and continued to admire how lifelike it looked. "Wow. Really beautiful."

"Yeah," he said.

She looked at him. He wasn't looking at his art, but at her.

"Beautiful," he said and inched closer. His arms slipped around her waist, and that's when he kissed her.

The kiss started out slow, a little sweet, but got hotter. As crazy as it was, she could almost feel his purr. His heart raced against her. His hand moved to the hem of her T-shirt and moved up to touch her waist. The feel of his fingers on her naked skin had her melting closer to him. Had her wanting . . .

He pulled away and took in some quick fast breaths. "Sorry," he said, looking at her, his eyes bright with passion.

"For what?" she asked.

"We should take it slow, right?"

And it was a question. He waited for her answer. And she knew what he was really asking.

A part of her wanted to tell him no. She wanted this. She wanted to feel the magic of it now and not wait. But wisdom said not to rush it.

She nodded. "Slow's good."

"Okay," he said. "I promise to behave."

She grinned. "I'll try to do the same."

He laughed. "So you're having a hard time keeping your hands off me?"

"Yeah," she said.

He pulled her against him. "Good." Passing a finger over her lips, he said, "I guess we should go paint."

"Yup," she said and pulled out of his arms, even when staying there was so nice.

They both stepped back inside. "Can you stay on a ladder this time?" he asked with a tease in his voice. "Or am I going to have to catch you again?"

She grinned. "Maybe this time I'll catch you."

"Oh, I'd like to see that," he said.

"You might be surprised," she said, wondering and just a bit worried what he'd really think if he knew just how strong she was.

They were almost in the kitchen when the chimes started. They seemed to notice at the same time, because both of their smiles faded at the same instant.

"Told you," he said.

Fredericka listened. The sound wasn't so sad this time. It was almost . . . almost romantic.

Was his sister watching?

Looking over her shoulder at the chimes, relief struck when she didn't see her there. When she looked back at Brandon she recalled her need to help the spirit pass over. Holiday had said that oftentimes, if a person was murdered, they stayed here to get justice against the person who'd killed them.

Brandon walked into the garage to collect the paint that must have been delivered that morning.

"Have you told the police that you think this old boyfriend could have hurt her?" she asked.

"Oh, yeah. Why do you think he came over the other day? He was outraged that I told the police that he could be responsible for her being missing."

"Why do you think he would have hurt her?" she asked, grabbing one of the ladders and following Brandon outside.

He set his ladder down beside the porch. "Because two days before she went missing she told me that they'd had a bad argument and that she was going to break up with him. She even told me that she was . . . kind of afraid of him."

He passed a hand over his face as if to wipe away his frustration. "I got upset and told her she sucked at picking boyfriends. I told her it was because she had daddy issues. And while I was telling the truth, it hurts that my last conversation with her was me criticizing her."

Fredericka put her hand on his shoulder. "I'll bet she knows you just got upset because you were concerned."

"I hope so," he said.

They spent the next two hours painting, working side by side. They talked about art and their plans for the gallery. He asked her to send some photographs of her pieces so he could start posting things online and hopefully drum up some business. She found herself getting excited about the prospect of selling some of her work.

Around five, when the sun was slowly sinking behind the western sky, she finished off one last section and told him she'd better start packing up her things. She got ready to go wash her brush.

"Why don't I take you out for dinner?" he asked. "It's the least I can do for you helping me."

She wanted to say yes so badly, but her gut said she needed to get back to Shadow Falls and see just what crap Cary had set out for her this time. She moved into the garage where she'd seen a sink, a perfect place to wash out the brush. He followed her.

"How about a rain check? Maybe Friday evening?" she offered, knowing Thursday was the full moon and she really shouldn't be seeing him again until afterward, especially when temptation was present.

"Then it's a date," he said.

"Great."

"What about tomorrow?" he asked. "Can you come by and help me plant the flowers?"

She hesitated, knowing she shouldn't, but damn it, she didn't want to go two whole days without seeing him. It was only when she was with him that she felt happy.

"Sure," she said.

"You don't have to," he said as if he'd noted her pause.

"I want to," she said as she turned on the faucet and stuck the brush under the stream of water. "I won't be able to come by on Thursday, though. I have to . . . study for a big test."

"I could always help you study," he said and moved in close. His hip brushed against hers as he held his brush under the water as well.

She felt the tingle of his touch. She dropped her brush and faced him. Leaning in, she lifted up on her tiptoes and kissed him. His brush dropped to the bottom of the sink with a slight thud.

His arms came around her and she held on. After several long seconds, and before she wanted to, she pulled away. "If I came here to study, I'm afraid I wouldn't remember a thing, but . . . how blue your eyes are, or how your smile is just the slightest bit crooked, or how good your lips feel on mine."

He smiled. "You're probably right." He pressed a finger over her lips. "But I'll see you tomorrow?"

Yeah," she said. "As long as the creek doesn't rise." *Or Cary doesn't do something to prevent me from coming.*

As she drove away, Brandon stood on the porch waving. But as she pulled past the house, her gaze automatically shifted to the side of the house where she'd seen his sister twice.

Her breath caught when she saw her there again, kneeling at the flower bed. In her rearview mirror, she saw Brandon move inside. She drove away slowly, remembering Holiday's advice.

You need to talk to her. When you see her next time, approach her. Ask her if she remembers what happened to her.

But holy hell, Fredericka didn't want to do that. Nope, not even a little bit.

Then she remembered Brandon talking about his sister. How he wanted to find out what happened. Fredericka owed it to him to do this.

She pulled over and parked. Getting out of her car, she walked down the street. Linda still kneeled at the flower bed. The closer she got, the colder it got. Chills crawled up Fredericka's spine.

Stopping about five feet from the spirit, Fredericka forced herself to speak.

"Linda?"

When she didn't answer, Fredericka spoke again. "I just want to help."

The woman shifted back just a bit. "I'm dead, aren't I?" she asked, then she slowly looked over her shoulder.

Half the woman's face was beaten to a pulp, her eye dangled out of the socket.

Fredericka screamed. When she went to step back, she tripped over her own feet.

She landed on her ass, and was still screaming, butt-scooting backward, when Brandon came running over.

"What happened?"

Panic still gripped Fredericka. She glanced back at his sister, but the woman was gone.

"I . . . I . . ." If she told him the truth, he'd think she was nuts. "I dropped my phone and I . . . saw a bug."

"A bug?" He held out his hand.

She got up without his assistance.

He looked puzzled. Disbelief brightened his eyes. "You don't seem the type to be afraid of a bug."

She searched her mind for something more credible, but nope, nothing came, so she stuck with it.

"It was big," she snapped. "I . . . gotta go." She took off.

He called her name, but she ignored him. When she drove off she saw him standing in the same spot, staring as if . . . as if he didn't buy her bug excuse.

And right beside him was his sister, waving good-bye, her eye still dangling against her cheek and the front of her sundress stained in blood.

As disturbing as that was, more disturbing was the fact that as she went to turn off Main Street, she recognized the car behind her.

Cary.

Chapter Twelve

After tossing and turning most of the night, Fredericka jolted awake an hour late, Wednesday morning. "Crap!" Bolting out of bed, she realized class had already started. She went to her closet and gathered her clean clothes.

She'd spoken with Holiday when she'd gotten home yesterday and told her that now Brandon's sister knew she was dead.

Holiday had given her some pointers on how to encourage the spirit to open up. *Just talk to her, don't freak out.*

Right! How could one stand there and have a discussion with someone whose eye was dangling out of their socket and not freak?

As a matter of fact, it had been Holiday's warning that the spirit may come to see Fredericka, versus Fredericka having to go see her that had caused Fredericka's sleepless night.

Seriously, who could sleep knowing a dead person could just pop in? Well, Fredericka had finally cratered, after about four hours.

Of course, also keeping her awake had been Cary. He hadn't followed her all the way back to the camp last night. No, he was smarter than that, because someone might have seen him and had she chosen to tell Holiday about his obvious stalking, then the camp leader might have believed her.

Finally dressed, she ran a brush through her hair.

Between Cary's ire, and the trouble he was causing, and ghosts, you'd think she might just throw in the towel and stop seeing Brandon. But nope. And it wasn't just about the position at the gallery, either. Or because she was too damn stubborn. Though that was part of it.

But it was mostly . . . him. How just being with him made her smile. How with him, she didn't feel so . . . damaged.

She felt . . . beautiful. Feminine. And happy.

She glanced at herself in the mirror, noting she even looked happier.

Which meant this afternoon, she'd go back to Brandon's and . . . well, try to look a ghost in the eyes. She'd try to help him find the answers he needed.

Holiday's words echoed in Fredericka's head. *Linda Hart needs to cross over. Usually they stay here for a reason. And her brother needs answers. Everyone needs answers.*

Did Fredericka need them?

Pushing that from her mind, because it hurt too much to think about, she slipped on her boots and went back to thinking about this afternoon. Spending time with Brandon.

She'd be extra careful when she left, just to make sure Cary didn't follow her.

Somehow she was going to have to warn Brandon, too. Not that she really believed Cary would hurt him. Everyone knew that messing with humans could get you in a world of trouble with the Were Council. Cary might be an asshole, but he wasn't stupid enough to risk his job and way of life just to get even with her. At least she hoped not.

God, she really hoped not.

Looking at the clock, she just dropped back down on her bed. No use interrupting math class when she'd only attend a few minutes.

She tried to relax for a few minutes and then headed out to attend her second-period class. After English she had lunch, and then, ready to face Cary, or at least telling herself she was, she went to her history class. The second she walked in, he met her eyes, and she got a sense he had something else up his sleeve. There was just something cocky about his smile.

Fifteen minutes later, she'd almost convinced herself that she'd simply imagined it. But then Burnett James, Holiday's vampire husband, half-owner of the school, and an agent for the Fallen Research Unit—basically the FBI for supernaturals—walked into the class. While everyone here considered the man fair, he had the presence of a hungry pit bull in a meat market.

His gaze shifted around the room and came to rest on Fredericka. And it wasn't a restful gaze, like a simple hello. Her gut tightened and her instincts said the shit had just hit the fan.

Mr. James spoke to Cary, and then motioned for Fredericka to come with him. Picking up her books, fighting the urge to start screaming: *I didn't do it,* she followed Burnett through the door. She looked back over her shoulder and saw that cocky smile touch Cary's lips again. Fury rose up in her chest.

What the hell had he done this time?

Fredericka sat across the desk in Holiday's office, staring at the evidence placed before her. Supposedly, Miranda, Kylie's roommate, had found it pinned to their cabin door after lunch.

"I didn't do it," Fredericka said, looking down at the picture of Kylie Galen with a doodle of a knife drawn through her chest, the word DIE written across the front. The edges of the photograph were burnt as if someone had used a torch. Probably her torch, too.

On Fredericka's lips were the words: *Cary did it.* But she didn't say them. Why waste her breath? They wouldn't believe her. Not without proof.

And she didn't have any.

"The edges look as if someone used a torch," Burnett said. "Has anyone had access to your shop but you?" His head tilted to one side as if to hear her heartbeat.

"Not that I know of," she said and she didn't look at him because . . . because she didn't want to see disbelief in his eyes. Oh, he would know she was telling the truth, but everyone knew that some people just excelled at lying. He probably thought she was one of them. Why not? She was the daughter of a rogue, after all.

Oh, she could remind Holiday that she'd lost a key, and anyone could have gotten in there. She could tell her about her realization that she and Cary were through, and that he was having a hard time accepting it. But again, what did that prove?

"Fredericka." Holiday said her name. "I know you've had a lot on your mind lately. With your father's death and then the ghosts. I think maybe—"

"I didn't do it!" she repeated. "I don't hate Kylie anymore."

"But you used to hate her, didn't you?" Burnett asked, as if testing her ability to lie.

"Yes, I used to hate her. Not anymore." She closed her hands into tight fists. Not angry at Holiday or Mr. James. Her fury was directed at Cary.

"Why didn't you show up at math class this morning?" Mr. James asked.

"I overslept," she said, and even to her ears it sounded like a lie. "Are we finished here?" she asked, wanting to go for a long run. Wanting to feel oxygen burn her lungs, until the burn of anger in her chest subsided.

"No, I'm not finished," Mr. James said. "What are you not saying, Fredericka? You are holding back. I can tell!"

She inhaled and tried to fight the sting in her eyes. Not just from her emotions making them bright, but from tears. Tears of injustice.

"I'm supposed to go help Brandon Hart plant flowers in front of the gallery. Can I please be excused?"

"No!" Mr. James snapped. "You will not leave here today until you start talking."

She tilted up her chin, inhaled his vampire scent that instinctively annoyed her senses, and met his bright eyes.

"What does it matter what I say? I'm the daughter of a rogue. You've already got me down as guilty!" Would her father's sins ever stop haunting her?

She stood up and walked out.

She heard Mr. James call her back, but then she heard Holiday say, "Let her go."

Fredericka couldn't help but think that Holiday would be happy if she did go. Far away. If her shadow never fell on the school again.

Tears of anger, of frustration, burned her eyes and she headed for the woods to run until it hurt to breathe.

She ran five laps around the property. The perfect blue sky peered down at her through the trees as if mocking her angst. The smell of the forest, of the wet earth, just reminded her of a certain artist and his woodsy scent.

Each time she came close to the fence, the temptation to jump over it and go see Brandon hit. She didn't. Because that would just make her look guilty.

After about three more laps, her lungs struggling to breathe, she collapsed on a large rock by a stream. Only a little more than twenty-four hours until the full moon offered her escape from the hurt, but it couldn't come soon enough.

She pulled her knees up to her chest and hugged them. Then she closed her eyes and let the tears flow freely.

Once she'd cried it out, she pulled her phone from her pocket and texted Brandon.

Sorry. Can't make it today. See you Friday.

She hoped she could see him Friday. Hoped by then she'd figure a way out of the jam Cary had put her in.

She got a text right back.

Damn. I was looking forward to seeing you.

Me, too.

Everything OK?

No,

she typed. Then deleted it. The last thing she wanted was to get Brandon involved in her problems. He had enough on his own plate.

> Fine. Except missing you.
> Miss you, too. How did you get under my skin so fast?
> Sorry.
> Don't be. You make me . . . happy.

Closing her eyes, she held the phone to her heart. His message offered a slight reprieve from the pain collecting there. What she wouldn't give to have him hold her right now. To feel the sense of happiness sneak into her chest and chase away all the pain, the injustice that seemed to be a legacy left to her by her father.

A few minutes later, she jumped off the rock and started back to her cabin, but that's when she heard it again.

The rush of water.

What did the falls want with her this time?

It was dark, almost seven, and her clothes were still wet from the falls when Fredericka stepped up onto the cabin's front porch. Somehow the trip to the falls had led her to this idea. Had it come from the death angels? Maybe. She just hoped it worked.

The door swung open before she knocked.

Della, her vampire eyes already a bright lime green, stood there staring at Fredericka. "Just take your wolf ass away from here. I swear to God, if you lay one finger on Kylie, I'll have you whimpering like a pup."

Fredericka held her chin up. "I didn't do it."

"Really?" Della said, but with her head still tilted to the right to hear Fredericka's heartbeat, she looked puzzled.

Fredericka inhaled to find out if Kylie was here. When the chameleon's scent was absent, Fredericka asked, "Where is she?"

"Like I would tell you," Della said.

Fredericka frowned. To make this plan work she needed Kylie. The same girl she was being accused of threatening. She just prayed that Kylie didn't believe it. Because if she did, she'd have no reason to help Fredericka.

"Let her in," a voice called from inside.

Fredericka recognized Miranda's witch scent, and her voice. For some odd reason, she felt she had an ally in the girl. And right now, Fredericka could use all the help she could get. Though, she didn't have a clue why the witch would agree to help.

"Can I please come in?" Fredericka asked.

Della didn't move, except to look back over her shoulder, at Miranda. "Why should I let her in?"

"Because I believe her," Miranda said.

She does? Fredericka lifted up on her tiptoes, to see Miranda standing by the kitchen table.

Della huffed. "Yeah, but you still believe in Santa Claus, too!"

"Just let her in," the witch said.

Della stepped back, but she gave Fredericka a hard, cold look. "I'm watching you."

Fredericka rolled her eyes and moved in. Rumor was that Della was one kickass vampire. Oddly, Fredericka wasn't afraid of her. If Kylie liked her, the girl couldn't be all bad.

Fredericka walked all the way inside to stand beside her newfound ally, Miranda.

"Where is Kylie?" Fredericka asked the witch.

"Don't answer her." Della shut the door and came into the kitchen.

Miranda smiled and ignored the vampire. "She and Lucas ran to the store for Holiday. But she should be back in a few minutes. Sit down." She walked over to the fridge and pulled out two Diet Cokes. She held one out to Fredericka and one to Della. "You want one?"

"Thanks." Fredericka reached out and accepted the drink and sat down. Then curiosity got the best of her and she looked up at the witch. "Why do you believe me?"

"Now there's a good question." Della plopped down in the chair at the end of the table.

Chapter Thirteen

Fredericka waited for the witch to answer.

"I don't know," Miranda said and popped the top of her soda. "Sixth sense, maybe."

"Like that's dependable," Della said and opened her soda.

"Just ignore her," Miranda said. "We have to do that all the time. She's difficult. It's not her fault. A bitch bug crawled up her butt accidently. We love her anyway."

Fredericka looked at the vampire who shot the witch the finger. The two of them were famous for arguing, but something told Fredericka they were the kind of friends Fredericka could only dream of having.

"I really didn't do it," she told Della. "Kylie and I have made amends. I don't wish her any harm."

Della tilted her head again to listen for lies. "Okay, if you didn't do it, who did? Who wants to hurt Kylie?"

Fredericka hesitated to answer, but decided if she was going to tell Kylie—and she was—she might as well tell these two. She had a feeling they shared everything. "I don't think anyone is trying to hurt Kylie. It's me they want to hurt."

Kylie walked in right then. "Who's trying to hurt you?" She went straight to the refrigerator and got herself a drink.

"I didn't leave that picture," Fredericka said, not sure how much the girl had heard.

"Oh, I know that." The confidence with which Kylie said it brought some emotion to Fredericka's chest. Was this what it was like to have friends? That they just believed in you when no one else did?

"Thanks. Not everyone thinks that," Fredericka said.

"If you mean me, I didn't say I believed you did it," Della said. "I'm just being cautious. It's part of a vampire's nature."

Fredericka looked at Della. "I didn't mean you. I mean . . . Holiday and Mr. James."

"They don't think you did it either," Kylie said and dropped down in a chair.

"Yeah, they do, but that's not important. I came to see if you would help me . . . help me prove it to them." Fredericka noticed all three girls looking at her. "No one will get hurt. It's completely safe."

"Well, you just took all the fun out of it," Della said.

"Would you shut your trap and let her finish?" Miranda snapped.

"What's your plan?" Kylie asked.

At seven the next morning, Fredericka slowly walked into the cabin where she had history class. She inhaled to make sure Cary was there. He was.

She didn't pick up any other scents, which was good. *Please let this work.*

With her nerves firing, she walked toward the back where he usually hid away in his office. But then she stopped. Better if it took place out here.

Just to get his attention, she dropped her books on his desk. She heard him scuffling out of his chair. No doubt, he'd already picked up her scent and knew it was her. Considering tonight was a full moon, and a were was at his strongest right now, it wasn't the ideal time to do this. But she had to clear her name.

"Look who showed up early." He leaned against the door frame. "Have you had a change of heart?"

She felt her pulse racing, praying this worked. She'd spent most of the night trying to think of exactly how to play this. Exactly what to say.

"Why are you doing this?" she asked.

"Doing what?" He offered her his cocky grin.

"What is it going to take to stop you?" she countered.

He let his gaze move down her body, in a totally indecent way. Then he inhaled again, as if checking to make sure no one else was around and deciding whether this was a trick.

It was a trick. But she prayed he didn't figure that out.

"You know what I want?" he said after testing the air.

"No, I don't know. Because honestly, I don't think you even like me that much. You're going to Europe as soon as school's out instead of staying here with me."

"I told you I wasn't going to be gone all summer. Not that . . . we have to wait until summer to get to know each other." That look appeared in his eyes again.

"I thought you were worried about your job?" she said.

"That was before."

"Before what?" she asked.

"Before I knew exactly the type of relationship we would have."

"And what kind of relationship is that?" She felt the sting all the way to her toes.

He shook his head. "You are a daughter of a rogue, Fredericka. You know we can't have a real relationship. But I can give you what you need so you don't have to throw yourself at some human."

It took everything she had not to go for his throat and tie his freaking vocal cords around his neck. "He's my boss."

"He was your boss. You're going to tell him that you changed your mind."

"I signed a contract," she said, not sure how much she needed him to say.

"You will walk away from him!" He moved in and grabbed her elbow. His fingers dug into her forearm. "Or I'll get your ass thrown out of this school. Do. You. Hear. Me?"

"*I. Hear. You!* Release her!" Burnett's voice boomed into the room before he became visible. As long as he held Kylie's hand, no one would see or hear him. Obviously, he'd released her. He became visible . . .

and his presence held more intimidation than his voice. Within seconds, he had Cary against the wall, his hand around his throat.

"You will pack your things and be out of here before class begins. And don't you think I won't report this. Your teaching career, Mr. Cannon, is history!" Burnett seethed and dropped his hand.

As Cary gasped for air, Burnett looked at Fredericka. "Are you okay?"

"Fine," she said and didn't realize until then that she was rubbing her arm where Cary had held her.

"Kylie, can you walk with Fredericka to the office?" Burnett asked. "I still have a few things to discuss with this piece of shit."

"I'm sorry," Fredericka said to Holiday a few minutes later. Kylie had left. Burnett was still escorting Cary off the Shadow Falls property.

"What are you sorry for?" Holiday asked.

"I brought on all this trouble."

"He brought on all this trouble, young lady. You didn't do a thing. Except not tell us what was going on."

"I thought I could solve it myself."

Holiday sat up in her chair. "No, you were afraid to trust anyone else. There's a difference."

Fredericka looked down at her lap. Holiday was right, but . . . "I went to Kylie."

"Yeah. I suppose that was a step."

Mr. James walked in. He looked down at Fredericka. "Don't ever let a man treat you like that," he growled.

She nodded and bit back the need to apologize.

He looked at his wife. "Did she take it?"

Fredericka got a feeling she knew what they were talking about.

Holiday shook her head. Burnett sat on the edge of the desk, opened a drawer, and pulled out an envelope. "You know, most weres are more afraid of being afraid than they are actually afraid. You're an exception."

She looked at him, her mind racing to understand his meaning. "Is that a roundabout way of calling me a coward?"

"Are you?" he asked. "A coward?"

She wasn't really angry, just annoyed. "You two," she said, pointing to him and Holiday, "act as if by reading this, it will fix something. There's not—"

"Oh, hell no, it won't fix shit. You can't fix the past, Fredericka. But you can learn from it." He paused. "You can get answers. Some of us would love answers."

"Look . . ." Holiday started to speak up, but her husband shook his head at her. "Let me finish," he told his wife and faced Fredericka again.

She stared up at him, not really following him.

"I've never told anyone this other than my wife, but I was found at a garbage dump when I was six weeks old. And I'm not too proud to tell you that it hurts like hell knowing I meant so little to my parents. Especially now that I have Hannah and know how precious children are. But if I had an envelope that could tell me something, I'd read it so fast your head would spin. You know why? Because . . . I know that what I imagine has to be worse than the truth."

Tears filled Fredericka's eyes; partly for the strong man baring his soul, and partly for herself. Right then she understood why so many of the students respected this man.

"But it is worse," Fredericka said. "I already know that. I told myself he was dead all these years. It was easier believing that than . . . than thinking he just abandoned me."

Burnett inhaled. "Look, Holiday spoke with the friend of your dad who brought this envelope. She knows some of what is in here and she tells me that you need to read it. And my wife," he put his hand on Holiday's shoulder, "knows her shit. Trust her. I know it's hard. When people have let you down in life, it's hard to trust. It took me forever to learn that. But I finally did. I realized that you can't let the past control you or define your future. This is your life, Fredericka. You define what you are by how you live, but to do that, you need to let go of it. Read this."

He held out the envelope. Fredericka's hands shook, but she took it.

. . .

At eleven fifty that night, her blood fizzing, preparing for the upcoming shift, her heart reeling from reading her father's letter, Fredericka started out to meet the other Shadow Falls weres. As she moved through the woods, she lifted her face hoping to catch Lucas's scent. He wasn't nearby yet.

She'd heard he'd been looking for her earlier, but she'd spent the afternoon and evening working in the shop, trying to get her necklace sets finished. Now, however, she needed to explain why she wouldn't be running with the pack tonight.

Standing in the midst of the woods, night noises filling the dark silence, her phone dinged. Earlier, she and Brandon had been texting back and forth. She'd been tempted to go see him this afternoon, but with her emotions heightened and the slight physical changes due to her upcoming shift, she worried he might notice something. But as the night grew darker, she started worrying about something completely different.

Brandon's safety.

Now that Cary couldn't hurt her, would he go after Brandon? Before she'd assumed Cary cared too much about his job to do something stupid. Now he didn't have that job.

She'd warned Brandon about Cary—the best she could. Telling him only that the teacher had quit and was upset, and that she'd explain later, but for him to be careful.

She was unclear about what all she could tell him. She knew she couldn't tell him she was worried her teacher would show up at his house as a were.

Cary wasn't stupid, he knew that crimes done by weres when they were shifted were often overlooked. At least by the Were Council, but not so much by the FRU.

And yes, Burnett had informed her that he'd warned Cary that he would be keeping an eye on his every step. But was Cary arrogant enough to think he could get away with anything?

She pulled her phone from her pocket, and saw Brandon's name. She read his message.

You're probably asleep, but I just walked outside and realized
what tonight is. No wonder I feel so . . . antsy. Do you ever feel
that way during a full moon? If you're still awake, go peek at it. It's
beautiful and somehow alluring.

She stopped and looked up at the moon through the trees. Would
it be so wrong to tell him the truth? She recalled Holiday saying it
could be bad. *Could. Could be bad.* Which meant there was a chance
it could *not* be bad?

So caught up in her thoughts, she didn't pick up the scents or hear
the footsteps until they were right behind her.

Startled, Fredericka swung around, a growl on her lips.

Chapter Fourteen

Lucas and Will, another were, moved in.

"There you are," Lucas said, his voice deep and his frown apparent. Then he glanced at Will. "I'll meet you in a few minutes."

As Will treaded off, his footsteps almost silent on the damp earth, Lucas's unhappy gaze fell back on her. "What's going on with you?"

She waited until Will was far enough away not to overhear her response. "What's wrong?"

"You know what's wrong!" he growled, and even in the dark night with only a few moon rays to add light, she saw his blue eyes bright with familiar frustration. For sure, she'd heard that tone from him so many times—always when he'd been giving her hell about the tension between her and Kylie.

To his credit, most of those times Fredericka probably deserved his anger, but it hadn't stopped it from hurting, and more importantly, she didn't deserve his attitude this time.

And with her emotions on her sleeves due to the lunar energy, Fredericka's hackles rose. "If this is about that picture of Kylie, then you need to pull your head out of your ass, because I've been cleared of that charge! I wouldn't hurt—"

"I know that," he interrupted. "I'm talking about Cary Cannon, and your not coming to me when he started acting like an ass! You're

like family to me. And I'm the leader of your pack. You should have
come to me."

"I . . . I went to Kylie. You two are attached at the hip, so it's practically like going to you." Oddly, she hadn't even considered going to
Lucas. And maybe she should have. The pack leader was there to help,
but her problems with Cary were . . . relationship based, not werewolf
based.

He frowned. "It's not the same."

"Almost," she said, realizing it felt kind of good knowing he cared.
"I'm glad I ran into you. I'm going to run off somewhere after the turn.
I'll catch up with you guys later."

His frown tightened. "What's his name?"

"Excuse me?" she asked.

"His name. This guy, the gallery owner that you have a thing for."

"Kylie told you?" she asked, but strangely she wasn't really annoyed.
When explaining Cary's behavior to Kylie, Miranda, and Della, Fredericka had mentioned Brandon. Barely mentioned him, but all three
of them had picked up immediately that there was more to it than she
was willing to say.

"Spill it, were," Della had said. "And don't try to lie, because I'll
know."

They'd finally gotten her to admit that he was . . . well, hot, and
drove a motorcycle, and was, well . . . really hot. Then she'd told them
he was part were and how he'd kissed her. She probably shouldn't have
told them that, but . . . it had felt kind of good.

All three of them had announced they were coming to the gallery's
open house just to get a peek at the new hot artist in town. As crazy as
it seemed, Fredericka had felt as if she'd been a part of something that
night. A girl something. Like maybe she might even become friends
with them. It seemed almost impossible, but she could dream.

Lucas cleared his throat, drawing her back to her problem at hand.
"Yeah, Kylie told me about him. We're joined at the hip, remember?"
Lucas said.

Fredericka rolled her eyes. "Hips don't have ears." She waited for
him to warn her against getting close to a human, but then recalled

Lucas was different. He himself was breaking the Were Council's rules and was planning on marrying Kylie. Fredericka admired him for that.

"Does he shift?" Lucas asked.

"No," Fredericka said.

"Does he know you . . . ?"

"No," she said. "He doesn't even know that he has were blood. I mean, I think he senses it, but just hasn't accepted it."

Lucas shook his head. "But that's where you're headed, isn't it, to see him? Why? If he doesn't know, this is not the way to tell him."

"I'm not. I'm going there to . . ." She hesitated one second, then decided she might as well tell him. "I'm going there to protect him. I'm scared Cary might try something."

As soon as the shift was complete, Fredericka's paws hit the dirt and she moved with the wind. She wanted to get to Brandon's as soon as possible, before Cary did—if that was his plan. Of course, she could be wrong, as Lucas had pointed out, but she didn't want to chance it.

Brandon was . . . already too important to her.

As always her muscles burned and ached a bit after a turn. But it was a good pain, like someone rubbing a sore shoulder. Pushing herself into a full-fledged run worked the soreness away. Soon the liberating feeling of being in her were body took over.

As she ran, cutting through the woods, hiding in shadows as she darted through neighborhoods to get to his house, a sad thought hit. Brandon would never feel this. Never know the freedom of shedding his human form and seeing the whole world through different eyes.

Then she remembered how it had felt to ride his motorcycle, a sense of freedom and power. Had he subconsciously turned to riding to experience something that gave a similar sensation to shifting?

As she neared Main Street, she picked up some lingering were scents, not strong enough to know for sure if they were Cary, but enough for her to push herself to move faster.

She was less than a block from Brandon's home and gallery when the were scent grew stronger. Inhaling, the hair on her back stood up as she recognized the scent. Cary was already here.

Knowing how fast a were could kill a human, her speed grew faster.

A growl rose from Fredericka's throat and she prayed she wasn't too late. Now with the gallery in sight, she spotted Cary in wolf form leap over the back fence. She charged, her hind legs pushing against the ground as she flew over the fence after him.

He must have sensed her, for her paws hadn't hit the ground when he pounced. Their bodies met midair and the fight began. Unprepared for his attack, his jaws clamped down on her neck.

Thankfully, the fall to the ground offered her a chance to escape before his sharp teeth ripped into her flesh. She rolled once on the ground, shot up onto all fours, and growled. He already had his stance, ready to pounce. His eyes glowed orange, but no doubt hers did as well.

He had more weight on her, and probably strength, but she'd never backed down from a fight and had lost few. His lips curled up in a menacing growl, and she sensed he wasn't just out for blood. This was a fight to the death.

He charged again. They met in midair. His weight knocked her to the ground. He landed on top of her, his teeth cutting into her side. Pain had a howl slipping from her lips. She turned, sinking her teeth into his neck. Blood, his blood, spilled on her tongue. His jaws released and his yelp brought her pleasure. But she knew she'd barely broken his skin.

He bolted back; for one second she hoped he was satisfied that he'd left her injured and would leave. But his menacing growl said otherwise. He didn't plan to stop. One of them wasn't going to make it through the night. By no means was she backing down, but with the wound in her side, she accepted her odds were not great.

A cloud must have shifted in the sky, because the wooden wolf statue seemed almost spotlighted. Anger rushed through her with the thought that if she failed, Cary wouldn't stop with just her. He'd go after Brandon.

A surge of adrenaline fueled her fury. She wanted to live. Wanted to protect the artist whose hands had made the wolf. She wanted to know his kisses, to spend time basking in his smiles.

She attacked. Her mouth found the spot on his neck and she buried her teeth in deep. He pulled away, but not before she tasted more blood.

He howled, his eyes growing brighter. His breathing labored. At least now they both fought with their own wounds.

Suddenly in the distance she heard several other wolves. Fredericka recognized those howls. Lucas and some of the pack had come after all. But they were too far away to stop this now.

Cary pawed at the ground, as if ready to finish it. She lowered her head and growled, telling him she wasn't going down easy, and ignored the pain in her side.

Suddenly something flashed past. Fredericka knew immediately it was a vampire. And not just any vampire, but a certain half-Chinese vamp whom Fredericka had enjoyed diet sodas with just a few nights before. Then landing beside her was another vamp, or rather a chameleon in vamp mode.

If anyone had told Fredericka that she would have been happy to see vampires on a full moon, she would have thought them crazy. If anyone had told her that Della and Kylie would have come to her rescue, she'd've called them a liar.

Cary's hair stood up on the back of his neck and he growled at the two vampires. The howls of her pack echoed closer and Fredericka saw when Cary knew he was beat. His orange gaze shot to the fence, and he leapt up and over six-foot slats of treated lumber to escape.

"That's right. Run, you chicken-shit dog!" Della said, sneering after him, her canines extended and her eyes glowing neon green. The two vampires' gazes shifted to Fredericka.

"You okay?" Kylie asked, her eyes fading to their soft blue color.

Fredericka nodded. Her wound was not fatal, but it would have kept her from fighting at her best, which might have allowed Cary to finish her off.

"You go," Kylie said. "We'll hang out here to make sure he doesn't come back."

But then Della muttered something, and they both flashed off.

And that's when the light on the back porch flashed on.

The sound of the back door opening echoed in the night.

Every were instinct inside her told her to run, to leap over the fence. Every Fredericka instinct told her to stay.

Chapter Fifteen

Brandon stepped out onto the porch, wearing only a pair of navy boxers. His hair was mussed, his eyes heavy from sleep. The moon brushed against all his bare golden skin. She noted his muscles seemed more pronounced than before. He might not shift, but his body still grew stronger due to the moon.

Fredericka couched down a bit, hoping he could read her body language that she wasn't there to hurt him. She knew the exact second his gaze found her, because he gasped. Yet it didn't seem to come from fear, but perhaps awe.

He moved slowly toward her. When he got a few feet from her, he held out his hand. "It's okay. I won't hurt you."

In her heart, she knew it to be true. She let him touch her. He turned his hand over slowly and ran his fingers over the top of her head. As a wolf, she'd never been petted by a human, and it felt wonderful. And for the first time she understood the few weres that actually hung with humans while shifted.

"It's not you, is it, Nana?" he asked.

Fredericka's heart jolted. He knew.

He dropped down on his knees, and looked her right in the eyes as if searching for her identity. Fredericka got a feeling she should go. But not before saying good-bye.

She moved in and brushed her unwounded side against his arm.

"Don't go," he said. But she couldn't stay. She could hear Lucas and several others in her pack nearing the other side of the fence.

She went to give him one more brush with her snout when he ran his hand down her other side.

He pulled his hand back quickly, glancing down at the blood. "You're hurt."

She moved away. Looking back one more time, she saw his sister standing behind him. Thankfully, her eye was in place.

Fredericka nodded her head at the woman, then leapt over the fence.

Burnett had Cary picked up the next morning. Because he hadn't actually killed anyone, and it came off just as a fight between two weres, Burnett couldn't arrest him, but Burnett promised to put the fear of God in him. Knowing Burnett, she didn't doubt his ability to do just that.

Fredericka was both excited and nervous about seeing Brandon. After her first class, she ditched school, and went to talk to Holiday.

"He knows." She told her about what he'd said to her the night before.

"But he doesn't know what you are, right?"

She dropped down into the chair across from the redheaded camp leader that she'd come to respect. "I don't think so, but I want to tell him."

Holiday exhaled. "You really like him, don't you? And not just as a boss?"

Fredericka didn't deny it. She told Holiday about his scars, and how she'd never shown anyone her own scars and yet she'd shown him. "I know it sounds crazy, but it almost feels like I understand him better because we both have them."

The fae leaned back in her chair. "It doesn't sound crazy, but . . . it's best if you let him come to the realization himself. Hearing someone say this can really mess with a human's mind."

"But what if he never comes to the realization, or never says it aloud?"

"From what you told me, he's close," Holiday said. "Don't push it." Then she leaned forward. "Have you seen the sister again?"

"Briefly last night. But I . . . might see her today."

Holiday nodded. "Remember what I said. Stay calm and try to get her to talk to you."

Fredericka stood up to leave. She got to the door when Holiday spoke up.

"Did you read it?"

Fredericka turned around. "I can pay my tuition now. He left me over a hundred thousand dollars in the bank." She noted Holiday's surprise. "Didn't Marissa tell you about the money?"

"No," Holiday said. "She told me the reason he left you with Lucas's father was because he had enemies after him and his biggest fear was that they would take you to hurt him."

She nodded. "He wrote that in his letter." She swallowed the lump of hurt that swelled in her throat. "I still say he was wrong. He should have at least told me."

"People make mistakes," Holiday said.

"He was a hit man for some human mob boss."

"Some of those mistakes are worse than others," she said, sadness in her voice.

She hesitated to say it, but because it was the one thing that made her a bit less angry, she forced the words out.

"Did she tell you how he died?"

"No," Holiday said.

"He'd been hired to kill someone. He didn't know until he went there that it was a girl. A young girl. He couldn't do it. Instead, he went to the girl's father, who was the real target, and warned him. My dad wrote me in a letter that she reminded him of me. He said that he knew if he didn't do the job, the person who hired him would come after him, but he did it anyway because he felt as if it was his way of redeeming himself."

Fredericka felt tears sting her eyes and she saw similar tears appear in the camp leader's green gaze. Then Holiday spoke. "He gave his life for someone else. He wasn't all bad."

"I guess not." She started out, then turned back. "Thank you for encouraging me to read it. It still hurts. But you were right. It helped."

She almost called Brandon to tell him she was coming early and then decided to just surprise him.

Much to her dismay, he wasn't home. Or he wasn't answering his door. For one second, she worried Cary might have gotten to him.

Snatching her phone out, she dialed his number. By the second ring she was panicking, then he answered.

"Hey," he said. "If you're calling to cancel, I'm not hearing it."

She chuckled, relief washing over her, the sound of his voice pulling a soft emotion to her chest. "No, I'm calling because . . . I came early. I'm here and you're not."

"I'm in Bayberry . . . about an hour north of Fallen, at a storage shed my sister had. She had some of my stuff here from years ago."

"Art?" she asked, thinking he could have other pieces to add to the gallery.

He paused. "No. My . . . grandmother's things," he said. "She had a diary."

She swallowed and her heart raced. "Really?"

"Yes. She wrote some really interesting stuff," he said. "And some of it . . . some of it reads like . . . it was written to me."

"Really?" she said again because she didn't know what else to say.

"Yeah, I'll tell you about it when I get there."

"Okay." She bit down on her lip.

"Go on inside. Wait for me, okay?"

"Yeah. But it's locked," she said.

"There's a key under the fake dog poop in the front flower garden."

"Fake poop?" She laughed.

"Yeah. My sister's idea. I'm gonna head out. See you in a bit."

Fredericka found the fake poop and unlocked the door. She'd barely gotten the door open when, in the corner of her eye, she saw a flash of yellow, the same color of Linda's sundress, disappear into the kitchen.

Pushing back fear, Fredericka hurried inside, and followed her.

Only Linda wasn't there. Or maybe she was, but just not showing herself. The cold from the room sent chills up Fredericka's arms.

Remembering Holiday's advice, she forced herself to speak. "Linda? Can we talk?" *And please have both your eyes in their sockets.*

The sound of the wind chimes from the other room filled the cold air. Fredericka walked into the front room where the chimes hung.

"Brandon told me you made these," she said. "They are beautiful."

She waited to see if she would show herself. She didn't. But the chimes kept playing.

"I want to help you," Fredericka said. "I want to help Brandon. He wants answers. And . . . answers are good things sometimes."

Still nothing.

Then the chimes stopped ringing. Like really fast. The dead silence of the room reminded Fredericka of the other time when . . .

She heard a car stop in front. She heard the motor cut off. Then she heard footsteps treading across the front yard.

Moving to the front door that she'd left open, she confirmed what she'd feared. The man standing in the side yard looking between the two houses was the same guy she'd seen in the car a couple of days ago. The man Brandon said was Linda's old boyfriend. The same one Brandon believed killed Linda.

Then he swung around and started for the porch. Fredericka probably should have been afraid, but all she felt was fury. This man had taken Linda's life.

He stopped when he got onto the porch and looked at her, still standing in the doorway. Looked at her the way disgusting men looked at women. The hair on the back of her neck rose, warning her that this man was trouble.

She checked his pattern to make sure he wasn't anything more than human. He wasn't. But she noted his pattern was murky. So her perception of him was right on target.

She took a small step back, but not so far he'd think it was an invitation to come inside.

"Hey, gorgeous. Where's Brandon?" He moved in closer and even leaned against the door frame as if he was too sexy to stand on his own two feet. But holy shit, what she wouldn't give to knock him on his ass and give his ego a good squashing. Squash it like the no-good worm he was.

"He'll be here shortly," she replied matter-of-factly, if not a bit cold.

"Can you give him a message for me?" He reached out to touch her hair.

She stepped back and glared at his hand.

"Sorry, it's just so pretty. Girls like you make guys wanna touch. And be touched. I even have a few scars if that's what turns you on."

Her hackles rose up so fast, she had to hold back a growl. "Does your message have anything to do with Linda and her disappearance?"

His demeanor changed from guy-on-the-prowl to pissed-off murderer. Changed so fast, she suspected this guy either had mental issues or was a user of some badass drug. Or maybe both.

"Yeah." He leaned in. So close she could tell he'd had garlic for dinner last night and had overlooked his oral hygiene. Then he put his face right in hers. And that was the wrong thing to do. Everyone knew you didn't get in a were's face.

Well, not everyone knew, but she didn't mind teaching the lesson to this ignorant human.

Before she started initiating that lesson he spoke again. "Tell Brandon to stop telling these stories to the police, or they'll be looking for his body!"

She tilted up her chin, showing him she wasn't afraid, and well, maybe egging him on. "You know, that's a threat and I think it's against the law."

His eyes glittered with rage. He caught her by her arm. She could have dodged his reach, but nope, she actually hoped he'd give her a little something to justify what was coming.

His hand tightened. "No, sweet ass, that's not a threat. It's a promise."

She lifted one eyebrow, leaned in just a bit, and looked him dead in the eyes. "Wanna hear my promise?"

Chapter Sixteen

His hand tightened on her arm.

"I promise that I'm gonna find out what happened to Linda, so your butt will rot in jail. Oh, yeah, I also promise you that this is gonna hurt!" She lifted her knee with were force and got him right in his gonads.

The man went down to his knees. Between gasps for air, she heard him call her a few names. However, what she mostly heard were the wind chimes playing a beautiful song.

She stepped back and shut the door, and looked back at the chimes. She still didn't see Linda, but she knew she was there. "You liked that, didn't you?"

The chimes played louder.

"Please talk to me," Fredericka said five minutes later.

Linda's killer had managed to get his sorry ass and sore balls into his car and drive off. Fredericka walked around the house talking to a ghost who apparently had disappeared. The chimes were still silent. Not the dead kind of still from before, but just silent.

Suddenly remembering seeing Linda outside by the flower bed several times, she walked out.

As she cut the corner, she saw her, sitting there, hugging her knees. Eyes all in the proper sockets.

"Can we talk?" Fredericka asked.

The spirit looked up. "Why can you see me and no one else can?"

"I guess I'm supposed to help you."

She smiled. "I like what you did to Brice."

"He . . . hurt you, didn't he?" Fredericka asked.

Linda nodded and her gaze moved to Fredericka's arm. "He hurt you, too."

Glancing at the bruises, Fredericka said, "This is nothing. But if you can tell me about what he did to you, maybe I can make good on my promise to him. To get him arrested before he hurts anyone else."

Linda inhaled. "This is where I am."

Fredericka didn't understand. "I know, I see you." She moved in a little closer. She heard a car pull up in front of the house, a different-sounding motor than the one she'd heard the creep drive away in. So she ignored it, because she didn't want Linda to disappear. "Remember I saw you the other day, too."

"No, not this me." She touched her chest, pressing her hand over her heart. "The other me."

The other you? All of the sudden Fredericka understood. "You mean . . ."

Linda nodded. "I was . . . planting the flowers, early in the morning before it got too hot, and he . . . dropped by. I'd broken up with him and he didn't want to accept it. He yelled at me, then he . . . took my shovel and hit me with it." She glanced at the flower bed. "The shovel is in there, too. And I think I scratched him, so there should be proof under my fingernails."

"I'm sorry," Fredericka said, her chest aching and suddenly wishing she'd neutered that bastard instead of just bruised his boys.

"Me, too. There was so much I wanted to do. But I think . . . I think it's gonna be nice where I'm going. Isn't it?"

"I think so," Fredericka said. She wished she knew more, wished she could offer Linda something more, but she didn't know for sure, and the last thing she was going to do was lie to a dead person. "I'm kind of new at this, but Holiday—a friend who does this a lot—said you would be happier there."

Linda stood up. "Will you take care of Brandon? He's a good guy. Oh, he pretty much takes care of himself. He had to because of his mother. But since he's met you, he's been happier. A lot happier. He needs that. He deserves it."

"He makes me happy, too," Fredericka said, and right then she heard the footsteps behind her, followed by his voice.

"Who makes you . . . Who are you talking to?" Brandon asked.

Linda moved a little closer. "You can tell him. He knows I'm here. He talks to me. But I don't think he hears me. That's why I started playing the chimes."

"I didn't hear your motorcycle." Fredericka turned around.

"I drove Linda's car," he said, looking at Fredericka a little strangely. "How's your side?" he asked.

"Fi—" She gasped a little.

His gaze went to her forehead. He was attempting to read her pattern. "Your . . ." He touched his forehead. "It's different."

She just stood there.

"My grandma told me how to . . . I never tried. I thought, everyone in the family thought she was crazy." He continued to stare at her. "Then she wrote it down for me. In the diary."

He pushed a hand through his hair. His blue eyes looked puzzled and wide. "Don't stand there and let me think I'm crazy."

"No, I . . . You're not crazy. You are . . . part were."

"Part?"

She nodded. "You're like seventy-five percent human and then were and a little fae."

"She said that, too." He nodded. "And you . . ." He squinted again. "You're full were?"

She nodded.

He blew out a big sigh then took a long gulp of air. "Shit." Then he looked at her again. "That really was you last night, wasn't it?"

She nodded.

He stood there as if thinking. "Can I change into . . . ?"

"I don't think so. I don't know a lot about what mixed bloods can and can't do. But I know someone who does."

He seemed to contemplate what she'd said. "The school? That's what . . . ?"

She nodded.

"Why didn't you tell me?"

She shrugged. "I was . . . told it was best if you came to the conclusion."

"Okay." He stood there for a second, as if a little overwhelmed, and finally said, "Damn!"

Then he smiled.

She smiled back.

Then he kissed her.

She kissed him back.

And then when that ended—after several glorious seconds, he asked, "Who were you talking to?"

"Just tell him," his sister repeated and Fredericka winced because she'd forgotten she was there. And that kiss hadn't been one a sister should have seen. Not even a dead sister.

Fredericka hesitated. How much could he handle in one day? Should she lie? But she needed to tell someone so they could . . . find the body. Didn't she? She glanced down at the flower bed, trying to think.

"Hey," Brandon said.

She looked up. Oh, hell, she sucked at lying. "Your sister. I was talking to your sister."

"Do you want to press charges?" the sheriff asked, looking at Fredericka's bruised arm. Two officers walked past, rolling yellow tape. They had just started digging, looking for Linda's body.

"Nah, I . . . think I got even." She'd told them about busting the man's balls. So far nobody seemed to blame her. "I mean, unless you need me to." Standing on the porch, she glanced at Burnett in the front yard talking to Brandon.

Right after she'd told Brandon about seeing Linda, she'd called Burnett for advice on what to do next. He'd shown up ten minutes later with instructions on what to say to the police. Then he'd hung around to make sure it all went smoothly.

Basically, she'd told the truth. Leaving out the ghost part, and perhaps exaggerating the boyfriend's interest in the flower garden on the side of the house. And it worked like a charm, just as Burnett said it would.

"Why don't we wait and see what we find here," the sheriff said. She could tell he was still doubtful, not that she blamed him. He hadn't seen the ghost with her eye hanging out.

Fredericka nodded again and looked at Brandon. She'd noticed him checking out everyone's forehead. His gaze shifted and landed on her.

He smiled and that was all it took for her heart to fill with some warm emotion. She'd never been one to believe in sappy shit like love at first sight, but she couldn't deny she'd been drawn to Brandon from the start. Then again, he'd been shirtless and wielding an axe. Most women would have been drawn to him.

Suddenly voices rose at the side of the house. One of the officers called the sheriff over. The words weren't said, but she knew, and so did everyone else.

Linda's body had been found.

She saw the look of grief cross Brandon's face. While she knew he'd wanted to find answers, it still hurt. Considering her own unearthing of answers, she understood that all too well.

When she saw him walk through the garage to go inside, she went in herself.

He was standing in the front room, beside the chimes. She moved beside him and wrapped her arm around his waist.

"I'm gonna miss her," he said, his voice tight.

"I know," Fredericka said.

After a few minutes of just standing arm in arm, he looked down at her. His blue eyes were misty with tears. "How did I get so lucky to find you?"

She just grinned. "I'm the one who's lucky."

"Do you believe in fate?" he asked.

She nipped at her bottom lip. "I don't know."

He ran a finger over her lips. "Don't worry. I believe enough for the both of us."

She took in a big breath. "There are still things about me that . . . that you don't know. My dad . . . he was rogue. He did a lot of bad things. And in the were world if you were raised rogue, then you are considered—"

"Stop." He shook his head. "Do you really think that's going change my mind about you?"

"I just want you to know in case—"

"All I need to know is you." He brushed a strand of hair off her cheek. "I know we just started . . . but I've never felt this kind of connection with anyone. Don't you feel it?"

"Yes," she said. "I do. But . . ." She hesitated and then forced herself to say her fear. "What if what you're feeling is just because I'm were? There are a lot of were chicks out there with good family history."

"I got a feeling there's only one Ricka. And do you think I'm looking for family history? I've got a pretty messed-up family history myself. I'm looking for someone who makes me happy. Who can make me laugh. Who understands art. Who knows what a scar is . . . and isn't. I'm looking for someone who with one look can make my heart feel whole. And that's you. You do that for me."

She smiled. "And that's you," she repeated. "For me. I'm still just a little scared."

"Don't be." He leaned in and kissed her. The kind of kiss that tasted like promises, love, and a future.

Oh, hell, maybe Fredericka did believe in fate.

Read the series that started it all.

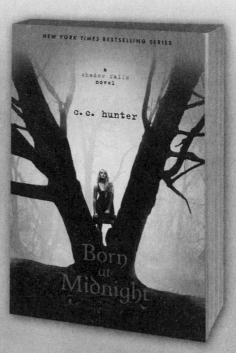

Available now

DON'T MISS C.C. HUNTER'S NEW SERIES

SHADOW FALLS:
After Dark

SHADOW FALLS

After Dark

Reborn

NEW YORK TIMES BESTSELLING AUTHOR

C. C. HUNTER

BOOK 1

SHADOW FALLS

After Dark

Eternal

NEW YORK TIMES BESTSELLING AUTHOR

C. C. HUNTER

BOOK 2

St. Martin's Griffin